THE DRY DIVER DROWNINGS

THE DRY DIVER DROWNINGS

A. CARVER

CONTENTS

A MAP OF THE PITCHWATER BUILDING

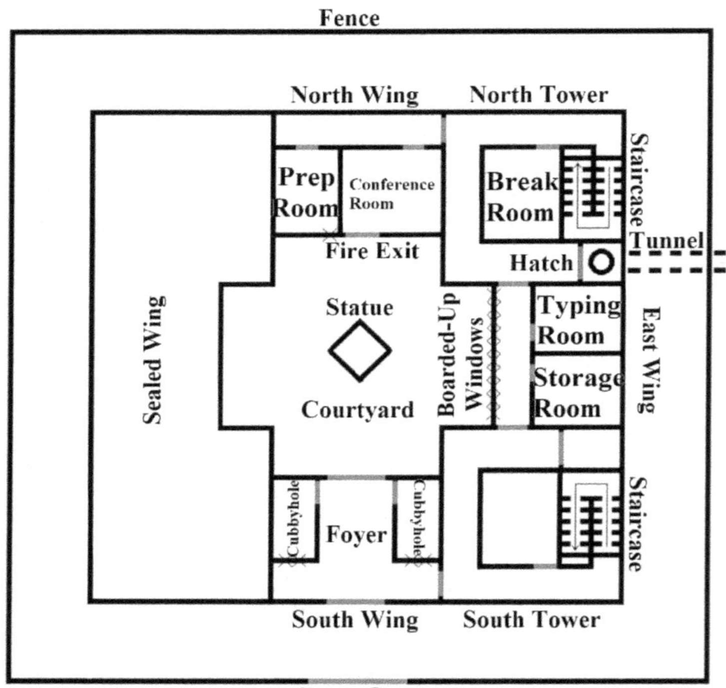

SILVERFISH
"Episode 6"

Footsteps crunch through dead leaves. The camera, chest-high, follows a narrow beam of light sweeping from trunk to dead trunk. There's nothing to distinguish the blood-vessel branches from the night sky above; no moon or star to light this fool's errand.

"Has to be around here somewhere," a boy's voice mutters above the camera. The torch swings in wide, frustrated arcs.

A shadow steps into the torchlight; the camera takes a moment to refocus, revealing a girl wrapped up in a long coat, hair tucked beneath a woollen hat. She looks out of place in the woods at night, but she's where she's meant to be; she has a camera strapped to her chest too. "What does the map say?" she asks.

"The map," the first speaker says, trying not to sound too exasperated, "says nothing, because this place isn't meant to *exist*."

"Right, sorry, I forgot," the girl says, and she's swept off camera as the search continues. "This still feels new to me…" Her words trail off; then there's a soft pat nearby, the sound of a hand on the cameraman's shoulder. "Wait; shine over there – is that it?"

The torch fights through a lattice of trunks, and at its limit it finds a flatter surface; picks out a rectangular outline tucked away among the trees.

"Yeah – yeah, that could be it! Nice catch!" the cameraman says, and then there are two pairs of footsteps jogging through the leaves, the camera's eye dipping now and then as the bearer dodges a trunk or hops over a particularly prominent root.

And then they're there – a low, narrow shack, little bigger than a phonebooth, unobtrusive, yet amiss in the trackless woods. The roof is corrugated iron; there are no windows, but on one wall there's a door. The torch and camera flash briefly on a rusty catch, an even rustier padlock lying broken in the leaves; and then a gloved hand reaches forwards and pulls the door open. Inside there's nothing – at first; but on the floor there's a raised plate of metal, heavy, circular, looking like a submarine hatch. "Bingo," the cameraman whispers.

The girl is beside him; he steps back so the camera catches her face. She's wide-eyed with surprise. "Oh my gosh. Somehow I just didn't really believe it…" She darts a look at the cameraman. "Will it really open?"

"Only one way to find out," he says, and the camera catches him flipping his torch to his other hand and then reaching down, grabbing a handle set on one edge of the hatch. The girl is grabbing another, and then with a whine, with a groan of ageing metal, they're heaving it open.

Beneath is a black hole. It's even darker, somehow, than the forest outside. There's the first rung of a ladder leading down, but no trace of what it leads to.

"That looks so scary." The camera flicks up to the girl as she speaks, her eyes fixed on the pit.

"Listen… you don't have to come." His words draw her attention. "You can stay here. Guard the entrance. Just in case… I don't know, in case something happens."

"No way something *isn't* going to happen," she replies. "And hanging out alone here? Like that's not going to be scary too?" She shakes her head. "No; I'm in. 'Cause you know what's the scariest thing of all?" Her voice falls low, serious. "Having to go through life never understanding what happened to me. What's still happening to me."

The camera dips in a nod. "Alright," the bearer says. "Then, let's go –"

The last word is cut off in a gasp. There's a noise nearby, the tap of something sharp on metal. Again, a few seconds later. Tap, tap, tap, getting closer…

It's coming from the shaft. Slowly, shaking, breath coming quick and shallow above, the camera moves, the torch points down the pit…

And for just a moment it sweeps across something down there – a hulking shape of metal and grimy fabric. It climbs the ladder –

"It's him!" the speaker yells, his voice coming high and panicked, and the girl screams. "Close the hatch, damn it, close the hatch!"

There's a blur of movement, and then the heavy metal hatch slams down with a deep and resounding boom, like the echoing toll of a bell. There are clamps on the side to fasten it shut, and the girl is on the ground flipping them closed –

"There's no time, just run!" the cameraman cries, grabbing her by the arm and pulling her up. She stumbles and they're both falling out of the shack, a carpet of skeletal leaves rushing up to meet them with a rattle as the camera hits the ground. The one filming flips over onto his back, the camera spinning to focus on the square shape of the building looming over them like a tombstone…

"What are you doing?" the girl yells as she scrambles up. "We can lock him in!"

"No, we've got to run," the cameraman says, hauling himself up. "It'll only slow him down –" The camera, the torchlight settle on the doorway – on the hatch. "Oh no…"

Even with only half the clamps shut, the hatch lid shouldn't be able to rise. And it doesn't. But something is rising anyway – rising through the surface, through the metal, as if it were only water.

A gloved hand, first – a bizarre hand, with only two broad fingers to its thumb, and one of them tipped with a hook-like claw – and then a whole arm, clad in loose, baggy rubber… A second arm follows, and, pressing on the ground, they begin to draw up the shoulders and torso of a whole body – a saggy shape smeared with dirt and mantled with a heavy ring of metal, studded with bolts, with tubes and pipes, surrounding a great iron ring for a neck…

But above that neck there is no head.

"Dry Diver," whispers the cameraman; and then water begins to run down the glass of the lens, and the camera cuts out.

CHAPTER ONE
THE SOUND OF THUNDER

A few days before the disappearances
Neither in the woods nor at night, a girl a little younger than the pair in the video paused in the middle of a lonely country road, first to switch her shopping bag to a different hand, and second to look at the lowering sky and hope the rain would hold off long enough for her to get back to her great-aunt's house.

Alex Corby was living a mercifully quiet life, in spite of other people's best efforts. After several years of her parents pushing her to be more outgoing when she would rather be at home reading (mostly a book, often the internet), her first serious attempt at being outgoing had resulted in sufficient catastrophe for her to have wrangled an extended stay with her great-aunt in the country instead. Since the great-aunt also would rather be at home reading (almost always a book, just occasionally the internet), this suited both of them nicely; and all the more so because, by a strange coincidence, the great-aunt had been mixed up in the catastrophe, too. Both had been present in that eerie castle on the coast where four people had met their deaths in bizarre circumstances; and both had played a role in finding the truth behind a murderer's illusions. And now Alex felt she could be quite happy with nothing like that ever happening to her again.

Great-Aunt Cornelia disagreed. She had waited more than a lifetime for a *real* mystery, not one of the ones in her books, and would grasp with both bony hands for more while she still had time in this world. But unless you're a true crime stalker, you don't go looking for mysteries. They come to you, or not at all. Alex turned up the drive to her great-aunt's home, and frowned. The first raindrops were beginning to fall, and there was a car pulled up to the front of the house.

Calling it a "house" was underselling it a little. Cornelia Crow lived in a building as remote and eccentric as herself, a gatehouse attached to the remains of a covered bridge which had once crossed the broad river behind, leading to a now-neglected stately home. It was the sort of building which looked something like a stately home or a castle in itself, stone-built, with an asymmetrical pair of pointed towers casting a horned shadow on the brightest day, and narrow windows glaring suspiciously out at the world; and the inside was cramped and labyrinthine, all the more so because Cornelia had walled each room and corridor with bookcases. Alex's bedroom – nominally the spare bedroom and actually the spare library – had taken some rearranging before it let in actual sunlight, which caught and scattered on the spiralling dust.

But the point was that this was not a house to which people came. It was a relic in the middle of nowhere, whose only visitors were parcel carriers bringing more books and the occasional online grocery order where there was something Alex hadn't been able to find in the village – which was where she had been just now. It wasn't the longest walk, but it felt a lot longer with a heavy raincloud catching up with her and a heavy grocery bag alternating arms. Great-Aunt Cornelia appeared to subsist almost entirely on sandwiches, so Alex was having to learn to cook in order to eat her favourite dishes again. It was strange how full the days seemed sometimes. She hoped whoever the visitor was wasn't about to disrupt things.

It was a pretty old car, she noticed as she got closer, early raindrops bouncing off her coat and sneaking into her bag; she didn't know much about cars, but she knew what was out of fashion. Back at school, some of the students taking driving lessons had second-hand cars like this. Was this… for her? No, there was no way; she didn't have her license yet, and Great-Aunt Cornelia knew that, because Alex complained about it every time she did the shopping. Then Alex noticed that there was actually somebody sitting in the car. This had a lot to do with the fact that the person sitting in the car noticed her, too.

"Hey there!" He was getting out of the driver's seat, a boy not enormously older than herself. Her learner driver theory was closer than she thought. "We just got here, so I didn't realise you weren't home yet. I'll take that."

He lifted the shopping bag from her arm without asking and carried it across to the doorstep, where he dropped it. The distance was about five feet. He appeared to believe he had rendered Alex a great service in doing this.

"Thanks," Alex said absently, her mind more on whether she had any idea who he was or what he was doing here. She didn't have her great-aunt's photographic memory, but she was still pretty sure she had never seen him before in her life. Still, there was a polite way of getting more out of him. "I'm Alex, by the way," she said, and waited for him to introduce himself.

Instead, he looked confused. "Alex?" he asked. "Are you sure?"

"Um, yes, I am sure," she said. "Were you expecting someone else?" On balance, it seemed like he didn't really know what he was doing there, either.

Rain began to slick their hair as she waited. The boy rocked back and forth on his feet, and Alex realised that, beneath his friendly demeanour, he was actually quite tense. "She said your name was Cornelia."

Alex put the pieces together. A girl had come to the house looking for Cornelia, and hadn't thought to inform her companion that Cornelia's next milestone in age was getting a telegram from the Queen. That was a weird, unlikely combination of circumstances –

And then two things happened. The first was Alex's heart plummeting as she remembered there was exactly one person for whom this combination of circumstances made complete sense. The second was that the people in the house heard them talking, and were opening the heavy front door to meet them.

Peering down from the arch of the doorframe was the face of Cornelia Crow, her narrow skull of a head seeming to float unaided in the unlit corridor which her black dress faded into, and her half-lidded eyes giving at once an impression both of haughty disinterest and great scrutiny. As usual she stood ramrod-straight, taller than she had any excuse to be, and beneath her head then only her bony hands would have been visible clasped atop the silver head of her cane, had there not been the worst person in the world standing right in front of them.

The girl with her hand on the door was someone Alex had only met once, but that had been more than enough. Someone who thought of herself as an author but who only wrote dark and blood-drenched fanfiction, and who thought of herself as a detective but wasn't interested in people. Someone who had accused Alex of murder and threatened her with a knife. Someone whose very name began with a "why", which was the question Alex was asking herself right now.

"Hello, Alex Corby," grinned Yva Dysart.

CHAPTER TWO
SYMPATHY FOR THE DEVIL

A few days before, a few minutes later
The gatehouse kitchen was a cold and business-like room which existed for the exclusive purposes of quickly and efficiently preparing meals and tea, and entertaining visitors who hadn't been promoted to the warmth of the parlour. Like the rest of the house, it held only two chairs; a tall grand chair for Cornelia, and a stool which was now reserved for Alex but which had previously been labelled "for guests". A guest was occupying it now, leaving Alex standing up and making the tea.

She didn't mind so much being put upon by her great-aunt, who though not exactly infirm had earned the right to figuratively put her feet up (which literally she would never do). Being put upon by Yva Dysart, on the other hand, left Alex grinding her teeth.

"So what are you doing here?" asked, not Alex, but Yva, who was acting for all the world as if it were her home and Alex were the visitor.

"I live here, Yva," Alex said, rattling a spoon around the cups. "Maybe you should have deduced that."

"Alex," began Cornelia rather grandly, "is my 'carer'." She didn't physically make an air-quote gesture but left it very clear that it was there. "It is a little bit demeaning, but a fine excuse to share some mystery novels with a really promising young detective."

"You used to share those books with me, CC," Yva growled. Her mood always did flip at a moment's notice.

"Alex is also very diligent about some of those household chores I may have allowed to slip a little," Cornelia went on, nodding at Alex as she handed her her tea. "I imagine such activity would be less to your tastes, Yva?"

Yva looked mollified. "I *do* try to avoid doing those. Maybe I need an Alex."

Alex slammed down a cup of tea in front of Yva as hard as she could without spilling it. "What about your friend?" she asked. "The one you left in the car again. He drove you here, after all."

"Oh, him?" Yva said dismissively. "He's my boyfriend."

Alex spilt her tea, and even Cornelia's cup jumped a little in her hands. Alex shocked easily, but it was very unusual for her great-aunt to lose her composure. This turn of events merited it. *Yva has a boyfriend*, Alex thought, as she ran a hasty cloth over the counter; somebody she genuinely likes, and who, amazingly, likes her *back?* Alex didn't have a boyfriend. Or a girlfriend. Granted, she did not feel this as a loss, but by comparison it felt somehow unjust.

Yva, watching the pair of them, furrowed her brow. "You two seem surprised," she said cautiously.

Cornelia and Alex looked awkwardly at one another. Even the old lady seemed to be struggling for words. "Yva dear," Cornelia said at last, "I confess you have never struck me as being... interested in romance. Or equipped for it." She sipped her tea, gained her stride. "You regard others as beneath you by default. You are hypercritical of people's flaws but respond poorly to the same treatment. Your attitude to friendship is transactional and unaffectionate. To put it bluntly, you lack warmth."

It was a devastating analysis from a woman who refused to tell even the littlest white lie, and it would have broken Alex. Yva, on the other hand, appeared unmoved. "True," she shrugged. "But we get on."

Alex had a hard time imagining this; but she was curious. "What's he like?" she asked. "You haven't actually told us his name yet."

Yva cocked her head, as if Alex's very curiosity was mystifying. "His name is Reef," she said. "He's also a creative type, so we can talk about that. Pretty serious about his career, so we can talk about that too. Guy with a lot to prove."

"Okay," Alex nodded slowly. "I can see it, I guess..."

"Particularly after his previous girlfriend dumped him, so probably this is a rebound thing," Yva went on, quite spoiling the effect. "I don't think he's over her."

Alex winced. She might dislike Yva, but this seemed incredibly sad. "Yva," she said carefully, "don't you think you... I don't know, deserve better?"

"Well, *obviously*," Yva snorted. "But I've got better, right here," and she tapped her forehead, "so an accessory like him is just a means to an end."

"Transactional," commented Cornelia, as Alex shook her head. Alex liked books with romantic subplots, and this was not like the books at all. "Now, Yva dear," Cornelia continued, "You did not, I presume and hope, come all this way just to tell me about your dysfunctional private life. You came here for a purpose, and I would rather like you to tell me what it is before I have to bribe you with a rare book."

Yva grew eager. "If I get to the point, will you *reward* me with a rare book?"

Alex tried to sit on the counter, and succeeded on the second attempt. "It would be better if you just got on with it," she said.

Yva rolled her eyes, and got on with it. "Have either of you heard," she said, and she leaned forwards so the shadows were in her eyes, "of Dry Diver?"

"No," Alex said.

"No," Cornelia said.

Yva slumped back with an exaggerated sigh. "I was hoping to skip the exposition," she said. "It's..." She frowned as she calculated how few words she could get away with. "A creepypasta vlog cryptid."

Cornelia turned to Alex. "This is gibberish," she said. "I may use the internet, but I do not care to be online enough to understand such jargon. Does this nonsense mean anything to you?"

"I think so," Alex nodded. She didn't mind being that online. "A creepypasta is like a scary story, but on the internet. A vlog is a blog, but on video. And a cryptid is just a monster that paranoid people think might really exist?"

Yva nodded along. "Close enough," she said. "Basically, Dry Diver is a monster that this guy came up with for a creepypasta contest a year or so ago. It looks like someone in an old-school diving suit, but its gimmick is that it can pass through walls and the ground like it's swimming through water – and hence the name. Also, it has no head for some reason."

"In my day," Cornelia interrupted, "we had such things, too, only we called them 'ghosts'."

"Yeah, but ghosts are dead," Yva pointed out. "Cryptids are the new big thing which you've got to chase if you want to get noticed. Which is where I come in, because," and she grew noticeably more enthusiastic, "there are a bunch of fan-made Dry Diver web shows and Reef's is the biggest, and I inveigled myself into the team as their new writer!"

The rattle of rain on the narrow kitchen window became accompanied by a beak-like clicking. "*Fantasy*," Cornelia tutted. "Oh, Yva. I *am* disappointed."

Yva's face fell. "No, no, it's not like that!" she exclaimed. "I'm just doing it to get my foot in the door to a real career. *And* since I took over the writing I've been trying to seed a hidden mystery explanation! I'm still a mystery writer, I am definitely going to be a rich famous award-winning mystery writer! My books *will* be in your library!"

Looking at Yva's desperate, pleading face with her wide eyes fixed on a Cornelia who was sipping her tea in silent thought, Alex was also reminded that Yva did, in fact, have a vulnerable side. She might spend most of her time acting as if she was the only human being who mattered, but it was a whole different story when it came to Cornelia, the one person whom Alex knew Yva sincerely admired. Alex suspected this had to do with Cornelia basically embodying what Yva fervently desired to be – a genius who didn't need to care what anyone thought and could just sit around reading mystery novels all day. Until she reached that point, Yva needed the validation which came from impressing Cornelia.

Yva's pride was like a balloon: Eye-catching, full of hot air, and easily popped.

Wait, that was two different kinds of balloon. Well, forget it, Alex shrugged. She wasn't the writer here. "Where exactly are you going with this, Yva?" she asked.

Yva scowled at her. "I have to explain the background or you won't understand the important bit," she said. "But since you insist, here it is: Basically, my team's series, *The Dry Diver Drownings*, is filming a crossover episode with the second-biggest series, *Silverfish*. Neither team is much above the level of a bunch of kids messing around with cameras, but theirs has slightly more gloss, and they have the actual creator of Dry Diver on side, so it's kind of a big deal – for what it is, at least." She drew herself up straight on her stool. "And, CC, I am proud to offer you the opportunity to come along and watch the whole thing happen as my guest at the filming location."

"I decline," Cornelia said immediately, and set down her empty cup in its saucer. "Now, Yva, if that will be all –"

Yva looked absolutely crestfallen. "But – but you have to come! I asked you nicely!"

"Strictly speaking, you didn't actually ask," Cornelia replied. "But let me see if I have the gist. These are amateur productions, are they not? Everyone involved is a young person. Probably they are very tiresome and modern and likely to patronise their elders. Furthermore, this is a horror series, you say? I imagine you will be filming in some lonely spot at night. It will be cold and unpleasant and quite probably damp." She leaned back in her chair, and clasped her hands. "So you see that there is very little to appeal to me in your proposal."

"But you have to be there!" Yva cried. "Maybe *I* could bribe *you*? I could write you a short story, or, or I have some new mysteries by Anthony Horowitz which are quite good and you probably don't have copies yet –"

And as Yva begged and pleaded and Cornelia watched unmoving above her, Alex narrowed her eyes and tried to understand what this was *really* about.

It certainly wasn't about doing something for Cornelia. Yva admired her a great deal, but her relationships *were* transactional; even if she was doing something for another person, it was with the hopes of getting something out of it. So what was it? Did she want to show off to Cornelia, perhaps? Or was there something she could only achieve if she had someone with her…?

"Yva," Alex interrupted, and the two combatants turned to look at her. "What's your ulterior motive?"

Bullseye. Yva actually looked disconcerted. "Why would I have an ulterior motive?" she asked, not actually denying it.

"You're a good liar, Yva," Cornelia remarked. "You speak the truth so unconvincingly that the lies are perfectly camouflaged."

"But it's pretty obvious that this isn't about Great-Aunt Cornelia," Alex said. "It's about you."

Yva was silent for several long moments. She didn't meet their eyes, and her fists clenched. Eventually, through gritted teeth, she growled, "I need someone to help make me look normal."

Alex's mouth fell open.

"Explain, please," Cornelia directed.

Yva ground her teeth and looked mutinous. "I'm not stupid," she said. "I understand that people find my personality… offensive. That they don't like who I am and let that colour their judgement. That it doesn't matter if I say the truest or the most reasonable things in the world if people don't want to hear it." Her gaze sunk lower, and her tone, too. "Everyone says to just be yourself," she muttered, "but apparently they don't mean me."

Alex felt an unexpected chord of sympathy sound in her heart. "My parents say the same thing to me," she said softly.

"They're all idiots," Yva said bitterly. "Everyone's an idiot. Well, almost everyone," she added, darting a look at Cornelia. "Anyway, the point is that I am *trying* to give people the impression that I am a normal boring human being with a bland vanilla personality. Starting a relationship is part of that." She looked up, her expression stern. "And for this crossover, I have to get it right. Some of these guys have talent, like, actual talent – not me-level talent, they can't write for salt – but we are talking about people who are going to swan straight into the creative industries. *The Dry Diver Drownings* and *Silverfish* are breakouts and they're starting to attract attention from some big fish. There's talk of a sponsorship deal. I need to be making contacts, and to do that I need to look sociable."

Alex was frowning. "No offence, Yva, but aren't we like… a bit young to be worrying about this sort of thing?"

Yva turned a bitter glare upon her. "Your parents love you, don't they," she said bluntly.

Straight for the jugular. Alex stared. Although she and her parents didn't really see eye to eye, they loved each other all the same and would always support each other; but it hadn't even occurred to her to consider how Yva Dysart might relate to her family…

Did Alex's great-aunt love her?

The question was so sudden and so embarrassing that Alex quickly suppressed it.

"Giving me the silent treatment, are you?" Yva resumed, and Alex came back to reality. "Whatever. The fact is, *my* parents have made it pretty clear that the day I turn eighteen they're turning me out on my ear; so you'll forgive me if I have my eyes on the prize." Her face contorted with tension. "This crossover *matters*. I have to get noticed for the right reasons."

"And your proposal for how to go about this," Cornelia elaborated, "was to bring along an old lady of no actual relation to you."

Yva looked quizzical. "Yes? So people see that I am capable of having normal relationships, and also that I am kind to the elderly?"

Cornelia exhaled, slow and long. "This may require a second cup of tea," she murmured.

"I'll do it," Alex said.

"Make more tea?" Cornelia's face brightened. "You *are* good, Alex."

"No," Alex corrected, "I mean I'll go to the crossover with Yva."

There was a moment of silence, and then both Yva and Great-Aunt Cornelia turned to Alex with uncannily similar expressions of stupefaction. "*You* will?" Yva said, as if Alex had just announced she was planning to climb Mount Everest.

"I guess I will," Alex replied, feeling actually a little bit surprised in herself; or perhaps she was more surprised that Yva had actually managed to make herself look sympathetic.

Yva Dysart clearly had problems. Maybe they came from a personality disorder, maybe she'd had an abusive childhood, or maybe she was just a bad person. But, Alex thought, we all have parts of ourselves that we don't reveal. If Yva can walk the walk and talk the talk of a good person, does it matter what she's really like? And if she acted well enough, the act might even become the real thing.

Alex couldn't help herself. She wanted to help Yva.

"Okay," Yva was saying, slowly. "That might work too..." Gradually, a familiar grin began to open across her face. "You're good at acting supportive, and people seem to like you for it –"

"There won't be loads of people there, right?" Alex asked quickly; her one qualm.

Yva shrugged. "Should be fewer than ten."

"So, nine," Alex replied.

"Including us!" Yva clarified, and Alex figured that wouldn't be so bad. "It'll be fine. It'll be more than fine. The more I think about it the more perfect it is; having you as my guest would really, really work!"

"A good start," Alex suggested, "would be to stop calling me your guest and start calling me your friend."

Yva reacted as if somebody had just shown her a spider. "I *guess*," she said, and began rummaging in her pockets. "It's in a few days, so I'll e-mail you the details. I'll have Reef pick you up –"

"I notice," Cornelia interrupted, after a long span of silence, "that nobody has asked me how *I* feel about this."

Alex and Yva went still. Although Alex was nominally her great-aunt's carer, her great-aunt was also pretty much her legal guardian. She had the power to tank this whole idea if, for whatever reason, she didn't like it. "How *do* you feel about it?" Alex asked, without a clue what the answer might be.

Great-Aunt Cornelia turned towards Yva. "Is this business taking place in a safe and public location?"

"No," Yva said.

"Is there going to be a responsible adult present?"

"No," Yva said.

"Is everything you're doing completely legal and above board?"

"No," Yva said.

The old lady finished her tea. "Splendid," she replied. "Were I your age, I might really have been tempted. Go on, Alex. Have an adventure while you're still young. You'll always wonder what you would have missed."

What Alex would actually end up wondering was just how much difference her presence made on that ill-fated filming trip. Did fewer people die, because of her? Or perhaps, did more?

CHAPTER THREE
EXIT ONE DETECTIVE

Night of the disappearances, 9:58pm
Just as Cornelia Crow had anticipated, the filming was set for midnight; and with just over two hours to go it was already raining. Alex, clad in her longest and least flattering raincoat, leaned her head against the car window and watched the headlights gliding by and the raindrops trickling down. The situation recalled the last time she'd travelled in these conditions, and for a moment, the droplets took on the hue of blood. At least it wasn't snowing this time.

"So," Reef said stiffly. He'd admitted when he picked her up that he hadn't long since passed his driving test, and he was doing everything stiffly. Alex braced for death every time he took a sharp corner. "How did you and Yva meet? She never told me."

Yva wasn't there. She lived close enough to the filming site to walk to a rendezvous point, and had sent Reef hours out of his way to pick Alex up on his own. He insisted he didn't mind, but Alex had made a mental note that her first tip for Yva should be that there was a difference between a boyfriend and an errand boy.

"We met on a book forum online," Alex began, piecing together a sugar-coated version that wasn't just all lies. "Yva was, um, a major player in the community, and we spoke now and then. And then there was this big offline meet-up, and..." She paused, wondering what words could possibly wring something positive out of that bleak day. "It was a bonding experience."

Reef nodded firmly. "That sounds like her. She was a huge Dry Diver fangirl, too."

Alex didn't say anything.

Reef hesitated, and then tried to resume the conversation. "And what about... you know..." He took his eyes off the road to jerk his head towards the back seat.

"I'm not deaf, you know," came an imperious voice, and Alex looked over her shoulder to see Great-Aunt Cornelia scowling forward.

Cornelia had decided to come at least partway along at more or less the last minute. She didn't care to leave Alex wholly unchaperoned, she said, but as luck would have it apparently a bookshop near to their rendezvous point was holding a midnight opening for something or other, and she had stated her intention to get inside and browse the mystery shelves until the crossover filming had wrapped up. In retrospect, part of Reef's stiffness probably came from having her constantly glowering at him in his rear-view mirror.

"Um, they met the same way," Alex expanded. Great-Aunt Cornelia's taste for murder mysteries was quite insatiable, and Yva was good at churning out complicated ones. "My great-aunt recommends old mysteries that Yva might be inspired by. They're like a two-person book club."

"It's in my interests for young Yva to fulfil her dreams of becoming an author," Cornelia added. "Her plotting has great potential."

"Yeah, don't I know it," Reef said, and he smiled. "I used to handle the writing side of *The Dry Diver Drownings*, but I didn't really know what I was doing. I've learned a lot from her."

Alex had done a little bit of homework, actually having watched the most recent entry in *The Dry Diver Drownings* in advance of the filming trip to prepare for her role as a close friend of Yva's. The oeuvre was surprisingly slim; a mere eight videos, comprising not even two hours' worth of material. It must have caught the zeitgeist somehow, showing up at just the right time to resonate with people. Alex didn't know exactly when Yva had come in, but the most recent three videos were a considerable jump in duration compared to their predecessors, so that was probably it. The instalment she watched was half taken up with Reef and another boy poring over a conspiracy wall of thumbtacks and post-its and print-outs and miles of string, exchanging theories, rumours, dreams about the extensive lore of their series; the other half, a doomed excursion by twilight through woods and lamplit streets while the monster stalked them, culminating in Reef's disappearance from a dead-end alleyway.

Dry Diver itself only appeared in shadows and blurry glimpses, and Alex was glad of it. It was actually quite effectively creepy; a distorted, hulking shape lurching past distant doorways or reaching out from the walls…
Alex shook her head. She scared easily, and hanging around with strangers and Yva at midnight was not the right time to be getting

jumpy. "And you?" she asked Reef, continuing their conversation. "Where did you and Yva meet – and just what is it you like about her?"

"Oh, she showed up on the sidelines while we were filming Entry 5, and came up and introduced herself!" Reef explained. "Really enthusiastic and wanting to play a part. I was in kind of a bad place at the time, but we got talking and just kind of clicked." He actually grew quite animated, taking one hand off the wheel to gesture, which was one hand more than Alex liked. "She threw herself into Dry Diver, body and soul. Made herself indispensable. It's only been a few weeks, but I couldn't do without her."

"I see," Alex murmured. He hadn't really talked about Yva's personality at all... "So, how would you sum her up in one word?"

"Hmm. She's..." He paused for thought. "Quirky."

Alex turned away so he wouldn't see her rolling her eyes. Cornelia was dead silent.

Somehow they managed to survive the remaining largely silent hour or so of the drive, and Alex was relieved when the bright lights of the small town of Kilinan came into view. Soon they were riding through the orange haze that passed for streetlighting on the roads leading to the bookstore where they were due to meet Yva. Alex recognised the last street they drove down from *The Dry Diver Drownings* Entry 8, and that video's lingering menace was probably why she screamed when somebody stepped out into the headlights.

Reef slammed on the brakes and they screeched to a halt what felt like far too close to the person now staring straight down their bonnet. They were wearing a hood, but a few gasping moments and Alex realised it was Yva.

"I wish she wouldn't do that, though," Alex heard Reef mutter, as she twisted in her seat to check on her great-aunt. Cornelia was rubbing sorely at the shoulder beneath her seatbelt, but stopped when she noticed Alex watching. Before Alex could ask if she was alright, her passenger door was pulled open.

"You're in my seat, Alex," Yva said, by way of greeting.

"You could have waved," Alex said, forgoing helloes and useless arguments and just unclipping her own seatbelt already.

"Needed to make sure you saw me," Yva answered, swinging a rucksack off her back as she squeezed in past Alex. "Hi, CC! Pleasant drive?"

Alex caught sight of Cornelia's glare as she climbed into the back seat. "We'll take a taxi home, if you don't mind," the old lady sniped. "Rather than trespass any further upon your time than necessary."

Alex saw Reef bite back a response, his knuckles tenser on the steering wheel than she would have liked as he set off again. She didn't say it out loud, but that taxi sounded like a good idea.

"Pugmire Pages is just around the corner," Yva explained, as they turned it. "Huh. Bit of a crowd."

In retrospect, the fact that the bookshop anticipated enough custom for a midnight opening might have tipped them off that it would be busy. A caterpillar of raincoat-wearing, umbrella-sporting fans and their parents trailed up the street, headed by a man in a reflective jacket guarding the doors until midnight. Reef pulled in across the road, and the four of them craned their necks through the windows.

"Hmm," Cornelia muttered, and checked her watch. "I confess I had imagined a smaller-scale affair, something which might reward arriving early. But that fellow on the doors looks rather serious about his role."

"There's still an hour to go until midnight," Alex said, and bit her lip. "Plus however long it'll take to get everyone inside. I wouldn't like you to be at the back of that queue, Great-Aunt."

The old lady sighed. "We'll just have to wait, I suppose," she said. "Fortunately I always bring a book with me."

"We can't delay the filming," Reef said sharply, with an urgent look at Yva.

"Can't look bad in front of the *Silverfish* gang," Yva agreed. "Hmm. Reef, maybe you could drop us and our stuff off at the rendezvous, then drive Cornelia back here, then leave her in the car while you walk to the site –"

"*Or*," Alex said, "we could just try and persuade him." She looked around. "You know. Appeal to the goodness in that security guard's nature."

The other three had the most cynical looks on their faces.

"Well, we can at least *try*," she insisted.

Yva sighed. "I guess we're early for the filming anyway, so we might as well chance Alex's stupid plan. But when it fails, I vote we just sneak around the back and find a lock to pick."

They disembarked, and the four of them walked across the road in a body, Cornelia cloaked and regal beneath the most enormous umbrella, bat-wing ragged. They marched straight to the head of the queue, Alex trying not to notice the ugly looks they were being given by those at the front.

"Stand aside, my good man," Cornelia instructed, with a haughty gesture towards the doors. "I am here now."

Perhaps she was hoping to be taken for visiting royalty, or a visiting author, which is the same thing. The man at the head of the line, with a security company logo on his jacket and on the cap he wore pulled down over his face, didn't even bother to look at her. "Back of the line," he said.

"I assure you it is only me and not these hangers-on," Cornelia insisted.

"Back of the line," the guard repeated.

"But I am very old, and in need of somewhere to take the weight off my feet and undertake some pleasant reading for a few hours," Cornelia explained, an ever-so-slight whinging tone entering her voice.

The guard lifted his cap, revealing a lined and weathered face white with stubble. "Join the club," he growled. "Back of the line."

"But I will die of exposure," Cornelia complained, "and my death will be on your conscience."

"Your choice, not mine," the guard continued. "Back of the –"

Alex thought it was high time she contributed, this having been her idea. "But we can't take her where the rest of us are going – and," she invented wildly, "my great-aunt so wants to be here for tonight's event."

"Yeah, my grandma's an epic fan of whatever series it is you're shilling here!" Yva piped up. "Probably a trilogy!"

The guard narrowed his eyes at her, and then transferred his gaze back to Cornelia. "And that series would be?"

"Eh…" Cornelia and her satellites cast a searching look down the queue. Many of those waiting were cosplaying as mermaids, but with witch hats.

"She's very forgetful," Yva stage-whispered, crowding the guard's attention again. "It's her age, you know. But it always brings her such joy to read the latest book in *Mermagic Mischief* or whatever, even if she can't remember the last one."

Cornelia's cane twitched violently in the direction of Yva's shins.

The guard glared at the four of them, before letting out a long, drawn-out sigh. "How much of that is true?" he asked.

"All of it," Alex said.

"None of it," Cornelia admitted.

"Leave me out of it," Reef muttered.

The guard stood there for a few moments, his eyes hidden by his peaked cap, rainwater dripping off it and onto his shoes. Then he turned and made a swift gesture through the glass, and Alex and Yva shared looks of triumph as someone came forward to unlock the doors. The guard blocked the surging crowd as the door opened a crack and Cornelia stepped forward, and then with a last "Have fun, Alex; I forgive you, Yva," she was gone. A collective groan rose from the crowd as the door slammed shut behind her.

"See?" Alex asked, as she, Yva, and Reef walked away. "Appealing to the goodness in human nature actually worked! …I'm surprised too."

"Feels more like lying through our teeth worked," Reef said.

"Get used to it," Yva said. She looked as happy as Alex had ever seen her. "There'll be a lot more of that where we're going."

CHAPTER FOUR
GOING UNDER

11:11pm

"Team Dry! Great to meet you in the flesh," smiled the young man stepping forward to meet them. In his early twenties, in a casual-smart-casual ensemble, and in a hotel car park, this was Matt Silver, the creator of Dry Diver and head of the *Silverfish* web series. "Reef Evans – good effort, really impressive for fanwork, can't thank you enough for preparing the ground," he said, pumping Reef's hand whilst slapping his shoulder. "And Yva Dysart – you're quite a catch, *The DDD* really stepped up in quality when you came along," Matt continued, effortlessly switching to another handshake after initially having moved in for a hug. Reef scowled at him behind his back. "And Chase Ferrier – you look very different on camera, I have to say."

"Uh, I'm not part of Team Dry," Alex clarified, also resisting the threatened hug. "I'm Alex Corby. Yva's friend."

Matt looked momentarily discomfited, and Reef and Yva's lips curled in a sneer which told Alex maybe they had more in common than she thought. But then Matt burst out laughing. "I'm just kidding you! Sorry, Alex – good to have you here, the more the merrier." Yva rolled her eyes at Alex, and Alex couldn't disagree with the sentiment. "Now," Matt said, swivelling about on his heels, "where *are* you hiding Chase, then?"

"Should be here any minute," Yva said. "He's got his instructions. He knows we're meeting up here before we move on."

"Hope he doesn't let the side down!" Matt grinned. "The rest of Team Silver are on location already. Like you, Reef – preparing the ground." He drew in a vigorous breath and looked up at the sky as if he could see the stars behind the clouds, or wanted to drink the rain. "Certainly have come a long way, haven't we? I knew Dry Diver had potential; bit of a diver myself, as it happens, and you see things underwater that you wouldn't believe... I wanted to bring some of that to dry land, remind people that you don't have to be in the water to drown." He exhaled loudly. "And now here we are, about to film *Silverfish*'s biggest episode yet!"

"And *The Dry Diver Drownings*'s," Reef reminded him.

"Right, right," Matt breezed. "You're important too, to give the backstory for why Bianca is part of *Silverfish* now – like a spin-off! Yva, Alex, you won't have met Bianca Marsh, will you? Top star. Destined for Hollywood, with her looks and her talent. Shouldn't have let her go, Reef!" Matt wagged his finger. "But your loss is our gain!"

"I didn't let her go," Reef said, through gritted teeth. "She dumped me."

"And I must say, it's big of you to have got over it and moved on," Matt said, clapping Reef on the back slightly too hard. "You're both seeing other people now, so I expect complete professionalism from the two of you!"

Reef frowned. "She's seeing someone else? Already?"

As they chattered, Alex drew Yva a step back to whisper. "Did I hear this right? Your boyfriend's ex is part of the other team you're filming with?"

"Yeah, that's right," Yva nodded. "Snapped her up pretty quick. Can't blame them, objectively."

"This seems like a tremendously bad idea," Alex muttered.

Yva cocked her head. "Why?"

Alex didn't even know how to start explaining, so it was fortunate they were interrupted – or rather, Matt was interrupted, mid-flow, and began staring across the car park. "That's Bianca's car over there! So she's been here all along. Must not have seen us. Come on, then – Bianca, oh Bianca!"

The four of them trailed across the car park, Matt marching right across the path of a passing car. Alex didn't see how anyone could have missed at least hearing them, as Matt Silver didn't seem to have much in the way of volume control; but clearly they were heard now, as two people stepped out towards them from between Bianca's and a neighbouring car. Bianca, in the lead, was unmistakeable; Alex hadn't cared for the way Matt had mentioned her looks before her talent, but it was true that she wouldn't look out of place edited into a poster for any Hollywood movie, and she carried herself with absolute confidence. The person behind her was quite different; almost skulking, in fact.

Bianca, meanwhile, was smiling up a storm. "Hey, you guys! Didn't see you over there. But look who I ran into!"

She stepped aside to reveal the person with her; a boy hunched, hands shoved in his pockets, looking as if he didn't really want to be noticed. Faintly familiar.

"Oh that's convenient," exclaimed Yva. "This is Chase, Alex; you see, Matt wasn't far off. Hey, Chase! Guess who Matt mistook Alex for!"

Alex and Chase exchanged the looks of people who didn't want this conversation to be happening.

"Well, Bianca, I won't say I'm not pleased to see you," Matt said, folding his arms. "But you were meant to be at the *other* rendezvous point. The rest of the team will have gone on ahead without you, you know."

"Oh, was I?" Bianca asked, taking it in her stride. "Sorry, my mistake! Guess I wanted to meet the new faces."

"Hi, Bi," smiled Yva, attempting to deploy a casual nickname. She leaned forward to shake Bianca's hand. "I'm Yva Dysart, the best writer here and your ex's new girlfriend."

Bianca's smile wavered uncomfortably. Everyone's smile wavered uncomfortably.

Alex let out a little laugh. "Oh, Yva, you're always so… so you!" she stammered, and the tension dissolved. "I'm Alex, hi. Yva's friend. So glad to be here; I thought it," she waved her arms desperately, "all sounded so interesting…!"

Bianca smiled benevolently at her, and then turned, with obvious reluctance, to Reef. They looked at each other with attempted impassivity.

"Bianca," Reef nodded at last.

"Reef," she nodded back.

Reef shoved his hands into his pockets. "Heard you're seeing someone."

"Huh," Chase, next to him, frowned. "Sounds like none of our business."

"You heard wrong, anyway," Bianca sniffed.

"Now now, children," grinned Matt. "We're all adults here. I won't tolerate any awkwardness from the two of you, so kiss and make up."

"Perhaps we had better be going," Alex interrupted, more loudly than she normally would.

"Yes, we had," Yva agreed, with a pointed look at Reef. "We're on a schedule, remember."

"Keeps you in line, doesn't she, Reef?" Matt joked, elbowing Reef in the ribs.

For all that she increasingly felt Reef had serious character flaws, Alex respected his restraint in the moment. "This way," he said, and led them back across the car park, gritting his teeth.

"We're downsizing to a single car at this point – Reef's is the least conspicuous," Matt explained, turning and walking backwards. "Brings back memories, eh, Bianca?"

"Is there a reason we shouldn't be conspicuous?" Alex asked; her memories darting back to Yva admitting that the operation possibly had something legally dubious about it.

Reef unlocked the car, and Matt moved to take shotgun without asking, despite Yva's best efforts. He paused halfway into his seat, and sucked in his lip. "Well…" he led off, with a gleam in his eye. "Normal folks tend to get unjustifiably suspicious about teenagers gathering in lonely places at the dead of night. That's why we're doing this in steps, shedding that bit more baggage at each step."

"Speaking of baggage," Yva said, gesturing at the poky vehicle, "this car only seats five. And there are six of us."

Reef and Matt were already in the front, and Bianca had taken the seat directly behind the driver, quite possibly as it meant the least engagement with said driver. That left two not enormous seats to go between Alex, Yva, and Chase.

"Hmm!" said Matt, twisting around in his seat to look. "I don't suppose anyone wants to sit on my lap."

Alex and the other four gave this statement the attention it deserved. "Chase," Yva ordered, "get in the boot."

This option seemed worse even than sitting on Matt Silver's lap, and Alex was as startled by the suggestion as she was that Chase didn't immediately refuse. He merely looked over at the narrow boot, and exhaled through his nose. "Why not one of you?"

Yva glanced at Alex, and for a fraction of a second Alex could tell that she was seriously considering it. "No," she decided at last, "friends don't ask friends to curl up in the boot with all the equipment." She gave Chase a pointed look. "Coworkers do, though. Boot."

Chase trudged around to the back of the car muttering darkly about being a kidnap victim.

"Your team spirit is really something," joked Matt, as Yva not-so-subtly pushed Alex into the narrow middle seat. She cringed apologetically in Bianca's direction; Bianca politely shuffled over about a centimetre to make more space. "I don't think I pay my team enough to ask them to get in my boot!"

Yva looked suddenly alert. "Wait, you guys get paid?"

Reef revved the car as noisily as he could, and they were off.

It was a short drive, though it felt longer with the constant bickering in the front as Matt tried to give directions to somewhere, Reef explained irritably, he had already been. They quickly passed out of the streetlights; stuffed into the centre of the back seat, Alex could make little of the dark roads, and since Yva wasn't one for small talk, she thought it would be a good idea to build bridges with Bianca. "So hi," Alex said, turning her head towards her with the limited motion any of them had in that cramped back seat. "You're Bianca, right? Everyone's been saying you're a pretty great actor."

To Alex's relief, Bianca took up the stream instantly, rather than letting it be awkward. "Everyone? That's flattering," she said, smiling freely. "It's not like I grew up going to drama school or anything, but the way things are going I might be able to make a career of it."

"Nice to have that assurance, I guess," Alex replied, having absolutely no idea what she was going to do with her own future. "So like, how did you get into acting?"

"Through Reef," she said, phrasing it like an admission of guilt. "I thought what he was doing with Chase seemed kinda cool. He didn't want me in at first, but Chase convinced him to give me a shot." She grinned. "And then I got the acting bug! It's fun to be another person, just for a little while."

"I'm the same with books; it's like an escape," Alex nodded. "I think I'd get stage fright acting, so I've never tried..." She left out any mention of the various lies she seemed to end up telling, including the fact that she was only pretending to be Yva's friend at that moment. "But I guess you've acted with both teams already," she continued, "so this should come naturally to you."

Something indefinable shifted in Bianca's mood; or perhaps had already shifted. "Yep," she replied, and there was noticeably less warmth in her voice, "comes naturally." And then she turned and faced fixedly out the window, leaving Alex to wonder where she had gone wrong.

Thinking about it, it was probably when Reef had come up. He certainly wasn't over Bianca; and while she had been the one who had left him, it seemed some sentiment lingered, and not necessarily a good one.

Alex began to get the uneasy feeling that their breakup had been quite ugly.

"We're here!" cried Matt, leaning forward and pointing at something indistinguishable through the car windscreen. "That's the Karswells' car. Pull in."

Reef didn't really need the instruction, but he pulled in ahead of the other car and made a show of it, carefully tucking himself into the lay-by as if he had something to prove. Perhaps he did. Even the other car was more impressive than his, from what little she could make out as the five of them disembarked. They appeared to be on a minor countryside road where the last of the streetlamps had petered out long ago; and only the interior light from the two cars could distinguish the person standing outside from the countless skeletal trees screening the lay-by.

Bianca was out of the car like a shot and waving. "Hey, Viggo! We made it."

Viggo didn't really look like a Viggo. He had a slight build and hair that spilled untidily around pierced ears. "Hey," he said. "Thanks for texting, Bianca. Wondered where you were."

"Leo and Tara already gone ahead?" Matt asked, and Viggo nodded. "Well then," he said, clapping his hands, "let's get walking."

"With our equipment, Matt," Reef said tersely.

"And more to the point," Bianca interrupted, "with Chase, if you'll let him out of the boot already."

Alex was ashamed of how easy it had been to forget about him. "I'll get it," she said, and hurried around to the boot, part of her feeling that maybe it should have been her in there after all. She flipped it open with a heave, and almost screamed.

Chase was in the boot, alright. But he wasn't alone. Reaching from behind his prone figure was a man-like shape of grimy fabric and twisted limbs, clawed hands and a head replaced with bolts and valves and tubes –

It only lasted an instant, that grotesque tableau of a shadow and a cradling shape; and then Chase was unfolding himself and sliding out of the boot, and stretching his arms and legs. "Thanks," he mumbled. "I take it you like the costume."

It was Dry Diver, the other figure in the boot; but a Dry Diver deflated and vaguely comical. Just a costume, after all – but a good one. "It's really well-made," Alex admitted. "Is that proper metal?"

Chase looked as if he might have smiled, if he felt more like it. "We blew our entire excuse for a special effects fund on a real historical diving suit, and I patched it up and modified it in my mum's workshop. Even got it back to being airtight; that's a breathing tube, see?"

Alex tilted her head, seeing how one of the myriad flexible tubes winding up and over the shoulder had an open end. "So how do you fit in? I mean, without the head?"

"Taller than it looks," Chase admitted. "The arms and shoulders are built up on the inside, and we use fishing-line to move the –"

"It'll have to wait, Chase," Reef interrupted, marching up to them. "We need to get moving. You've got the bodycams?"

Chase rolled his eyes. "Like I'd forget," he said, and reached behind the costume to retrieve a couple of digital cameras attached to a complicated set of dangling straps. "May as well get these on now."

Alex peered into the boot for anything she could carry, but the cameras and Dry Diver appeared to be it. "Don't you have those, uh, boom mics, I think they're called?"

"You overestimate our competence and budget," said Chase. "We can dub something in later if there's a problem."

As he and Reef strapped themselves in so the cameras were mounted in the centre of their chests, Matt came wandering up; his mouth opening in an O of exaggerated surprise. "So that's the famous costume!" he said. His voice actually went a little quiet. "Wow, it's actually very good. Almost like the real thing."

"Real thing?" Alex asked.

Matt ignored her, still in his own world. "You know, we started off with a suit too, but we could never get it to look quite right." His face brightened. "But then we found out how amazing Tara was at CG, and threw it out. Put us back on top!"

Yva popped up from behind him and snorted. "CG is too easy," she said. "Practical effects are all that matters."

Alex raised her eyebrows. She hadn't imagined Yva having an interest in film. Maybe it was something she'd picked up from Reef... or was putting on for him. Or maybe, as a mystery writer, she just had a thing for sleight-of-hand and clever magic tricks.

Matt grimaced comically. "Guess we'll agree to disagree!" he said, as if even that prospect excited him. "Okay, follow me, children, into the dark woods! I promise I won't lead you astray!"

Reef hauled out the Dry Diver costume and helped to arrange it onto Chase's shoulders as if he was giving it a piggyback ride; Viggo moved to help but Chase waved him away, for all that it looked heavy. And then Matt had flicked his phone into torch mode and was marching off into the woods in a seemingly arbitrary direction, leaving the rest of them scrambling to keep up – first Bianca and Viggo, then Reef and Chase, and Alex held Yva back to form the rear guard. They were a strange group, dressed more for a hike, with hats, long raincoats, gloves; but they followed an incompetent path, leaving a crashing and crunching wake of smashed twigs and scattered leaves, veering around trees, ducking under low limbs. It was a cavern of branches.

"Hey, Yva," Alex murmured softly, as they stomped along the barely-lit non-path; a single glance back, and she already had no idea where they'd come from, saw no trace in the dark of the road or cars. "Creepy or what?"

Yva tried to raise an eyebrow. It was clear she'd been practising since her last attempts. "The woods?" she asked. "Or Matt Silver?"

Alex was presently undecided on whether Matt was creepy, or just incredibly bad at reading the room. "Both."

"*So* creepy," agreed Yva, loud enough to be overheard but fortunately not. "Still think I'm that bad?"

Alex considered this as she danced awkwardly around roots. On balance, she was actually finding Yva astonishingly tolerable on this trip. Perhaps Yva was really learning. Or perhaps it was because they didn't have a mystery to argue over.

"You're not doing badly so far," Alex admitted. "There's a lot you can get away with if people think you're joking, for what it's worth. I'm curious, though" – she lowered her voice yet further – "what exactly happened between Reef and Bianca?"

Yva couldn't ignore that Alex was deliberately lowering her voice, and, mercifully, lowered her own. "Their breakup? No idea. Reef doesn't talk about it, but sometimes he whines about how underappreciated he felt. Chase just won't tell. He doesn't like me very much."

Alex bit back an entirely unnecessary sarcastic comment. Yva didn't need encouraging to feel antagonised.

"We're he-ere!" Matt's sing-song voice echoed from up ahead, accompanied by at least two equally loud shushes. Alex craned her neck to see through the last of the trees, where several beams of torchlight were illuminating –

A rickety shack with a corrugated iron roof, rusting away, falling apart, a single door sagging on its old hinges. As she tramped up, Alex found it hard to be impressed, except at how successfully unpleasant the murder hovel was.

Matt clapped his hands in the dim light. "So, we've all seen this place before on video, but I know it's some of our first times here, mine included. The atmosphere here is' – he breathed in deeply through his nostrils – "exquisite, don't you think?"

Nobody volunteered anything, so Alex did. "It's certainly spooky," she said, "but not quite what I was imagining." She frowned. "You mentioned a Leo and Tara. Are they in there? Is it bigger on the inside?"

Matt looked delighted. "I see somebody hasn't seen our latest!" he enthused. "You are in for a treat, Alex. How do you feel about," and he waggled his eyebrows as he pulled the door open, "secret passages?"

And a ring of torchlight shone upon a reinforced metal hatch in the ground, like something from a submarine, yawning wide open; a hole in the ground leading into the earth.

It was actually pretty cool. Also even spookier.

"Okay, that's worth seeing!" Alex agreed, as it now seemed to be her who was expected to do the reacting. "Is this a bunker or something? Like an air raid shelter?"

"He did say *passage*," Yva corrected. "It leads to a place called the Pitchwater Building, even deeper in the woods. That's where we're going."

"It's fully fenced off on all sides," Chase added, in an undertone. "No other way in or out but the passage."

"Uh…" Alex's remembered the legally dubious aspect of the whole exercise, and her anxiety started to spike. "Are we trespassing? Isn't this breaking and entering?"

"We aren't *breaking*," Bianca answered, in the manner of somebody who had already pictured themself explaining this to the police. "This hatch was unlocked when we found it!"

"Really it's just urban exploring," Viggo added. "If anything we've made it *more* secure."

Matt seemed pleased by this. "See this padlock?" he asked, nudging a padlock hanging off a clasp on the hatch. "We put that there. There are two copies of the key, one with Team Silver and the other with Team Dry, so either of our teams can get in independently for filming work. *Silverfish* got in first, of course; the latest log used the hatch."

"But it's just been me and Leo and Tara so far who've actually been *in* the building," Yva piped up. "We joined up earlier in the week to go over the place and figure out the best filming spots."

"And so those two got saddled with the set-up," Viggo said. "Not that there's much; but from what Leo's told me, you wouldn't want to be alone in there."

"Well, we'll be alone together!" Matt grinned. "I'll go first! Last person through shuts the hatch behind us!"

There must have been a ladder just out of sight in the darkness, for Matt seemed to hop down and then slide out of sight. Bianca quickly moved to follow him, and then Viggo in turn; all dipping down into the darkness and being lost from sight in seconds.

"Come on, Alex," Yva said, dragging her forwards. "But before we go, let's save these idiots from their own stupidity." She leant over the hatch and grabbed the padlock still hanging off one of the clasps. "Better not leave this up here," she said, "or anyone could just happen across the place and snap it shut, and then we'd all be trapped."

"Good idea," nodded Alex, because the whole affair didn't need to get any more menacing. She'd been trapped in an isolated building with Yva before, and it wasn't an experience she cared to repeat.

Reef smiled. "Thoughtful of you, Y," he said.

Yva shrugged, and dropped the padlock down the hatch. A distant "ow" echoed up.

Alex sighed. "Okay, I'll go down and apologise," she said, and peered into the hatch until she found the ladder. It looked as though it went down quite a way. "Yva, you do realise Great-Aunt Cornelia couldn't possibly have used this ladder?"

"Huh," Yva blinked, as Alex tentatively sat on the edge and swung her feet for the rungs. "Good thing I got you instead, then."

"Just great," Alex muttered, and putting her hands on the cold, abrasive metal, she climbed down into the abyss.

CHAPTER FIVE
HONEST LIES

11:29pm

The shaft was more or less pitch-black, so it was impossible for Alex to judge how far she ended up climbing, when all she could do was put one foot down and then the other, reaching for a rung she could only have faith was there. It wasn't a long climb, though; the pit probably only went a storey or so deep, enough that anyone randomly digging in the woods to lay power lines or hide bodies was unlikely to reach it. It probably wasn't a minute before the shaft opened and she reached Matt, Bianca, and Viggo waiting at the bottom, in a hall of flickering torchlight. Viggo was rubbing his head.

"Sorry about that," Alex apologised. "Her fingers slipped."

"Apology accepted," smiled Matt, and Alex supposed she could hardly complain if both the apology and its acceptance were delivered on someone else's behalf. "Yva has quite a sense of humour! We could hear her from down here."

Alex faked a laugh, resenting for a moment all the smoothing-over she was doing for Yva's sake before realising that it came more from her own instinctive dislike of conflict. She was in this now; whatever it took to have a pleasant time.

Not that it was a promising setting for a pleasant time. By way of changing the subject, Alex flashed her phone's torch about to get a sense of her surroundings; bare concrete behind her back and beneath her feet and sheets of corrugated metal arching over her, forming a corridor wide enough for two people to walk shoulder-to-shoulder forwards, where lay a blackness her torch couldn't reach the end of.

"So I take it this tunnel leads to the Pitchwater place you mentioned?" Alex asked. "This seems like an... unusual feature."

A shape dropped down next to her, and Alex jumped. "That's because it was a government building," Yva said, straightening up. "Spy offices or something like that, the sort of thing which meant it wasn't on any maps. Reef and the others are investigating it for links to Dry Diver; there are rumours of dark experiments and people going missing, and it seems like the whole place was abruptly shut down."

Alex frowned. "Okay, and what about in real life?"

"Oh, that's the same," Matt said, "apart from the Dry Diver elements. Blurring the boundary between reality and fiction is what people love about this form of horror."

Alex could not believe these people. "We are trespassing in a *secret service black site*?"

"It's cool! This place was shut down decades ago," Bianca explained. "It's just another abandoned building now, only a little harder to get into – which is perfect for what we're doing."

"Yeah, we had Matt give us rock-solid assurances before we agreed to this," Viggo nodded.

"And just in case," Matt interrupted, "if anyone asks later, we were filming somewhere *completely different*, and just *pretending* it was the Pitchwater Building, even though it actually is."

"For verisimilitude," Yva said, and Matt nodded.

Alex was thinking that she really, really, *really* should have asked more questions about this going in, rather than just assuming Yva was exaggerating about it not being completely legal and above board.

Chase and Reef had dropped in at this point, one with the Dry Diver costume and the other closing the hatch behind them, and so Matt clapped his hands. "Without further ado, then, let's go and meet up with the others! Hurry, you know what Tara's like about schedules!"

A schedule. Yva had mentioned it before. As Matt led them once again into darkness, albeit slightly more easily navigated darkness, Alex once again fell into step with Yva. "So what is the schedule? Your text said we'd be back with my great-aunt at about 2am at the latest?"

"It's a filming schedule Chase and Tara blocked out – start at twelve, finish at one, in theory. It's really for the actors, the rest of us are tagging along just in case," Yva explained.

"And hopefully for fun," Viggo chipped in.

"Like I could just not have you here, Y," Reef said, and Yva smirked.

"Besides, I do have a job here," Viggo went on.

Chase's voice rose up from behind them. "Porter?"

Viggo grimaced, but Alex could tell it was a sympathetic grimace, from one porter to another. "I was thinking getaway driver."

Bianca turned to look at him. "Your brother still hasn't passed his test?"

"I know, right?" Viggo said, sounding tired of hearing about it. "You can imagine how that makes him feel."

"Your brother – that must be Leo?" Alex asked.

Viggo nodded. "Yeah. You'll know him when you see him, trust me."

"Roles can be a little blurred in these sorts of productions," Matt's voice echoed from up ahead. "We all chip in where we can. Leo and Bianca are our leads, for example, but I'll be putting in an appearance today. And I'm sure everyone pulls double-duty in a smaller team like Team Dry."

"True," Yva admitted. "Even I've been learning a little movie directing. Me, a writer!"

"Helps to be multitalented in this jobs market!" Matt called back.

Yva made a finger-snapping motion. "You're right! Jack of most trades, master of all, that's me!" she enthused.

"That's not how that saying goes…" Chase's lonely voice echoed from the back of the line.

The banter dried up as they continued their way down the long, dark corridor. Alex started to bite her lip. Conversations in which she was out of the loop made her feel nervous, but in this place the silence was even worse; buried underground, walking an unknown distance in a concrete coffin, their procession of seven a kind of island in light with shadows ahead of them and darkness pursuing… An idle and unwelcome question entered Alex's head, whether the tunnel was as airtight as the Dry Diver suit Reef was carrying.

"Anyone claustrophobic?" Matt called. "Never mind, we're here."

Alex could hear that she wasn't the only one letting out a sigh of relief, and indeed she now got the impression that Matt was actually a lot nervier than he let on – at least, if the rate at which he was rattling up the ladder which had appeared ahead of them was anything to go by. She let Yva push ahead this time as the crews hauled their way up, with considerably less reluctance than they had climbed down, and used the time to smile nervously back at Chase and Reef. "Time to get cracking?" she asked.

"Guess so," Chase muttered. The reflected torchlight gave the pair of them queasy expressions, though in Chase's case having the filthy Dry Diver suit slung over his shoulders probably didn't help.

"Are you okay carrying that thing up the ladder yourself?" she asked, pointing at it. "I can help... somehow, probably."

"No need," Reef said. "Chase doesn't let anyone but me and him touch it." He paused. "Not that we don't trust you or anything."

Chase rolled his eyes. "We'll handle it. You go ahead."

She went ahead, to the haunting accompaniment of Matt Silver's echoing, dwindling calls of "Helloooo, Lee-oooo, Tah-raaaa...?"

It was silent by the time she reached the top of the ladder. She surfaced in a room not unlike the shack, a narrow space scarcely bigger than a cupboard which plainly existed solely to house the hatch, with paint peeling off concrete walls and bare light fixtures hanging smashed from the ceiling. A metal door hung open ahead of her, giving way to an empty corridor little brighter than the tunnel she had just left, in which the four people who had gone ahead were standing silent.

Too silent, with all torches shining on a single wall which had been slathered in slashes of red-painted letters.

DIVER WILL GET YOU

Alex tilted her head, and flashed her phone at the opposite wall.

LEAVE OR DRY

Ah.

"Trespassing is one thing," she said, in a shaky voice, "but I don't much like vandalism."

Yva cleared her throat. "So. Thing about that, Corby." She licked her lips. "These weren't here last time we visited. They've been added since the location scouting."

During which time there had been exactly two keys to the padlocked hatch, one with each filming team.

"Oh," she said quietly.

Somebody was trying to send a message. And she didn't understand what it meant.

CHAPTER SIX
CRUEL LOGIC

11:35pm

Matt Silver coughed nervously, and clapped his hands again. "Okay! Guess somebody decided to get a little proactive. Bit unsubtle for *Silverfish*, but we can work with this." He turned down the corridor as the last two members of the party clambered up to join them, carefully hoisting the Dry Diver costume between them. "Team Dry, really, you should consult with us before adding these embellishments…"

"What embellishments?" Reef asked sharply. "None of us have been here since the location scouting. Yva returned the key to me the same night."

Matt's voice grew a little higher. "Well, *our* key's been with the Karswells since the location scouting."

"We definitely haven't given it to anyone," Viggo interrupted.

Alex looked from one team to the other. Bianca was glaring in their direction with outright suspicion written on her face… "M-maybe," she piped up, "somebody managed to get in here through the fence? Maybe a tree fell and knocked a way through?"

"A random vandal," Chase said. "Who knew about the Dry Diver filming."

Alex's simulated reassuring smile wavered. "They might have overheard something…?"

"Speaking of overhearing," Matt said, pulling out his phone, "I'm wondering why we haven't heard from Leo or Tara. They were long ahead of us; very irresponsible of them not to text me about this. Perhaps Dry Diver really did get them!" He flashed a grin which, just this once seemed to have something false about it. "Viggo, you haven't heard anything?"

"No," Viggo said slowly, but he checked his phone anyway. "No. I'm texting him now."

"You've got reception?" Alex asked; this had been a problem for her before, but Viggo nodded, and a surreptitious glance at her own phone screen showed the same. Well, at least this time, if anything went wrong, they could call for help –

"Maybe they did it," broke in Yva.

37

The others looked at her. "Did what?" asked Bianca.

"Painted the message," Yva said, and Alex felt an uneasy motion in her stomach.

Yva had a theory.

Bianca frowned at her. "Why would they do tha—"

"There are a limited number of explanations for this graffiti," Yva said, tapping the wall with her phone, "and even fewer that take into account Leo and Tara being silent on it. One is that they did it. That's the simplest, but also the most boring."

"Yva," Alex interrupted, "maybe this isn't the best time —"

"The second explanation," Yva continued over her, "is that somebody waited near the shack until Leo and Tara unlocked the hatch, then followed them through the tunnel and left this message after they'd already passed through, so they don't know about it yet. That's the cleverest, actually." Yva nodded to herself. "No idea *why* it would happen, but it's more important that the explanation be interesting than plausible."

"She's in writing mode!" Reef said quickly, before Alex could intervene. "Detective fiction is Yva's hobby. You're all in for a treat. Got any more for us, Y?"

Yva frowned. "Just one right now," she said, and Alex closed her eyes as she saw a familiarly unpleasant smile creep across Yva's face. "And that's that there *is* a trespasser, and they attacked Leo and Tara the moment they stepped —"

"So you're finally here."

And Alex caught just the briefest flash of disappointment on Yva's face as every torch swivelled away from her and to the other end of the corridor, where they alighted upon a person who had just walked around the corner. It was a short girl wearing a wet raincoat and wet knees, because the raincoat was also short; and she had an expression of faint annoyance on her face which looked more or less permanent.

"Tara!" Bianca brightened. "We were just talking about you."

"I heard," she said. "I see you've seen the graffiti. Leo thought it was hilarious and begged me not to spoil it for you."

"Sounds like Leo," Viggo said, and the other members of Team Silver nodded. How easily, Alex thought, a sinister mystery could be resolved. Out of the corner of her eye, she saw Yva pouting.

And yet –

"So whodunnit, then?" Chase spoke up.

"Beats me," Tara shrugged. "But the two of us did a quick check over the building and went around the entire fence. Looks like vandals got in somehow, as there's been a few windows smashed and things dragged around; a little repair work, too. But the fence is intact, so," she shrugged, "who knows. There's definitely nobody else hiding here."

"Any damage that would interfere with the filming?" Matt pressed her.

"No," she shrugged again. "Now that I *would* have texted you for."

Matt visibly relaxed, and with him, so did the rest of the party; Alex included, for all she reflected that it didn't make sense. There was still a mystery; they were just choosing to overlook it…

"So where's Leo hiding?" Viggo asked, leaning in a doorway beside Alex.

Tara's eyes sought out Alex, and then rolled irritably. "Pulling his usual party trick," she said.

"Yeah, do we have to do this every time?" muttered Viggo, down the corridor.

"Oh come on, we only get one chance per person to pull this!" complained Viggo from beside Alex. "How come I got all the sense of humour?"

Oh. "You have a twin," Alex said to Viggo.

"No, *I* have a twin," said, presumably, Leo.

Yva tutted in an old-ladyish manner she had probably copied from Cornelia. "Such a cop-out solution," she said, giving Alex a sidelong grin. "Knox's Tenth, right?"

"I resent that, Yva," Leo grinned, stepping forward into the corridor to join them. He was dressed identically to Viggo, and also styled identically, which looked as if it took a surprising amount of work for at least one of them. "Just imagine the convenience for camera tricks, pranks, exams!"

"It's always me who does the exams," Viggo said.

Leo punched him on the shoulder. "That's what you get for being two minutes younger."

"Real twins don't care about that," Viggo muttered, very quietly.

Well, just two last people to be introduced to; better make a good job of it, Alex thought, as she turned a smile in Leo and Tara's direction. "Hi, I'm Alex; Yva's letting me see all the exciting filming action and stuff. Um, I don't have a twin, but if I did I'm sure we'd prank people sometimes, because why miss out on an opportunity, right?" She sensed herself starting to babble and hoped somebody would say something.

Leo nodded at his brother. "See, cute chick gets it."

Alex mentally withdrew her hope that somebody would say something. "My name's Alex, actually."

She caught Bianca rolling her eyes. "Just ignore him, Alex," she said. "Leo's been warned about this before, *haven't you, Leo.*"

Leo mimicked her eye-rolling. "Whatever you say, Ms. Lead Actress Prissyboots," he said. "Not everyone's as uptight as you."

Yva made a noise of disgust. "I had to put up with this guy for an hour on the location scouting," she said, jabbing a thumb at him. "What a pain."

Fortunately most of the assembled seemed to take this remark in good humour. Alex didn't, but for once, she actually preferred agreeing with Yva Dysart. Hell must have been freezing over.

The conversation was broken by the cacophonous echoing of clapping as Matt called for attention.

"Well," Matt clapped again, "looks like the entire merry band has assembled! And with," he checked his phone, "ooh, a good twenty minutes to spare!"

"Time to take a breather," Leo said.

"And shake off your coats," Tara snapped. "They're all wet, and that'll mess up continuity if we have to do a retake. We've set up a break room around the corner here..."

She led them down a windowless corridor and around two right turns, past a doorway and into a corridor which terminated in a stairwell and an open into the room they must have been circling.

"What's the layout of this place?" Alex asked, trying to get her bearings. She was sure it was simple, but surrounded by darkness and doors the building felt like a maze.

"Like the Pentagon, if it were the Square," Yva answered. "Four wings joining four towers with a courtyard in the middle. This is the north-east tower, but we're just calling it the north, because the westside towers and wing are entirely sealed off. A lot's sealed off, actually –"

"We checked during the location scouting," Tara called over her shoulder. "The rooms on the upstairs wings are all locked tight, and only this floor and the two remaining towers have been left fully open."

"Which is why we're filming exclusively at ground level – Team Silver in the north wing, Team Dry in the east," Matt said, as he turned into the break room. "Well well well, Tara! What's this?"

Alex braced herself for another disaster. Instead, the windowless, concrete break room, lined with scattered chairs and defunct water coolers, was lit up by a flickering and surprisingly cheery glow emanating from the centre. A set of nine chairs had been arranged in a circle around a rickety table, in the centre of which, incredibly, sat a birthday cake. It was quite unmistakeable; two tiers high and oozing jam, slathered in pale buttercream, with more candles merrily blazing away than Alex could count offhand and a roughly-piped message in the centre: *HAPPY BIANCA DAY.* ...On closer examination, it had probably started out as "*BIRTHDAY*" before somebody got distracted.

There was also a long, sharp knife lying next to the cake. But that would come later.

"What's Bianca Day," Yva asked flatly. But a nudge in the ribs quickly got her following Alex's lead of spinning around to clap an ad hoc "Happy Birthday!" at Bianca with the rest of the group.

"I assume it *is* your birthday," Alex followed up afterwards.

"It was yesterday," Reef said; and flushed angrily at people's attention. "I'm allowed to remember stuff like that."

Matt was assessing the cake with a critical eye. "Interesting," he murmured. "Not what I expected, Tara – but you've outdone yourself."

"Yeah." Tara was suddenly looking extremely awkward. "Matt told me to get snacks for the joint filming, but I knew it was close to Bianca's birthday, so, why not both. I - I allowed time in the schedule to get everything set up, and waited to hear you in the passageway before I lit the candles…"

"We can sing the Happy Birthday song," Matt beamed. "Don't worry, the copyright expired a few years ago."

"No, don't do that," Bianca commanded, whose view on birthdays as excuse for bizarre public embarrassment was clearly as negative as Alex's. "And Tara, you shouldn't have…"

"Of course she should," Leo grinned. "Just because you're shy doesn't mean the rest of us don't deserve cake."

"No, I mean you *really* shouldn't have," Bianca repeated, and her tone was so sombre that the atmosphere began to die. "I'm sorry, Tara. I went vegan a few weeks ago."

The cold room went quite silent. One of the candles flickered out.

"Oh," Tara said in a small voice. "I, uh. I used a lot of dairy in this."

"*Awkward*," stage-whispered Matt.

Alex hurriedly spoke over the snigger Yva was about to give. "It was still a lovely gesture, Tara," she said. "And I'm sure Bianca appreciates the thought –"

"Oh, absolutely," Bianca chimed in. "I'm flattered, Tara, totes flattered. And, since I'm not the kind of vegan to get flustered about other people's diets, I'm going to sit here and enjoy watching the rest of you eat it."

Tara's head shot up. "Really?"

"*Really*," Bianca nodded. "And there's a great vegan café in town, so one day I'll return the favour. And hey, if nothing else, I'm taking my birthday wish before any more candles blow out." She stepped up to the cake and, in a single smooth movement, bent over it and blew out the remaining candles, plunging the room into temporary darkness until people pulled their phones out again.

Matt slapped Bianca on the back, coming dangerously close to pushing her face into the cake. "That's big of you, Bianca, really! So good of you not to let your principles get in the way of us having a good time."

"It *will* be much easier to cut it into eight pieces than nine," Tara admitted.

"More for the rest of us!" Leo chimed in.

Matt snapped his fingers, and even that he did loudly. "It's just like the old puzzle!" he exclaimed. "You know. How few cuts does it take to divide a cake into eight pieces?"

The atmosphere relaxed, and people began to collapse into their chairs. "I remember that one," Chase spoke up, quietly using himself to separate Reef and Bianca. "It's three, right?"

"That's right," Alex nodded. You didn't get into reading mysteries without having come across a few logic puzzles. "I forget why. I think you cut it into quarters, and then the third slice is…"

"Across the middle," Reef interrupted. "You cut through the side, so each quarter becomes half as tall."

"No, you can't do that," Tara protested. "Not here. There's jam between the layers. Half of us wouldn't get jam and the other half wouldn't get enough buttercream."

"You move the pieces," Leo said confidently. "After the first two cuts you stack the quarters in a pile and cut all of them in half with a single final cut."

"No!" Tara repeated. "You'll squash the lowest pieces and ruin the writing!" With a tut of frustration, she reached down beside the cake and picked up the knife. "I'll just cut the cake norma–"

"I can do it in one slice."

The bantering dialogue suddenly dropped to dead silence, as if somebody had taken their speech bubbles and popped them like balloons. Alex felt her eyes bulging as she turned her head to look at the one person who could possibly make such an absurd pronouncement:

Yva Dysart had a theory again.

Here was the disaster, like a runaway train charging to a collision; and Alex could see that it was all going wrong but couldn't see how the train was going to get there yet, what route from A to B there was that she could possibly intercept…

"Your first mistake," Yva said, speaking calmly, nodding to a nonplussed Matt, "was failing to set more specific parameters for the problem. Usually this puzzle asks only for straight cuts, and for all the pieces to be the same size. That's why it has to be a round cake, too."

She casually reached across the cake, pinched the knife blade between two fingers, and gently tugged it out of Tara's hand.

"Without those specifications, there's actually another three-cut solution," Yva said, her voice still so even and reasonable, as she flipped the knife so the handle was in her palm and lowered the glinting blade into the cake. "The traditional two cuts to begin with – like the opening moves to a chess game. Then you'd use a *curving* slice to cut a ring around the centre of the cake – leaving you with basically a smaller cake in four pieces, and an outer donut-shape cake, also in four pieces. They wouldn't be the same size, not without using some maths, but it'd impress most people and that would be enough."

The knife smoothly cut straight through the centre of the cake, and approached the three-quarter mark – and there it was, the shark-like grin of somebody who thought she was the cleverest person in the room. "But why settle for three slices" – and the blade twisted suddenly in her hand – "when the same rules let you get away with even fewer?"

Yva's cut through the cake, originally straight as an arrow, now curved like a fish hook – and then turned back on itself in mere moments, forming a shape like a musical note. The cut crossed its original path – turned another half-circle, and once again crossed through…

"If a curving cut is allowed, if pieces of any size are allowed, you only need one cut! And so long as you make them small enough, you can cut *an infinite number of pieces*!" Yva exulted, her knife's serpentine path finally reaching the cake's edge, its terminus; and she sat back, proud as Lucifer, beaming at the cake she had carved into a kind of helix-pattern, a ladder of alternating crumbling semicircles… "Everyone gets jam. Everyone gets buttercream. And the writing remains intact. It truly is the definitive solution."

Yva put the jam-gored knife down. Set her index finger and thumb against her chin, cocked her head, raised a single eyebrow – and posed. "Impressed?"

CHAPTER SEVEN
DRY DIVER'S CUE

11:44pm

"Yva is really, *really* sorry," Alex insisted, some minutes later after everyone had synchronised their watches and departed, leaving just her and Tara tidying the wreckage by phonelight; an activity nobody else seemed very enthusiastic about and Leo had actively suggested they not bother doing. But Alex didn't much like littering either.

"I worked. *Really hard.* On that cake," Tara scowled, holding open a bin bag while Alex swept paper plates and plastic forks into it.

"I can tell, and it was totally delicious, even if the pieces were… in pieces," Alex replied. She stood up and brushed her hands, which made it less obvious that they were shaking. "Yva just… gets carried away."

Tara looked up at her with narrow, bitter eyes which looked as if they'd been trying not to cry. "She's not a child. None of us are."

"Well, we aren't adults, either," Alex said, thinking of what Yva's parents planned to do with her.

"I mean she's old enough to apologise *herself*," Tara said, "rather than standing outside the door and sending her mum to do it!"

They both looked across the break room. The break room doorway no longer had a door in it, and Yva was quite visible standing in its place, where she had been hovering the entire time.

Alex subtly gestured to her to apologise. Then she did it again less subtly.

"I am very embarrassed about what happened," Yva said, in a flat and unconvincing tone. "I promise I'll never do another bad thing."

"You still didn't say *sorry*!"

Yva's ability to fake an apology appeared to get worse in proportion to how much it mattered. "I regret any offence you may have felt –"

Tara let out a growl of frustration, and shoved the bin bag into Alex's hands. "New plan: You two do something *useful*," she said, storming over to a corner of the room. She came back with something which looked like a small metal toolbox, which she dropped into Yva's hands. "Go collect up the phones."

Alex, tying off the bin bag, frowned. "Phones?" Her own was propped up on a chair and serving as a lightbulb.

"Team Silver policy," Tara said. "No phones on set. We do have *some* professionalism here. Phone off, in the box, drop it here when you've got all nine. I'll start."

She pulled out a phone from deep within her coat. Unexpectedly from its owner, it was in a pink case with cat ears, or possibly devil horns. As Tara switched it off, Alex noticed that her lock screen image appeared to be a photograph of herself and a smiling Bianca on set, and tactfully decided not to ask about it.

"Is that you and Bianca?" Yva said.

Tara dropped her phone in the box and slammed the lid. "Filming starts in fifteen," she said. "Get going."

And she herself got going, picking up one of several identical torches standing on a table near the door – Matt had insisted on providing one each – before beaming herself out, leaving Alex and Yva alone. Alex side-eyed Yva for what felt like a long few seconds.

"I can't believe they weren't impressed," Yva said at last, and Alex rounded on her.

"*Yva are you even trying*," she hissed. "Because I am! But I came here to *help* you, not to do all the work *for* you!"

Yva had the decency to look awkward. "Look, I'm new to this, alright?" she said defensively, dropping the box on the table. "It's inevitable to make a mistake here or there when you're new to something that doesn't come naturally. You have to remember that my talents lie elsewhere."

"That is debateable," Alex shot back. For a moment it was really satisfying, and then she regretted it. "I take that back. You do have talents, people skills aren't among them, but… you just need to try harder to understand other people's points of view. Have you ever tried that? Tried honestly to imagine yourself as someone else with their personality and dreams?"

"I did once, for a writing exercise," Yva said, and made a face. "It felt gross."

"Do it more often. Figure out what other people want and avoid conflict."

Yva cocked her head. "Like you, letting everyone walk all over you?"

"I don't let everyone walk all over me," Alex retorted. "I just try to keep the peace." She paused, and sighed. "It does feel that way sometimes, though."

"Sounds like you need to try harder too, at putting yourself first," Yva pointed out. "You can't feel other people's feelings or live other people's lives. At the end of the day, the only one who matters is you. By which I mean me."

So that was how Yva thought. And when you put it like that, she wasn't wrong either, Alex reflected. Even so… "You're just going to have to pretend that we're both right," Alex said, "and find a balance between what *you* want, and what everyone else wants, like the rest of us." She paused, and added slyly, "Think of it as detective work."

Yva visibly brightened. "Deduce the other person's agenda, and strategise around it? Why didn't you say so before?"

Alex rolled her eyes. Good enough. "Then let's get started," she said, tapping the box on the table. Picking up one of the two remaining torches, the size of small maces, she retrieved her own phone to switch it off and set it alongside Tara's.

And just for a moment, the image of the mystery graffiti flashed into her head. She was making a mistake – already, a fatal tactical error –

She dropped the phone into the box. If anyone else, absolutely anyone, refused to offer theirs, she would take her own back. But if it was a mistake, at least they would all be making it.

Yva followed suit. Her phone wasn't even a smartphone. She really did have it bad.

Alex shut the lid, and gestured at Yva to take the box. "Come on. Be nice to people, and they'll think you're a nice person. Simple, right?"

And it *was* simple, to start with. Yva, who knew where everyone was supposed to be, directed Alex around shadowy corners to the east wing where Reef and Chase were making their preparations; a dilapidated office with "Typing Pool" on the door, off an empty corridor leading from the doorway near the tunnel. The architecture appeared to be roughly the same wherever you turned your torch: Concrete walls, narrow and barred and often boarded-up windows, and heavy metal doors which had once been built to endure break-ins but had been left open in the abandonment; for furnishings, decaying office chairs, collapsing desks, filing cabinets lining the rooms. In low light it was appropriately spooky, and the narrowness of the exterior windows plus the surrounding woodland left Alex reasonably confident that nobody was going to notice their trespassing; and she was coming to think of the Pitchwater Building as a surprisingly smart pick for the whole filming exercise.

It was when they reached the north wing and Team Silver that things started getting weird again.

"Tara's in there. Do not disturb, she's in one of her moods," grinned Matt, jabbing his thumb at a door with a sign marked "Conference Room". The layout of the north wing was similar to the east, except this time with the rooms on the inner wall and the corridor windows looking out to the fence and the woods – the former just visible, if Alex flashed her torch close to a cracked and barred window, as a great barrier of high metal rods each twisting into a spike. The rattle of rain on the windows was a constant accompaniment, underlying every spoken word so they had to speak just that bit louder.

"I'll go see what's up with her… after I turn this in, of course," he said, wriggling his own phone in front of them, as flashy and chrome-edged as the digital camera on his chest. "Can't break my own rules, after all!" He placed it into the box, and surveyed the other phones with open curiosity. "Once we wrap we should try to guess the person from their phone. Whose is this brick?"

Alex could clearly see Yva restraining herself from slamming the lid down on his fingers, and gave her a silent nod.

Matt vanished into the conference room with a squeal of old hinges, and Alex and Yva continued towards an open doorway which cast a rectangle of light across the darkened corridor. The wide office space that was Team Silver's prep room was unusually cold and largely empty, as revealed by several torches which had been left on a chair, shining in all directions; one of which was illuminating Viggo as he tugged and tweaked at Bianca and Leo's clothes.

"Hi," Alex said, walking in. "Um, what are you doing?"

"I'm prepping them," Viggo said, tightening Leo's camera straps and looking him over. He stepped back, and looked at the effect. "And we're done."

Neither of them really looked any different than they had when Alex had last seen them, save for the digital cameras they too now had strapped to their chests, and which Alex couldn't help noticing looked considerably more expensive than Reef and Chase's. "You make it look easy," Alex remarked.

Viggo gave an awkward smile. "To be honest, I have no idea what I'm –"

Leo physically thrust forward to speak over him. "Our filming philosophy..." The tone he adopted was instantly reminiscent of Matt Silver. "...is that the more amateurish the process, the more genuine it looks." He paused, and smirked. "Which handily means we don't have to work too hard for it, unless your name is Tara Gill."

"On which note," Yva interrupted, rattling the box, "phones for the poor, phones for the poor, hand them over quick."

Leo checked his watch. "You're right, my cue's coming up," he said, and he and Viggo began rifling hurriedly through their clothes.

"Here's mine," Bianca said, holding her phone out to Alex, who frowned. Bianca had taken a long step away, out of the torchlight, and to take her phone Alex had to do the same. And when she did so, she felt Bianca's free hand on her upper arm, squeezing quite tight.

"Quick question," Bianca murmured, just quietly enough not to be easily heard over the sound of Yva rattling the phone box. "Reef and your friend. Are they, like... okay, together?"

Alex took a sharp intake of breath, and glanced involuntarily at Yva. She was quite distracted trying to be patient with Leo, who in his haste was actually slowing himself down. "They're, uh... They..." How was she supposed to answer this question whilst, first, covering Yva; second, not actually having any real idea what they were like together; third, not telling too enormous a lie? "They seem happy," Alex compromised. "Reef thinks she's amazing. He says he can't do without her."

Bianca's expression was lost in darkness. "Huh," she said, and let go of Alex's arm. "Good. I'm happy for them."

The sincerity in her voice would have been really convincing had she remembered to put it on sooner than halfway through her statement.

"And that's everyone, let's go!" Yva called from across the room, seeing the last phone in Alex's hand and giving the metal box an impatient jangle. She breezed past, acquiring Alex in her wake, with a last cry of, "Things are taking way too long to start happening!"

It did indeed feel high time for the cameras to start rolling. Alex waved her torch over Yva's shoulder to light the way as they jogged back towards the break room, but the darkness of the cold corridors was beginning to get that bit more predictable and navigable and they were back in moments. Yva dumped the phone box just in the doorway, replacing it with the last of the torches left there. "I think I handled that well," she was saying as Alex caught up, tossing the torch in mid-air and only just catching it. "Not even you can have any complaints, Alex."

She switched the torch on and flashed it experimentally around, and Alex was just preparing her reply when the torchbeam swept over a lurching shadow on the back wall and Yva really did drop it.

The torch hit the ground with a jarring crack and the light went out. But Alex had already swung her own torch like a sword in the same direction, as if it could somehow fend off the shape she saw there.

Dry Diver – hunched over the table where they had cut the birthday cake...

"Is it moving?" Yva's voice came out beside Alex. "You saw it move too, right? Damn it, where's that torch gone."

Alex didn't move her own torch one inch. She thought she had seen it move, too – that diving suit with its lumpen form and misshapen neck. She wasn't going to give it an inch so long as she wasn't sure. It would be scary if she saw it move; but the thought of it moving unseen in the darkness was even worse...

But it didn't move, not again. Beside her, Alex could make out Yva straightening up from the floor, the metallic glint of the torch in her hands. There was a rapid noise of its switch being clicked. "These things are so *fragile*, the cameras are the same," she growled, producing no light. "This is not my fault. Since when was that thing in here?" She paused. "Is someone inside it?"

"I don't think so," Alex said, cautiously. "I think your torch just made a moving shadow."

Yva seemed to consider this. "I'm going to touch it."

She stepped into the torchlight, and Alex followed, the beam guiding them the long steps across to the centre of the room. Dry Diver remained still and dead, and Yva stretched out with the dud torch and gave it an experimental tap. Then a harder one.

"It's empty," she reported, ditching the dead torch on the table. "It's obvious if you get close, the costume's too flat. It's just been propped up."

Alex let out a sigh of relief. "So we just scared ourselves," she said, and tried to laugh. "Easy to do around here."

"That's where you're wrong," Yva said. Her expression was out of the light, and Alex didn't like to picture it, for her voice had taken on a low, angry note. "Somebody else scared us. This costume has no business being here, Reef and Chase like to keep it close –"

There was a small, metallic noise from behind them. Just a quiet clink, but it made Yva pause, as if she was wondering whether she'd really heard it. Alex began to turn the torchbeam –

And the sound of running footsteps echoed from the corridor before the light had even reached the doorway, fleeing at speed.

"After them!" Yva yelled, and Alex was off before she had time to think about it.

She wasn't a fast runner, but neither was anyone in those tight and echoing corridors. She hurtled out of the break room, collided with the wall and bounced off it, shifted in the direction the echoes were following; they stumbled as they twisted away from the north wing's doorway, and as Alex bounced off the same corner in pursuit her torchlight caught a blur of movement taking the next bend at speed. She kept up the chase, hearing the footsteps hesitate at the junction between the east wing and the tunnel –

She bounced off one last corner, and with her torch showing only the empty corridor and the hatchway ahead she skidded to a halt at the doorway to the east wing, and cast a lance of torchlight down it.

"Watch where you're pointing that!" complained a voice, and it took Alex's own eyes a moment to adjust to the sight of a person – Reef, standing calmly in the middle of the corridor hefting an office chair in both arms.

"Did –" Alex had to stop to wheeze in a few deep breaths. "Did someone just run past you?"

Reef looked puzzled. "No?" he said. "I heard running, but that was just you, right?" He looked towards the typing room's wide-open door, angling a torch which he held awkwardly between a couple of fingers. "Nobody's been down here since Leo a minute ago, right, Chase?"

Chase emerged from the room, staggering with a heavy office chair on each arm and his torch in his teeth. He shook his head stiffly at Alex before shoving past Reef and crab-walking down the corridor. Reef reached for the door and swung it back across the corridor, briefly blocking the way before it shut; ahead, Leo appeared from a second doorway, standing aside to let Chase pass into what was plainly being used by the team as a storage room.

Alex wanted to ask more questions, but she was suddenly too busy leaning against the wall and catching her breath. Why did she always end up running in her stupid cases? Detecting was supposed to be a mental pursuit, not a physical literal one.

It took her a moment to realise that she had started thinking of the night at the Pitchwater Building as a "case" – and herself as its detective. And she didn't like one bit what that suggested, what she suspected.

Yva had jogged into view in time to hear much of this without exerting herself so hard. "Can't hear anyone down the tunnel," she reported. "Reef, why is Dry Diver in the break room? You guys take better care of it than that."

"The break room?" Reef frowned, peering through the chair he was carrying; past him, Chase returned from the far door and shouldered his way past Leo, who was watching curiously. "Chase, what did you put Dry Diver in the break room for?"

"I didn't," Chase protested. "Did you?"

"Of course not, we've been together the whole time prepping this room," Reef snapped.

"Relax, you two," Leo spoke up, strolling their way. "And here I thought *I* got filming jitters. We're starting in a minute and I'm still not sure how I'm meant to be playing this. Like, when you show up, am I meant to be scared, or more curious?"

"Explain it to him, Reef," Yva commanded. "And Chase, get the costume."

Silently, Chase complied, his expression sour as he pushed past Alex and Yva. Reef and Leo disappeared into the storage room at the corridor's end, and then there were two. Alex flashed her torch at Yva, just high enough to see her eyes.

"Is something going on here, Yva?" Alex asked.

Yva's face was a blank; but in Alex's experience, that meant she was thinking. "I don't know," she answered. "I don't want to get my hopes up. But with the graffiti, and now this – and especially with everyone doing their best to stop thinking about how it doesn't make sense…"

"What just happened, even?" Alex wondered. "Why was Dry Diver moved? Why was somebody following us? And where did they go?"

Yva's brow furrowed. She looked angry, which was her way of being confused. "Not the tunnel, I know that much," she said. "Reef and Chase vouch for each other, and there's no way they're smart enough to get anything past me. But Leo couldn't have got past them, nor anyone else."

Alex chewed her lip, resisting the compulsion to do the same to her nails. "I don't like this. Somebody's trying to be clever …"

The sound of shuffling footsteps grew clearer behind them, and Chase emerged from the corridor, heralded by his torchbeam, the Dry Diver costume slung empty over his back.

"About time, Chase!" Yva said loudly, pointedly looking at her watch and tapping it. "We should be starting any second!"

"Yeah, yeah," he muttered.

"I'll get that, Chase," Reef's voice echoed, stepping out and meeting Chase midway. They exchanged the costume and Reef vanished into the storage room, and Chase, looking a little better with the weight off his shoulders, returned back up the corridor and slumped up against the closed door of the typing room, a little way from Alex and Yva.

"Is your costume okay?" Alex asked.

"For now," he said; and, after letting out a sigh, grew expansive. "We left it by the tunnel earlier, so maybe one of Team Silver thought they were being nice by moving it. That's what I figure."

"When, though?" Alex replied. "From the break room we came straight to you and Reef down here, and then up to the north wing to see Team Silver." She hadn't noticed if the costume had been beside the tunnel entrance when they'd gone to collect Reef and Chase's phones, though; she'd been keeping her torchlight on the floor and couldn't see that far into the darkness.

Chase shrugged. "It's all screwy. This place messes with your head." He looked at his watch, and straightened up with a jump; he was actually quite tall and the effect was dramatic. "It's time," he said, and clicked off his torch and turned down the corridor just as the storage room door opened. "Cue, Leo! Come on in!"

Chase swung the typing room door out into the corridor, and with rhythmic footfalls the actor jogged up. Chase watched him in and slowly shut the door.

"And that's Leo," Yva said, and turned to Alex to explain. "He does his bit in the typing room for a couple of minutes, I won't bore you with the exact figure, and then Reef goes in. For this one we have to be strict on timings, to make sure he's facing exactly the direction given in the script when Reef opens the door. We'll have to be quiet when that happens, but otherwise these soundproof rooms mean we can talk as loud as we like out here. It's a similar story for the rest of Team Silver and their bit in the north wing, and then later on both sets of actors join up."

"Not much room for retakes," Alex said.

Yva laughed. "Idiotic, isn't it? We're amateurs, so we have to get it right first time!"

They chatted for a couple of minutes, Yva enthusiastically outlining the story arc she and Matt had planned, and how easy it was to blend the lore of each series when they already left so much to the imagination. Down the dark end of the corridor Reef emerged from the storage room, the beam of his torch trained on his watch, and he jogged up with his footsteps an echo of Leo's.

"Just made it," he breathed. "Yva, how do I look?"

She pointed Alex's torch-bearing arm at him and reached up, brushing at his dishevelled hair. "Golden," she said, and it looked for a moment as if they would kiss; Alex, looking aside, shared with Chase a brief and accidental glance of incredible discomfort. But the moment passed, Yva checking her watch in the torchbeam instead.

"Quiet everyone; torches off," she murmured. "Five seconds."

Alex clicked her torch off, and Chase's was already off; Reef kept his on, shining it at the typing room door as Chase moved aside. Alex mentally counted down the last seconds, and then Reef took a deep breath, pressed a button on his bodycam, and opened the door.

The corridor went dark, the open door blotting out Reef's torchlight as it separated him from Alex, Yva and Chase. Only his fingers on the door's edge could be dimly seen as he took a step forward.

Then, silence; a silence that stretched uncomfortably.

"Are you real, or just another hallucination?" Yva prompted in an undertone.

But Reef didn't say the line. Leo didn't say anything, either. All was silent from the room, and after a few moments Reef pushed the door to enough to shine his torch back at Alex and the others, and switched his camera off.

"You saw Leo walk in here, right?" he said, his voice high and strained.

"Yes, *obviously*," Yva retorted. Her face turned towards Alex, who gave a tentative nod.

"Couldn't miss him," Chase added.

Reef shone his torch back into the room, and stepped out of sight. Then they heard him draw his breath in sharply. "Can you three come in here?" he said, still in that strange, taut tone. They did so in a rush, as if hurrying could somehow change the result...

With three torches now on, the room was revealed as a medium-sized office that evidently had once housed a number of secretaries; but now it was just an open square room lined with desks and shuttered filing cabinets, and with the same narrow, barred, and inescapable windows looking out onto darkness. With some of the furniture moved out of the room by Reef and Chase to create a clearer filming environment, it looked barren; not quite without places to hide, but certainly without any to someone who was actually looking. Their torches could reveal only two things: Another torch, unlit, rolled against a table leg in a corner of the room – and, just a step from the doorway, the digital camera Alex had seen strapped to Leo's chest, lying discarded on the floor.

But it was clear that no human being was in the room.

Chapter Eight
The First to Dive

12:05pm

"…I don't get it," Chase said, flashing his torch all around. "I practically touched him. He can't have left."

Reef took the few steps over to the fallen camera and picked it up, turning it over curiously. "You never took your eyes off the door?" he asked.

"I never took *myself* off the door. He's in here," Chase retorted.

Alex, for her part, had dropped to ground level and was shining her torch under all the desks, into each corner of the room, even at the bare concrete ceiling. "I don't think he is," she said, trying to keep her voice from shaking. She'd seen this before; been there where people had vanished from rooms locked or guarded. But in those cases, the one who had vanished had always left someone behind – a victim. The number of people had decreased from two to one.

Going from one person to zero? It couldn't be done.

"I'm checking the walls," Chase muttered, moving to the nearest one and running his hands over it. "Then the floor. Then the ceiling. Spies worked here. There has to be a secret passage –"

"It's not a secret passage!"

The words came in almost a scream, and three torchbeams flashed to the doorway. Yva hadn't budged from there; she was standing squarely in the doorframe, legs apart, both arms extended, bracing herself in the entrance like a barricade. She was breathing hard, and the sight of it set Alex's own heart beating harder in a panic.

Yva was furious. And when she was furious, she was dangerous.

"Secret passages are stupid," she hissed. "They're cheap. They're third-rate. They're not the solution to this mystery. Chase, you prove they aren't here. Reef, check the windows, make sure the glass is fixed and the bars are solid. Alex, check every filing cabinet in case he's a contortionist and folded himself up or has prosthetic limbs and removed them to hide himself inside."

Those were all unbelievably silly solutions, but you had to rule them out. As Reef ran to the windows, Alex stepped to the nearest bank of filing cabinets and tried first one drawer, then the next, then the next. All locked, or empty, or, like one with a drawer standing open, filled with sheaf after sheaf of decaying, mouldy, unreadable paperwork; and across the room, Reef was tugging hard at every bar behind which rain clawed at the windows, Chase poring over the joins between walls and floor…

"No dice," Alex reported to Yva, when they reconvened a minute later. "No cigar. No thing."

Reef and Chase nodded. The three of them were correct. There were no secrets in these filing cabinets. There were no unfixed or unbarred windows in the room. And there were certainly no secret passages in the building.

Yva had her teeth gritted. Alex could have sworn she saw a bead of sweat. She herself didn't feel much better. "Ideas. I need them. Give me generic solutions."

"He hid behind the door and slipped out behind us," Reef suggested.

Yva scowled. "That's wrong and you know it," she said. "The door opens out into the corridor so there's no behind to hide in."

"He hid under a desk next to the door, then, and slipped out behind us," Chase said.

"I never moved from this doorway. I barred it the moment you three stepped inside," Yva answered.

"He slipped out in the darkness just as Chase was closing the door, or as Reef was opening it," Alex attempted.

"Even I don't think anyone's that stupid!" Yva yelled.

Reef walked across the room and bent down, straightening up with the fallen torch. "But he was here," he said, looking at it. "You three saw him walk in, and his stuff's here." He gazed into the bulb and flicked the switch on the torch repeatedly, but it gave no light.

"I'll guarantee that it's impossible that Leo left," Chase said firmly.

"Nothing is impossible," Alex said. "I mean, nothing that really happened is impossible."

Yva nodded. "Leo was in here; so either he's still here, or he left. Which means that somehow, unbelievably…" She took a deep breath. "Leo Karswell has pulled a fast one on me."

"On all of us," Alex said. She felt that cold sweat, too, now; but it wasn't anger that gnawed at her. It was fear. Cold, petrifying fear, that stiffened her legs yet set her heart racing as if she should run. She wasn't sure why. It was just a prank, right? Leo was going to pop out of an air vent any second now to laugh about how he'd fooled them.

But the last time she'd seen a prank this good –

Wait a minute. If he wanted to laugh about how he'd fooled them, there was a way of doing that without him being in the room at all.

"Did he record anything on the camera?" Alex asked. Chase looked at her, confused, and Reef and Yva exchanged looks. "I mean, that is his camera, right?" she went on. "And he was in here alone for a couple of minutes. He might have recorded something."

Clap. Clap. Clap. Yva, bizarrely, was giving her a slow clap. "Finally," she said, and her mouth formed a familiar grin. "I was hoping you would ask the clever question, Alex. That's the one lead we have yet to pursue, and I think it'll pay off. There had to be a reason his camera was unfastened, after all. Reef, would you do the honours?"

Reef had set the camera down on a desk, and now he picked it up and switched it on, flicking through the options. "You're right," he said, his voice tight. "There's one file on this camera – a movie. He started recording."

Without needing any instruction, Alex, Yva, and Chase gathered beside the desk, shoulder to shoulder. Reef carefully set the camera back down on the desk, swivelled it to point the screen their way – then pressed a button and joined them, an audience of four as the recording began to play.

SILVERFISH
"EPISODE 7"

A fuzzy grey view comes into focus as the same typing room, seen at chest-height and in torchlight, with a digital time and date superimposed in the corner; the same dusty desks arranged against the walls, the same grimy filing cabinets. The windows are dark behind their bars, reflecting back the glare of the torch pointed at them; it quickly moves away, panning across surfaces thick with filth, looking for something. The camera shifts wildly and the torchlight moves with it, peeking into pigeonholes, filing trays...

At one point the view skates across the metal door, firmly shut and letting in not a glimmer of light or sound, and then it's onto the filing cabinets – and there is a clang, a sudden deafeningly loud clang in the silent room, as one drawer after another is tried and found locked. But eventually one comes open, heaped with cracked and mouldering pages. "Bingo," Leo says softly, and a gloved hand reaches into shot and starts rifling through folder after yellowing folder –

Then there's another noise. A muffled clang, like the filing cabinets, perhaps like the door to the room. That's where the cameraman instinctively turns to face, leaving the cabinet drawer open as he jumps to his feet and spins.

The torchbeam shines across the room and towards the door. It's still shut, but somebody has come in anyway; somebody with metal boots which clang on the floor in rapid steps, shining-wet arms flying akimbo as their owner hurtles across the room –

Somebody without a face.

The cameraman turns and races for the window, fixed and barred though it is – but then with a heaving impact he's brought low, and the camera clicks off.

CHAPTER NINE

12:07pm

Alex and Yva, Reef and Chase, stared silent at the camera screen for quite a few seconds after the recording finished. The only voice was the hiss of rain upon the windows.

"*Excuse me?*" Yva said at last. "Was I really just shown this?"

Alex, still staring at the blank screen as her mind tried to process what she had just watched, had the same question. It was plainly, blatantly impossible. In fact, it was worse than going from one person in the room to zero; it had gone from one to two and then two to zero!

"But that's *my* Dry Diver costume!" Chase said, his voice getting deeper as he got angrier. "Reef, what –"

"Are you *accusing* me? Your best friend?" Reef shot back. "That's *not* our costume, and I know it's not because it was in the storage room with me the whole time I was going through my lines. What, you think I put it on and swam through the wall like Dry Diver?"

"No, but –"

"Team Silver had a costume," Alex interrupted, before their argument escalated. "Matt told us, remember, Yva? So if your costume's still in the storage room –"

Privately, of course, she considered the possibility that Reef had indeed been wearing the costume, exactly as he'd said. But it didn't explain how he got into the typing room, so the Team Silver theory was just as plausible.

"Of course it's Team Silver's costume," Yva spoke up. "And you know how I know that? Because they – are – pranking us." She stabbed her finger into her hand like a knife to emphasise each word. "This is them trying to prove they're smarter than me. They're hijacking my script!"

As a theory, it was completely paranoid and egocentric. And yet, Alex actually found that idea something of a relief. She didn't like being the sort of person who always feared the worst, but her experiences of the impossible had always led to the most brutal possible result. But just because she'd seen impossible murders before, didn't mean that this was going to be another one. Why would it be? The chance had to be miniscule. And come to think of it, the very fact that there *wasn't* a body made it more likely to be a prank...

Reef looked troubled by the idea, though. Hurt. "That does sound like something they would do."

"No it doesn't," Chase retorted. "I don't know about all of them, but at least one of them wouldn't agree to it. Bianca wouldn't, Reef, you know that."

Reef's expression darkened. "No, I don't know that. And neither do you."

"We have to crack this problem. We have to catch them red-handed to show they can't humiliate me like this," Yva was going on. "I don't believe that bunch of all-money-no-brains imbeciles could come up with something clever. And having the *cheek* to set up one impossible situation and then leave the video behind showing it's doubly impossible!"

"No, nothing's changed," Alex said softly.

Yva looked disconcerted. "What are you talking about?"

"I mean it's still the same problem," Alex explained. "If Leo could get *out* of the room, somebody else could get *in*, right? In fact, if they took him away, they just took him out the same way they came in."

Chase gave a cautious nod. "Figures," he said. "If the attack was staged, of course they left together."

"It might be the same problem," Yva acknowledged, "but it's not *necessarily*. There might be a way you can only use to leave and not enter, or vice-versa. Actually," she went on matter-of-factly, "I already came up with a non-reversible theory about how they got in. That's why I was treating it as two problems."

"Non-reversible – as in, a way they couldn't have used to get out?" Alex asked. Why?

Yva nodded. "Leo didn't check thoroughly around the room in the video; particularly not at floor level. We also don't know how good a look-round Reef and Chase gave this room when they were clearing the excess furniture. Dry Diver" – she caught herself – "the person in the Dry Diver costume could have been there the whole time."

Alex looked over to a dubious Reef and Chase. "Do you two think that could be –"

"Hi?" called a voice from behind them, and it was such an unexpected voice that Alex span around almost in alarm. Standing in the doorway, with his torch lowered so as not to catch them all like the deer in the headlights they were, was positively the last person she had expected to see. Especially not with such an innocent expression on his face.

"*Leo*," Reef breathed; his voice taut as wire. "How did you get out?"

Leo's face dropped into a habitual look of apology. "Sorry to disappoint you, but Leo's actually the one I'm looking for. It's just me, Viggo."

Alex untensed, and could feel the others doing the same. Of course it was just Viggo. *He* certainly hadn't mysteriously disappeared, after all.

But what he might have been was in on the prank.

"Viggo. What a pleasant surprise," Yva said, unconvincingly. "What brings you here?"

"My brother, like I said," Viggo replied. "I'm at a loose end while Matt and Bianca are filming, so I thought I'd see how you were getting on." He flashed his torch around, looking vaguely puzzled. "Are you done already? Where's Leo?"

He sounded genuinely oblivious. Alex couldn't exactly spot a liar at twenty paces, but she tried to read him, nonetheless. Was he really out of the loop? Or was he just putting out a feeler, to see how they'd answer after falling victim to the twins' prank? At any rate, just as certainly as it was Viggo standing before them, they certainly couldn't answer the question –

"He's gone to the toilet," Yva said.

Alex looked at her as if she'd gone insane. Well, they couldn't answer the question *honestly*, at least.

"He's... gone to the toilet," Viggo repeated, slowly.

"Yep," Yva repeated, with absolute confidence. "At the towertops. He's been here before, remember? So he knows that they still have running water and everything."

Viggo continued to stare blankly at her. "But he's meant to be filming again in a couple of minutes."

"No better time to go," Reef interrupted. Alex caught him throwing a wink at Yva.

Viggo continued to stare at them, his eyes hidden, like theirs, in the shadow where the torchlight did not reach. He, too, was probably silently theorising; and was he as silently suspicious of Team Dry, Alex wondered, as they were of him? Whether he was in on it or not, would he accept their lie, or break character to dispute it?

What he did was to give a sigh, and lean one shoulder against the wall. "I don't understand my brother sometimes," he said, running his hand through his hair. "Well, Reef, you'll want to head over to the north wing for your next scene. Leo had better be back for that; Tara really wants to get it in a single take with Matt and Bianca's bit."

"Then we'll be off," Yva said abruptly. "We'll go with you, Reef. Chase, guard our stuff. Viggo –"

Viggo shrugged. "I'll just stay here and wait for Leo to get back, I guess," he said. "Better than Tara inventing something for me to do." He wandered in, shining his torch for somewhere to sit down. "The rain sure sounds heavy. It's a good night for Dry Diver."

Alex followed the beam of his torch, and noticed two important things. One was that the broken torch was gone, and come to think of it, the last she had seen of it was in Reef's hands. The second was that the *camera* was gone – and given the positions of everyone in the room, she was certain that Yva was holding it behind her back.

So that was how it was going to be, was it?

The four of them, Alex and Team Dry, stepped out of the room leaving Viggo behind. Out of his line of sight, Yva unzipped her coat and openly stuffed the stray camera inside.

"Wait," Alex said quickly. "We should just check on –"

She nodded her head in the direction of the other room, the storage room. Yva looked at her for a few moments, and then gave a silent nod. They moved down the corridor to the second doorway and stopped outside it, directing their torches cautiously in.

He was still there – Dry Diver. The storage room looked like another open office space with a kitchenette in the corner, now just a shallow sink and a rusting stove, and beside those and behind a barricade of stray chairs Dry Diver sat facing them at a desk with its head stump resting against the countertop behind. Seeing it watching them from a table in torchlight was eerily reminiscent of the scene in the break room.

"Sorry, Reef," Chase shrugged peremptorily. "Guess I was being paranoid."

Alex noticed that Reef didn't accept the apology. Instead he simply said, "Keep an eye, Chase. Especially with him next-door." He lowered his voice. "From now, he's the enemy."

"If you say so," Chase nodded, and settled himself into a chair by the door. "Should've brought a book with me," he muttered, but Reef and Yva were already marching away. Alex trailed in their wake, past Viggo, the "enemy," leaning against a desk looking as bored as Chase.

If she hadn't been in a hurry, she might have thought to suggest they hang out. If she hadn't thought it wasn't her place, she might have thought a lot of things. If she had only known –

"You probably shouldn't have touched that torch, Reef," Yva said, as they passed into the tower corridor. "It's evidence. If this were a crime, you'd be ruining the fingerprints."

"Everyone here is wearing gloves anyway," he replied, waving his own.

"Hmm. True," Yva said. "The police really shouldn't have let slip about fingerprints existing; they made themselves a sword, but gave the criminals a shield..." She looked back at Alex. "You're quiet, Alex; more than normal, I mean. Are you thinking something important?"

They paused at a shadowy corner, and Alex, caught in torchlight, gave a slight nod. She had moved on from her regrets – she knew from experience that she would be better off dealing with them later, when she would have more of them but also more time – to dwell on the problem of the disappearance again.

The scene in the room... It was odd. There were a couple of odd things about it, things which didn't fit, or made no sense, or should have been there; not all of which she could put her finger on right now. But it was definitely the same room as in the video; there was no question of it having been filmed elsewhere...

"Spit it out already," Yva interrupted her thoughts.

Well, better give her something, then, Alex thought; and spoke. "I'm wondering why Leo's camera was left near the door when he was attacked near the window."

Yva's face blanked. "I hadn't considered that angle," she murmured. Slowly, she began to lead them on towards the north wing, Reef struggling to keep his torchbeam ahead of her while she moved automatically. "They wanted to make sure we couldn't miss it, perhaps."

They turned into the north wing, and Reef seemed to have something to add. "You know what I think is sus?"

They didn't hear what he thought was sus, because the nearest door swung right open in a flood of torchlight and almost knocked Yva over. Closing, it revealed Bianca, who swung her torch at them and jumped.

"Watch where you're going, idiot," Yva snarled, regaining her balance.

"Damn –" Bianca hurriedly grappled at the bodycam she was wearing, and bipped it off. "Sorry," she said, although Yva's criticism actually hadn't made any sense. "The corridor's supposed to be empty."

"It certainly was!" Tara came storming down the corridor, having apparently heard the commotion. "Matt's still filming in there; a step or two further, and you'd have ruined his take! As it is we'll have to cut Bianca's footage a couple of seconds early."

"We're sorry, too," Alex broke in. This time she wasn't just trying to smooth things over. "I'm sure if Leo had been with us, he'd have made sure we were more careful."

She was putting the cat among the pigeons.

"Leo?" Bianca repeated; and flashed her torch through the three bodies ahead of her. "Where's he got to?"

Tara, at her shoulder, snorted. "That creep is a liability." She paused for a moment. "I'm glad we're mostly girls here so I can say things like that."

Reef nodded. "I get it. Guys shouldn't hit on someone else's girl."

He didn't get it, but it seemed like explaining would take a while, so they resignedly moved on.

"But seriously, where is Leo?" Bianca asked.

"Toilet," Yva said.

"He couldn't wait?" Tara's face was a picture. "Was this after you finished filming?" A panicked expression swept across her face. "Before? Tell me it wasn't before."

"After," Alex said quickly. If someone was trying to disrupt filming, trying to keep things on track might draw them out. That, and while she wanted information, she didn't want disarray.

Besides, Tara hadn't offered "during" as an option.

"Where are we on timing?" Reef asked. "I lost track while we were" – he darted a look at Alex and Yva – "waiting."

They huddled together in the island of torchlight, and Tara checked her watch. "Matt'll be filming for the duration."

"It's a multi-bodycam scene set in the conference room," Yva explained, for Alex's benefit. "Matt's filming a single continuous take, first with Bianca and then Reef and Leo, while they're *also* filming. Everyone's footage gets used, so it all has to match; a single mistake, and everyone starts over from scratch."

"Right now Matt's giving a big monologue to the camera," Tara went on, "and we've blocked in ten minutes for it – but it's the one thing we left flexible, because Matt still hadn't decided how he was going to play it." She bit her lip. "He should have chosen before, but it's his screen debut and he keeps having 'ideas'… Either way, *you*," she pointed at Reef, "need to be ready for him to open this door from the five-minute mark. With Leo."

"What if Leo doesn't turn up?" Alex asked.

Bianca gave her a strange look. "Why wouldn't he?"

Was it that she was in on the prank? Or was she out of the loop, but suspected already that there was a loop to be out of? Was there a loop at all…?

"As one of the writing team," Yva interrupted, "I say do the scene without him. He's superfluous, he's just there to introduce Reef and transition to the next scene. Cut him."

"He might still show up," Reef said. He turned to look directly at Bianca and Tara. "Who knows?"

"That reminds me," Yva said. "You started saying something, before we were so rudely interrupted, Reef."

"Yeah," Reef replied, still looking at Bianca and Tara. "But we'd better discuss it in private."

"We'll use the prep room, then," Yva said, pointing to a barely visible doorway at the dark end of the corridor; the neighbour to the one Matt was now filming in. "Come on, Alex, I'll bounce some ideas off you for Reef's new lines."

Reef cleared his throat. "*In private*, Yva," he said, staring meaningfully at her.

She stared back, blinking, for a few moments. "Oh, right," she said. "Hold the fort, Alex." She and Reef started moving down the corridor.

Tara lunged ahead of them. "You literally have a scene in minutes, Reef," she cautioned. "By that time *you* need to be out here – and *we* need to be in there."

"Yeah, what's so important it can't wait?" Bianca asked.

Reef gazed at her with a suddenly sly look on his features, ugly in the half-light. "You weren't this slow on the uptake when you were with me, Bianca," he said, a faint smile plucking at his lips. "We want to be alone. Got a problem with that?"

Alex didn't care for his expression, and it looked like Bianca didn't either. "Whatever," she mumbled, and turned away from him with a toss of her hair.

Yva drew Alex near as she passed. "Tell me if something happens. And try to get something useful out of them," she said in an undertone. As their torches reached the doorway, Alex caught a glimpse of the wide cluttered room with barred broken windows before Reef pulled Yva ahead of her. "So long, Alex! Reef, this had better be good," and then her voice was cut off with a slam of the soundproof metal door.

Alex stared at the door, trying not to think about what Yva and Reef might be doing on the other side. Just discussing whatever Reef had noticed about the disappearance, she hoped. It was amazing how quickly she had turned around from pitying Reef for having Yva for a partner. Sure, Yva was bad; but there was something naïve about her badness, and her relationship with Reef made Alex uncomfortable.

Suddenly the door opened again, mere seconds later, and from out of the invisible Yva reached and seized Alex's wrist. "On reflection, if I leave you on your own you'll just run off and find clues without me," she said, "so I'm making sure you stay right here." Alex could only stare in bewilderment as Yva drew both their arms out to their full extent and retreated into the darkness. "No listening in, though!" The door closed on Yva's elbow, and in the dark she commenced muffled whispering.

The tableau in the corridor had grown intensely surreal; a maze of crossing torchbeams through which Bianca and Tara were staring at Alex as she hung like a dog on a leash. It was embarrassing enough that Alex found herself no longer caring if she asked personal questions. "So, how did you all meet? Team Silver, I mean," she asked, having cast about for a relevant subject that might shed some light on the dynamics in play. "I know Reef's team was all just people he knew…"

"Uh…" Bianca took a moment to readjust herself to acting like nothing was unusual about their situation, which she did with aplomb. "For me, just as soon Reef put online that I was leaving the series, thank you Reef – I got an e-mail from Matt Silver, like *immediately*, asking if I was really gone or if it was just part of the story. He said if I still wanted to act they'd be happy to have me, and, well," she shrugged, "I did!" She turned to Tara. "I thought it would be weird, starting with people I didn't know, but you've done so much to make me feel welcome, Tara."

Tara looked at her feet, lacking her usual composure. "Haha, um, I would do it for anyone… I mean not *anyone* but…"

"And you, Tara?" Alex interrupted, to save her from herself. "How did Matt get the team together?"

"I was a fanartist," she said. "I make CG models and animations. It's my hobby – well, I make a little money on commissions." She said that last part in an undertone. "Matt contacted me after seeing my Dry Diver tests and asked if I wanted to work with him on a new series. …He also said if I didn't he'd send me a cease and desist, but I think he was probably joking." She frowned. "And the Karswell twins preceded me. They'd put out a video of their own, and had it fly under the radar; but Matt is obsessive about fanwork and has seen just about every one of them – and he noticed that they lived not far from him. So it made sense to join up."

"So Team Silver are all strangers to each other," Alex said. "It's the opposite of Team Dry."

"We never actually called ourselves Team Dry," Bianca pointed out. "Matt just started using that name when he came up with this crossover idea." She looked through a barred, pitch-black window, nothing to be seen but rain spatter. "Which I was against, but…"

"What's Matt's actual formal role on your team, anyway?" Alex asked.

"Showrunner," Tara answered. "Otherwise known as a little bit of everything and a lot of telling people what to do. Which is good. Someone has to set a direction."

Alex tried smiling at her. "I heard you did a lot to keep people in order, too."

She rolled her eyes. "Someone has to," she said. "Even when Matt's not filming, he's not a very orderly person. So I keep everyone on-schedule so we aren't trespassing long, I work out logistics. When we're done I take the cameras home and edit everything into sequence, and *then* I add the visual effects, do any new modelling and animation work and insert *that* –"

"One thing I've learnt – with both teams – is that there's always one person who ends up doing most of the heavy lifting," Bianca said. "You'll never see her on-camera, but Tara carries this team on her back." She gave Tara a soft smile. "You're the one we *really* can't do without, you know."

Tara, her blushes almost luminous in the shade, mumbled something inaudible and looked at her feet.

"So who's that person on Reef's team?" Alex asked Bianca, sparing Tara's blushes.

"It's Chase, of course," Bianca said. "Even now –"

"Ahhh!" Tara screamed, out of the blue.

"Bloody hell, Ta, what now?" winced Bianca, who had jumped about a foot in the air.

"It's five minutes! We just hit the five minute mark and Leo's not here and Reef's still kissing in there!" Tara exclaimed, looking completely panicked. "If Matt opens that door before we're ready we'll have to retake everything. Think of the schedule!"

"Oh, is it time?" Yva's voice called loudly from the other end of Alex's arm. "We'll talk about this later, Reef, now get out there!"

The door was shoved open and Yva marched out, dropping Alex's wrist. Alex winced; she had a tight grip. Reef followed shortly after, straightening his coat.

"What ever happened to 'no snogging on the job,' Reef?" muttered Bianca, scowling at him.

"That was your rule," he muttered right back.

"And we weren't snogging, we were just talking," Yva said.

"Who cares! Reef – get over to the other door and turn your camera on, everyone else in the prep room," urged Tara, physically ushering them down the corridor like a gaggle of geese. Reef stepped aside as Tara pushed the girls into the room, and she pulled the door shut almost to a crack and peered out. "Point your torches away from this door! Reef's torch should be the only light in that corridor," she ordered back at them. "What is Leo *doing*?"

"Giving you an excuse to fire him from the team?" Yva asked. Of the three of them, she was the only one without a torch; and her voice came from the darkness.

Tara gave her an angry glare from the doorway – and then did a double-take, looking more thoughtful. "That… is the most interesting thing you've said all evening."

Bianca shone her own torch up at her face so they could see her more clearly, and Alex, stepping closer to Yva, followed suit; lit up like candles, in that room of shadows and rainfall, lit up like demons in the dark. "Do you think Matt would go for it?" Bianca said, her voice low and conspiratorial. "Do you think Viggo would?"

"Is he honestly that bad?" Alex asked.

"Yes," Tara said.

"Yep," Bianca said.

"Yeah," Yva said. "Like, I know I'm not your idea of a great judge of character, but if I told Reef even half the stuff that guy tried to pull at the location scouting, he would go berserk."

"I only agreed to location scout with him because I knew there'd be another girl there," Tara nodded. "Ditto with going ahead to the site tonight, because *you* were meant to be there, Bianca." A note of hurt entered her stiff voice. "Where were you? I managed to keep his hands full the entire time, and the graffiti distracted him, but –"

Bianca's eyes widened. "Ta, I am *so sorry*. I had to be somewhere, but I should've thought…" Her voice trailed off, and she sadly dipped her torch.

Alex looked around the circle of faces – Tara by the door, a sliver of Reef's torchlight catching her hair; Bianca nothing but a shadow; Yva at her shoulder, dark and leering face watching with interest. Alex wondered what they thought she herself looked like. "Does Viggo know about this?" she asked softly.

"He can't *not*," Yva said.

"He won't do anything, though," Tara replied. "He's a parasitic twin. He just goes along with whatever Leo says."

"Do you think we could get him to stay on the team without Leo?" Bianca suggested.

Tara chewed her lip. "Maybe."

"Sounds like it might be good for him," Alex said.

The conversation lapsed, and Tara lit up her digital watch. "Oh *no*," she whispered.

Alex exchanged a quick glance with Yva. What now?

"We just hit the ten-minute mark," Tara whispered. "Matt's *improvising*."

Bianca groaned. "Brilliant," she said. "Just brill. I warned him! Didn't I warn him about knowing what you're doing before you turn on the camera?"

And that was when Alex realised. With a sharp intake of breath, she looked quickly at Yva and saw a gleam in her shaded eyes, too.

It was happening again. They were standing in the dark, waiting for Reef to enter a room where somebody was filming alone, and something *wasn't right*…

"So, these rooms are all soundproof, right?" Alex asked, shining her torch around the walls.

"In theory," Tara replied. "Not this one, because," and without taking her eyes off the corridor she pointed her torch towards the far wall, "the windows have all been smashed." True, the bars over the windows reflected a rainslick appearance, more droplets dashing in around them like bullets; a sight hidden only from view where maintenance staff had boarded up a single window at the near side.

"Then how do we know Matt's okay?" Alex said.

The room fell silent again, but this was no lapse in the conversation, no awkward pause. In daylight it might have been an innocent enough question; but in the dead of night, in a strange abandoned building, in a storm, Alex's words carried a sinister suggestion.

"What do you mean," Bianca said, with deliberate emphasis, "how do we know he's okay?"

Alex shrugged; tried to act casual. "I just mean that some strange things have already happened, right?"

"The graffiti, the vandalism," Yva supplied. "You say you looked, Tara – but can you *really* be sure there isn't a tenth person lurking somewhere in this building?"

And that suggestion was openly sinister.

"A tenth person can't have got in," Tara said firmly. "It's impossible."

"Then who left the graffiti? Who vandalised the place?" Yva asked, with a dark grin.

"Even if a tenth person couldn't get in ahead of you," Alex said – recalling an idea of Yva's that scared her – "there's no reason someone couldn't have *followed* us in, right?"

Rain prickled in the shadows; the cold air bit. Alex couldn't see Bianca and Tara's expressions, not well; but what she could see looked as worried as she was. They no longer felt safe.

"There's an entrance to the courtyard on the opposite side of the building," Tara said; more to herself than to the rest of them. "We could make our way around there and peek through the conference room windows. No interruption to filming necessary."

"Or we could just," Yva made a sweeping gesture, "go in."

The rain chose that moment to intensify, like a signal to remain inside and comparatively dry; puddles began to stretch towards them from beneath the barred windows. Tara took a nervous glance out of the door and into the faintly-lit corridor, where Reef was still waiting; and where time kept ticking forward, with not a word nor a sign from Matt Silver…

"Leo's not back yet, either," Alex added. "We're already off the rails."

Bianca looked to Tara. Tara looked at her watch.

"This had better be good," she said quietly, and pushed out into the corridor.

Bianca, Yva, Alex followed suit. Reef, still hovering outside the door where Matt was filming, flashed his torch in their direction. "Tired of waiting?" he said. "Me, too."

Yva went to his side. "Reef," she said, "how much of that did you hear?"

"Not much, with your door only that far open," Reef pointed. "But I got the gist." He bent closer to her, and whispered, not quietly enough, "Do you think this has something to do with –"

"We'll talk about this later," she cut him off. "The point is, either Matt's unwell, or he's messing us about."

"Neither of which I signed up for," Tara said. "This is a trainwreck. We're taking a look and seeing what we can salvage."

And, her decision made, she swiftly reached forward and pulled the conference room door open; and the group of torchbeams blazed in like a searchlight.

Revealing a camera lying discarded in the centre of the room.

CHAPTER TEN
THE SECOND TO DIVE

12:27pm

"Somebody explain this to me," Tara said. She marched into the room without a moment's hesitation, ignoring the camera, turning her torch around the walls. "Matt! Come out!"

"It's no use, Tara," Bianca said, following her in and putting a hand on her shoulder. "There's nowhere to hide in here."

It was true. The room was larger than the one Leo had disappeared from, but emptier, too; it might indeed have once been a conference room, but the long table in the centre had been flipped over like a beetle and now waved its narrow legs helplessly in the air, and office chairs had been shoved into corners or overturned. Alex followed them into the room and scanned its surroundings herself; but there weren't even desks to hide under this time. Anyone in the room would be completely exposed to a person shining their torch around at random, and Alex tried it herself to make sure. And so far as floor, ceiling, and walls went, then just like with the typing room, they were solid concrete…

"But that's impossible," Reef said. He looked shellshocked. "I was guarding this door the entire time. I'm still guarding it. And before me, all you were outside the door. And before that, Bianca was in here. So –"

"Don't get excited, Reef," Yva said, joining Alex. "Boringly, it's not impossible. Alex, point your torch at the corner. Not the tower side, the other side."

Alex did so, and all was revealed. "A fire exit," she said; and so it was, with frosted, wired glass and a metal bar across its middle which opened the door with a hard push. Damp marks had gathered around the doorframe, though it looked quite watertight.

She didn't get it. Leo's disappearance had been impossible, a properly good magic trick. But Matt's disappearance proved nothing at all.

"I don't know what you three are talking about," Tara spoke up, "but this is a huge problem. Why," she waved her arms in frustration, "did Matt leave? In the middle of his scene!"

"And why did he leave his camera?" Bianca asked, pointing her torch down at it, left forlornly in the middle of the floor. It looked mistreated, with scratches across its shiny surface.

Alex exchanged a look with Yva. Strictly speaking, it takes three points before you can call something a pattern. Just two points can be a coincidence, even a very elaborate one. So it was too early to say that events appeared to be forming a pattern. But even so –

Even so, the two of them had a more than confident idea of what they would find recorded on that camera. What was surprising, particularly given Yva's conspiracy theory, was that Bianca and Tara didn't appear remotely interested.

"First Leo, now Matt," Tara was complaining, half to Bianca and half to the universe at large. "We can't film in these conditions. I'm going after him." She marched towards the fire exit and shoved at the bar to open it. It did not open. It didn't even budge. "I forgot that this thing sticks," she was muttering, shoving and shoving without great effect. "Can't even get fire safety right in here –"

Alex instinctively moved to help; she wanted to see what was through the fire door, anyway. Tara gave her the briefest nod of acknowledgement.

"You're wasting your time! If he went out the fire exit, he could be anywhere by now," Yva called –

But then the bar went down abruptly between the two of them, and while Alex stumbled backwards Tara pushed past and out into the night. "Matt!" they heard her voice call, suddenly muffled in the rattle of the downpour. "You told me this would be a professional gig –" The door, swinging shut behind her with an uncompromising slam, stole the last of her words.

"Ta, wait – !" Bianca had caught up too late, and once again the bar wouldn't budge under a single person's arms. Feeling this could get boring very quickly, Alex regained her balance and once again between the two of them they got the fire door open. Bianca leapt out in pursuit, and Alex followed, leaving Yva and Reef momentarily in the lurch. In seconds they were stepping down from the hard concrete floor to...

Well, to a second hard concrete floor. Yva had mentioned a central courtyard, and Alex had pictured something with a grass border and a few flowerbeds and a walkway around a fountain, considerably overgrown but nonetheless a well-earned break from the colour grey. But this was a government office from the postwar years. The whole thing was nothing but an undifferentiated concrete plaza, with the odd iron bench here and there and narrow metal grates in the corners to manage the rainwater. Effective drainage and a complete absence of anything which might block that drainage were all that prevented the place from becoming a giant concrete swimming pool. There wasn't even a fountain, just a bulky and ugly statue of some unidentifiable great man of history, unidentifiable chiefly from having had his head broken off. The rain proved a more efficient fountain anyway.

A torch, however powerful, could only do so much under night and heavy rainfall. But swinging the beam high and around, Alex received an impression of enclosing walls rising several storeys up, with the four towers jutting in at each corner like giants looming over her cage.

There was no immediate sign of Matt Silver, anyway. Tara, hood up, was stomping around the statue to a set of double-doors on the opposite side; the only way out of the courtyard, the fire exit being one-way. ...Speaking of which, had they just shut themselves out of the north wing?

Alex spun around, her torchbeam passing over the barred or boarded windows and back to the fire exit – in which Yva had fortunately thought to post Reef, standing bracing the door open. Yva herself was following his torchbeam towards Alex – and she had picked up the camera...

Bianca, though, had dashed ahead to intercept Tara whilst Alex had been distracted. "Ta, come back, this is stupid!" she called, catching up with her before she could reach the door of the south wing; the rain falling in curtains around them, streaming down their coats and giving scattering reflections, gleaming like metal. "We can't all go wandering off. We should stick where they can find us..."

Tara's muted reply was drowned out by the shower of raindrops on Alex's hood. She took a step forwards and her shoe connected with something, a light object that rolled away; and her foot came down on the ground with a faint crunching sensation. She took a hasty step back and directed her torch at the ground, where it reflected back a strange glitter amid the puddles.

Shattered glass. And the object that had rolled away was yet another broken torch, with a smashed lens…

A splash to her side announced Yva's arrival, plainly more interested in the stray torch than in Tara and Bianca's muffled back-and-forth. "I wonder what these are supposed to mean, other than that Matt Silver is a cheapskate," she said.

Three broken torches, one at the site of each mysterious appearance or disappearance, was enough for a pattern; even if Alex had seen that one of them was rare moment of clumsiness on Yva's part. Alex raised her eyes to where Tara and Bianca's torchbeams crossed, and nodded in their direction. "Still think they're in on it?" she murmured.

Yva hesitated. "Their behaviour is irrational if they are," she said; "but that could still be to throw off suspicion. You can't ever judge based on behaviour alone. Personality doesn't matter in a mystery."

Alex would have disagreed – forcefully, even – but her torch had just caught the edge of something not quite blocked from view behind Yva.

There was something there, large and long and low, in the corner between the tower and the boarded-up windows of the east wing; and Alex pointed her torch at it, lying flat on the ground – about as long as a fallen human.

A coffin…!

Alex shook her head to get herself under control. No, of course it wasn't a coffin. That made no sense. She pushed past Yva to take a closer look, and it was just a filing cabinet, one which had had all the drawers pulled out and been shoved flat on the bare concrete, and which rain had filled to the brim. Vandals had clearly done a number on it. Alex glanced sidelong at Yva –

She should've been looking sooner. There was an expression on Yva's face which Alex had never seen before, pale and rigid and with eyes so wide it was alarming. She was actually frightened.

"Yva, it's okay!" Alex said, gently touching her shoulder. "It's just junk, a filing cabinet…"

A. CARVER

After the events they had been through together in the castle of Carver's Rest, after everything Yva herself had done there, Alex had never thought she would see Yva lose her nerve like this. The atmosphere in the Pitchwater Building was clearly getting to her, too; perhaps because it was so personal. This was supposed to have been her big chance… Whatever the case, Yva blinked and her expression became assertive again; and she brushed Alex's hand from her shoulder. "Let's get back inside," she said, dismissing the subject in a moment; and without another word she led Alex back to the fire exit, pushing past Reef and ignoring the expression of puzzled concern on his face. Bianca and Tara were coming back the same way, in any case.

It was a relief to be inside and throwing back her hood. The constant hammering of rain on Alex's coat had been oppressive, driving her down into the floor; even inside it seemed to pull at her as water dripped from her sleeves. The indoors was still tombstone-cold, but the very elements were not at war with her. The fire door swung shut and locked itself behind them with a solid and authoritative clunk.

But the din of the rain remained, muffled but constant, upon the windows; and it was easy to be drawn into the tense, increasingly paranoid atmosphere. As the five of them gathered in a circle of torchlight, Alex couldn't help glancing again and again over her shoulder at the shadows.

"Guys, I am so sorry about this," Bianca said. She looked genuinely baffled, for all that Alex kept reminding herself what a convincing actor she was supposed to be. "I don't know what Matt's playing at. If he needed to go, why didn't he just open the door and say something?"

"I'd have seen if he did," Reef emphasised. "Tara, too."

"He's right," Tara said. "I am not taking responsibility for this. Matt had better have a good explanation."

"Maybe there's an explanation right here," Yva said, and Alex heard rather than saw the grin in her voice. She was the only one without a torch, and it took a moment for Alex to realise that she was holding the camera. "Matt did leave something for us, after all…"

"Ah, I get it now," Bianca nodded. "If something happened, you'd expect it'd been caught it on film."

"And then left his camera…" Tara muttered, looking at it like a puzzle she couldn't solve.

Yva turned on the camera, the glow from the screen casting her face in a ghostly light, and buttoned away at its menus. "One recording," she said, and her brow knotted. "But it's partially corrupted."

"What?!" demanded Tara.

"See for yourself," Yva said, making no effort to let them see anything; so the four of them gathered at her shoulders. The playback screen showed the recording's date and time, starting midnight; but the duration was barely a minute and the thumbnail was only glitchy blocks of colour.

"That's not right," Bianca said; "Matt definitely had his camera on and recording the whole time I was with him." She looked to Tara. "Do you think it got dropped and that did it?"

Tara moaned. "Even the cameras are failing me."

"It's useless for the vlog," Yva agreed. "But let's take a look at what footage survived…"

Five faces leaned in. Yva, after a dramatic pause, set the playback going.

SILVERFISH
"EPISODE 8"

Squares of colourful static leap and dance until, with a crackle of sound –

There is the briefest hint of motion and the cut-off clang of metal as the door comes instantly to a close. The camera, chest-height, remains pointed at it for a few seconds, a circle of torchlight resting on the dull metal; but then both camera and torch swing around, drifting across the bare wall as the speaker strides away, catching the barred windows and the empty night as he goes, and for all that it might have been any door then the conference room is now coming into clearer view.

Then the torch and camera turn again, the light shining way across the room now, straight across the inverted table with its legs like stunted trees; and for no apparent reason the cameraman marches right down the middle of it, flashing the torch left and right as he goes, the scattered chairs casting long and slender shadows across the blank walls, the fire door firmly closed. After a few seconds the camera reaches the far wall, the circle of torchlight growing wider and wider until it does; then, with a restless motion, camera and torch flick around to point back across the room and the weary pacing resumes.

There is something maddening about it, that repetitive, echoing pacing across the silent and visibly empty room. It's as if the cameraman is on guard, or waiting for something.

The cameraman isn't even halfway back when there's a quiet clunk, like a door softly closing or a hard-soled shoe on the floor. The cameraman wavers for just a moment, then makes a rapid turn back in the direction of the fire exit –

Where the torchlight washes like water around the imposing shape of a diving suit, casting towards the fire exit a massive silhouette without a head. Before the cameraman can even react a gloved and clawed hand is reaching for the camera, and everything goes black.

CHAPTER ELEVEN
THE HAZARD DOOR

12:31pm

Alex, Yva, and Reef had some idea of what to expect, of course; but Bianca and Tara were stunned into silence.

"…How much of that was in the script?" whispered Alex.

"Everything up to you-know-who," Yva said. "Matt's waiting for his friends to return. He paces the room for a minute, then gets bored, takes off his camera, and gives a monologue about his tragic backstory."

"But someone else came," Reef said.

"Yeah," Bianca said; and she turned slowly to face him. "Someone wearing your Dry Diver costume."

Nobody moved when she made that statement. But Alex was acutely aware that they had gone from being a group of five, to groups of three and two.

"Is that what you think?" Reef retorted, his face twisting all too readily into a taut and angry one. "Our costume, is it? Like we've got a monopoly on Dry Diver costumes?"

"Matt told us that your team used to have one," Alex said to Bianca, trying to keep her voice calm; not interrogating, merely enquiring. "Do you know what happened to it?"

Bianca hesitated; turned to Tara. "I never saw it," Tara said, not meeting anyone's eyes. "Matt threw it away when he hired me."

"Or he said he threw it away," Yva grinned.

Bianca looked at her, eyes sharp as glass. "What's that supposed to mean?"

"What," interrupted Alex, her voice as loud as she could project it whilst remaining even, "do you think was going on in that video?"

"What's it look like?" Bianca answered, her voice hard. "Someone came in in a Hallowe'en costume and attacked Matt!"

Tara, eyes on the camera screen still, said nothing…

"How naïve," Yva said, with more than a hint of a sneer. "That's what they want us to think, sure. But this recording is simply a crude prank, as you would know if you thought about it for even a moment."

Alex thought, too; for the way Yva was speaking, the way she was placing all her emphasis on being logical and rational, made Alex sure she had some hard evidence in mind. It reminded her of Great-Aunt Cornelia making some effortless deduction.

Oh. It was obvious. "The fire exit," Alex said, and Yva nodded with approval.

"She's right," Tara said quietly. "It's a one-way door. Nobody can get in from outside, only out from inside."

"And the room has no hiding-places, and the only other exit was being guarded by both Reef and Tara," Yva summed up. "Which means that Matt Silver let Dry Diver in."

"But –" Bianca looked knocked off-balance, not sure which side of the fence to fall. "How would he do that? He never goes near it. He's not close enough to push the bar –"

"There are innumerable remote-control gimmicks you can invent with enough time and ingenuity," Yva said dismissively. "Some fishing-line looped around an arrangement of the room's furniture – or perhaps a telescoping pole he was unfolding outside of the camera view –"

"You're forgetting that the door takes two people to open," Tara said. "I pointed out that the bar sticks back when we were scouting this place."

"That does make the problem look like an impossible one," Yva admitted, though she sounded quite pleased at the thought. "But since Matt did leave, there must have been a way to circumvent it. That's just logic."

"I'm just going to check that fire door, actually," Alex said, unhappy at the prospect of a fire escape which actually made escape harder. You couldn't take anything for granted in a mystery, even that an unexamined door or window worked like any normal one would; and besides, it was a step that Tara and Bianca couldn't object to, either. She walked quickly up to the fire door, and ran her torch carefully along its edges, its hinges, the impenetrable glass and the metal bar. It all looked perfectly legitimate to her, nothing broken, nothing tampered with; and a couple of experimental pushes (with Tara's help) showed that there was no trickery with the bolt, either, which held the door shut when the bar was up, and retracted only when the bar was pushed down, from out of a small round shaft in the door jamb visible only with the door open. The bar was unusually stiff to push and took two people to open it, every time, but she was looking for things which made opening the door easier rather than harder. The concrete of the wall overlapped the door at the top and sides, and the door fitted snugly against the floor, so there was no hope of passing any string or wire around the edges. Alex even took the liberty of stepping out into the rain to inspect the door's outside face; but it was just a mirror image of the inner face, without a push-bar but with a small hook which could have been hooked on the outside wall to hold the door wide open – if the fastening had still been there, anyway. She had a feeling she'd seen modern fire doors do this with magnets.

"It's a normal fire door," she reported, back out of, if not the cold and the wet, then at least the wet. "No gimmicks."

"And there you have it," Yva concluded, giving her a look of delighted approval. "It doesn't matter how he did it – Matt invited his 'attacker' in, which means there was no attack, merely a low attempt to make us look stupid, just like Le –"

She tried to stop herself, but it was too late for that. The cat was out of the bag.

"Just like Leo?" Bianca filled in. "And what did he do?"

Alex looked at Yva and Reef, and shrugged. "Okay, cards on the table," she said, "exactly the same thing happened with Leo as with Matt. He walked into a room to film and vanished."

"And left behind another bogus video of him being attacked by Dry Diver," Yva added.

Tara cried out in frustration. "Has anyone done any legit filming tonight?!"

"Uh, me," Bianca said, with false brightness. "We can use that, at least!"

Tara let out a long, relieved sigh. "Knew I could count on you." Then she drew straight and stiff again, like a tightened bolt. "But what exactly is going on here?"

"You tell us," Reef sniped. "It's your team who are the problem."

"Don't look at us," Bianca said, staring right at him. "We're as clueless as you are."

"Or so you claim," Yva replied. Alex knew that she had a policy of, in general, not trusting anybody. But applying that when reading a mystery novel was different to applying it in real life.

"I would never do anything to disrupt filming," Tara said. "You're forgetting that this is a job to me. I get paid. You bet I take this seriously."

"Yeah like, Matt and Leo aren't our friends," Bianca added. "Even if they suggested some dumb prank to us, it's not like we're going to go along with it."

"You might if you were being blackmailed," Yva pointed out.

Tara snorted. "With what?"

That, Alex felt, was a surprisingly naïve remark from a girl who regarded herself as an adult and a professional. Alex was uncomfortably aware that there were plenty of things you could blackmail a teenage girl with. Uncomfortable enough that she felt it was high time to steer this argument away from unprovable accusations and towards something meaningful. "Okay, but what are we actually going to do about this?" she interrupted. "Two people are missing, and we're meant to think they were attacked by Dry Diver. What now?"

"I'll tell you what we're going to do," Tara said, crossing her arms. "We're going to do the exact opposite of what those idiots want us to do."

Bianca gave her a quizzical look. "So, what's that?"

Tara blinked in surprise, as if it was obvious. "We keep filming."

CHAPTER TWELVE
DERELICTION OF DUTY

12:33pm

"We," Alex repeated, "keep filming?" She exchanged a nonplussed look with Bianca.

"We keep filming," Tara nodded. "I don't know what *this*," she gestured to the camera, "is supposed to achieve, but I will not run around after a cryptid Matt Silver made up like we're in *Scooby-Doo*. Instead I'm going to do my job."

Yva looked stunned. "But that…" she said, "that was going to be my suggestion… And you just came out and said it…"

Reef put his arm around her shoulder. "It's fine," he said, giving her a gentle squeeze. "Anything to make us look the better team, right?"

"I suppose," Yva said, reviving. She loved being in charge, Alex knew. Alex suspected she was torn between going along with what she wanted to do or suggesting anything else just to be original.

Bianca was also looking conflicted. "What about Chase and Viggo?"

"What about them?" Alex echoed. "Last we saw them, they were just… waiting."

"We left Chase in our storage room, guarding the Dry Diver costume, if that makes you feel any better," Reef said, with his eyes narrowed. "And as for Viggo –"

He hesitated, and looked at Yva.

"Go on," she said, with a nod. "Tell them the idea you told me earlier, when we were alone together." She looked aside at Alex and gave her a grin. "He has a *theory*, bless him."

Alex felt her eyebrows raise. A theory, huh? She herself didn't have much of a theory of her own yet; she needed more clues. The prank theory explained most things, but it just didn't *feel* right…

Feelings don't matter in a murder mystery. Yva would say that, Great-Aunt Cornelia would probably agree – but intuitions mean something. They mean that, on some deep unconscious level, you've noticed an element which doesn't fit. An inconsistency in someone's behaviour, an explanation which doesn't quite match your observations. Those feelings could be wrong, and Alex, who had a serious tendency towards social anxiety, often was wrong when she invariably felt scared and embarrassed in perfectly ordinary situations. But nothing that was happening that night was ordinary.

Reef, meanwhile, was looking a little awkward himself, with all eyes on him, as if he was about to perform an important scene for a big audience. After pausing to put his thoughts together, he finally spoke. "We don't even know," he said, "when we're really talking to Viggo."

So it was a twin theory, then. Alex supposed she should have seen this coming. "But what difference does –"

"Twins," Yva began loudly, "are the solution to all sorts of bad murder mysteries."

Alex rolled her eyes, and waited. Yva was adopting Great-Aunt Cornelia's habit of giving mystery lectures.

"It's always a variation of the same thing," Yva went on. "X's alibi is a lie because it was actually his twin Y, etcetera. It's even one of Knox's Ten Commandments for murder mysteries that you can't introduce twins at the last minute as an explanation." She grew a fox's hungry smile. "But if you introduce them near the *start*, it's fair game. In fact, it's a certainty that there'll be twin shenanigans involved."

"Why are you talking like this is a murder mystery book?" Bianca asked, her voice uneasy. "Nobody's been murdered – and this isn't a book, either."

"I'm simply preparing the ground," Yva said haughtily.

"Yes thank you Yva, I knew all that," Alex broke in. "But what I was trying to say was, what difference does it make which twin we're speaking to? We know they're both here, after all."

"It matters," Yva said, speaking as slowly as if she were explaining to a small child, "because it means one of them can disappear for a long time while the other plays both roles. So we believed it was Viggo who appeared shortly after Leo disappeared, remember? But it might just have been Leo again, and who knows what Viggo has been up to all this time?"

…That was worth checking. Alex turned to Tara and Bianca. "When did you last see Viggo?"

They exchanged confirmatory looks with each other. "I was the last," Tara volunteered. "He loitered with me in the prep room next-door after we all separated to start filming. But I sent him to guard the corridor because his breathing was annoying me."

Yva nodded, as if this made perfect sense. "So if the 'Viggo' we met was actually Leo again, the real Viggo has been out of sight for a long time now. Of course, they might also have substituted earlier, such that the 'Leo' filming was actually Viggo, and vice-versa."

"Yeah, I don't know if I buy them swapping places," Bianca said, her expression dubious. "They're too different for that."

And again, Yva responded with one of those unpleasant, knowing grins. "Oh, and you know them intimately, do you?"

"We're all actors here, Bianca," Reef said coldly.

Alex felt that this line of inquiry had probably outlived its usefulness, and intervened before Reef and Bianca could make yet another uncomfortable scene. "Well, either way, both twins have been out of sight for a while now," she pointed out. "Maybe they're plotting something, maybe they aren't. But weren't we going to do some filming instead of worrying about their plans?" Honestly, anything to keep this mismatched group from arguing again.

"Very sensible. Thank you for reminding me," Tara said. She stepped into the middle of the group, assuming command from the centre of attention. "Just as you actors have your lines memorised, I have the schedule memorised, and we'll be just in time for the next scene requiring only the two actors we have here."

Only the two – *oh great*, Alex thought. She had backed the wrong horse.

Yva answered the unasked question. "It's the Reef and Bianca argument scene."

As Alex slumped, Tara seemed to brighten considerably; possibly it was the prospect of getting some work done and regaining a little normality in the abandoned building in the middle of the night. "Bianca and Reef, report to the prep room for filming, please!" she ordered, looking pleased mostly with herself. "At least we know *this* scene will be a good one, with Bianca in it."

Bianca pursed her lips. "I don't like this scene."

Tara's expression fought with a new emotion. "But… if you felt this way, why didn't you complain to Matt?"

"I did," Bianca said shortly. "He told me he was relying on me to be mature about this."

"So you have your answer," Yva said breezily. "If Reef can be mature about this, so can you."

Bianca's lips pressed tight. "If that's how it is…" she muttered, and swept wordlessly away towards the corridor, silhouetted by her retreating torchbeam; Reef following behind with a last backwards nod at Yva.

"I'll monitor from the corridor," Tara declared, business-like again. "The scene doesn't call for the door to be either open or closed, so we can leave it ajar." She looked sidelong at Alex and Yva, particularly the latter. "You two will need to leave a wide berth."

"Then we'll monitor the windows in the courtyard," Yva announced, and Alex's jaw dropped. "With guards on all sides, nothing suspicious can happen this time."

"That… is a good idea," Tara nodded, cautiously. "Turn off your torches, stay behind the boarded window, and keep quiet unless it's an emergency."

"Um, were you going to ask me about this?" Alex asked

"But somebody needs to guard the windows from Leo and Matt," Yva said – and, adopting an especially plaintive and whining tone, continued, "and you wouldn't abandon your only friend, would you?"

Alex was quite certain that Yva had misspoken, and had meant to say that Alex was *her* only friend. Yes, surely that was what Yva had intended. Even Yva wouldn't simultaneously plead with and belittle her, right?

Alex took several deep breaths and tried to remember what she was meant to be getting out of this exercise. Right, the inimitable feeling of having done a good deed. Never quite so appealing once you're actually doing the work rather than just making the offer.

"Of course I'd never abandon you, my only friend," she said stiffly; and, deciding that if she was going to be roped into this then she could at least be doing it her way, she added, "let's go the long way around, and say hi to Viggo and Chase before we leave through the south wing."

"Euh –" Yva looked tongue-tied – but then she found her sickly-sweet smile. "Whatever you say, *friend*."

"You two are so weird," Tara said, and stomped off after Reef and Bianca. Alex took one last look around the conference room before she, too, left. The camera had vanished.

They were back in the tower before Yva spoke again. Her voice was dead flat, as if she too was getting tired of acting. "What did you really want to go this way for?"

"To say hi to Viggo and Chase, like I said," Alex replied, guiding them around the dark turns. "They might have seen something in the courtyard."

"Not through these windows, they won't," Yva said, as they turned into the east wing. Alex's torch passed from one window to the next which had been boarded up firmly on the courtyard side, the bars looking out only on wide sheets of plywood.

"You know, someone's taking care of this place," Alex said. "Perhaps that's your tenth person. Hi Viggo!"

She swung her torch into the typing room where they had left Viggo, the same one from which his twin had seemed to vanish. Doing so gave her the eeriest sensation of déjà vu. This was brought about largely by the fact that the room was, once again, quite empty.

"Okay…" Alex said. "I've decided not to be alarmed by this."

Yva tilted her head. "Is that something normal people can do? Just decide to feel a certain way and then feel it? I wish I could do that. It would be a huge help on the times when I actually do feel something and it's unpleasant."

"It's more of an aspiration," Alex replied, and began walking down the corridor again, trying not to increase her pace. "Hi Chase!"

The storage room again came into partial and shadowy view, and again there was only the lolling figure of Dry Diver left slumped at the far wall to greet them.

"…I'm also aspiring not to feel alarmed right now," Yva said. "Does it show?"

Alex gave her the full beam. She did indeed look unusually tense; and Alex felt strange, empathising with her.

"It kinda does show, actually," Alex said.

"Huh," Yva said, and forced a grin. "Guess I need to work on my own acting. You go first, okay?"

Alex had never thought of herself as the brave one. Nor had she thought of Yva as cowardly, come to that. "Since when did you ever want someone else to take the lead?" she asked, looking quizzically at Yva.

"When it started being a question of pranksters hiding around corners to jumpscare us," Yva answered. "We're not on a case here, Alex. *Yet*," she added, in an undertone.

The thought of people waiting to jump out at her did Alex absolutely no favours as she set foot into the south side of the Pitchwater Building, an area she had yet to explore. The south tower was a mirror image of its northern counterpart, with a closet on the left in place of the entrance to the tunnel, and a corridor that crooked multiple times around the sides of a single central room. Alex found herself leaning out of each turn, shining her torch at an angle that illuminated as much as it could around the corner.

It was just as they had reached the door to the south wing that they heard it. The rooms of the Pitchwater Building might have been soundproofed, but the bare concrete surfaces of the corridor left sounds echoing; even the sound of softly murmuring voices. Alex stopped to listen, straining her ears to catch that faint drone that wavered like a dying flame.

Yva gesticulated down the corridor. She didn't need to say it. The noise was coming from that way. Dipping the torch to the floor, treading lightly, they crept cautiously along afraid now not of being surprised but of being the ones doing the surprising.

Past a closed and irrelevant door, they reached one of the staircases to the upper floors – a steep straight flight that followed the outer wall before turning twice and continuing on upwards. The voices were louder now; they must have been at the very top of the flight, just out of sight. But if you just silently took first one step up, then another, until the upstairs landing came into view…

"Oh, it's just you two," Yva said out loud, guiding Alex's torch to shine them full in the face. "What an anticlimax."

Standing shielding their eyes at the top of the stairs were Viggo and Chase. Alex found herself at once relieved, and strangely disappointed. Their disappearances hadn't lasted for long.

"And it's you two, too. Sorry, can you not point that in my eyes?" Viggo asked, and Alex lowered the torch out of Yva's grip. "Thanks. Anything the matter?"

"No," Alex lied. She didn't want to make a habit of it, but pretending that everything was okay just came so naturally to her. Perhaps that was aspirational, too. "What about you two? Just taking a walk?"

"Kind of," Chase said, the camera on his chest scattering torchlight up towards his face. "Decided to hang out together rather than in separate rooms, and Viggo asked me to help look for Leo. Safety in numbers."

"Safety from what?" Alex asked. "Dry Diver?"

She'd meant it as a joke, but all it did was betray her own nervousness. More than that, it betrayed Chase and Viggo's, too. "You shouldn't be scared of Dry Diver," Chase said, looking deeply uncomfortable. "It's not real."

"Or so they say," Viggo said quietly. "I asked Matt, once, where he got the idea – and he said it was from life." He swallowed. "And he wouldn't explain any more than that…"

For all that Alex tried to be rational, and knew that Matt Silver was surely just teasing him – it wasn't something she wanted to hear in the dark. "Any news on Leo?" she asked quickly.

"No sign up here," Viggo supplied. "I'm starting to get worried." His face was a knot of concern, and Alex wondered if he was the only person in the building who cared about Leo. Or perhaps, like everyone else, he was more worried what Leo might get up to on his own. "Have you seen him?"

"Not *obviously*," Yva said, implying something that Alex couldn't deduce. "So you two have been together the whole time?"

Viggo looked at Chase and shrugged. "I guess we have," he said. "Why?"

Yva looked sidelong at Alex, who read the suspicion in her eyes. So *that* was what she meant by "Not *obviously*." Take Viggo and Chase accounting for one another; then the various permutations of herself, Yva and Reef, Tara and Bianca in the prep room or the corridor outside it… It added up to alibis all round for Dry Diver's appearance in the conference room with Matt – with one exception: Leo Karswell.

Although there were other possibilities. Alex could feel them stirring in the back of her brain, waiting for her to pay attention to them. Bianca, for instance –

"I'll tell you why," Yva went on – and her expression grew suddenly fierce. "Because Chase, did you forget you have a *job* to do?"

Chase was taken aback, and almost dropped *his* torch, too; and his eyes flashed to Viggo. "I –"

"Guarding our Dry Diver costume, *remember*?" Yva said, with a curl of her lip. "What would Reef say if he knew you'd been sneaking around behind his back, hmm?"

Chase looked really quite distressed, and Alex felt she had to do something. "Seriously, Yva, don't be so hard on him!" she interrupted, and gave Chase her most apologetic look. "Sorry, Chase, we're all kind of on edge down here."

"No. I get it," Chase said, and in the space of a moment he had closed himself off, his shoulders hunched and his eyes staring at the ground; his body language totally uncommunicative. "My responsibility," he muttered darkly, and hurried around the staircase without a backward glance.

"I guess I'll just keep searching for Leo on my own, then?" Viggo said, blinking at Chase's receding back. "Alone? In the dark?" His eyes darted to Alex and Yva. "Unless you two want to join me."

"We'll pass," Yva answered. "You go make your movements uncorroborated."

"Good luck," Alex added. "If you find him, we'd like to talk to him."

"Not what most girls say," Viggo said in an undertone, and he and his torchbeam turned out of sight up the stairs; a distant call of "Leo?" echoing their way before receding into silence.

Yva turned to Alex. "After all," she said, once they were quite out of earshot, "if nobody was guarding the costume, then it *could* have been ours in Matt's video. It's unlikely, but we can't disprove it."

"Even if a different one was used in Leo's video," Alex said. "Hey, if it was Leo wearing the suit in Matt's video, who was it in Leo's video?"

Yva shrugged. "Viggo? Or Leo, maybe, if Reef is right about Leo having been Viggo and vice-versa. Once that theory is in play, it doesn't really matter which is which."

Alex wasn't sure about that angle. They may have been physically identical, but the twins sure didn't have identical personalities. "How do the timings work out on that?"

Yva shrugged. "One of the things you learn when you start paying attention to crime is that human perception of time – along with all other witness testimony – is so unreliable that it's actually useless," she said. "Unless it's an old-school mystery with alibis about train timetables and other objective events, I don't bother paying attention." She paused in thought. "Do you think Tara will buy that if we use it to explain why we took so long?"

Oh, right, they were going to the courtyard! "Not if we keep hanging around here!" Alex said, and in a moment they were off again, Yva leading them straight back down the corridor and to the door to the south wing. This proved to be entirely occupied by the foyer of the building, a wide open area with a large pair of entrance doors in the centre of a wall to their side, fronted with more wire-mesh windows which would let the light in and little else; one of them was ajar, and Alex figured this must have been how Leo and Tara had left to check over the fence before the rest of the group arrived. Opposite was an identical pair of doors leading to the courtyard, set between two small rooms in the corners – reception desks once, but the glass panels communicating between them and the foyer had again been boarded over, leaving them completely enclosed. Broken glass crunched beneath Alex's feet.

The courtyard was as wet as it had ever been; there was no way you could spend more than a couple of minutes out here without the rain making its way through your coat. Alex hoped it was a short scene Reef and Bianca were filming.

Had the Dry Diver suit been wet?

It hadn't occurred to Alex to look closely at it, either of the two times they'd checked on it after a disappearance. She'd been distracted by the fact of it having been there at all; or of Chase not having been there. But certainly whichever Dry Diver suit had been in and out of that fire exit would've got soaked in the courtyard, even if the waterproofing had protected the person inside; just as it would have been obvious if anyone had been out there recently in a coat. Unfortunately there was nothing to hope for in the way of wet footprints as clues, as the nine of them had muddied the corridors with those already.

So forgetful, Alex! She hadn't thought to ask Viggo about Team Silver's original Dry Diver suit, either. Perhaps when she next saw him. Or perhaps by then the pranksters would have got bored and given themselves up…?

She shelved the thought as she and Yva reached the glassless bars of the prep room, their latest filming site. The passing of their torchlight brought Reef to the window, looking as if they were visiting him in prison. "What took so long?" he asked Yva; if nothing else, he always looked concerned for her. "Everything okay?"

"Nothing to worry about," she said; Alex was glad she didn't mention that Chase had neglected his possibly unnecessary and definitely boring duty of guarding the Dry Diver suit. "You all ready to go?"

"Yep," said Bianca's shadow, obscured in the back of the room; keeping her distance from Reef. "Tara's getting antsy. Says she thought you'd have been quicker to watch us do a scene you wrote."

"From an original idea by Matt Silver, to be clear," Yva corrected.

"Don't let us keep you!" Alex said brightly, in case this was going to run and run, like the raindrops running into her hood while she had her face upturned.

Reef nodded, and vanished from the window. Yva pulled Alex over to where a solitary rectangle of ply blotted out bars and broken glass, placing the pair quite effectively out of sight, and grabbed at the torch to switch it off.

"And, action!" she heard Tara's distant yell.

Silence in the room. Then a muffled exclamation. A pause, and then a further exclamation. Then an exchange of voices, indistinguishable; indeed, barely audible…

Alex quickly came to the conclusion that she was not, in fact, going to be experiencing much of the scene at all. With her hood over her ears and the rain beating a steady rhythm upon it, her hearing wasn't great. In fact, why be so generous? It was downright appalling, she couldn't hear any more than a murmur. There might have been just one person in the room talking to themselves, for all she knew. Meanwhile all she had for entertainment was the curtain of rain falling in the vast concrete cell of the courtyard, like a giant gutter.

She glanced at Yva, standing beside her. Yva was leaning as close to the open windows as she could get away with, clearly straining to hear. "Why did you think this was necessary again?" Alex whispered, as quietly as she could afford over the rain. "We could've just stood in the next room with the fire door op–"

"*Shhh!*" hissed Yva with a sudden lurch of the head. "They're getting to the good bit!"

It had better be good, Alex found herself sulking. But then the muffled voices in the room jumped in volume, and what they said got very interesting indeed.

"And I'm asking you again, why did you abandon us?!"

It was Reef. His acting seemed to have got better since the last *Dry Diver Drownings*; his voice was straining with passion, and hurt and bewilderment contested for the upper hand as he pleaded with Bianca.

"Because I was in danger with you!" Bianca screamed back, her voice breaking with pretended distress. "You were being so reckless, I was *scared* of you! Scared for the people around you!"

"I'm *so* good at this," Yva whispered, turning to Alex with absolute glee in her eyes. "I wrote this with the double meaning of Bianca also having left Reef in real life. So meta!"

"Yeah, I got that," Alex nodded grimly. Just like Yva. Just like Yva, to write something like this without realising it had the power to cause genuine hurt to her actors...

"But you're still in danger *now*!" Reef was roaring. "You took right up with those guys, and just look at what's happening! You really think you're safer here?"

"But I didn't *know* that!" Bianca cried, her voice a choking mess, and Alex could really picture the tears running down her face like the raindrops on her own. "I needed to keep doing what I was doing to try and understand myself, and I thought Matt and his friends would be safe and supportive and everything you *weren't*!"

"I was *always* supportive of you!" Reef bellowed. "You just didn't want to know!"

Yva frowned. "Hey, they're going off-script."

Alex took a sharp intake of breath. So *that* was why this performance felt so heart-wrenchingly tense. They weren't acting.

And Reef was going on and on, screaming his heart out like he'd bottled it up, given it a shake, and fired the cork like a bullet...

"This is your fault! You did this to humiliate me!" he shrieked, his voice jumping an octave, a sob leaking into the last word. "All because you wanted to be with *anyone but me*! Admit it, *you cheated on me!*"

The only answer Alex heard was a scream – and then a trampling of stumbling and desperate feet, and the deafening slam of a door that made the window's boarding shiver.

CHAPTER THIRTEEN
THE TRAP CLOSES

12:43pm

"But that's not how this scene's supposed to end!" Yva exclaimed, outrage writ large on her face. "They're *ad-libbing*! Actors, I ask you!"

But Alex was already pushing past Yva to the unblocked windows, reviving her torch to shine it through the gaps in the bars. The door was swinging, and there was nobody inside; just the distant resound of racing feet.

"This is why adaptations can never supersede the original text," Yva was still rambling, until Alex seized her hand.

"We have to go after them," she said.

"If only to get out of the rain, sure," Yva grumbled, but Alex was already scanning for any quicker way in than the long way around she had led them on. But the windows were all barred or boarded, and a quick, hopeful tug on the catch on the fire door did of course not pull it open. The only way forward was back, pulling Yva past the stifled statue and to the south wing doors.

They stepped inside, threw back their hoods, and shook off their coats; and then they were marching back off into the tower, back into the corridors, Alex hurrying ahead.

"I notice you are taking the lead," panted Yva, as they veered through the dark. "What exactly are you thinking you're going to achieve? Because I was just going to yell at them."

Alex stopped on the spot. Okay, maybe this was a useful thing to explain to a person trying to feign normal emotions. "These people are hurting," she said. "I get that you don't feel sorry for them, but somebody has to try and help."

Yva had a look on her face as if she was trying to solve a puzzle. "If you say so, but why is that *your* responsibility?"

"Like I said, *somebody* has to try," Alex repeated. It helped to convince herself, too. "And with a lot of the others hiding, or wandering around…"

Yva released an expression of undisguised contempt. "Right now, I'm just done with these people, all of them. Completely useless. Even with my own goals, I am on the brink of walking right out of here."

Alex took a quick look around, flashing her torch left and right along the corridor; just in case somebody was hiding, she supposed, to try and catch her out. "Being totally honest," she whispered, "I get that too. I just want to run away from their problems; I hate looking at what these arguments and these stupid pranks are doing to everyone. But..." She sighed. "We've got to try. It really is that, or leave. We don't have anything else to do. Everything's kind of fallen apart."

"This whole thing was a mistake," Yva agreed. "I couldn't have known that, but Matt Silver should've known better."

"It was his idea?" Was that a clue? Alex shook the thought off; she was getting distracted. "Forget it; let's go find them. Before anyone else disappears."

But as ever, Alex was destined to be disappointed.

"Chase?" she called, as they entered the east wing. "Uh, you might want to come with us. Reef and Bianca have..."

She trailed off as she drew level with the room he was supposed to be guarding; and for the third time that night, her torch shone only on the immobile hulk of a modified diving suit. Dry Diver was alone in the room.

"I suppose it was too much to ask that a person would stay put," Yva said, sighing dramatically. "Even Dry Diver went on walkabout earlier." She grinned. "Suppose it got Chase, too?"

Alex shuddered. "Don't say that," she whispered. "Besides, there's no camera." Dry Diver had always left his victims' cameras behind, after all. Still, this was so ridiculous it was disturbing, or possibly vice-versa. How long ago had they left Chase? Five minutes? Ten?

"Bianca?" called Alex, as they stepped into the north tower. "Tara?"

"Reef!" Yva yelled.

No answer, came the stern reply. They walked right around to the north wing, but their calls found it silent, and the torch found it empty; both rooms, deserted.

"So has everyone just disappeared now?" Yva asked. An increasingly dark expression began to storm her face. "So, they were all in on it… and *I'm* their target."

"I'm sure that's not true," Alex said quickly. "We could hear that they ran off, after all. Bianca was upset, and Tara and Reef will have followed her…"

"But Chase too?" Yva shot back. "I'll only allow so many coincidences before I stop suspending my disbelief, Corby!"

She had a point. It was a point Alex had been trying not to think about; it made her too uneasy…

But then a thought struck her, and she felt the tiniest stirring of hope. Because now that nobody was around and everything was in such a mess, she could get away with things she'd been explicitly told not to do.

"It's fine. I have a plan," she said, and Yva paused her fuming. "I'm going to ring Great-Aunt Cornelia."

The clouds dissipated in an instant, and a smile of genuine pleasure took their place on Yva's face. "The maven of mystery! That's a plan I can actually get behind. She's sure to have some ideas about the disappearances."

"Yeah," Alex nodded, a little guiltily, "but also she might give us an excuse to leave."

"Better and better," Yva said. "Wanting to rub the solution to those disappearances in Leo and Matt's faces is a big part of what's keeping me here, but it'll be easier to solve in CC's parlour like a proper armchair detective."

The break room where they had left the phones was only a few steps away, a straight shot from where they were now; and yet somehow, this last walk wound Alex's nerves almost to the point of snapping. Yva was right. One extraordinary thing, perhaps two, she could allow; but a whole seven people vanishing into the darkness was too much for her to credit to an innocent series of pranks and upsets. The whole thing felt staged, or somehow arranged, as if they were all just so many playing pieces on a gameboard being moved this way and that by an invisible hand… Alex didn't realise until she'd stopped just how much her pace had increased, and she almost fell.

There was no Dry Diver in the break room this time; nor anyone else. It would have been a relief to see a friendly face, but Alex wasn't sure she counted any of these people as friends; strange days, when Yva was the comfortingly familiar presence. Regardless, there was nobody to raise an eyebrow as Alex opened the lid of the phone box and plunged her hand in.

And recoiled, gasping, her hand ice-cold and with the sense of something repulsive crawling over it –

With the sound of dripping.

"What now? Why is your hand wet?" insisted Yva, squinting in the dark. Alex aimed her torch at her hand, glistening with damp; it was only water, and nothing worse – but right now, just water was bad enough that Alex felt she might never look at it the same way again. She shook it off and dried her hand on her leg; and then slowly pointed her torch back into the box.

It was invisible at first glance, but unmistakeable to the touch. Somebody had filled the box with water, almost to the brim, and all nine phones were lying deep in it, refracted out of their real positions.

"But that's vandalism," Yva said, the truth dawning on her. "That's not a prank, that's actual property damage! I can't *afford* another phone!"

Her hand dove into the water and pulled out her own brick of a phone, and she began frantically pressing every button. Alex retrieved hers a little more slowly, and with a sense of futility. It wasn't panic driving her now; it was a slow and infectious dread.

Their phones were dead. So were the other seven. And all Alex could think of was that dreadful day in a remote clifftop castle with Yva and Cornelia, out of mobile range and with the landline and router sabotaged.

It looked as if Yva was starting to get it, too. The anger and frenzy were slipping off her face, replaced by a stone-chiselled seriousness. Alex was a little surprised that Yva, thinking the worst of everyone, hadn't jumped to this conclusion sooner.

Somebody in the Pitchwater Building was playing a dangerous game. It was time the pair of them stopped playing along.

Yva turned to Alex and met her eye. "New plan," she said: "We just go, right now."

"Agreed," Alex said, and they took off as one for the tunnel. Forget Yva's reputation. Forget consoling the distressed. Forget the disappearances, forget it all, because events had taken a turn for the downright *sinister* and it was time to be out before it endangered them personally.

The message was still slashed in red upon the walls. *LEAVE OR DRY DIVER WILL GET YOU…*

If only it could have been exciting – running through the night-dead corridors, ensnared in an enigma. On past occasions like this, Alex had felt it her duty to stay and solve the mystery. But those occasions bore several differences to this lonely night. The first difference was that she'd had Great-Aunt Cornelia to guide her. The second was, to put it bluntly, that she had been quite sure she was in a mystery and not a slasher.

And that was probably why Yva was reacting differently, too.

"You loved Carver's Rest," Alex said abruptly. They had reached the hatchway, and Alex had kindly let Yva push in and be first down the ladder, not that its black depths looked any more appealing than the rest of the haunted house. "You loved every second of it. You never once took any interest in trying to escape." She crouched at the lip of the tunnel, her torch pointed down at Yva as she practically slid down the ladder. "You're really scared, aren't you? For yourself."

"Who else would I be scared for?" Yva snorted. Her feet hit the concrete floor and she waved Alex down with an impatient gesture. "I may not be the most emotionally intelligent person, but I'm a genius in all other respects. I know full well that I've ruffled a few feathers here. There are loads of people in this building with a motive to get at me – and suddenly they're all mysteriously out of sight? I don't buy it."

Alex struggled down the ladder, one hand occupied with their last torch, because if she dropped that they really would be in trouble. "Somebody's trying to cut us off," she said. "From the rest of the group, and from the outside. So why just let it happen, right?

"Right," Yva agreed. "If I'm the target, the last thing I want to do is the first thing they expect. Wait, does that make sense? Never mind." She shook her head irritably. "Point is, the best thing I can do to get my own back is get clear, and tip off the police to sort the lot of them out."

Alex dropped the last few rungs. It was quicker than trying to do it properly. "And Reef?" she asked, straightening up.

"Reef's a big boy. He can handle himself," Yva said. "All that matters is coming up with a good excuse to feed him by the time we next meet. You can help with that."

"I'll try," Alex said, and pointed the torch down the tunnel; expecting for just an instant a monster to be there, instead of more distant darkness. "Think you can lead us back through the woods?"

"Yep," Yva said as they took off, only technically not running. "Then we can follow the road back into town and grab the old lady, use her phone to grab the police and a taxi home…"

She trailed off. Their footsteps trailed off, too. For in the island of torchlight cast ahead in the long tunnel, something had just washed up on shore, limp and wet.

The torchbeam had settled on a foot. A foot laid flat on the floor, dripping, with a leg leading up to a prone form obscured in the darkness…

Wordlessly, they took careful steps forward, and the whole body came into view. It was soaked through, the water still dripping off it, pooling on the floor around the tall form with one hand at its throat and the other outstretched and yearning for the ladder a few inches away.

It was Matt Silver. He was lying quite still.

"This is part of the prank, right?" Alex felt her breath coming fast and heavy now. "He's going to jump up and say boo to us, right?"

"This is why Cornelia has a cane," Yva said, her teeth like a vice. "I don't want to have to touch it unless it's not going to get up…"

She took another step forward, another, even slower and more silent than those before; and with the edge of a toe she nudged the body before her. Then another, more forceful nudge; and finally a kick in the ribs to make certain. Her foot squelched, and the body did not react.

"He's not acting," Yva said quietly. "He was a terrible actor, anyway." Alex almost thought she sounded relieved.

"You mean – he's –" Alex felt her throat closing up.

Yva stepped over to Matt's head and knelt down, touching his hair, looking at his face, his throat. Alex was horribly glad she couldn't see his face –

"Yes," Yva said, and her voice was strange, her tone flat. Alex couldn't tell how long she spent examining him; bending his fingers, lifting him slightly to see his front. "Yes," she repeated at last, "he's dead. But *how* he died…"

"You don't know?" Alex whispered. Yva was an amateur forensic researcher. She had spent hours looking at pictures of dead people.

"There are minor injuries; a blow to the back of the head, scratches to the face," Yva replied. "But no obvious signs of fatal injury – not that there would be, in a case like this."

"What case?" Alex was afraid to even ask.

Yva answered her anyway, turning to meet her eyes. "A case of drowning."

You don't have to be in the water to drown. Somebody had said that to her before – Matt, in fact, within minutes of their meeting; and now he had died to prove it. She had heard something else like it, too, a long time ago. Where was it, and what had it meant…?

LEAVE OR DRY DIVER WILL GET YOU.

Alex was done thinking. She was past Matt's body in a few steps and lunging for the ladder, hauling herself up it, the torch gripped between one finger and a thumb while the others manhandled her upwards.

The hatch was above her, and she spared a hand to shove at it –
Clank.

The hatch raised just an inch or two, and then clanked as if it had hit an obstruction. Scarcely believing, Alex pushed again and again, as if maybe something that had fallen on it could be pushed out of the way.

But then she heard a lighter, almost fluid set of clinks; and she saw it. Running between the clasps on hatch and lid was a short loop of gleaming chain, and the two ends of chain had been snapped together with a hefty padlock. It wasn't the padlock the teams had used before, either; that was still at the foot of the ladder. This was a padlock to which there was no guessing who had the key.

That had been the third difference, between Pitchwater and everything else. In her past adventures, Alex had had no *choice* but to stay put, because the alternative had been taken away from her. But that was no longer a difference; the disparity had been erased. No matter what the words on the walls said, there was no leaving now.

Alex slowly returned to the base of the ladder. Yva was waiting there, eerily calm, an almost expectant expression on her face.

"We're trapped here," Alex said. "With a dead body, a murderer, and no way to call for help."

And, as if a switch in her mind had been flicked, Yva looked as if she couldn't have been happier about it.

"It's happening," she whispered, her voice almost shaking with delight. "It's finally, finally happening. I finally get to be the detective!"

CHAPTER FOURTEEN
MURDER AT LAST

12:50pm

"You get to be the detective?" Alex repeated. "Matt's been murdered, and that's your takeaway?!"

"Of course," Yva said. "We need one, don't we?"

Alex supposed she was right. It was Carver's Rest all over again. If leaving the building or calling for help were out of the question, that left catching the murderer as the only choice that could protect themselves and everyone else. But it still felt like madness to be turning on the spot and walking away from the body, and back towards the Pitchwater Building.

"This changes everything," Yva enthused. "We've established that I'm not the target, which means I've got nothing to fear. And Matt's death upgrades the whole sordid business to an impossible crime mystery, which is my speciality."

"You only come up with them, though," Alex pointed out. "You don't solve them. It's not the same thing."

"And *that*," Yva said, pointing at Alex, "is where you come in."

And with Carver's Rest in mind, Alex had a pretty good idea of where this was going. "You want me to be your Watson," she said.

"Exactly!" Yva beamed. "I knew I was right to keep a hold on you while I was conferring with Reef. It means I can clear you of suspicion – and vice-versa, I guess. If I'm going to solve this mystery, I'll need an assistant who's almost as competent as myself, and if you're good enough to Watson for Cornelia, you'll do. But this time, *I'm* Cornelia Crow."

The prospect plainly gave Yva immense pleasure. Yva had always idolised Great-Aunt Cornelia, Alex knew, and now at last had come a self-indulgent opportunity to award herself her dream role.

"I'm Cornelia Crow, but remember, you're still Alex," Yva added, continuing in the same vein. "You're not me, or anything so glamorous as that. I'm Poirot, you're Hastings. I'm Drury Lane, you're Patience Thumm. I'm Daisy Wells and you're Hazel Wong."

"Hazel is cleverer than Daisy," Alex said. But this was stupid. She was getting like Yva, bickering when people were in danger.

"Fine, have it your way – but do some detecting already. How long ago did Matt die?"

Yva scowled. "Too recently. I can't narrow it down much more than sometime after we found him gone. Not within the last few minutes, but that was obvious; we'd have met the murderer in the tunnel."

"Although the murderer could have left through the outside hatch," Alex pointed out. "And then padlocked it behind them to stall reporting of Matt's death."

Yva licked her lips. "Huh. That's true..." she murmured. "But it doesn't add up. Stalling on reporting it won't get anyone an alibi because we know the time of death window – roughly midnight until now. And we'll soon find out if one of us has gone home and left us trapped, so it would be obvious that they were the murderer."

"The murderer probably is one of Team Silver or Team Dry," Alex admitted. "A random outsider doesn't seem likely, even if it is possible."

"And lastly, there's the evidence of the padlocked chain," Yva said. "Didn't you notice, Corby? You can only padlock the hatch if it's shut – which means you can only do it from the outside. But if you use a short chain..."

"It gives you enough let to do it from inside the tunnel," Alex realised. "You just open the hatch an inch or two and stick your hand out."

"Exactly," Yva grinned. "It's not *proof* that the murderer is inside Pitchwater... but it is *evidence*. And enough evidence is proof."

They had arrived at the Pitchwater end of the tunnel. Alex shone the torch up the ladder, and was relieved to see the other hatchway still open, at least. Even if she was still trapped in the building, it was far better than being trapped in the tunnel. "So what's your theory?" she asked. "It has to be one of the twins, right?"

"What has to be one of us?"

A head was thrust into view at the top of the ladder, and Alex tensed, in spite of herself; after all, if it had a head, it wasn't Dry Diver. No, it was Viggo. ...Probably.

"I heard you two talking. What are you doing down there?" he asked, his hair hanging down around his face. "Is that where everyone else is, too? I haven't seen anyone in a while."

"We're on our own, too," Alex answered. "Everyone else just kind of ran off, and –"

"Don't lie to him, Corby," Yva said. "We know where *one* person is, at least."

Alex darted her a nervous look. She'd been wondering how much they should let on about what had happened, and she and Yva hadn't had a chance to confer about it yet.

"Come down here, Viggo," Yva continued. "You'll want to see this for yourself."

"Uh, okay." Viggo began to descend the ladder, Alex lighting his way. "Is something going on that I should know about?"

Alex grimaced. "Yes," she said. "You probably wouldn't believe us if we told you. Everything about tonight is unbelievable."

Viggo landed beside her, looking extremely confused; unless he was Leo, and just acting. Or unless he was Viggo, just acting; or Leo, confused. There were too many possibilities and not enough proof.

"It's down the far end," Yva gestured. "We'll wait at the top."

"I'm so sorry, Viggo," Alex said.

She couldn't begin to think how to break the news to him; but he seemed to get some glimmer of an idea, and his face drained, some of his confusion giving way to fear. And then he turned and jogged away down the corridor, the beam of his torch dancing with him until it was all that could be seen.

Yva was already halfway up the ladder. Alex followed suit.

They arrived at the top, Yva taking a few steps away from the hatchway, the better for her echoes not to be overheard. Alex joined her; and Yva said, as casually as if nothing had happened, "So you were telling me your own theory about the twins."

Alex struggled for a moment. "Did you send him to see his friend's body just so we would have more time to theorise?"

"You yourself said that he wouldn't believe us if we told him," Yva shrugged. "And we do have to avoid showing our hand to our suspects, letting on how much we've guessed. It's not like he's in any danger down there or anything. So, your theory?"

Alex really hated how often Yva's callousness had a point to it. But she was trying to be a detective. Half of that was detecting evidence; the other half, deducing conclusions. "Leo, or whichever twin disappeared during filming, is the only one unaccounted for while Matt disappeared," she explained. "Forget how they did it; nobody else could have showed up in a Dry Diver costume in Matt's video. So Matt was collaborating with that twin, and left with them; so most likely they killed him."

Yva was nodding along. "That makes sense. It's very boring, but it's the simplest solution, and there's no evidence against it right now. But there are other possibilities; to be frank, in light of Matt's murder, I'm now reconsidering the prank angle."

"You mean Leo and Matt really were attacked?" She was right; Matt, they now knew, *had* been attacked, though the form of the attack remained mysterious. "And Dry Diver came the wrong way through a one-way fire exit?"

"Why not?" Yva answered. "It's no more impossible than Matt opening a two-person door alone. Plus..." A glow of quiet excitement came into her eyes. "It's more interesting this way."

Of course Yva would think of it like that. But did it actually make a difference? That was what Alex was wondering. "If it wasn't a prank," she said slowly, "that widens the pool of people who might be involved. Because Matt would only have pulled a prank with someone he trusted."

"Whereas now we can consider Chase as a suspect," Yva said. "After all, who was alone with the Dry Diver costume this whole time?"

"Meant to be," Alex pointed out. "He was actually with Viggo the whole time."

Yva's eyes dulled. "I forgot. That idiot," she muttered; but she recovered in moments. "Chase and Viggo together, then, as they were together subsequently. Or just one of them, forcing the other to give them an alibi."

Chase and Viggo working together wasn't any more likely than Chase and Matt, though. "Why would they do that?" Alex asked. "It doesn't make sense."

Yva rolled her eyes. "You're the one who does *motives* and *human nature*. You work it out. Later, because right now I just came up with another suspect: Bianca."

Bianca? It had crossed her mind. "You mean," she said slowly, "maybe she did her scene with Matt in double-quick time, left the room without alerting Tara, then ran around to the opposite side of the building, put on a Dry Diver costume and came in again through the courtyard?" She thought about it. "We don't have proper timings for anything, but that sounds way too tight. We were in the east wing, so on the outward leg she'd have to go through one of the upper floors to avoid us. And she'd have had to dispose of Matt and the costume before exiting into the corridor and running into us, too."

"She would've needed an accomplice," Yva agreed. "Tara, most likely, who was out of sight during the same period. One of the twins would've worked too, but then it's not as new a theory."

Alex's mind was still turning over the possibilities of Bianca. "Hold on a second," she said, as another possibility slowly came into focus. "Bianca works with the prank angle, too. I've no idea why she'd have done it, but – well, remember that Bianca doesn't actually appear on Matt's recording because of the file corruption. So what if they never filmed it in the first place? Tara watched the two of them into the filming room – but then Bianca left through the fire exit with Matt's help, got her costume on while he rigged the door to somehow open from outside, and then they staged the attack on camera." She had an idea that this point could be developed somehow, but right now she was on a roll. "They dropped Matt's camera until they were sure the file had been corrupted – it didn't matter how much, just so long it was a tiny bit glitched then we'd assume the rest had been eaten – and then they stowed the costume together, and…"

"And then Bianca killed him," Yva nodded. "How and where, or how she had time to shift his body, I couldn't say. But that's not the interesting part, so with any luck she'll just confess it later when we prove she did it."

Even if the exact timings were vague, it all seemed so tight. Alex had been checking her watch throughout the evening, and nobody seemed to have had more than about five or ten minutes to move around unobserved. "How long does it take to drown someone?" Alex asked.

"More time than you'd think," Yva said. "Just like any form of asphyxiation. Ten minutes – maybe even more, to be sure…"

For a moment, the two of them wore identical expressions, troubled and frustrated. It was starting to seem as though there were more impossibilities than just the appearances and disappearances…

And then their island of silence was disturbed. An unearthly, haunting sound, the echo of a strangled cry, reached them from the tunnel like a banshee's wail.

Viggo now knew that Matt Silver was dead.

"Could be fake," Yva said dismissively. "Almost everyone involved in this case is an actor, remember."

"Almost everyone involved in this case is a teenager! And a human being!" Alex said, aghast. "Yva, maybe your feelings work differently, but you can't assume that's the case for everyone!"

Yva fixed her with a stern glare. "Even so," she said, "someone is lying. Probably more than one person, actually. So if you don't mind, I'll leave it to you to determine who's sincere, Little Miss Motive."

It was so frustrating to Alex. Spending time with Yva was like spending time with an alien. That wasn't Yva's fault, and so long as you understood it, she wasn't that bad. When she was actively trying to fit in, even if she didn't do it very well, she could pass for just being a bit odd. But the moment the normal rules of society were suspended, she seemed to feel completely validated in giving up all pretence and becoming her worst self – because another seemingly normal person had done the same.

Distantly, from the depths of the tunnel, they heard the approach of hurrying footsteps. "Viggo's back," Alex said. "At least *try* to be considerate. If only to make detecting easier."

"Yes, yes," Yva grumbled. "He could have had the decency to walk. We haven't even *considered* the possibility that the prank and the murder were unrelated."

Alex grimaced. Now *there* was a can of worms that just about doubled the difficulty of the problem facing them.

Clanging footsteps, missing a rung and stumbling to correct it – and Viggo's head was thrusting its way into the torchlight, specks twinkling on his piercings and under his eyes. His expression was distraught, his eyes as wild as his hair. "What *happened*?" he croaked. "How did Matt die? Why are we locked in?" He looked around urgently. "Has anyone even called the police?"

"Our phones are as dead as Matt Silver," Yva said smoothly. "Now calm down, please, and answer a few questions –"

But Viggo was plainly in no mood to be calm, and Alex stumbled back in alarm as in a single swift movement he lunged forwards and seized Yva by the collar. "You want me to *calm down*?" he demanded, his voice breaking on the last note. "You've been acting like a psycho this whole time! What were you two doing down there? *Did you kill him?*"

"We're the only two people here who *can't* be murderers," Yva said, her voice even and uninterested even as Viggo was lifting her onto the tips of her toes. "Unlike," and here she grinned mockingly, "the man with his hand on my throat."

Alex stood a step away, frozen, with absolutely no idea how to respond. She didn't do violence. She hadn't taken self-defence classes. She couldn't fight him off if he was that frantic –

But she could try using her head, and saying something. She didn't know much about Viggo, but was there something she could say that would get through to him?

She had to try, and Alex cried out as loud as she could. "Let her *go*, Leo!"

The words echoed through the hallway like a whole host of Alexes calling out, and Viggo stopped dead. For all that Alex had talked about being considerate, it was an underhand move; but the occasion called for it. His eyes widened, as if he could see himself; and in an instant he had loosed his hand on Yva's collar. It was as Alex suspected.

"Interesting," Yva said, straightening her collar. It was as if she had merely stepped off a bus. "So, Reef was right. You *are* Leo."

"No I'm not!" Viggo exclaimed, his voice trembling. "I'm *not*!"

"You've got the wrong end of the stick, Yva," Alex explained, and Yva frowned. "This is Viggo. I'm almost certain."

Leo had emphasised his and Viggo's status as twins; Viggo had, if anything, done the opposite. Alex suspected that there was really only one of them deliberately styling himself to look as identical as possible to his twin. Viggo wanted to be his own man; Leo wanted a stunt double. Alex wouldn't have been surprised if Viggo had got the piercings specifically to try to stand out, only for Leo to follow suit.

Tara had called Viggo a parasitic twin, but perhaps it was the other way around.

"I'm so sorry," Viggo whispered. "I swear I'm not like Leo."

"There's no need to apologise," Yva said. If anything, his break into physical violence seemed to have deeply pleased her; for once she had the moral high ground. "If I had really felt threatened by you, I would have reached forwards and pulled out your eyes."

Viggo looked at her, his eyes frightened now, his face drawn. "But what *is* going on? And where did everyone go?"

"That's what we're trying to find out," Alex said softly.

Some they would find out sooner than others. It had been drowned out at first, but now the sound of feet running flat-out was echoing towards them, in answer to Alex's call. "Take your hands off her, Leo!" roared Reef, as he crashed around the corner from the corridor.

"False alarm," Yva said, and he stopped and swayed on the spot. "About time you showed up, though. Where have you been?"

"Following Bianca and Tara," he said, with a pause to catch his breath. "They ran off deep into the building and I lost track of them."

"Why did they run off?" Viggo asked. "Why did everyone?" Fear tugged at his voice again, like a nagging thorn. "What's been happening all this time Leo's been missing?"

"Look, *a lot* is going on, and I hate repeating myself," Yva spoke loudly, "so let's just get our hands on Bianca and Tara and Chase, Leo if he's not still hiding, and then I only need to do the one recap."

"Matt Silver has died," Alex said. The full story was a long one, but there was no excuse now for keeping any essential facts hidden; and certainly not just for convenience. "We found his body at the end of the tunnel... and found that somebody had locked the hatchway in the woods and destroyed our phones, too."

"What?" Reef gasped, darting an astonished look at the hatch. "Down *there*? How?"

"I would need to perform a full post-mortem to be sure," Yva said, "but nobody's going to let me do that, so my preliminary conclusion is drowning."

"Drowning? That doesn't make any sense," Viggo said, shaking his head like he was coming around from a bad dream. "There's nowhere to drown around here. How do you *know* all this?"

Yva scowled. Alex knew she hated being challenged. "Cyanosis," she said. "For you laymen, his face went blue from lack of oxygen. Also he's wet through, including the inside of his mouth. Froth around the lips. No other mortal injuries present. Slight wounding to the head and face." She began to look frankly irritated. "Look, it's a really hard diagnosis, okay? Even for professionals."

"*Could* it have been anything else?" Alex asked. It was an important point to clarify. "Don't get me wrong; I trust your forensic skills, if nothing else. But is there no way he could have been poisoned, maybe?"

Yva rolled her eyes. "Nobody poisons anyone anymore, Corby. It's too difficult to get your hands on anything interesting, and believe me, I've tried."

Viggo blinked rapidly. "Um, what?"

"For research purposes only, of course," Yva added.

This did little to assuage Viggo's concerns. Or Alex's. But it was time to be moving on. "The important point right now is that four of us are still missing," Alex said. "And it looks like somebody very dangerous is locked in here with us. We need to group up and make a plan to escape." She hesitated. "There's just one thing I'd like to check first."

In the dim aura of torchlight, Alex could see Yva attempting to cock an eyebrow. "Ah-ha," she said quietly. "Now wouldn't *that* be interesting…"

Yva was already a dangerous step ahead, and just as well, as this was an idea Alex didn't like to put in words. Instead she led the others quickly around the corner and into the east wing – past the typing room where she now feared to tread – to the storage room, to swing a light from wall to wall.

Stack after stack of chairs. A stove so tarnished it no longer reflected light. A crusty sink, with a tap that dripped with maddening regularity.

And no Dry Diver costume. Not a trace of it. Just a blundering path through the forest of chairs from sink to door.

Alex tried to speak; had to force it. "We need to find the others," she breathed, "as soon as possible."

It was the correct course of action, and the three people around Alex nodded in unison. It was just a shame it was too late for some. The dangerous individual responsible for Matt Silver's drowning had already attacked two other people – and the night was far from over.

CHAPTER FIFTEEN
BEACHCOMBERS

1:07am

"So where did you last see Bianca and Tara?" Alex asked Reef, once they had hurried back to the junction by unspoken agreement.

"They went up the tower," he answered, gesturing in the direction of the stairs. He seemed glad to speak of anything other than the missing Dry Diver. "I thought they made for the next floor, but they got away from me somewhere. They were legging it the whole way and the echoes could've come from anywhere."

"It's as good a place to start as any," Alex said, and pointed her torch ahead and into the sea of darkness surrounding them. "Everyone, keep together, and let's go."

It couldn't take too long. Tara had told them earlier that, above the ground floor, everything outside the towers was locked; so each wing was just a glorified corridor. Bianca and Tara couldn't have got far. Nor Chase. Nor Leo. Nor anyone.

Which made you wonder why they hadn't been running into each other more often.

Alex looked over her shoulder at Reef, following alongside Yva whilst Viggo lagged behind. "So where exactly have you been?" she asked.

"You ask a lot of questions," Reef said, his eyes suspicious. But then he sighed, and turned away. "But that's fair. I've just been wandering the corridors, calling out for Bianca. ...I guess I understand why she might not have answered me."

"Weird that I never heard you," Viggo said, as the four of them turned up the first flight of stairs and began to climb.

Reef shrugged. "I never heard you either."

"We'll check people's movements once we have everyone rounded up," Yva interrupted. "There's no point in doing interviews on the go. We're going to do this properly, like in a real mystery novel, and interview everyone individually. That's my detective method."

"That wasn't your detective method last time," Alex said.

"My detective method is individually tailored to the particular situation," Yva pronounced.

115

"Wait," Viggo spoke up, at the back of the line. "'Last time'?"

Alex felt this was a question better left unanswered for the time being, and they turned midway up the flight of stairs and at last reached the next floor in silence. Waving her torch right and left, Alex found that it seemed indeed to be a complete duplicate of the layout of the floor below, with a further set of stairs on one side and a long corridor on the other. The corridor presented three choices, with a door nearby that would lead to the equivalent of the break room, a turn in the corridor that would circle around it, and a further door straight ahead into the second floor's north wing.

"I had to check all of those whilst chasing Bianca and Tara," Reef said. "Must be how they got away from me."

Alex wondered just how hard they had been trying to get away from him. Moreover, just how hard he had been trying to keep up with them.

"Bianca!" Viggo called, stepping out in front. "Tara!" He paused, listened to his echoes bounding away, unanswered. "Leo?"

"You up here, bro?" called Reef.

It was hard to imagine their cacophonous cries going unheard; calling at the tops of their voices, the echoes came as loud as if there were speakers hidden in the walls. But they had a lot of ground to cover, and in barely-broken darkness the corridors felt unending.

"How many storeys does this place even have?" Alex asked, aside, to Yva. "I didn't think it would be important, so I didn't ask."

"Four for the wings. The towers go one higher," Yva said. "Even with a lot of rooms locked, it's a lot to search… if people don't want to be found."

There were still as many people missing as found. Even with four or five storeys' worth of building to get lost in, it was difficult to believe that the scattered people weren't bumping into one another. It suggested that they were sticking to one spot rather than moving around – or more cynically, as Yva had suggested, that they were actively trying to remain hidden. The thought made Alex shudder; but that seemed to be the case for Leo, at least. He was probably the person it most worried her to have sneaking around on his own.

But that was a good point: Those who were missing might have people they didn't want to be found by. Reef wasn't popular with

Bianca and Tara; and Viggo's voice, identical to Leo's, was tantamount to a trap. Yva wasn't much better. So, Alex thought, she would have to take the lead herself, then. The prospect made her hesitant. Normally she would only put herself in front if somebody else had told her to. Or if she did it without thinking at all.

"Tara? Bianca?" Alex called, and went ahead down the corridor. She didn't make a point of shouting, and her raised voice sounded strange and cracked, not herself; like hearing your own voice on a recording. "Can anyone hear me?"

"Everyone!" Yva yelled, moving at pace to keep up. "We need you! There's a killer on the loose!"

Alex swung her torch around to aim it in Yva's face. "Not. Helping."

"It's important knowledge!" Yva protested. "I wouldn't want anyone to keep something like that from me. Like you did once."

"Uh, is anyone going to explain what happened to you two before?" Viggo asked again.

"Let's just say we've been around the block," Yva answered. "This is not our first rodeo. Once bitten, decidedly not twice shy. In other words, yes, we totally have detective experience."

Alex kept quiet and kept moving, waving her torch down one empty corridor after another. Yva hadn't mentioned the details, probably because they made her look bad; and Alex wasn't inclined to fill in the gaps for much the same reason. Catching killers was something to be proud of, but not, in her view, something to boast about. It couldn't undo what had been done.

If she could stop what was happening here before even one more person got hurt, that would be worth something. But somehow the murderers always seemed to get away with everything they wanted to do, until the point at which they would have stopped anyway.

By this time the group was moving through the east wing in short order, since it was effectively just a corridor. Yva tried every locked door as they passed, just to be sure, but they didn't even budge in their frames, and the keyholes were cobwebbed and filthy. There wasn't a single false locked door in the entire building. Nobody could hide that easily. But it was as they rounded a corner in the southern tower that Alex caught her first glimmer of light.

There were doors separating the towers from the wings, but so far they had customarily been left open, pushed flat against the adjacent walls such that she'd barely noticed they were there. But at the junction to this floor's south wing, Alex's torchlight fell on a door that was closed.

"Finally! I was beginning to think everyone had snuck out through the tunnel before it was chained shut!" Yva exclaimed. She pushed past Alex and waded through torchlight to the door, leaving Alex wondering why you would close a door in a place like this, when anyone could open it and all it showed was that you were there. "Now we're getting somewhere," she said, and with a brutal motion kicked the door open –

Or so she imagined would happen, anyway. But instead the door simply resounded like a gong, and Yva hissed and danced around on the spot with her foot in the air before abruptly remembering she had company and putting it down again. "I'm okay," she said quickly, trying not to wince as she put weight on it.

That, at least, was a lie not worth challenging; and nobody did, but Reef hurried forwards too. "What? Is it locked?" he asked, incredulous.

"No, it budged," Yva insisted. The true keys to the Pitchwater Building, long-unused, were well outside the fence and wouldn't be used to lock or unlock any doors that night. "There's something blocking it." A frightening grin flickered across her face. "I wonder if it's a body…"

"Don't say that," Alex shivered. With one person dead, and three others missing, the chances of stumbling across a dead body seemed sadly high; but Alex didn't want anyone to die. Especially not in the locked-room mystery which a corpse blocking a room's only exit would imply.

"There's only one way to find out," Reef said; and, taking a few steps back, ran at the door shoulder-first. It gave a little with a thud and a scraping noise, like a chair being pushed back on an uncovered floor, and Reef stood back, rubbing his shoulder and readying himself for another attempt. Viggo approached to join him, pushing the hair out of his eyes.

"Shouldn't the detectives be going in first?" Alex asked Yva.

"You're right," Yva agreed. "And I've been building up the strength for this sort of thing – as have you, judging by all that shopping you were hauling around at Cornelia's. But…" She shrugged as Reef and Viggo rebounded off the door with a crash. "Letting the normal people feel useful is a good thing, isn't it?"

Alex thought there was a little more to it than that. Frankly, Yva seemed not terribly interested in this particular problem. Had she deduced something? Alex hadn't time to ponder the problem as a second joint charge from Reef and Viggo had sent them crashing through the doorway, and she and Yva hurried forward.

Reef and Viggo were sprawled half on the floor and half over a chair and table that had been used as a makeshift barricade. Clambering over them and those, Alex found herself illuminating a mostly open space like the south wing foyer beneath them, with a pair of cubbyholes in the corners, yellowing blinds hiding the windows, and a wide space lined with chairs. Sweeping her torch over the furnishings, Alex got the impression of something like a classroom, or more likely a space for giving presentations; it reminded her vividly of school.

"There's nobody here," she said.

"Or nobody trying to be found," Yva said, with a grin on her mouth that seemed to turn and waver with the moment, like a windsock. "You two!" she yelled back at Reef and Viggo. "Stay where you are, block the door! Make sure nobody can slip past! And Alex, you know the procedure," she went on. "Leave no stone unturned…"

The shuddering of Alex's torchbeam betrayed the trembling of her heart. The torch shook in her hand as she passed it slowly along the walls of the grim concrete room, lined with faded and peeling wallcharts, or with blank space. There couldn't be nothing in the room, but she pleaded silently with an uncaring reality for this not to be another disappearance, or for this not to be something worse than a disappearance, even as Yva was chanting "Please be a locked room mystery, please be a locked room mystery, please be a locked room mystery…"

And then she saw it. A huddled shape, far across the room, balled into the corner like junk and tossed beneath a table…

Tara and Bianca.

CHAPTER SIXTEEN
FLOTSAM AND JETSAM

1:16am

Tara and Bianca. Alive.

Yva couldn't contain her disappointment.

"But it would've been such a good mystery!" she exclaimed, as Alex stared and Reef and Viggo approached from behind. "The door barricaded from the inside! No other exits! The door too tight a fit to allow for manipulation with string! Granted, I can think of at least three explanations…"

"Are you two okay?" asked Alex, ignoring Yva's rambling and approaching the two beneath the table.

Bianca had balled herself up, legs drawn against her chest like a barrier, staring out with terrified eyes. Tara was crouched beside her, but shielding her, ready to move out in a moment; and she stepped out now. "Physically? Yes," she said, "which I personally credit to deciding to barricade ourselves in here. Come on, Bianca, you can come out now," she murmured, kneeling and reaching out a hand to Bianca. "I trust Alex, at least. She's the not-insane one, remember?"

"Bianca, are you alright?" asked Viggo, stepping forward into the light. "It's me, Viggo. Not Leo. We don't know where he is…"

"…I'm okay," Bianca said at last, though her voice was breathy and high. "I just needed…" She trailed off, looking around the group. "Where's Chase?"

"We don't know," Reef said; he looked like he wanted to say something else, too, and then it all came out in a rush. "I'm really sorry about earlier, Bianca, I just lost it. I'm so sorry."

Bianca didn't look at him. She just stared off towards the entrance to the room, keeping her torch fixed on it; and occasionally flicking it away towards the shadows.

"So what exactly made you two lock yourself up in here?" Yva asked. "Given what's been happening, it makes sense. But I don't know how you two *know* what's been happening."

"Oh, have *more* things happened?" groaned Tara. "Things have been getting real freaky around here."

"Yes, we noticed," said Yva drily.

"Did you?" said Tara, deadpan even with her nerves taut. "Did you see Dry Diver crawling up the walls? Or a ghost with a bloody head dragging itself up the stairs?"

The room fell silent.

This was too much, Alex thought. It wasn't that it was overwhelming; it was that it genuinely stretched her credulity. It was like two different stories colliding by chance…

When the silence was broken at last, it was by Viggo. "Are you kidding?" he asked. "I really hope you're kidding. You're not kidding, are you."

"It was when we were upstairs," Bianca said. Her voice was quiet; or perhaps muted, stunned. "After we'd shaken Reef off – I don't know how we did that. I needed some time to calm down, so we'd just been wandering a while, and I – I looked out the window. To see if the rain had stopped. Tara was just ahead of me, and so I got up real close to the glass – there aren't bars on the top-floor windows, at least not on the courtyard side, it must be too high up – and I turned my torch off so I could see through. At first I still couldn't see a thing. But…" She took a deep, steadying breath. "Then my eyes adjusted, and it seemed to rise out of nowhere. Dry Diver, with its neck stump shining, and black water pouring off it as it inched up the wall – and lurched towards me –"

Alex, thoroughly unnerved, didn't know what to think; so she darted a look at the others to try and guess what they thought. There was a dream-like quality to their faces in the ambient torchlight; Yva looked impassive, quite blank as she took it all in; Reef, beside her, was failing to hide a look of alarm; and Viggo was plainly bewildered.

If Alex could have seen her own face, she might have thought it looked frankly sceptical. She was prepared to believe a lot, if only because some people out there had come up with some very clever tricks before now. But this appearance sounded frankly hallucinatory. It couldn't even have been staged, because how could anyone know that Bianca would have run off to the one specific point where this had been set up? There was the impossible, and there was the unbelievable…

What did it mean, then? Was Bianca behind everything that was happening that night? And was this latest sighting simply a lie, an overreach too far that broke suspension of disbelief?

"And what happened then?" asked Alex.

"I – I cried out," Bianca admitted. "Almost at the same time as it came for me... I completely freaked, to be honest, and got out of there with Tara as quick as I could."

Reef switched his torch over to Tara. "Did you see any of this?"

Tara shook her head. "I was looking the other way," she said. "But we *both* saw the ghost. It was a little after. Bianca had calmed down enough for us to have a serious discussion about aborting this whole event. We were going to grab our phones, tell anyone else we ran into, and just leave through the tunnel. But as we were going downstairs..." She hesitated; as if even she didn't believe what she'd seen. "We'd just come around a corner and our torches lit it up with no warning. It was slumped, I guess, one arm over the banister, the other clawing ahead – that's just my impression. What I remember is the way its body glowed green, and..." She paused, choosing her words with great care. "Its face was just a curtain of blood."

Viggo let out a quiet groan. Alex felt like doing the same.

"And that time we both panicked," Tara finished. "We ran for the first door we could close behind us and barricaded ourselves in. We were prepared to wait until daylight if that's what it took."

"I'm glad we found you," Viggo said. "Listen, you two have to know –"

"And which tower was that?" pressed Yva, totally speaking over him.

"South, this floor. Right outside here," Tara said. "But Bianca saw Dry Diver near the north tower, from the east wing. Fourth floor." She hesitated. "We're doing detectives now, right? It probably matters."

Yva's frown deepened with her thoughts; and after a moment she jerked her head sideways and looked at Alex. "What do you think?"

Alex thought first of all that it was progress if Yva actually *cared* about what another person thought, though of course she didn't say so. "The ghost is... *odd*," she said. "It doesn't fit. Like, everything else that's been happening here has been to do with Dry Diver, right?

As if someone wants us to think Dry Diver is real." Appearances and disappearances in guarded rooms, Dry Diver attacking people on camera, a drowned body in a place where nobody could have drowned them… "But a glowing ghost with a broken head doesn't fit," she concluded. "It doesn't match the theme."

Yva nodded. "I had a different reservation about the ghost," she said. "All the Dry Diver incidents are either impossible, or impractical. But there's nothing difficult about crawling up a flight of stairs."

"I'm sorry, but who cares?" Bianca broke in. "Someone's turned this whole place into a haunted house to scare us, and it's worked. Can we please just get out of here?"

Alex grimaced. The cold and empty room suddenly felt a lot smaller. "I'm sorry too," she said, "but since we split up things have gone long past being just pranks."

"Our phones have been shorted out, and someone's put another padlock on the hatch in the woods," Viggo stammered, "and – and Matt's dead. He's been drowned."

Bianca clasped her hands to her mouth. Tara drew in a deep, sharp breath. "You're sure," she prompted. "You've seen him yourself." ·

Viggo nodded miserably. "Worst thing I've ever seen."

"Yva's looked him over," Alex explained. "She knows what she's doing. We're trying to figure out what happened."

"I see," Tara said, her eyes narrowing as she began to process what she had learned. "Somebody's planned all this…"

"And that's why we're trying to get everyone together, under observation," Yva declared. "There's just Chase left. Forget Leo, honestly. He's the prime suspect."

"Leo wouldn't do this!" Viggo blurted out. "I know he's not the best person, but he's not a psychopath. He's got no reason to kill Matt, or, or do any of this!"

"Then our investigation will prove him innocent, won't it," Yva replied. "For now, we need to find Chase – and I want to examine the place where Bianca saw Dry Diver. So, let's kill two birds with one stone. Show us the way, please, Bianca."

Bianca looked instantly at Tara. Tara nodded, and showed the way instead, leading as they trailed out of the room in single file;

first Tara, then Bianca, Yva and Alex after them, Viggo and Reef as the rear guard…

It was the long way around, but nobody objected as Tara led them away from the south stairs, where the ghost had been seen – though Yva nudged Alex to shine her torch that way, and cast a lingering look in its direction. And then they were once again marching through the dark and echoing building, a river of torchlight through the corridors, the silence broken only by calls for Chase from Bianca and Alex, and the odd, lonesome call from Viggo for his brother.

"We're here," Tara eventually announced. They were at the upper end of an east wing corridor, identical to the rest but for the lack of bars on the courtyard windows.

"Why does this place have to be so anonymous," Alex muttered, not really intending to be heard.

Yva, of course, heard. "Losing your way?" she asked.

Alex shook her head. The one advantage to the Pitchwater Building's copy-and-paste design was that you couldn't get lost. "Maybe losing my will to live," she said. "It feels like we haven't moved at all. Like we're in Purgatory."

"You'd rather the vandals had made more of a mark past ground level?" asked Tara, raising an eyebrow better than Yva ever could.

"Why didn't they?" replied Alex. "It's almost like –"

Almost like it's the only place that's important.

Alex stopped dead, feeling as if she had just thought something important, too. Vandals had torn up the ground floor, smashing windows and moving things around. The crossover shooting had also been planned for the ground floor only, but that had a script and an agenda; it wasn't decided on a whim. Dry Diver had been targeting the shooting, and so it too had been following a kind of pattern in targeting the ground floor only.

And yet Dry Diver had also appeared here, in this random, unmarked spot on the fourth floor. Did that mean something?

A particularly deafening call for Chase from Reef brought Alex blinking back to awareness – to find Yva scrutinising her. "You've gone quiet," she said. "Quieter than your usual quiet. What are you thinking?"

Alex opened her mouth, trying to calculate in a few moments just how much was safe to let on in front of a group of people who were also suspects in a murder. But someone else spoke instead, with a "Hello?" and a beam of torchlight cutting down the corridor across them.

And Bianca stepped forwards into that light.

"Chase!" she cried, and there he was, squinting into a sudden barrage of torchbeams; stark against his shadow, with a momentary look of alarm on his face as Bianca swept him into a stifling hug. "Sorry," she said, releasing him after a few tight moments. "But it's so good to see a friendly face."

Alex glanced to her side to see all three of Yva, Reef, and Viggo starting to say that *they* were a friendly face, only to think better of it.

"Same to you," replied Chase, meeting her eyes for a moment before stepping into the corridor. Once out of Bianca's arms, his face had resolved into a look of apprehension, as if he wanted more than usual to be somewhere else. "I was just downstairs. Where have you all been? I've looked everywhere."

"Where have *you* been?" Yva retorted. "Your staying power for guard duty is in the seconds."

Alex might have tried to be a little friendlier, but then again, Chase *had* just lied to their faces.

"Fine, I admit it," he groused, "I got rattled. Nobody had come anywhere near our Dry Diver costume, but Leo was still out of the picture – and although you denied it when we met up on the stairs, it was obvious something else had happened. So I decided to do some sneaking around of my own."

"How did all these people not run into each other?!" hissed Alex, half to Yva and half to the uncaring universe. A moment later, she realised her faux pas: That was another clue.

"Sorry to say, Chase," Viggo spoke up, "but you've missed a lot. I'm glad you're okay."

"Uh, thanks?" he said; and, meeting their eyes, seemed to be seeing for the first time the drawn and harrowed faces around him. "What's going on?"

"Oh, we're just looking through this window," Yva gestured, "to see if we can see Dry Diver."

Chase's reaction was extraordinary. He reeled as if he'd been slapped in the face, and stared back blinking. "Did – did you really just –"

But Yva was ignoring him, turning to the window. "Even if we all turned our torches off, it would be hard to see through," she said, putting her face up against the glass. "Alex, could you lend me your torch?"

"Are you going to use it to smash the window?" Alex asked.

"Yes," Yva said, holding out her hand.

Alex sighed. "At least use the handle end," she said, passing it over. "We can't afford to break another torch."

Perhaps the others thought they were joking, or perhaps their nerves were at breaking point, but as Yva thrust the torch's long handle into the window with a crashing and a rain of broken glass then every last one of them either jumped a foot off the ground or let out a tiny scream. Some, both.

"Did you really have to do that?" gasped Bianca, leaning against the wall and panting for breath. "You nearly gave me a heart attack."

"Yeah, sorry, whatever," Yva said dismissively. "Just imagine how scared you'd be if there really was something out there."

She flipped the torch in her hand and pointed it out of the window and flicked it on, and the torchbeam bounced like the hammering rain off the decapitated copper throat of Dry Diver suspended in the void.

Alex's memory of what happened in the moments that followed was hazy and confused; an awareness of recoiling in blind panic, a salvo of screams and contorted half-seen faces, until with a high-pitched whirr the diving suit blinked out of sight without her understanding what had happened –

And then, seconds later, a tremendous scream of smashing metal; and then only the hushed roar of the rain on everything, and quiet sobs and panting breath.

Alex became conscious of herself pressed back against the cold concrete of the wall. Viggo was a few steps off and poised to run; and only Tara restraining her was keeping a hyperventilating Bianca from again fleeing in utter terror. Reef had thrown up a fist and was braced for useless combat, Chase crouched in the doorway and ready to push off –

Even Yva had taken a few steps back, and if she showed none of the instinctive fear of anyone else present, no sign of fight-or-flight, Alex could see her tensed at every joint. "I take it," she said, "you all saw that."

"Great detecting," gasped Alex, trying to steady herself; reaching out and putting a hand back on her torch. "We saw it. I don't know if we believe it."

"But what –" stammered Viggo, words tumbling over themselves to get out of his mouth, "what was it – what happened – and *how* –"

"I daren't guess how," Yva said, her hand holding a steady light out on the night and the flickering raindrops, until Alex slipped the torch from her fingers with surprising ease. "How he climbed up… But I think he fell."

"We need to take a look," Alex said, pushing the words out with her heart in her throat.

"Take a – take a *look*?!" shrieked Bianca, her voice high and piercing in the corridor and the night. "But that was Dry Diver. Dry Diver!"

"Dry Diver isn't real," Chase said, his voice hollow.

Viggo licked his lips, the sound wet and unpleasant. "I've read about something, a thing called a *tulpa*," he said, "that's an imaginary thing which becomes real – if you only believe hard enough –" In the torchlit corridor, his voice was barely louder than the rain. "Some people think lots of cryptids might be tulpas. Some people think Dry Diver –"

"It's an *empty suit*!" Alex cried. "It's somebody puppeting an empty suit, and there's only one person it can be –"

"Then let's prove it," grinned Yva, seizing Alex's arm and pulling her in the direction of the stairs.

Another race through the darkness, their careful train collapsing into a frenzy of dashing feet and chaotic torchlight, with anyone not held tight becoming impossible to track in the flurry of legs and maddened faces briefly seen –

A minute later they burst out through the fire exit, into the rain. It was heavier than ever, but nobody cared anymore, even as it streaked their hair and splashed up around their ankles. Alex had one hand in Yva's and her other on her torch, and as they rounded the last corner she darted the beam briefly up the wall of the building, to where the shattered window high above was just about visible, in a corner adjacent to the north-east tower where a trickle of water reflected gold –

And then she lowered it down, falling like Dry Diver to the shape below. The crumpled shape, like a marionette thrown upon a brick and smashed –

Dry Diver had struck the filing cabinet, the one stripped and left in the rain. One side of the cabinet had sheared off with the impact, water spilling out around the costume's twisted limbs, and the same blow had ripped a great ragged gash down the costume from shoulder to stomach and hurled it aside. It lay at Alex and Yva's feet now, face-up if it had a face –

Alex's mind was all too slow at putting the pieces together; too reluctant. The force of the blow which the falling costume had struck – the way the should-have-been-empty legs bent – the curious fullness of its trunk –

But there was no illusion left when her torchlight fell upon the hole in the costume and saw what was peeking out from behind.

It did have a face.

She gasped and her hand spasmed in Yva's grip. "There really is someone in there!"

Yva whipped her head around. "Reef!"

He stepped forward in an instant, as if waiting to be called to action, and hunched low over the body, fingers slipping as he worked the tubes and fastenings around the heavy neckpiece of the suit. In a few moments he had wrenched the entire thing loose and tossed it aside, mouthpiece and breathing tube trailing like viscera, and was pulling open the costume's wide gashed throat –

And recoiling with disgust at what he saw, as a cry of horror rent the air where Viggo stood.

It was as if it was the soaked face in the costume that had screamed, a howl of agony from the harrowed form with the staring eyes and torn face; because it looked so much like Viggo's face. Leo Karswell lay entombed, his arms pinned at his sides by the reams of padding around the costume's shoulders and sides, blue and bloodless and dead with the rain still falling on his unblinking eyes.

"This – this is what a dead body looks like?" choked out Reef, his eyes riveted to the corpse. "This is what you've seen so many times?"

"I don't understand," Tara said, in a low, uncomprehending voice, as Bianca wheezed into her hands and Viggo curled up into a silent, shaking shape. "Why is he wearing that? How did he climb up there? What was the point?"

"That's not what happened," Alex said quietly. She was no amateur pathologist, no forensic scientist; but she'd picked up enough to tell that Tara's version of events had a deep and irremediable flaw. "Yva – what do you say?"

Yva squatted down, and stared fixedly for a few drawn-out moments before reaching into the costume. "I'm checking for fatal wounds," she said, "but I don't expect to find anything except maybe another blow to the head." Eventually she looked back at Alex, and her expression, at last, was serious. "It's asphyxia again; it's drowning. And given that he hasn't bled a drop from that wound, I'd say he's been dead for a while."

Shaking, Alex checked her watch. Nearly half-past one – but it wasn't the time of death. "How long ago –"

"Pallor mortis," Yva answered. "Over half an hour ago. Perhaps a lot longer." She looked back from the body with switchblade swiftness. "Just like Matt, he might have died anytime since we saw him last."

The rain slicked Alex's hair to her face, so it fell like bars across her eyes. "So," she said numbly, "if Leo wasn't behind all this – who is?"

The pair turned, and looked out upon the rainslicked faces around them – at Reef with fists balled against an invisible enemy, at Bianca wide-eyed and terrified and Tara with a vice-like grip on her arm, at Viggo paralysed with grief, at Chase half-out of the fire exit and deathly pale.

"We're in deep trouble, aren't we?" Alex asked.

"Oh, yes," said a hoarse voice; and a beam like a headlight flooded across the courtyard and caught them all blinking in its fire. "You kids are in very deep trouble indeed."

Alex stood petrified, Yva agog at her side, everyone stunned as they stared towards the courtyard doors, where a craning shadow limped towards them through the rain with a torch the size of a skull hanging from its fingers. As the shadow drew closer and entered the range of their own torches, the nauseous green of a reflective jacket glowed into life – beneath a gaunt face and hairless crown stained red where the rainwater trailed from a long and ragged wound…

CHAPTER SEVENTEEN
THE TENTH PERSON

1:28am

A tenth person in the Pitchwater Building; Bianca and Tara's ghost. He was an old man, his head bald from age rather than choice, but Alex could see that he was far from frail; he retained a stocky build without a trace of fat. The ease with which he hefted an outsize torch in one hand while with the other he passed a sodden handkerchief over his still-oozing head wound testified to his fortitude. But the wound had clearly been a bad one, and he grunted in discomfort before turning his torch and his gaze on the corpse alongside the seven young people.

"Dear, dear me," he growled. "Kids never learn, do they. Put a warning sign and a lock and a fence in front of them, and what d'they do but go trespassing in dangerous old buildings anyway. And now look at where that's got you: One of your little friends is dead. What a tragedy."

"Who are you?" croaked Yva. "What are you doing here?"

Alex frowned. "Isn't it obvious?" she whispered. Yva may have been blindsided by the tenth person; but then, she'd never been that good at thinking outside the box.

They'd speculated about it, investigated and ruled out ways such a person could have got in – but because the building was supposedly abandoned and forgotten, nobody, not even Alex until now, had ever considered the simplest and most obvious answer to how there might be an additional person in there with them:

"You're a night watchman, aren't you?" Alex asked.

"No questions!" the tenth man grunted; which Alex took as tantamount to a yes. "I'll ask 'em. Now, you're all coming inside with me. Jump to it!"

They jumped to it, filing ashen-faced past the watchman as he pointed them to the foyer doors, keeping his torch and his distrusting eyes on them the whole way. At last they all huddled in a dripping gaggle in the centre of the foyer, feeling very much like what the watchman considered them to be: A group of scared children.

"Alright!" the watchman boomed, splitting the silence like a hammer to an egg. "Now it's time for a few questions: Mine." He drew a chair from near the wall and settled into it with a deep groan, placing the torch on a table next to him, still pointed towards the seven wayward delinquents before him. "First off," he said, and pointed to his head; "which of you was it what shoved me?"

"Someone attacked you?" asked Reef, looking among the others.

"Well I didn't push me bloody self over, did I?" the watchman roared in a sudden fury; and then winced in pain and passed the filthy handkerchief over his head again.

"Are you okay?" a faint voice spoke up; Bianca, peering out from behind Tara. "We saw you earlier, I think – but you looked half-dead –"

"I'll live," he muttered. "Now, any of you going to 'fess up ever? Which one of you thought you could throw me down and leave me in the rain?"

But only an anxious silence came, as Alex glanced through the crowd, and tried to think who, and why, and when. If he'd been in the rain, this almost certainly had to have happened in the courtyard; but when had that been possible?

The watchman sniffed, and shifted his weight. "Not surprised you won't talk, I suppose," he muttered. "Besides, like as not it was that dead boy in fancy dress, doin' something else reckless with you lot as his audience, seeing as it's him I was following when they got me."

"*Leo* pushed you?" Yva looked incredulously around at Alex and Reef, as if torn between being overjoyed that this theory was bearing some fruit and bewildered because it didn't make sense. "But he was already –"

"Oi!" The watchman pointed his thousand-lumen torch at her eyes, and she broke off, wincing. "What part of me asking the questions do you not understand? Alright, next one." He held out an empty hand. "Which one of you took my phone? Hand it over."

Silence followed, for an increasing number of drawn-out seconds, until at last Yva spoke up and said, "Obviously it was the same person who attacked you."

Their interrogator put a hand to his forehead, though Alex suspected it wasn't his head wound hurting him this time. "Give me strength," he muttered. "Alright. *Any of you*, then, hand over a phone." He stretched out his hand again, and shook it impatiently. "I've gotta call this in and get the police."

"We don't have them," Chase spoke up.

The old man fixed him with a hideous glare. "Don't give me that rubbish –"

"Our phones were all destroyed," Alex explained, taking a step forward. "We got in through the tunnel but someone locked it behind us. We've been trapped in here for a while now, and" – her voice caught in her throat – "it's two of us who have died, not just one."

"*Two?*" came a sudden high voice; and Alex turned to see Chase, gone paler than ever. Of course; they hadn't got around to telling him… "You mean – Matt too?"

"Oh my heavens," the watchman muttered, "you're a proper little bunch of psychopaths, aren't you?"

"No, only one of us," Yva said; and, with her eyes narrowed, added, "and maybe it's not us, but *you*."

"Eh?" spluttered the tenth man, putting a hand on the back of his chair as if to rise. "Where d'you get off saying that?"

"A number of curious events have taken place tonight which call for time, and knowledge of the building, which none of our number appear to possess," Yva said, reeling off this précis of the situation with complete calm. "As for that wound, you may in fact have given it to yourself – or perhaps one of your victims fought back."

"You – you – how dare you!" bellowed the watchman, leaping to his feet with his chair clattering over behind him. "Why, I –"

But leaping to his feet had been a bad idea; his voice trailed off, and he swayed for a moment before his knees slipped out from under him and he went tumbling to the floor. Alex didn't even think before rushing to his side. "Are you alright?" she asked, trying to lift him; he was heavy, but he'd landed well and seemed to be coming around, pushing himself up on one grazed arm. "Try putting your arm around my shoulder –"

And at that close range with the others' torches on their faces, both their eyes widened, as she recognised him and he did the same.

"You're the guard from Pugmire Pages!" she exclaimed, as the guard gasped, "You're the little girl with the great-aunt!"

"Wait, really? Are you serious?" Yva broke in, striding forward and peering into the man's face. "But that's so unlikely! Reef, come here, you recognise him too, right?"

Reef, stunned into silence, nodded rapidly.

Alex helped the guard back into his seat while Yva stood there doing nothing. "Thanks," he mumbled, rubbing tiredly at his head. "Need to get this seen to, I s'pose. Thought I could manage…" He sighed, and looked up at Alex. "Were you liar girls telling the truth this time? About you not having phones, and being trapped in here and two of you dying?"

"I'm afraid so," Alex nodded.

The guard let out a long, wheezing groan, and the age came back into his slack cheeks and deep-sunk eyes. "Alright," he muttered. "You're clearly not such a bad sort. You go and run back through the woods to town, then, and get the police. I'll keep an eye on the rest here."

"I'll go with her," Yva hastily volunteered.

"Not much I can do to stop you," he grumbled. "Let me just give you my keys…"

He reached a set of cracked fingers into one of his pockets, and his face drew taut. His other hand thrust suddenly into his opposite pocket; and then both started patting across his torso like roaming spiders.

"Naturally," he rumbled, and let his arms fall limp. "They're gone too."

"Naturally," Yva echoed, surveying the five others, the remains of Team Silver and Team Dry, with open suspicion.

Alex was desperate. Freedom had seemed, for just a moment, within their grasp…! "Can you remember," she asked, "if you left the front gate open? That's where you came in, right?"

"Right," he said. "And – I remember now, I *did* leave it unlocked." A faint light came into his eyes. "So maybe –"

Alex didn't wait for him to finish. She turned on her heels and ran for the front doors, Yva right on her tail. The two burst through and into the rain, and almost immediately crashed into the fence Alex had heard so much about. Only about a metre of waist-high grass and low shrubs from the crumbling walls of the Pitchwater Building, it was a multi-storey barrier of metal stakes, bound together with wire, each curved at the top into a cruel spike. The gate was differentiated from the fence only by a set of hinges and a heavy length of chain with a padlock binding the whole affair shut.

The chain was up and the padlock was set.

"No!" Alex cried, seizing the chain and rattling, hauling at it, as if there was the slightest chance of it just falling apart in her hands; but though going rusty on the outside, it was far too heavy-duty a piece of equipment for that. "But we're so close!"

"If I'm honest – which people usually criticise me for – I didn't really expect it to be that easy," Yva admitted. She looked at her distraught companion, and after a few moment's hesitation, gave her a tentative, experimental pat on the back. "Uh, there there, I guess."

"Thanks," sighed Alex. It was so close… The gaps between the metal posts were an inch wide at best, so there was no hope of slipping through; and she believed the two people who had checked around the whole fence earlier when they said it was all intact, as they were Leo and Tara and probably the least likely pair of the whole lot to be working together. Alex put her eye and her torch to the nearest gap, shining it through just in case there was anything, anyone, any building close by it might be possible to signal to; but there were only trees, hunched over a long-overgrown forest track rife with swaying weeds and encroaching shrubs and –

And a suspicious reflective glimmer. Litter? Alex pointed the torch at it and squinted.

"Can you see this, Yva? There in the light?" she asked.

Yva peered through the next gap over. "Got it," she said. "Looks a hell of a lot like a keyring with a bunch of keys in it." She paused. "I think that's a phone a foot or so behind, too."

"The attacker – the killer – just chucked them?" Alex asked. "And didn't keep them?"

"Could've incriminated them if they'd been searched," Yva supplied.

They stood there together, staring into the rainy darkness, at the keys that glittered beyond the iron curtain.

Just a couple of metres too far to be reached by any possible method.

Chapter Eighteen
Playing Detective

1:38am

"So, the good news is," Yva announced, as the two of them returned to the foyer, "that we know where your phone and keys are."

The others could be forgiven their surprise at Alex and Yva's return; they had been gone about ten minutes. Although it had taken very little time to establish that escape through the gate was impossible, Yva had insisted on following Leo's hours-old tramp around the weedy circumference of the building, checking for non-existent gaps in the fence. Alex's legs were now as soaked as if she had walked through a swimming pool.

It looked as if the others had been engaged in outlining the known sequence of events that evening to the night watchman – and indeed to Chase, who had been left behind by the most recent developments. He looked sick, almost as ready to collapse as the old man.

"You can't get them?" asked Bianca. "Are they past the fence?"

"Quite a way," Alex sighed. "We'd need a long pole to reach them. Like, a really long pole."

Tara let out a frustrated sigh. "I always said we should be using tripods. We might have had a chance with one of those."

"But then you lose the found-footage element," Yva frowned. "And that helps to disguise amateurish camerawork. It's important."

"Are you lot bickering about your little films?" the watchman snarled. "We've got more important things to worry about!"

Indeed they had, Alex reflected; and for all that the tenth person was a new suspect, he was also a new witness. "Since we're all in the same boat here," she said to him, in the same ultra-nice voice she'd employed at the bookshop, "what's your name? And why are you here tonight?"

He glowered at her suspiciously, before crossing his arms and leaning back in the chair. "Name's George Sanderling," he said. "Private security – and keyholder for this old place since they closed up shop." He surveyed the seven young people around him. "As to what I'm doing here – well, you didn't think there wouldn't still be folk keeping an eye, did you? Since my business at the bookshop was done and dusted, figured I'd walk across and give it a once-over."

"Isn't that quite a walk?" asked Alex, recalling the car drive over.

"Not if you go the *proper* way," he countered. "It's a straight shot through town to the old driveway, unlike that tunnel, *which is supposed to be a secret*."

Reef stepped into the ring of torchlight, and cleared his throat. Alex got the sense he'd been waiting for the chance to do something, to play a role; the others had all slumped on seats or on the floor, Tara still shadowing Bianca like a bodyguard, Viggo curled up and alone in his grief, Chase sitting staring at his hands and looking very small and very quiet. "So what do we do now?" he asked. "I'm guessing none of us are expected home tonight. Nobody's going to raise the alarm until morning – and who would know where we are?"

"No matter how understanding your parents are," Tara said, "they're not going to let you break into an abandoned government office. Of course nobody knows where we are."

"Great-Aunt Cornelia doesn't know *exactly* where we are," Alex said, looking over at Yva, "but she knows we're nearby. If it goes more than a couple of hours without us checking in, she'll get worried and call the police."

"What, the Iron Great-Aunt? Get worried?" Yva asked. Her face went slack as she considered the prospect. "Hmm. Flattering to think she'd be worried about me. More practically, she can identify Reef's car, she could pass those details on…"

"So you think we'll be rescued before dawn?" Bianca spoke up; her voice wavering, but clear.

"I'm sure of it," Alex nodded, trying to look considerably surer than she really was. Would Great-Aunt Cornelia manage not to get carried away in her reading? Had she bothered to pay attention to what Reef's car looked like?

"So we just sit here?" Reef asked, glancing anxiously at a still-silent Chase.

"With a few hours to spare? Of course not," Yva scoffed. "Actually, now that we're all together, this is the perfect opportunity."

Viggo looked up, blinking to clear his eyes. "For what?"

Alex looked again at Yva, and her eyes, by contrast, were shining. For Yva, there were only ever perfect opportunities for one thing. "For detective work," Alex said, answering the question herself.

"Exactly!" Yva beamed. She gazed hungrily around the room, as if expecting her audience to be just as excited as she was. "We'll wrap this ugly business up in time to hand the culprit over to the police when they arrive – which will also draw their attention away from any trivial trespassing complaints."

George, the watchman, groaned deeply and shifted his weight. "Think you're a little detective, do you?" he grunted. "Run around spying on your neighbours and finding missing pets, huh?"

"*Actually*," Yva retorted, drawing herself up in a haughty manner which Alex was certain she had copied from Great-Aunt Cornelia, "I'll have you know that Alex and I have solved four murders."

That was the sort of thing which made people look up and take notice. Reef didn't manage to look surprised – of course, if Yva had boasted to anyone, it would be him – but the remaining five people in the room wore expressions ranging from amazement to disbelief to outright suspicion.

Merited suspicion, perhaps. What Yva had said was not, strictly speaking, completely accurate; for one thing, Alex and her great-aunt had done the solving, while Yva's contribution might charitably be described as "helping". Or perhaps the charitable way of describing her role might be to leave it out altogether. But the point was that the murders had been solved and Yva had been there.

"Are you serious?" croaked Chase at last. His had been the suspicious face. "Or is this another prank?"

"I never prank," Yva retorted. "Alex and I are legitimate great detectives."

Alex coughed. "Well, amateur armchair detectives, maybe." This, however, was not the time for reticence, and she straightened up and tried to wear a more confident mask. "But we do know what we're doing."

"People who say that, usually don't," grunted George. But he didn't object.

"So what *are* you doing?" asked Tara.

Alex swapped a glance with Yva, and they turned aside for a moment to put their heads together. "Interviews first, crime scene investigation later?" she murmured.

"Having gone to all this work to get everyone together – interviews first," settled Yva.

It was about what Alex had expected – and also, in a way, about what Alex had *sus*pected. For a good stretch of the night, everyone standing in front of them had supposedly been roaming the upper floors; and, with perhaps one exception, they all claimed to have seen neither hide nor hair of each other. Alex was prepared to accept a few coincidences and near misses, in such a large and unlit building – but the layout was simply not that complex, especially with a lot of it locked up. The interweaving movements of the six people in front of her formed a tangled knot; but with some careful unpicking, their trails could all be plotted. And that might shed some light on where Leo had been, and when he had got into the costume, and how he had died.

One of the people in front of her, *at least* one of them, was a liar. Reef, Chase, Bianca, Viggo, Tara, George – the murderer was in the room. The murderer was in front of her.

"We'll do what the police will do later," Alex said, trying to control her nerves alongside the situation. "We'll talk to each of you, in turn, in private, about what you've been doing and what you've seen; so we know who was where, and roughly when."

"The classic detective novel method," Yva clarified. "We'll try not to make it too boring for us."

"Hold on, hold on," said George, his voice as hoarse as the grating of his chair over the floor as he rose unsteadily to his feet. "I'm the responsible adult here, the only one. I'll be sitting in on these here *interviews*, if you don't mind."

Alex suspected that Yva would very much mind; but to her surprise, Yva just shrugged. "I suppose a little official verification wouldn't hurt," she said. "Having a bodyguard wouldn't hurt, either."

Alex also suspected that George was in no fit condition to guard anything, but didn't say that either. "So, we'll need a place to interview people, not too far away, but where nobody can be overheard..." She ran quickly through the layout of the Pitchwater

Building in her head – but the two reception desks partitioned off from the rest of the foyer had already caught her eye. "One of those two cubbyholes will do," she said, pointing her torch to the nearest. "It'll be a tight fit, but we'll never be out of reach, and with the windows boarded over they should be nearly as soundproof as anywhere else in the building."

"Objection," interrupted Yva. "Let's sequester the suspects in the cubbyholes instead. Like you said, there's just enough room – but this way gives the detectives complete control of all entrances and exits, so nobody can run off again without us noticing."

Alex nodded. That made sense. "They're too small each for five people, so we'll have to split the groups."

"Uh, girls and boys?" suggested Bianca.

"I concur," Tara echoed.

"Gender divisions are moronic," Yva answered. "It'll be Team Silver and Team Dry, like it's always been. Bianca, Tara, Viggo, you pick one; Reef and Chase, you take the other. Oh, and before you go," she added, "hand over your spare torches. You only need one in each room, and I want to put a light on all the doors."

"Good idea," Alex smiled, as first Viggo, then Tara and lastly Reef each handed a torch over to Yva. Enough impossible things had already been happening that it made sense to rule out any cheap tricks early; and on that note, she hurried over to each of the cubbyholes herself to shine a light over them before anyone went in. But they were perfectly nondescript little places of only a few square metres, no blind spots, no ventilation shafts, just a desk and a chair and a filing cabinet, some defunct equipment and some narrow drawers stuffed with perishing pens and mouldering stationery. That done, Alex watched first Reef and Chase into one room, then Bianca, Tara, and Viggo into the other, shutting them in herself while Yva carefully laid a pair of torches on the floor with their beams pointed squarely at each door, plus a third aimed at the courtyard doors. Alex then hurried to check that the south-west door was firmly locked and unusable (as indeed it was, the west wing and its associated towers being entirely inaccessible on this night); while Yva demanded George's torch to point at the tower door to the south-east, throwing that dark corner into sharp and eye-burning relief.

In a couple of minutes, they were all set. George had been directed to take a chair, put its back flush up against the front doors, and sit on it; and Alex and Yva had dragged a single desk and a pair of chairs to the very centre of the room, facing up towards the courtyard and the cubbyholes and with their one remaining torch pointing to a single chair in front of them. They took their seats, looked at each other, and nodded in approval.

"Time to solve a mystery," Yva grinned; and raised her voice to a bellow. "Viggo Karswell – enter!"

Her call echoed around the room like a stray bat, and gradually dwindled into silence. It was followed by a muffled snicker from behind.

"Testing the soundproofing?" Alex asked.

Yva slumped back in her seat. "Just go and get Viggo," she muttered.

CHAPTER NINETEEN
IN THE VORTEX

1:45am

"Name?"

Viggo squinted, and put up a hand to shield his face. The torch was aimed directly into his eyes. "Um, you know my name."

"We know his name, Yva," Alex agreed.

Yva sighed. "I was *trying* to catch him out," she explained. "Honestly, Corby, you've got a lot still to learn about detective work."

Alex suspected that the only thing Yva had ever learnt about detective work was to copy exactly what they did in the books, without change or regard to feasibility. She sighed, and leaned forwards over the table. "So, Viggo. I guess you know by now about everything that's been happening here tonight."

Viggo gave a short nod. "We filled each other in when you left us with George," he said. "About – about Leo disappearing, and then Matt. And everyone scattering into the building."

"You're Leo's twin. You're closer to him than any other person in the world," Yva said. "He told you what he was up to tonight, didn't he?"

"No!" Viggo gasped. "I swear! Leo didn't tell me anything – I'm sure he didn't *know* anything." His eyes, wide and shocked, flared with a hint of the anger he had shown earlier. "He's *dead.* Isn't it obvious he was a target, not a criminal?"

…Would Leo have told Viggo, if he was up to something? On the one hand, Alex didn't plan to try and judge the relationship of two people whom she'd only met that night and only seen interact for perhaps ten minutes tops. Viggo was the most reliable person on himself and Leo, period. But on the other hand, she'd seen for herself that they were hardly the stereotype twins she'd read in so many books, who went everywhere together and finished each other's sentences.

This would require a gentle touch. That would be tricky with Yva around, but then again the whole question of character tended to go over her head.

"I sometimes felt like you and Leo didn't see eye-to-eye," Alex said, as gently as she could.

Viggo shifted uncomfortably. "That's not fair," he said quietly. "I know what people think – that he was the boss of me or something. But we're just into not quite the same things. That surprises people, for some reason."

"I don't have a twin, but I guess there's a kind of pressure to be twin-like?" Alex suggested.

Viggo nodded. "Leo was really into that; all the twin tropes. Like a cartoon. I was always trying to come up with my own look, but then he'd copy my clothing, or my hair. I got piercings, so he did the same." He sighed; a deep, years-long sigh of pressure without a release. "Getting into this horror vlog stuff was the perfect excuse. He came up with every kind of camera trick that needed both of us involved and looking the same."

Alex frowned. "Wouldn't one of you have been in the Dry Diver costume?"

Viggo looked momentarily nonplussed. "No, you've got the wrong idea somewhere. We *had* a suit, but it was a prop, not a costume; stuffed like a scarecrow and with struts and stuff so it could stand on its own. And it was… kind of crap, honestly." He looked down. "Would've been nice of Matt to ask permission before he threw it out, though. To ask *me* permission, I mean."

This information wasn't a huge surprise – Alex had long since given up on the idea of a second costume tucked away in the Pitchwater Building, though there was still one other possibility – but something else in Viggo's manner was; and Alex noticed her eyes narrowing as she tried to read him, and attempted to be less conspicuous about it. It certainly wasn't something he was going to admit to, perhaps not even to himself – but it was plain that Viggo resented his brother at least a little; and Alex wondered how deep a wound it had made into his soul. Being Leo's twin didn't make him innocent; it might even be the one thing making him guilty.

Being a detective, by contrast, meant suspecting things she didn't want to think about anyone.

"Being identical" – and this time it was Yva speaking, with the giveaway smile she always wore when she thought she was being sly, and without any of Alex's reservations about the horrible things she thought – "must have been troublesome for you… given how notorious Leo was for his behaviour around girls."

"Notorious?" Viggo repeated – and that trace of anger flashed across his face again, just as they'd seen when he had found Matt's body. "Y-you make him sound like a criminal – but it's all a misunderstanding! Okay, he was pushy, he was bad with boundaries, he didn't know how to take no for an answer –"

Alex felt that that sounded increasingly damning, though she didn't say it out loud; but she couldn't prevent a grimace from crossing her face.

"– but!" Viggo continued. "But it was all just talk. He never touched any of them. I know he didn't!"

"Never?" repeated Yva. "Do you *know* that – or is that simply what he told you?"

The faintest flicker of uncertainty passed through Viggo's eyes; and was suppressed. "I *know* it," he repeated. "Leo always told me the complete truth. I would have known he was lying."

Yva was trying really hard to arch her brow. "And with your mysterious magical identical twin connection, you were as good as a polygraph, is that what you're saying?"

Viggo was trying to keep himself from growing too heated, but it was all there in the tension of his brow, his knuckles, the way his shoulders shook. "I don't know what a polygraph is, but I know when I'm being made fun of. Don't think I'm going to just sit here and take it," he said, his voice low. "And that's another thing – we aren't even *identical* twins. We just look close enough that people think we are; and Leo did whatever he could think of to bridge the gap."

"Oi, sonny," spoke up a voice from behind them – and Alex looked back to see George rising unsteadily from his seat. "Mind your temper. Won't do you any favours in this situation. I hear you've lost your twin, and I'm not going to diminish that. But save your lashing out for the one what done it." Viggo looked down at his lap; and George shifted his gaze. "And as for you two girls – move on. He answered your question."

"Okay, let's do that! Moving on," Alex said hurriedly. There was no point in continuing any line of questioning that was only going to lead to Yva antagonising their witness. Besides, she'd heard enough to tell that the question of whether Viggo was telling the truth about Leo probably wasn't going to be resolved – but it was food for thought, nonetheless. Had Viggo been working with Leo? Had Viggo been working *against* Leo? It was clear what Viggo's answer was. "So, the point is," she concluded, "that, according to you, neither you nor Leo were in on it – whatever 'it' was."

"Put simply, you don't know anything," Yva said, tapping her fingers impatiently on the desk. "You had no idea there was anything more to this night than a crossover filming event, and you haven't heard or seen anything out-of-place which might have a bearing."

Viggo met their eyes, and shook his head. "I've told you everything," he said emptily. "I've spent most of the time wandering around, with you two, or with Chase, or on my own – but I never saw anything, or anyone."

Alex thought about this. Viggo's movements, by his own admission, were essentially unaccountable. If he had seen no-one, no-one had seen him. But how could that possibly be true with as many as six people running around in a building which, with most of its doors locked, was not that complicated? "It's getting on for two o'clock now," she said, checking her watch. "Perhaps you could give us a run-down of your movements since filming started at midnight? It's not that we suspect you –"

"Yes it is," interrupted Yva, looking sincerely confused.

"– but if we know where you were, we know where the murderer couldn't have been," Alex continued, ignoring Yva's unhelpful if accurate interruption.

"Um, okay," Viggo nodded again; he seemed to be recovering himself, breathing evenly. "I think I can do this… So, at midnight, I was in the north wing with Tara, in the prep room. I'd been with her since like five-to or so, when Matt and Bianca split off to start filming in the conference room. But I was only there for a minute before Tara said she wanted to be alone and sent me to stand in the corridor and make sure filming wasn't interrupted. I waited there about ten minutes, and then came to the east wing to give Reef his cue – you remember."

Alex nodded, though she was actually thinking about those ten minutes in which Viggo and Tara were totally unobserved. But Tara was in a room with only one exit, right?

"I guess you two and Reef headed to the north wing at like quarter-past," he went on. "I waited for Leo for about five minutes, but… I didn't come here to just stand around doing nothing, and Leo had made the Pitchwater Building sound cool and creepy after he did the location scouting with Tara and you, Yva. So I decided to go for a walk and see if I ran into him – and Chase was looking all restless too, so I invited him to come with."

"You must have been with Chase for about a quarter of an hour," Alex supplied. "What do you make of him?"

"Chase? He's a cool guy," Viggo said, smiling shyly. "Like, Leo and Matt were all about this rivalry or whatever with your team, but just going around with Chase talking about nothing was… was probably the most fun I had all evening, actually." He looked dejected. "Chase kinda looked glad not to be thinking about the filming, too."

"Enthralling, I'm sure," Yva said, "but where did you actually *go*?"

"To the toilets, to check on Leo," Viggo answered. "They're up at the towertops, right? The two towers that are actually open, anyway. But turns out there's really only one toilet, because the door to the north one is stuck. Chase looks stronger than me, but he couldn't get it open."

"Right, I think that came up during the location scouting," Yva said. "So Leo could only have been in the south one, then."

Viggo frowned. "Leo having gone to the toilet at all was just something you made up, though."

Yva blinked at him. "Oh yeah."

"But we thought it was true, at the time," Viggo went on, his voice a little tense, "so we went to the south tower to check there too. No sign, so we came down again. Uh, putting it all together, in those fifteen minutes we went to the north tower and up to the top, then along the east wing fourth floor, then up and down the south tower. And that's where we hit you two."

"That was just after we'd decided to film the scene with Reef and Bianca," Alex recalled.

"I guess so," Viggo nodded. "When me and Chase didn't find Leo, I assumed we'd just missed him – but when you said you hadn't seen him either, that got me worried. I had no idea where he could've gone, but it made me think, like, what if he took a wrong turning and hit his head or something? We're not joined at the hip or anything, but he's always egging me to get involved with what he's doing – or, he *was* always egging me..." Viggo blinked rapidly, and moved on. "I just couldn't figure out why he'd have up and vanished. He hated being alone. So like, I didn't panic or anything, but I decided to do a proper sweep, check every floor and every wing."

"Very thorough," Yva nodded, approvingly. "So, that took you about twenty minutes before you met up with us again..."

Only twenty minutes? Alex felt jolted awake by the thought of it. At the time, it had seemed like forever; as if a great curtain of water had fallen between filming or investigating pranks, and the moment they had found Matt's body...

"Twenty minutes? That sounds right," Viggo nodded. "I checked my watch a few times, I don't remember the time *clearly* but it was all between, like, around twenty-five to one and five to. So, from where I met you at the south stairs, I did a kind of second loop. I went up top and checked the bathrooms again first, going north; tried the north bathroom myself, just in case, but that door doesn't budge. And from there I did the fourth floor properly; checking the tower rooms, going north to south looking over the dead-end wings, before heading down the stairs to the third floor to do it in reverse..."

"You zig-zagged," Alex said.

"Yeah," Viggo agreed. "Fourth floor, north to south; third floor, south to north; second floor, north-south; and then the ground floor –" He frowned. "Actually, there I thought I heard someone's footsteps to the north, but that was just you two in the tunnel, just before I met up with you. And you know where I've been since then."

"And you never heard or saw anyone else, in all that time?" Alex checked.

"Nobody," Viggo nodded. "Like, as far as I knew at the time, nobody was meant to be up there anyway – but it was *weird*, like I'd been left alone in the whole building..."

Alex's suspension of disbelief was at floor-height. In other words, it wasn't suspended at all. Viggo's survey of the building couldn't have been more tailored to clashing with people who'd been running around. It seemed as if anyone else upstairs would have had to be actively avoiding him, for him to have met nobody. It just wasn't believable.

But if you were going to lie, would you *really* say that you'd been so thorough, when it had the greatest chance of introducing a contradiction? ...Or was the boldest lie, in fact, the safest lie you could tell?

Alex couldn't suspend her disbelief. But she could suspend her judgement; at least until she'd heard from the others. "Thank you, Viggo," she said. "I think that's everything we needed to ask."

"One more thing!" exclaimed Yva, waiting until Viggo was halfway out of his seat before saying it. "You and Leo had been entrusted with Team Silver's key to the tunnel padlock, correct? Between the location scouting and tonight, which of you had it?"

Of course; Alex had almost forgotten. The graffiti. The vandalism. That strangely purposeful damage to the building which could only have been made by somebody with a key...

"Leo did," Viggo answered, looking darkly back at her. "But he couldn't ever have come back here without me knowing about it, you get me? He was only here for the location scouting, and tonight."

"Hmmmm," said Yva, with exaggerated suspicion. "Very well, Viggo, you can go."

"...Okay," Viggo said, slowly pushing back his seat as if expecting a second one more thing. "So, did all that help?"

Alex weighed her answers, and settled on the truth. "We don't know yet."

Viggo nodded. "Well, thanks for being honest this time, I guess."

"Oh, and another one more thing," Yva interrupted, as he passed through the shadowy border between the beam of light cast from their makeshift lamp and the other aimed at the door of Team Silver's cubbyhole; and he returned an unseen glare. "Send Bianca out when you see her."

CHAPTER TWENTY
THE GIRL WHO SAW ENOUGH

1:55am

Bianca Marsh… Alex nodded to herself. Unlike Viggo, who had seen nothing, Bianca had kept on seeing things – at least one of which, the climb of Dry Diver, seemed to be in an almost random location. Had she known where to go? Had her flight from that last disastrous scene between her and Reef, distraught and embarrassed, in fact been a talented actress continuing to act? Indeed, Alex had questions about what she'd been up to even before the two teams had scattered. "Good call," she whispered to Yva.

"It was?" asked Yva, looking surprised. "I mean, yes, it was."

…Was Yva's assertive confidence an act, too?

Alex didn't have time to address *that* mystery. Viggo had stepped back into the cubbyhole with Bianca and Tara, the door closing behind him with an audible click; and a few seconds later, it opened to reveal Bianca striding towards them. It seemed as if she had recovered her poise; for all the horror they had uncovered, perhaps learning that she hadn't merely been hallucinating her floating Dry Diver and her ghost on the stairs had helped. Alex noticed that she didn't so much as glance in the direction of George, though, lurking in the unlit shadows behind them.

"Well, here I am," she said. She sat down, straightened her clothes, and then with a frown straightened the torch to point away from her face; though she was taller than Viggo and not so easily dazzled. Indeed, she herself was now dazzling, and not just from the bright reflections off the bodycam she still wore; she had adopted a demeanour that could only be described as stately, authoritative. Perhaps she thought that if she acted brilliantly enough, the act would become the real thing. "What do you want from me?"

"I want to ask about the scene you filmed with Matt," Alex said.

They both looked surprised, Bianca and Yva; as if it hadn't occurred to them that the dark events of that night might have, indeed *must* have, been set in motion before they had ever found a single person missing. Yva caught on fast, though. "Aha!" she crowed. "Just what I was about to say. Bianca, describe your filming experience with Matt Silver; when you began, when you finished, how it went."

Bianca had quickly wiped the confusion from her face, and answered as if she had nothing to hide. "It was just a few minutes after you left. Leo had followed you two into the tower; Viggo stayed in the prep room, and I met Tara out in the corridor. Matt was already in the conference room and we were set to start filming at midnight, and Tara counted me in after half a minute or so. Matt and I filmed continuously for about fifteen minutes – which is long, but it's an important scene. Matt gets formally introduced as a character, and we learn that his creation, Dry Diver, had trapped him in the Pitchwater Building –"

Her voice caught as the parallel caught up with her. She'd just been talking automatically at that point, Alex could tell; but then they had both suddenly seen the uncanny harmony between the fiction and reality of Dry Diver's plotting. Yva appeared unmoved; but then again, there was a good chance she'd written that plot.

It was only a moment, and then Bianca resumed as if nothing had happened. "So. Matt and I filmed the scene. I find him there, we trade backstories, he begs me to go for help, and then I leave. And bump into you two and almost ruin the take."

"That's the trouble with found footage," Yva nodded. "You need long, continuous takes to sell it. There's only so much you can excuse through clever editing and fake glitches."

"Did you ever go near the fire exit?" Alex asked, trying to draw them back on track.

Bianca looked glad to be back onto the physical and tactile. "Oh, no," she said, her voice snapping back to normal. "I didn't need to, it's not in the script."

"That's true – about the script, anyway, I looked over all of them," Yva nodded. "Of course, what you *actually* did is unproveable." She gestured towards Bianca's gloved hands. "It's not like any of us are leaving fingerprints here."

So far as proof went, though, Alex had a brainwave. "Do you think you could show us the recording? It's just on there, right?" she asked, pointing to where the bodycam was still strapped in place over Bianca's sternum. "We don't have to watch it in real time, just fastforwarding through will do."

Bianca looked disconcerted again; it was so easy to forget those bodycams were there, when they were all togged up in padded coats and nobody had been filming for over an hour. "Um, sure," she said, putting her hands to the camera; and after struggling with the fastenings for a few seconds she got it free. "Go ahead," she said, holding it out to them. "Of course you have to check these things."

Alex reached over and took the camera from her, but her heart wasn't really in it anymore. The theory she had been nurturing – no, more a possibility than a full theory – centred on the fact that Matt and Bianca had been out of sight together while they were supposed to be filming, in a room with a fire exit granting them full access to the rest of the building – and no chance of being seen if they used it, given that the east wing's ground floor windows had all been boarded up. What could they have used this opportunity for? Alex had no idea. It didn't seem to have a bearing on Leo's disappearance, and it was difficult to imagine Bianca being strong enough to have killed Matt, wherever it happened; and moving Matt's body to the end of the tunnel was an even bigger problem...

But regardless, if Bianca actually had the recording of herself and Matt filming that night, it cleared her completely – not least if that single continuous shot had herself, Yva, and Reef putting in an appearance at the very end. And if she was offering it so freely, it was certainly there.

Still, it never hurt to check. Yva had taken the camera and switched it on, and navigated to the playback menu. "Just one recording," she said, showing Alex the screen; and she set it in front of them and pressed the play button.

The digital screen of the camera showed a dark corridor, barely lit by a ring of torchlight. The beam fell upon a familiar metal door, and a gloved hand reached forward to pull it open. The owner of the hand hurried in, not troubling to shut the door behind themselves; and for a moment there was only the hiss of rain as the torchlight fell on a long row of barred and black windows. Then an exclamation broke the silence. Camera, torch, and Bianca swivelled right, and there turning to face them in the room, through a wall of clashing torchbeams, was –

Reef Evans.

"*What*," Alex whispered, an echo of Bianca's exclamation on the recording – and then the pieces fell into place. "Bianca – this is the scene you filmed with Reef! Right before you all ran off!"

"What? No!" Bianca cried, grabbing the camera away from them midway through tinny exclamations of surprise and wonder from the past Bianca and Reef living again on the camera screen. "No, that's not supposed to –" Her calm face had broken up like a shattered mirror, and there was something desperate in her eyes. "…Ohhh. I deleted the wrong one."

Alex darted a glance at Yva. She looked positively ecstatic, eyes and mouth widened in feverish delight. "I'm sorry, you did what?" Alex asked.

"I." Bianca stared at the camera for a few long seconds, and then abruptly paused the playback; but her eyes remained on the silent screen. "After I'd stopped running – after the scene with Reef – when I was sure I was alone… I felt so stupid and ashamed. I just wanted to wipe that whole awful scene in the room with him from my memory… and it was a bad take, anyway. So I deleted it." She looked up at them, her expression really nervous now, as if she knew just what kind of trouble she was in. "But I wasn't all there. And I deleted the recording with Matt instead."

"…*Did you*," whispered Yva. "Did you *really*." Her face was alive with an unhealthy glee. "How *convenient*."

"I swear it was an accident," Bianca insisted. "I wouldn't have kept this stupid, stupid scene! In fact –"

"No, wait!" Alex cried, but Bianca's hands had already moved over the buttons; and the surviving recording disappeared into darkness. "That might have been evidence!"

Bianca froze. "Oh. Oops," she said. She looked down at the camera, as if a look would undelete what she had done. "But you can still retrieve like, metadata from these things or something? From the memory card?"

"I… don't know?" Alex said, looking at Yva.

But Yva was still wearing that "gotcha" face. "There's no proof," she said. "No proof of anything that happened in the room with Matt! And that means we can posit any theory we like, and you *can't contradict it* –"

"No, wait," Bianca interrupted. "Wait. I see where you're going with this. It's true that me and Matt were out of sight, *and* his film of me got corrupted. And it's true that you don't have to take me at my word." She clasped her hands, a business-like gesture which seemed more a way of anchoring herself, as if she were holding onto someone. "But you do have to take common sense, and it makes no sense for me to want to harm Matt. Because whatever else he was, he was the first step on my road to getting a Bafta one day."

"What about Leo?" asked Alex; since she had no answer to the question of why *anyone* would want to kill Matt – or at least, not one she was prepared to voice just yet.

"*Leo?* He –" Bianca interrupted herself, and whatever she was going to say, she replaced it with a more measured reply. "Leo was a creep," she said. "But he hadn't done anything criminal. And if he *had*, I would have gone to the police."

"Because the police have such a great track record on sex crime," Yva nodded, not even bothering to add sarcasm to her tone.

"I'm not talking about this," Bianca answered, totally shutting down the conversation. Her face was a mask, not putting on any act now, not even her real feelings. "I've said my bit, take it or leave it."

"Where did you go after running from Reef?" asked Alex, changing topic as abruptly as Bianca had left the previous one. Take it or leave it? She didn't have to do either, yet.

Bianca frowned. "Like, specifically?"

"Very specifically," Yva confirmed. "With timestamps, if you have them."

Bianca closed her eyes; whether in thought or frustration, Alex couldn't guess. "I can't give you times," she said. "Stopping to check my watch wasn't the first thing on my mind. But I know we started filming just before twenty-to-one, and were in there for ten minutes…"

"Five," corrected Yva. "Based on how the scene was blocked in, and how far through you actually got, that's how long it should have taken."

"That sounds right to me," Alex agreed.

Bianca was silent for a few moments. "Whatever, then, but it took too long. I hated that scene – even before Reef made it personal.

But fine, let's call it five minutes, and by that point I had had enough. If I'm honest" – and here she opened her eyes, and Alex was struck by the vulnerability behind them – "if I'm honest, Reef was *scaring* me. He made it too real. I stopped thinking about the script, and the camera, and Tara… and I just had to get out of there." She gave a short, tired shrug. "So, I ran."

"Up the north tower," Alex recalled, from Reef's own account.

Bianca nodded. "All I could think about was how to throw him off. I knew I'd get tired if I went all the way up, though, and the top is a dead end, so I got off at the second floor and ran all the way south. …But I could still hear his footsteps pounding after me, so when I got to the south tower I went upstairs again. And from there I kept on trying to throw him off."

Alex felt an uneasy sense of déjà vu about this story… "You zig-zagged."

"Yeah," Bianca agreed. "I'd go up a flight of stairs and run along the east wing to the opposite flight. By the time I got to the fourth floor, I pretty much collapsed, I was so out of breath." She paused, and nodded slowly. "But I'd lost Reef. And I wasn't thinking about the argument anymore, either."

"What time was it then?" demanded Yva.

"I don't know," Bianca retorted. "I couldn't have known it was important, and besides, all I could concentrate on was catching my breath. I don't even know how long it took Tara to find me."

Alex was instantly alert. "She wasn't with you? I thought the two of you were together the whole time?"

"Like I said, all I was thinking about was throwing Reef off," Bianca said. "I don't know about anything else." Light seemed to dawn upon her, and her eyes grew alarmed. "But I'm sure Tara can't have done anything to Matt or Leo! In fact, since *she* caught up with me and Reef didn't, she must've been right behind me the whole time." She gave a forceful nod, more to herself than to her interrogators. "Yes, now that I think about it, I'm sure it was barely any time at all before she got back to me."

"I see," Yva replied icily. "I will treat your information with an appropriate level of trust in witness testimony."

This, Alex knew, was no trust. The annoying thing was that she had a point. Back in their online days, Yva had employed a small arsenal of links to studies proving that human memory was really, shockingly unreliable… chiefly to back up plot twists in her fanfics. "So what happened once Tara caught up with you?" she asked.

"We both needed a few minutes before we could even speak," Bianca admitted. "Then we walked around the fourth floor a little, just… talking about what happened. I guess if anyone had been in the south wing or its tower, we wouldn't have noticed; but nobody else came up. I was worried that Reef might, but I guess he gave up on us."

"And then, at some point," Yva proceeded, "you looked through a window and saw Dry Diver."

"Yeah," Bianca said, and shuddered. "Leo… He must have been trying to scare us somehow. I can't imagine how he climbed up the wall. They don't exactly make places like this to be climbed. It almost makes me think…" She bit her lip. "No. It's stupid."

"Everything is stupid," Yva said. "There's no point holding out on us if you have a theory."

Bianca hesitated; and looked over her shoulder. The way she twisted her body looked almost involuntary, as if she couldn't help herself. "It almost makes me think," she said slowly, "that maybe it *was* Dry Diver. That it didn't climb up the wall, it swam up…"

Alex and Yva stared at her, in the silence and the dark. With the low lighting in the long room, the high ceiling, the shadows hanging like drapes, it was as if they were in a church at night; and Bianca had invoked the Devil…

"I think you were right," Yva said, her voice low and quiet.

Alex's head jerked towards her. "You mean about Dry Diver?!"

Yva rolled her eyes. "No, about it being stupid. Here's a real question for you, Bianca Marsh," and she put her elbow across the table and leaned forwards: "How is it that the one window you just *happened* to look through was the one where Dry Diver was hanging around?"

"*That*, I can explain," Bianca replied, all business again. "I looked through more than one window. I was already thinking about leaving, so I was checking every other minute while me and Tara were walking whether the rain had stopped. It was just that last one, by the corner of the tower and the east wing, where Dry Diver appeared." She elevated her head. "As you know."

Yva looked irritated. "Good answer," she conceded.

"So after that, you ran again – understandably," Alex said, keen to keep things moving. "Where did you go then?"

"Not far," Bianca said. "At that time – well, at that time, maybe I was less scared of Dry Diver than of Reef. I did wonder if I'd imagined it. Tara grabbed me as I was heading down to the third floor and asked what was wrong; and I think maybe she thought I'd imagined it, too, as that's when she got serious about the two of us leaving. She said I needed a mental health break." She gave a small smile. "Tara's a good friend. With a team full of boys, we have to look out for each other."

Alex strongly suspected that Tara wanted to be more than just good friends, but she let the point rest. "And from there you went straight down and crossed paths with," she gestured behind her, to the guard sitting with his back to the front doors, "George, right?"

"Right," Bianca nodded, looking sheepish. "Um, George?"

Alex looked back, to see George sitting up and taking notice. "What's that?" he said.

"I'm so sorry we didn't stop and help you!" Bianca called; their exchange was a few metres apart, and her raised and echoing voice sounded more pleading than she had perhaps meant. "We didn't think you were – I mean – we weren't thinking…"

George waved an arm in dismissal; he looked deeply tired. "Water under the bridge, kid. On my first night here alone, I'd have believed anything, too."

"You can be forgiven for anything if you're pretty enough, I see," growled Yva. "Back to the story, Bianca! Do you have any useful idea what time any of this happened at?"

"Actually," Bianca said, with a triumphant air, "*yes*. Obviously we checked the time when we decided we were leaving. It was a couple of minutes before one o'clock – and less than a minute after that we met George on the stairs."

"And from one o'clock you were barricaded into the south wing of the second floor," Yva supplemented, and Bianca nodded.

Alex mentally aligned this with Viggo's account of his wanderings. From roughly 12:35 to 12:55, Viggo had gone up the south tower, through the east wing to the north tower, and had then slowly zig-zagged back down to the ground floor, finishing back where he started. From roughly 12:45 to 1:00, Bianca (and Tara?) had, starting at the north tower, quickly zig-zagged up to the fourth floor, remained there for a while, then gone down the south tower to the second floor before diverging to the south wing.

The amount of time each party had spent roughly added up, when you considered that Viggo had covered more ground more slowly. But should they have run into each other? Alex decided to wait until she'd heard from the remaining interviewees before coming to a conclusion on that question.

"No further questions," Yva declared; and made another of those grand, sweeping gestures she might have copied from Cornelia. "You may go now, Bianca."

"Thanks, Bianca," Alex said. "You've been a big help."

Bianca breathed a sigh of relief; and in that moment, began to look a lot more ordinary, just a girl out of her depth. "I hope you're right," she said, and stood up. "You two are better at this than I thought. We're counting on you, you know." She hesitated for a moment, as if there was more she wanted to say; and then half-turned and pointed across the room. "Do you want me to send Tara out after me?"

"All in good time," Yva said smoothly. "We'll come for her when we are ready."

Alex raised her eyebrows at Yva, but she remained as stolid and unrevealing as a cement wall until the moment the door clicked shut on Team Silver's cubbyhole with Bianca behind it. "Why are we leaving Tara for later?" Alex asked, then. "What's your, like, interview meta-strategy?"

"Keep 'em guessing," Yva replied.

"Keep 'em – that's *it*?" Alex blurted out. "That's your logic? See them at random?"

"Do you have a better one?" Yva asked.

Alex really thought about it. Well, they'd already seen two members of Team Silver, and openly declared that they were leaving the third for later; so their options going forward were actually pretty limited…

"I guess it's fine so far," she sighed. "My own strategy would be to be reactive. We've had Bianca's account, so now we can check that against Reef's, and then check *that* against Tara's. We'll fit

Chase in there somewhere as well – last or second-last, because I feel like his story is just going to make everything much more complicated…"

"There's someone you're forgetting," a rough voice came from behind them. Alex and Yva turned to see George sitting up in his chair, one leg resting on the other, arms loosely folded and an alert incisiveness in his eyes. "*Me.*"

CHAPTER TWENTY-ONE
BEHIND THE SCENES

2:10am

George Sanderling. And why not? The watchman who had come from nowhere, on this night of all nights. He had been hovering around the fringes of their story since the beginning, way back at the bookshop, hours ago; but just because he had been there at the beginning, it didn't follow that he should return for the end. As long as they were trapped, there was no way of checking just when he had left the bookshop; and, therefore, when he had arrived at Pitchwater. Could he be the murderer, the one piece of the puzzle who jarred with the rest?

"Alright, we'll hear you out," Alex said, and swivelled her chair and her torch around to face him; Yva, this time, the one following suit. "You dropped a few hints earlier, Mr. Sanderling, but – what *are* you doing here?"

George gave a grim smirk, and began. "First off, lassie, I *worked* here at Pitchwater – way back, when I was just starting out. That driveway out there," and he thumbed at the doors behind him, "stretches all the way to the edge of town; used to be the whole wood was fenced off, and a guard post set up at the gate, and I was one of them. O' course, when Pitchwater was shuttered – I'm not saying when, that's classified – a lot of that was taken down, or fell down; but they still needed someone to watch over the place, in case they ever reopened, or needed some of the information that's locked up here. Now, most of the staff had been moved on elsewhere; I wasn't that important, but I was *trusted*, and in this trade that's what matters. So they handed me the keys, and a small monthly stipend to keep an eye on the place and make sure no one gets in."

"You aren't doing a very good job of it," Yva remarked.

George squinted at her. "That's because I'm just one man, on pay that hasn't been topped up since the end of the Cold War, working a second job in private security to make ends meet," he growled. "Of course people get in. Kids, vandals, small-time crims – they break in, I dip into the stipend to redo the locks they've broken or the windows they've smashed or the fences they've cut. Don't have the budget available to give the whole building the attention it needs, mind; I'm just papering over the cracks. Besides, break-ins are rare, and nobody's ever made any real trouble." He glared at them. "Until tonight, that is."

"Yes, tonight," Alex nodded. "The one night that actually matters – and you just happened to pay a visit? You have to admit, it's a bit of a coincidence."

"That's because it's not a coincidence," he said, his chapped lips set in a humourless grin. "When I said there were still folk keeping an eye, I didn't just mean me, you know. I'm the only keyholder, but there are other retired Pitchwater men in town who make a point of passing this way – and they reported lights in the building, twice in the past week."

Yva frowned. "To be clear, there was only one official night's location scouting," she said. "Tonight is only the second night any of us were meant have been here, and for most of the two teams it should be the first."

"That may be what you think," George replied, with curled lip; "but it's not as if your little friends have been telling you everything, now, is it."

Alex met Yva's eye, and Yva gave her a slight nod. They already knew it, but this was the confirmation. The vandalism in the Pitchwater Building hadn't been somehow overlooked by the location scouts, it wasn't the product of a freak tornado, and it certainly wasn't Dry Diver throwing a tantrum and scrawling on the walls. It was the work of a human being, one who shouldn't have been there.

Perhaps, one who *couldn't* have been there. Leo had one of the padlock keys. Reef, Alex remembered, had the other. That narrowed it down far enough to be suspicious.

But of course, there was a third man with a key to the building.

"What about the repair work?" Alex asked, breaking off her and Yva's silent conference. "Some windows have been smashed since the location scouting, but they've been boarded up again. Was that you?"

"I noticed that, too," said George, nodding towards the cubbyholes. "Vandals with a conscience! Nothing to do with me, kid; I haven't been here in months. Can't make head nor tail of it, myself."

Alex was starting to, though. She didn't know what it was all for – though she had a few keen guesses about some areas – but in her head, she had started thinking of the damage and repairs not as vandalism but as a curious form of set dressing.

It also occurred to her that disbelieving George was an option. Even if he'd told the truth about witnesses seeing lights in the building on multiple days – and that was something which the police were sure to double-check later – then there was no reason some of those lights might not have been his.

"That's the preliminaries," Yva said briskly. "Now, tell us about your movements, Mr. Sanderling – from Pugmire Pages, to that chair you're sitting in."

"Hm. About time," George muttered, and hunched over in his chair, clasping his hands; his eyes falling into deeper shadow. "Obviously, I was on the door of the bookshop 'til midnight, keeping those rabid children out and that old lady of yours in. You can check that. Once the doors opened, my business was officially done, but unofficially I was there a while after, sorting the brats into lines and keeping 'em from knocking things over, before I could finally walk out for good at quarter-past. You can check that as well. After that, getting here by the direct route is a half hour's walk or thereabouts – could've done it in twenty when I was younger, but that was a long time ago. Point is, some o' that you can check too, CCTV and so on. Let's say I walk into the building between a quarter and ten to one."

"Plausible," Yva nodded, "plausible."

"Believable," Alex agreed.

George looked at them with unseen eyes for a long moment before continuing. "Yeah, well, hold onto your hats, 'cause here's where it stops being believable," he continued. "I walk into the building, and what's the very first thing you think I see?"

Alex, remembering something George had said earlier, began to get a sinking feeling. "Someone wearing a diving suit."

"Top marks, girl," nodded George, the glistening edge of his wound bobbing in the gloom. "Top marks."

Yva goggled at Alex, her eyes as wide as maybe not dinner plates but egg cups, perhaps. "I don't believe it!" she hissed. "You were right. It isn't believable at all!"

"You're telling me," George sighed. "I didn't believe it myself. Just stood there as it slipped out into the courtyard, wondering if the day had finally come when I was starting to lose my marbles. I told you, didn't I, that you could believe anything in a place like this in the dark. But then I got a hold of myself. 'George,' I said, 'you may be going off your rocker, but the least you can do is make sure.'"

"So you followed it," Yva gestured over her shoulder in the direction of the courtyard, "out there."

"Aye," George nodded. "I walked straight across the room and out again through those doors. Couldn't see a thing for a few seconds, though, what with the rain playing havoc with my torchlight; but that's what diver boy had been waiting for, because the next moment I was shoved over like I'd been hit with a wrecking ball and knocked myself out against the ground." He pointed to his oozing head injury with a bitter smile. "As you see."

"But you didn't see who attacked you?" Yva pressed him.

"Nah," George said, shaking his head and then thinking better of it. "Would've made it too easy, wouldn't it? Well, from the sound of things, if I'd seen whodunnit they'd have surely killed me too, so I suppose you could say I was *lucky*."

His bitter sarcasm said everything about what he thought of his luck.

"So, how long do you think you were unconscious for?" Alex asked.

She exchanged a very careful look with Yva as she said this, and for once felt like the pair of them, thanks to Yva's medical knowledge, were on the same page. This question was a bit of a trap. It didn't feel like a very kind thing to do to an old man with quite a nasty injury, but it was a necessary thing to do, because what she and Yva had both learned was that if George, or anyone, had been unconscious for more than few minutes then it was quite likely that he had suffered lasting brain damage. That didn't necessarily mean he couldn't be talking to them right now. But his answer might make him their top suspect – or in need of urgent medical care.

In the event it was a moot point, because George gave an ambivalent shrug. "Couldn't tell you. To be honest, I'm hard-pressed to care about the fine details," he admitted. "I wasn't even aware of having come around – like when you're lying in bed in the night and realise you've been asleep and awake already, just without noticing it… I realised eventually that I was lying on the cold wet ground, getting colder and wetter every second, and that I needed to get inside or pretty soon I wouldn't be able to. How much of that was unconsciousness, how much was just grogginess – I don't know."

"Did you look at your watch when you awoke?" urged Yva.

George snorted. "Girl, a whole parade of divers could've come stamping by and I'd have scarcely noticed. A hundred percent of my energy was being spent on number one. You get in that situation yourself, you try and hold anything but a single, simple goal in your head. My goal was to get somewhere safe; and tend to myself. An' I did."

"And that was upstairs?" Alex asked. It didn't make much sense to her.

"That was one of them toilets, with a sink and a mirror and a lock on the door," George expanded. "Would have to be right at the very top of the towers, though, wouldn't they? Who designed this place? I ask you." He sat back in his seat with a grunt, and once again took out his filthy handkerchief to dab at his scalp. "Fortunately for me, you don't patrol a place like this for decades without coming to know it like the back of your hand. I could find my way around here in the dark – and that's just what I did. Had to. I'd left my torch behind in the courtyard, didn't pick it back up until I confronted you lot there."

"Oh no you don't!" interrupted Yva, looking as if she'd like to bang her fist on the table. "You don't get to skip to the end. You just leapt right past a whole half-hour between being seen on the stairs and showing your face in the courtyard!" She pointed a finger at him like the barrel of a gun. "Did you think I wouldn't notice?"

George looked wholly unimpressed. "Steady on," he said, staring unblinkingly at her. "That was just me giving a little piece of what's called *context*. If I hadn't, you'd have just asked me what about my torch, and I'd have had to tell you then, and so it would all have been a waste of time not telling you in the first place, like it's a waste of time you asking me why I was telling you. Sometimes when you're telling a story you can't tell every little detail in the order it happened."

Yva looked sulkily at her lap and her clenching fingers. "I know more about storytelling than you ever will."

Alex thought she had better step in. "You must have been aware of meeting Bianca and Tara on the stairs, though," she said. "It sounds… hard to ignore."

"Yeah, I'm not going to be learning your names," George said. "A couple girls ran across me as I was getting to the second storey, though. Maybe it was them other girls. Maybe it was you two. All I got out of it was a torch shining in my eyes and screams like banshees, and then me left blinking in the dark wondering again whether I'd been imagining things. Didn't help me, so I carried right on up to the top. Only when I was *safe* did I start getting my strength back." He paused, and his fingers moved on the handkerchief again. "Getting a splitting headache, too…"

Yva looked up impatiently. "And *then* did you look at your watch?"

"I'm getting there, alright?" George sighed, rolling his eyes. "*Yes*, once I'd got myself as washed up as I could with next to no light, I got a read off my watch; luminous face, you know. I went to round up you trespassers at twenty-past one, on the dot."

And Bianca and Tara had encountered him on the stairs just before one. Twenty minutes was a big gap – but he wasn't a well man. It all came down, Alex thought, to whether you trusted him or not. And Alex was beginning to think that she did trust him.

Paradoxically, she trusted him because he'd just made a very obvious mistake.

"Twenty-past one?" Alex asked. "You're sure?"

In answer, George thrust his closed fist towards her. Alex lurched back – but then he was rolling up his shirt sleeve, and revealing a heavy-looking digital watch. He pressed a button on its side, and the display lit up with a dim green glow. "Check your own watches against mine, if you're not happy," he said.

Alex shrugged, and held out her own watch, Yva following suit, such that they formed a strange three-pointed fist bump. And their watches *did* match – at least, as closely as it really mattered for them to do.

"I'm satisfied," Yva said.

"For once," muttered George, withdrawing his arm.

"Satisfied that you're either a liar or an idiot," Yva continued. "You noticed too, didn't you, Alex?"

Alex nodded over George's protestations. "It must have been nearer half-past when you confronted us in the courtyard. So, where were you for nearly ten minutes?"

"It gets better!" Yva broke in. "I've been keeping a *scrupulous* watch on my watch. At twenty-past one we were making our way to the fourth floor to investigate Bianca's sighting of Dry Diver."

"So at the same time we were going *up* the south stairs," Alex realised, "George should have been coming *down* them!"

"Hang about! Hang *about*!" George roared. "Alright, listen! I have a perfectly good explanation for this."

"They all say that," Yva said. "All criminals, that is."

Alex shushed her. "Come on, hear him out."

"That's right, hear me out," George repeated, his voice still raised. "Put yourself in my shoes for a minute. I'd just seen a man in a diving suit, been knocked down and left for dead, then assaulted by shrieking banshees on the stairs. So when I was heading down to the fourth floor and heard a whole gaggle of voices coming up towards me..." His voice dwindled and trailed away; and he looked quietly humiliated. "Well, what would you do?" he muttered.

Mere moments earlier, Alex had been alarmed by this man, with his bluster and evasions; but just as suddenly, she felt her heart go out to him. "You were scared."

"'*Cautious*' is how I'd put it," he mumbled. "'Sensible.'"

"It actually *was* a perfectly good explanation. That's rare," said Yva. "So... what did you do instead? Let us go past, and then make a break for it?"

"No!" George exploded, fierce as a landmine. But then the hot air drained out of him again. "Well, I *did* let you go past. But then I followed you to listen in, and get an idea of what I was dealing with – whether I needed to go for backup or not. Turned out, you lot didn't know what was going on, either. Then you all got scared by that thing out the window and ran off down the ground floor, so I hurried back to the stairs to catch you at the bottom."

"Keeping up, but keeping a safe distance," Alex said.

"In case, yeah," George agreed. "Headed to the courtyard, where the action obviously was, by the main doors. I thought, if worst came to worst, I could pick up my torch – which had been switched off, by the way, and not by me – and make my way out the front without being seen. But then it became clear that there'd been an accident and someone had died, and, well, at that point I had my responsibilities to think of. So I showed myself." He spread his hands. "And that's my little bedtime story for you kids. Don't see as it contradicts anyone else's, but who knows, there's time yet." His lips gave a sarcastic curl. "Any questions?"

He was right, Alex thought. His story tallied with the others'. Neither Viggo nor Bianca had been to the foyer or courtyard from the time George had entered the building, so neither would have run into him there. Viggo had come from the south and met herself and Yva at five-to, and Bianca had encountered George on the second-floor stairs a few minutes later, so it was feasible that Viggo had just missed him crawling out of the foyer.

But there was time yet, as George had said, and three members of the group yet to interview. The long night was far from over. So there was time enough for just one long-shot question.

"Do you have any grandchildren?" Alex asked. "Or great-nephews, great-nieces…?

If somebody in the building was *related* to George –

But George shook his head, and grew misty-eyed. "Nope. No grandkids, no kids, no wife or siblings or anything. It's just me," he said, his voice wistful. "I always wanted a family, truth be told. There was just one thing stopping me."

Alex took the bait. "What was that?"

George looked up, and met her eye. "I hate kids."

Yva stood up in disgust. "I'm getting Reef."

CHAPTER TWENTY-TWO
THE THIRD TO DIVE

2:23am

"So which of you is the good cop, and which is the bad cop?"

Alex shared a deadpan glance with Yva. No sooner had Yva brought Reef over from the cubbyhole he shared with Chase than he had opened with a bad joke. Perhaps he was just nervous – he certainly *looked* nervous – but it was nice to see that the two detectives were in agreement about his poor taste. "To be honest, I'm not sure jokes are appropriate given the circumstances," Alex said.

"But," Yva interrupted, "if you mean bad in terms of competence, the answer is self-evident."

Alex frowned at Yva. "I couldn't agree more," she said, although apparently they weren't so in agreement after all.

Even Yva seemed to detect her sarcasm, as she cleared her throat and changed the subject. "Listen up and take this seriously," she began, staring Reef straight in the eye. "Obviously, we know exactly where you were for the entirety of the actual filming period. You were under observation, mostly by me, practically every minute, so there's no mystery as to your whereabouts. But we have to be fair and consider the possibility that you are actually a diabolical genius, so understand that you are being treated as a suspect so long as we can't establish where you were after we all separated."

Reef gave a quick nod, his bodycam bobbing with him like a third eye. "Alright. I understand. So you want to know my movements, right?"

"From the time you were filming with Bianca," Alex said. This was going more smoothly than the other interviews, but they'd had plenty of practise.

Reef looked towards Yva, almost instinctively. "Filming with Bianca," he repeated, with a grimace. "Yeah, you heard how that went down. It was – and it was meant to be! – kind of a fiery scene… but," he held up his hands, "I got *too* into it. I said a lot of things in the moment that I'd been bottling up, and it figures that Bianca, well, bottled it." He had the decency to look ashamed.

"Why did you follow her?" Alex asked. It was something she'd been wondering for a while.

"I –" Reef gestured helplessly. "I just… it seemed like the sort of thing you should do, okay?" He seemed unable to meet their eyes. "She ran, and for one second I didn't understand what she was doing; but then I felt… I just felt like such a jerk. I knew how wrong I'd been, and I wanted to catch up and tell her I was sorry." He looked away, into the shadows. "I meant what I said, but I regret saying it. I've never wanted to hurt Bianca."

Alex snuck a glance at Yva to see how she was taking her boyfriend's confession of his deep, conflicted feelings for his ex. But Yva didn't appear to be bothered. "She had enough of a headstart to lose you," she prompted.

Reef nodded eagerly. "She got away from me in the dark – plus I didn't really know where she'd gone. I said earlier, right, that I was checking every room along the way? This place echoes so much that you can't tell where the echo is really coming from."

Alex wasn't at all sure she bought this, but they would have time to poke holes in Reef's story later. "What about Tara?" she asked. "She disappeared, too."

"Was she ahead of you?" prompted Yva. "Or behind you?"

"Um," Reef mumbled, his eyes darting away. "Thing is, I'm not sure? I didn't really think about her at all. I definitely didn't see her ahead of me… but I'd have remembered if she passed me." He frowned suddenly, a flash of darkness across his face. "How did Tara know where to go? Had Bianca already agreed to meet up with her somewhere?"

Some holes needed poking immediately. "But earlier you told us you'd been looking for both of them," Alex pointed out. "You kept on talking about Bianca and Tara like they were one unit, together."

"I've had time to think about it since then," Reef said. "At first I only knew that Bianca had gone, but then later I realised that Tara had vanished too – so I assumed they had been together the whole time. It's only since we found them again that I started wondering how that was possible."

But when did he realise that Tara had also vanished?

"We're getting off the subject of your movements," Yva said, giving Alex a stern look. "Bianca ran. You left the room after her. You didn't see Tara. Where exactly did you go? *Exactly.*"

Reef's tongue flicked across his lips. It was an unsettling move, like a hungry animal. "The north staircase," he began. "She didn't have so big a headstart on me at first, and I thought that was where I heard her going. But I looked in the break room on the way because I couldn't tell where she'd turned off, and that slowed me down; and then I got off on the second floor and checked the tower room there, and *that* slowed me down…" He looked tired out just remembering it. "At that point it was already hopeless. I was too far behind and I couldn't hear her footsteps any more. But" – he shrugged – "it felt stupid to just give up, so I kept going down the entire second floor like that, looking in on the north and south wings as I went. And then I ended up going up the south stairs…"

Yva groaned, and Alex felt like putting her head in her hands too. "Don't tell me," Yva said, "you *zig-zagged.*"

Reef looked taken aback. "Uh, no, not really," he said. "I was going to, but then I got to the top of the third floor stairs and realised that going on was even stupider than giving up. I had no idea where Bianca was, and she might even have gone back down for all I knew. So I went downstairs again."

"All the way down?" asked Alex.

"Yeah, all the way," he agreed. "I didn't zig-zag, I looped, pretty much back to where I started. I figured I'd meet up with all of you downstairs and think about how to salvage this messed-up filming trip… but," he muttered, "when I got back, the whole place was dark and silent. I looked in on the foyer and all the filming rooms, but nobody was there – not even the costume. I thought at first you were filming something else, but we weren't meant to be filming above the ground floor." He stared at Yva. "I – I was really worried about you."

"So what did you do?" Yva asked, impersonally.

Reef sighed. "Something actually sensible," he said. "Obviously *everyone* was moving around, circling after each other and chasing their own tails or something – so I decided to stay put. I went to the break room at the bottom of the north tower and stayed there, waiting for people to come to me." He looked at Yva, and his voice softened. "That's where I heard Alex shouting, and ran to help."

"How long do you think you were waiting?" Alex asked. "Did you look at your watch at all?"

"I glanced at it, when I sat down," Reef said. "It was ten to one, I think – but I wouldn't swear to it, I just looked out of habit." Some of the nervousness re-entered his expression, and his mouth twitched as he spoke. "I was paying more attention to how much time had *passed*. It must have been fifteen minutes before you showed up again, and I was getting desperate."

"Didn't you think that everyone might have left without you?" Alex asked. "If I'd been waiting that long, I'd have wondered."

"Without their phones?" Reef asked. "I don't think so."

"And so that's your whole story," Yva summed up. "You didn't see or hear anyone, or anything else important. Right?"

"Right," Reef said, with a cautious nod. "Looking back, maybe I *should* have kept on looking – but it didn't make sense to me that literally everyone had gone a different way." His brow creased as he looked down at his hands. "It still doesn't make sense to me. I tried asking Chase," he gestured back towards the cubbyhole, "what *he'd* been up to, but he clammed up and refused to say anything."

"And rightly so, as that would have been collusion and would have jeopardised the truthfulness of your testimony," Yva declared, pious in her detecting dedication. "We'll hear from Chase next, then. Send him out."

"You know, maybe we should have spoken to Chase first," Alex murmured to Yva. Across the desk from them, Reef was getting up and avoiding George's eye. "Now that I think about it, he was out of the picture for longer than anyone else – longer than Viggo, even. We could've used him as a sort of baseline for a timetable."

"Timetable mysteries are *boring*," Yva complained. "They're busywork best left to the police pen-pushers." She brightened momentarily. "But sometimes the author draws them for you, and you can work out something interesting."

Nobody was going to draw a timetable for Alex and Yva, of course; and it certainly wasn't necessary to solve the mystery. But if she had found the patience sooner to dredge up paper and pen from the neglected stationery cupboards, Alex might have learnt something crucial before she even put pen to paper.

"And the thing about Chase," Alex went on, paying no attention to Reef as he crossed the torchlight towards Team Dry's cubbyhole, "is that he was just down the corridor from the tunnel. We don't know where Matt Silver was drowned, but somebody had to move his body to the tunnel, and anyone in the east wing must have heard or even *seen* something! How long Chase was there before leaving again is a vital clue!"

"I can't understand how the body was moved at all and I'm *so annoyed*," Yva admitted, although the explanation was a simple one. "Moving a corpse is *slow*! Even someone really strong would have to be insane to risk dragging a body through a building with people on all sides!"

"I've been listening to this rigmarole, too," George's gruff voice echoed from behind them. "Far as I can see, it's nonsense, all of it. All that blundering about in the building while you were all apart – it doesn't matter. No matter which way you look at it, there isn't *time –*"

"Uh, guys?"

The voice broke in on them from across the room, a high voice with a hint of an echo. Though Alex had never really looked away from it, she switched her full attention back to the corner of the room where Reef now stood, full in the torchlight, one hand visible on the now open door to Team Dry's cubbyhole; and she knew that something was terribly wrong.

It wasn't the faint tremor in his voice which shook her, or the corpse-rigid grip of his hand on the open door. It was the uncharacteristic expression on Reef's face, his half-face staring straight into the room through the open door, to where Alex could not see.

He looked absolutely terrified.

Alex and Yva leapt up as one, their chairs clattering to the floor with startling violence; George rising behind them with a muffled profanity. In seconds they had crossed the fully-exposed room with its torches beamed at every door, where nothing could possibly happen, where nobody could move without them knowing about it –

The cubbyhole was just as Alex had last seen it, in the light of her same reclaimed torch; a narrow rectangle with only a few square metres of floor space, a skeletal desk, a flimsy chair, a filing cabinet with its drawers sagging open. Above the desk was what had formerly been a glass screen where the receptionist would have dealt with enquiries and filing, but it had been smashed and firmly boarded over; an old-fashioned telephone had long ago had its cable ripped from the wall and now lay in a discarded heap on the floor, rotary dial and handset separated by a spiral cord gone slack with use. The only anomalous things in the room were a lit torch sent rolling across the floor by the opened door; and a digital camera, a concession to a modernity which had otherwise passed the Pitchwater Building by, idly waiting in the centre of the desk.

The other anomalous thing wasn't in the room; or at least, it wasn't visible.

Chase Ferrier was nowhere to be seen.

"I just opened the door, and he was gone," Reef stammered, still staring into the room. "He was there when I left. How could he have gone?"

"He couldn't have!" Yva exploded. "He couldn't have, he couldn't have, *he could not have*!" She pushed past Reef and into the room, and now she seized the rolling torch to shine it like a peering eye into the blind spots and around the side of the filing cabinet as if there were space for a person there.

"This is Leo's disappearance all over again," Alex whispered. They had stood outside this door and watched Chase enter the room, and the entire time since then the door had been in full and illuminated view.

She couldn't see a way around it. She'd read her fair share of locked-room mysteries, but every single time it happened she was blindsided with incomprehension. There was no way out!

"Out, you lot. Let me see your faces," George's voice spoke across the room; he had opened the door to Team Silver's cubbyhole, and was counting them out one by one – Viggo, Bianca, Tara… "All present and correct," he growled, and stuck his head into the room himself. "And nobody else hiding in here, either."

"What's going on?" asked Bianca, her voice high and scared. "Where's Chase?"

Alex bit her lip. "We don't know."

They crowded around her, the remains of Team Silver, while George brooded in the background looking thoroughly stumped; and Reef stood awkwardly to one side with a cold sweat pouring off him. "How can you not know?" demanded Bianca. She pushed past Alex and stared into the room herself, eyes flicking from corner to corner. "Weren't you watching the whole time? How can you *not know*?"

"We also don't know," Yva said absently, peering into first one filing cabinet drawer and then another, pulling the top drawer all the way open to match the rest, "how we can't know."

"What are you looking in those drawers for?" asked Tara; frowning, over Bianca's shoulder, at Yva's strange search. "A person can't fit in there."

"We discussed this earlier," Yva said, her voice low and frustrated. "Contortionism. Prosthetic limbs. Also, Reef could have cut him up." Her eyes were wild now, shaking with suppressed energy like a boiling kettle. "He could have cut him up, and put the pieces –"

"*Shut up!*" Bianca screamed; and everyone stepped back from her as if pushed by a shockwave. "Shut up! Shut up! Shut up…"

Covering her ears, she dissolved into sobs, falling into a crouch on the floor. Tara hovered around her, looking like she didn't know what to do with her hands…

"Reef. Get over here," muttered Yva. "Help me move this."

She had her arms around the side of the filing cabinet. Reef responded mechanically, moving past Alex into the room; and together they twisted the heavy cabinet away from the wall, revealing its blank backside and a filthy rectangle of dust and cobwebs and dead insects…

"No ventilation shaft," Alex murmured. "Then maybe…" She pushed her own way in, walked to the desk; and pushed on the plywood board over the once-window, first gently and then with increasing firmness, hard enough to shove a person over. But, though it wasn't easy to tell, the board was firmly nailed into place; and certainly could not have been removed and replaced whilst they were interviewing suspects on the other side of the wall.

"I'm so angry that I'm not even angry any more," Yva said. She had passed through it into a kind of chilly remoteness, looking down on the world from a mountaintop above the clouds. "There's no exit. Locked doors and windows are one thing, but this time the lock is *us*. Just like Leo – we saw them walk in, and they were gone without walking out."

"Do you think," Reef stuttered – the first words he had uttered in minutes – "do you think, if you had spoken to him first – it would have been me who –"

"You're getting ahead of yourself," Yva corrected. "As far as we know, Chase escaped on his own – afraid of what we might deduce. He escaped justice."

"There's nothing else for it, then, is there?" Alex asked. She pointed at the object next to her on the desk, the object which she hadn't touched, as if it might burn her. "We'll have to look at the camera."

Reef stared at it. "You think –"

"I think we're all capable of basic pattern recognition," said Yva.

When a stray camera was found in the Pitchwater Building, floating adrift of the bodycam harness and the person who wore it, that only meant one thing – no matter how little sense it made. Dry Diver was trying to tell them something. Dry Diver was boasting…

The three of them pushed back through into the foyer. Yva was carrying the camera, and Alex heard a sharp intake of breath from Tara when she saw it. But nobody spoke a word. They silently formed a train, a strange funeral march, that followed in Yva's wake until at last she slammed the camera down with a hammer blow.

"This is a clue," she announced. "This is the answer. We're all on the same page now: None of us have any more private advantages or trivial secrets clouding our view of the crime." This wasn't true, as it happened, but Yva didn't know that. "So I need you all to watch carefully. Obviously I'm not expecting much, but if even one of you spots some tiny detail which can explain what's going on, I need you to speak up."

She switched the camera on. Navigated to the playback. A single video sprang into view. It should all have been so simple.

THE DRY DIVER DROWNINGS
"ENTRY 9"

Once again a door closes in the viewfinder's eye, metal like a prison gate. The camera is already moving, though, tracking a chest-height path down the corridor-width room, torchlight from the camera's side throwing every inch of the narrow and stuffy space into fuzzy but distinct relief.

Seconds later it's at the desk and the boarded-up screen, the opening that is closed. The torchlight shifts and a gloved hand comes into view as it twists, until it's wedged carefully in a corner of the desk and shining its light full out and down the room. And then it's the camera view which shifts and clunks, and the body of the camera lifts free; gloved fingers dance around the lens until the whole thing is turned around now, pointing straight at a chest with an empty camera harness. And then with a scraping of a chair the chest sinks and the body settles and, finally, the face of a person comes into view, blinking against the torchlight.

It is Chase Ferrier.

"Reef's gone," he says, in a low and strained voice; it's as if he's forcing himself to utter the words. "It'll be me next… But I'm tired of being the one to just sit quietly and wait. I have to say something. Even if just turning a camera on is a risk now…"

He looks anxiously over his shoulder, but there is nothing else in the room; just the black shape of a filing cabinet, the sliver of a door on the side wall. It seems like an instinctive gesture, uncontrolled, and Chase turns stiffly back to the camera with the air of a stormswept seaman lashing himself to the ship's wheel.

"I couldn't tell anyone – they'd never believe me," he whispers, "but in case something happens to me I have to leave a record, so people will know what happened… and so there'll be some meaning to everything I've seen and done tonight."

He takes a deep breath, as if preparing himself, or preparing his imagined audience, or as if building the suspense, like a magician at work; and then his words fall out in a rush.

"I finally understand what's been happening – how Leo and Matt disappeared – but the truth is so much worse than I could ever imagine. It's a nightmare! But I can't risk keeping it secret. The one behind all this is –"

A slight noise off-screen catches Chase mid-sentence, like a heavy tread. It clearly jars him and he darts a hurried look over his shoulder – but the camera view can already see behind him and all the way down that tiny room, and its few furnishings and only door haven't moved an inch. But the camera can't see behind the camera; and Chase can. In a fraction of a second it's clear that in looking away he has sealed his fate, because in looking back his eyes fly to something above the camera and he thrusts himself away with a cry of "No – !"

But his last act is indeed a meaningless one. He tips over out of sight but there's already something lunging into view to grab him, a dark and dripping shape like the trunk of an elephant, or some bizarre tube-worm from the abyssal depths of the sea. It's the distinctive two-fingered, hook-clawed arm of an old diving suit; and as it reaches down towards Chase, another lurches into view and settles over the camera, and all goes black.

CHAPTER TWENTY-THREE
OUT OF SIGHT

2:34am

Seeing his face made it worse. Leo, Matt – they had both kept their cameras firmly harnessed to their chests, and it made their disappearances and even the charge of Dry Diver somehow impersonal. Alex had thought she was numb to the impossible and the insane, but Chase had made it personal; and undeniably more inexplicable.

Alex found herself looking at the stunned faces of those around her – Reef with a face of stone, Bianca dizzy with grief, George bewildered by belief in hallucinations. Yva wasn't there. The second the video had ended, she had marched right over to the boarded-up screen at the end of the cubbyhole – the screen through which it seemed Dry Diver must have lurched – and was scratching and tugging at the sheet of plywood as if it would peel off like skin.

It was a good idea. If nothing else, detecting gave you something to do when you might otherwise go mad, and so Alex strode with equal swiftness to the door of the cubbyhole and pointed her torch back down it. The desk was pushed flush up against the boarded-up screen Yva was presently failing to remove; and the camera had been in perhaps the centre of the desk. There was no room for anyone to stand behind it, much less in a diving suit.

She walked silently out of the cubbyhole. Perhaps she would go mad anyway.

Viggo broke the silence. "So, does anyone have any way of explaining what we just saw?" he asked, gesturing futilely at the camera. "Were they all like that? I never saw the other videos. Were they all that impossible?"

"Um," Alex said, and bit her lip. "Pretty much."

"This one's the worst, though," Tara said. "We couldn't see Matt's face in his."

"We heard Leo speak, though," Reef added.

"I wasn't done talking," Tara replied. She had an expression on her face that was at once crafty and exhausted, as if she had a clever idea which she knew wouldn't work. "Seeing Chase isn't the worst part. The worst part is how *specific* the video is."

Yva, returning from her futile efforts at the firmly boarded-up screen, shot a look at her. "Meaning?"

Alex let out a long breath. "Meaning we're finally touching the elephant in the room, I guess."

Tara looked at her appraisingly. "Specific as in being in that particular room and saying the things he did. None of that was part of any filming plan… meaning it couldn't have been put together in advance."

And there they had it. The theory Alex had been quietly working on, the one idea that showed any promise of helping, simultaneously voiced and debunked. She spoke up and explained, working it through for herself, even though it felt like barring the barn door after the horse had bolted. "I'm sure we all thought it at some point: That maybe these videos were faked somehow, that they were pre-recorded by someone else and Leo and Matt had been tricked into putting the files on their cameras. After all, you can't see a person's face on a video they filmed with a bodycam. But that was really Chase, and he was really talking about tonight."

"Hold on there," George interrupted. "Supposing he was in on the plot…"

"He's not in on *murder*," Bianca sobbed. Her face was streaked with tears. "I know him, remember? We – we were all friends before. Chase hates the thought of people getting hurt."

Yva sighed dramatically. "It doesn't really *matter*," she said. "Fake videos couldn't get Leo or Chase out of those rooms. So it stands to reason that they're real."

"That doesn't stand to reason at all," Alex said. Yva was jumping to the conclusions she found most interesting, and it would do them no good whatsoever. "But what does stand to reason is that, *if* Chase was in on it, appearing in person on that video would be incredibly incriminating." She glanced at Bianca, still distraught, and Reef, still frightened. "Like, I hope he turns up fine, we all do – but what would it mean if he does?"

"Could it be mocked up? Like on a computer?" asked Viggo, still staring at the camera himself. "Like with those programs which can put a person's face on a video of someone else, or mimic their voice."

"You can do that now?" exclaimed George.

"It's not that," Tara interrupted. She didn't look happy about what she was saying, and seemed torn between sticking to the truth and not upsetting Bianca. "I do this semi-professionally, remember? I want to work in this field, and I've *studied* these things, so I know. What we saw in that video wasn't CGI, it wasn't manipulated, it wasn't dubbed over –" She stopped for breath, a deep and shuddering one. "That was all practical effects," she concluded. "Everything in that video was real."

"So… so what now?" Viggo asked. He looked shaken to his core. "Do we just start believing in Dry Diver? Or do we *already* believe, and that made it real –"

"No we don't," Tara hissed. Alex noticed that her hands were trembling at her sides. "I *might* be prepared to admit that there are some pretty strange phenomena in the world, maybe some things we don't understand – but a ghost in a diving suit in a spy base? Come on! We're only filming here because we *could*."

"But how do we explain it?" Bianca whispered. She clutched at Tara's hand. "How do we *explain* it, Ta?"

"We will explain it," Alex said. She didn't mean just anyone. One step took her next to Yva, a person she could once never have imagined standing in solidarity with. She looked back, and *great*, everyone was staring at her and thought she was going to give a speech. Being the detective was one thing, but being the hero was quite another. She took a deep breath, closed her eyes, and tried to mentally prepare herself.

"Some people are clever," she began. "I mean, *really* clever. They could trick you into thinking black is white and up is down. Luckily, a lot of them go into writing, or stage magic. Maybe both! But some of them? They go into crime." She glanced at Yva, one of those who had gone into writing; and Yva gave her an unexpected, approving nod. Alex returned the favour. "Yva was telling the truth earlier. We were there for the Carver's Rest murders, where four people died behind doors that had been taped over at every gap. It seemed impossible – but there was an answer, and we found it. Here, the locks are different; it's not tape guarding the doors, it's *us*. But we're not any more reliable than tape, really; we can be tricked too."

"Bully for you," George said. He didn't look terribly impressed. "But that's all talk. Do you actually have an explanation for how any of this could have happened?"

"I'll give you an example," Yva said. She looked pleased with herself, whether for having had an idea or just for being the centre of attention. "Chase's disappearance is possible if he and Reef and George were in on it."

Reef's face went rigid with alarm, and the surviving members of Team Silver took an automatic step away from him.

"Care to clarify that remark, missy?" George said, his voice deep as a well.

"I think I know what she means," Alex said. It wasn't a very flattering theory, but it was valid. "When me and Yva interviewed George, we turned our chairs around to face him. Chase could have left the room while our backs were turned – but Reef and George would both have seen him…"

Bianca had her hands to her face, staring through her fingers at Reef as if she wished there were bars between them, and Tara once again stepped between them. "Don't try anything, Reef," she warned him. "I knew you were a nasty piece of work. But there are more of us than there are of you –"

"Yeah, calm *down*," Yva sighed, rolling her eyes. Her expression spoke of an utter weariness with the stupidity of humankind – with just a hint of contented superiority. "I said it was just an example. I don't think that's actually what happened."

"Sure seems like it explains everything to me," Viggo said; he had adopted almost a fighting stance, glancing back and forth from Reef to George as if gauging which was the more dangerous.

"It really doesn't," Alex said quickly. "And it's a brute force solution anyway; it's not actually believable. I don't buy that three out of the ten of us would all collaborate on a murder plot."

Alex was right to be dubious. Three of the ten of them did not collaborate on a murder plot.

The tension in the room slackened. But only a little. What had been said could not be unsaid – and it was all too clear that all too many people in the room were perfectly prepared to believe that Reef Evans was a party to murder.

"So… what are you two going to do?" Viggo asked. He was still keeping his torch square on Reef.

Alex looked at Yva. "What we discussed earlier," she said. "Crime scene investigation, right?"

Yva nodded firmly. "There's one particular room that's especially suspicious. It's about time we had a look at it."

"Chase is somewhere out there, too," Alex reflected. "Leo and Matt travelled quite a way after they disappeared. He could be anywhere…"

"Now, wait a minute," George rasped. He took a step towards them, and drew himself up to his full and gangly height. "I'm not so sure I should let you girls go wandering off on your own. No good's come of it so far, and, well…" He rubbed at his stubble, trying to find the words. "I don't claim to understand any of what's going on, but seems to me there's something dangerous prowling about the Pitchwater Building tonight – maybe something that don't obey the usual laws of nature…"

"I'll go with them," Reef volunteered in a high, strained voice.

"No, you stay here," Yva commanded, and he trailed off. "*All of you* stay here," she expanded, darkly surveying the pool of suspects and witnesses and whatever else they were before her. "We should have done it this way from the start. We are the detectives. You people are the suspects. We can't trust any of you. But so long as we leave all of you in the same room together, the odds are that more of you are innocent than not, so the enemy won't be able to do anything. That leaves me and Alex free to detect."

She glared at the people gathered before her, Viggo and Bianca and Tara all in a group, Reef alone, George standing uncertainly before them. At last he gave a defeated shrug. "Your funeral," he muttered. "I'll keep an eye on this lot, then."

"Thank you," Alex sighed. Everything felt like a battle, and not only with the culprit. "Then we'll head out. We'll be back in…" She looked at Yva to check. "Half an hour?"

"Sounds right," Yva agreed, turning to their audience, "but give us an hour before you send out a search party. Not that I expect anything to happen to us, of course; it's you we need to worry about."

Tara nodded wanly. The rest stood silent. Probably every one of them was wondering whether they could *tolerate* another hour spent in such threatening company; let alone survive.

Alex and Yva had their torches at the ready; Alex her own, Yva the one left by Chase. The other five had all reclaimed their original torches, too. Ten torches, minus the broken pair found where Leo and Matt disappeared and a third dropped by Yva, still left them one each, so at least there was no question of their being lost in the dark. Alex decided not to worry what the battery life of these fragile things was. They made for the south-east door, and Alex took one last look at the five people they were leaving behind, distant and frightened on their islands of torchlight in the drowning shadows.

"Remember," Yva called back to them, "nobody leaves. No one! That way, nothing can or will happen!"

Something could and did happen. But not yet.

CHAPTER TWENTY-FOUR
UP, BUT NOT FOR AIR

2:41am

"I take it we're going to the towers," Alex said.

They had closed the door behind them, and were now soundproofed and effectively alone in the angular, pitch-black corridors of the Pitchwater Building – which meant it was time for a strategy meeting, or at least a torchlit huddle. It was all very well saying in front of the others that they were going to perform a crime scene investigation, but in actual fact they already *had* investigated the scenes of all three disappearances, and now had no plan whatsoever.

But the top floors of the towers with their unlocked rooms were the only places left that stood out. They deserved a visit. Yva clearly agreed. "That's the only thing that makes sense," she said. "To be frank, I couldn't care less about searching for Chase. Leo and Matt's bodies were dumped somewhere interesting where we would inevitably find them, so an active search is redundant."

"And if he's alive," Alex added – unlikely though it seemed, which was perhaps why Yva hadn't even considered it – "clearly he doesn't *want* to be found."

Yva shrugged. "Either way, it makes the tower heights the only places worth a serious look," she said. "They aren't very glamorous, but if the old American detectives could get a decent mystery out of grubbing around in apartments and alleyways, then I'm sure we can find *something*."

The nearest stairs were just down the corridor, so they set off. The two of them were alone again, but it was a different kind of loneliness from before. The first couple of times they had been alone in the building, it had felt strangely full of life, and they had known they were going from one occupied room to another, part of a team and part of a plan. Later, when everyone had vanished, that emptiness was a sinister thing, a surprise of nothingness. But now they were truly alone, advancing through emptiness without the expectation of coming across anyone. The hollow corridor had a new kind of silence about it, and their footsteps echoed away into the unseen as if they were inside a deep and trackless maze of caves; and the repetitive, copy-and-paste structure of the building, every corridor and stair looking the same, made Alex feel as if their journey might take forever, as if there was nothing unnatural about there being another stair and another landing over and over. It was a jarring thing to arrive at a numberless landing and have her torchbeam settle, where there should be a corridor, on a blank wall.

"We're here," Yva said; stating an obvious that felt strange. The top floor of the south tower; finally, a place which felt unfamiliar. A landing wound anticlockwise around the recess of the staircase, coming up against a narrow door after several turns, and then twisting again to lead away down a corridor.

Ignoring the corridor for the moment, Alex pushed open the door. It gave way to a slender room – perhaps about the size of the cubbyholes – which proved to be one of the bathrooms Viggo had been sent on a wild goose chase to, hours ago now. The toilet was at the far end, and like most things in the building that weren't made of concrete, it was made of dull metal; about halfway down the room, a pair of coathooks glinted on the wall, with the glass of a high and slit-like window opposite glinting back at them. The door banged alarmingly against something which prevented it from opening fully, and seeing Alex jump left Yva rolling her eyes.

"It's just the sink," she said. "Look." She pushed Alex through the door, with the air of a person pushing someone into a jail cell, and Alex tottered as she regained her balance. But it was indeed a sink jammed awkwardly into the space behind the door; and unlike a jail cell, the lock to this door was on the inside.

"This room seems…" Alex hesitated, trying to put her finger on what was bothering her. The whole room seemed off, somehow. "Extraordinarily poorly-constructed?"

Yva followed her in, and waved her torch around peremptorily. "It's like it's crammed into the only space they had left after designing everything else," she observed. "And only one per tower, for the whole building! The architect's a hack."

Alex turned her torch from one glimmer to the next. The lock was quite sturdy; a heavy bolt, more the sort of thing you'd expect to find on the door of a warehouse. The sink, by contrast, was an afterthought, its flimsiness evident by the dent worn into one corner from decades of people opening the door into it. "Still, there's at least one clue here," she said. "Or maybe more of an anti-clue."

Yva jammed herself into the same space as Alex, looking quite annoyed. "What are you talking about? What did I miss?"

They both hated being out of the loop on mysteries, so Alex explained as soon as she could get a word in edgeways. "The sinks in this place are so small," she said, gesturing. "It suggests – I mean, it *doesn't* suggest…"

"Got it!" Yva broke in, instantly as smug as if she'd thought of it first. "You mean it's too shallow to drown a person in."

Alex nodded. "This isn't something we've really talked about, but… there's nowhere to drown anyone in this place, is there? No decorative pond – no, I don't know, a well or anything…"

Yva glanced down the room. "I wonder if there's enough water in the toilet for that."

Alex wrinkled her nose. "Gross," she said. She still checked, though; there wasn't.

"We need to sit down and have a proper theorycrafting session," Yva decided. "But let's finish looking around first."

"Yeah, we have to be nearly at the point where we have enough clues to solve the mystery," Alex agreed. "We've been almost everywhere! At least the others are safe."

But not yet.

They left the bathroom. Following the corridor took them nowhere interesting, as it proved to terminate in very short order, separating the bathroom from another room and coming to a halt in a blank wall with a single window, glassed and barred as was the norm. Having been turned around so many times she had started losing her bearings, Alex made a point of peering out of it, and her torch just managed to bring out a hazy view of a grey, featureless rooftop; that of one of the wings, the south one, she thought. It was strange to think that the others, Reef and Bianca, Tara and Viggo and George, were housed deep below. There was no way to access the rooftops, as was evident from the filth of ages, ruins of birds' nests, the weeds and lichen which had somehow managed to take root in that stony expanse. The last door off the corridor revealed simply another empty meeting room, table and chairs thick with dust, and windows clawed by the heights of trees.

Which left them one tower down, and the other to go. As Viggo claimed to have done, Alex and Yva dropped downstairs and cut up the east wing, heading for the north tower. This one would lack novelty, but had one marginal point of interest.

"You remember the significant feature of this next tower, don't you?" Yva asked. It was as if she was quizzing Alex to make sure she wasn't losing track.

"Yes, Yva," Alex droned. "This is the one where the bathroom door is stuck, right? Chase tried it, and later Viggo did too."

"*Allegedly* stuck," Yva corrected. Cold and silent and pitch-black as it was, her attitude made the building feel almost like a school after dark. "As we've seen, the bolts on those doors would keep anyone out. Just like the government, security before comfort! Very sensible of them."

Alex ignored that remark. She had remembered something else. "It's not just Chase and Viggo," she began. "You said you remembered the stuck door from the location scouting, right? Was that something you found yourself, or was it Leo, or Tara?"

Yva stopped and dropped behind into the shadows, so suddenly it startled Alex.

"What's wrong?"

"Just trying to remember whether it was Leo or Tara who told me..." Yva muttered. "Damn it! I didn't know it would be important, so I didn't store the information."

"Oh. That's a shame, I guess," Alex shrugged. But she got the sense that Yva was silently beating herself up about this lapse, and added, "You never know, maybe it *isn't* important!"

"Maybe," Yva said. But in the torchlight, her expression had taken on an unsettling grimace... They walked on in silence, past the smashed window beneath which Leo's body lay.

The north tower was, as on all other floors, a mirror image of its southern counterpart; and though everywhere felt unknown when seen only in torchlight, it was a slightly surreal experience for Alex to be walking around a strange backwards version of the place she had just been, the landing turning right instead of left, room and corridor on opposite sides. Perhaps this was how they liked it, those Cold War spies; constantly reminded of the strange twilight world they inhabited on the other side of everyday life. Life was a bit like that for a detective, too.

The door to the bathroom was shut. "Well, moment of truth," Alex said to Yva, and she pushed the door. It swung open easily, revealing a bathroom not unlike the one she had been in a few minutes before; only with a door that swung the other way, colliding with a sink on the wrong wall, with a window on the reverse side.

"It *isn't* stuck," Yva said. "Not even a little bit! So, who lied? Everyone?"

Alex swung the door a little, her fingers touching the bolt on the other side; one no different to that in the other bathroom. "How easy would it be to lock a door like this from the outside, Yva?"

Yva strode over, and took two quick glances first at the bolt and then at the doorframe. "Trivial," she said dismissively. "That's not the issue. *Unlocking* it again from the outside is the issue." Her torch swept down the length of the bathroom, and she took a quick intake of breath. "But something *obviously* happened here! So this wasn't a waste of effort."

Alex followed her gaze. At first she didn't see it; but here there was only one coathook opposite the window – and the second had been torn out of the wall, and now lay on the floor some distance away with one of its screws missing.

"The scene of a struggle, I think!" Yva continued, looking pleased at the prospect. "And look, these taps are loose." She jiggled them demonstratively. "The combatants must have knocked into the sink in their throes!"

"What's that?" broke in Alex, her own torch catching something stuffed behind the sink. She reached down, and her hand came up with a loose coil of metal wire, spooling away on the floor to apparently quite considerable extent.

Yva made a noise like a balloon expelling its air, one which in any other person Alex would have classified as a squee. "That's actual fishing-line!" she squealed. "Actual, legit fishing-line straight out of mystery novels! Strong as anything and practically invisible!" She stared down into the tangle, and gasped. "The ends are knotted into loops and everything!"

It was such a change to see Yva so animated, enthused with innocent glee, that Alex found herself infected with it too. "Now *this* is a clue!" she said. "Great-Aunt Cornelia says the best mysteries are the ones you can solve without needing them, but I really think clues are the best part." She looked across the room and found the window, though letterbox thin, free of glass as she expected. "Leo's body must have been hoisted up, right? That window looks out on the courtyard, *right*?"

"Yeah, yeah!" Yva agreed, bobbing her head with reckless abandon. "And everyone's wearing gloves, so no worries about hand injuries from the wire or anything!" She punched the air. "This mystery rocks so much!"

"Okay, wait, hold on. I thought of something," Alex said, starting to come down from her high. "So now we know how he was pulled up, how was he let down? It happened right in front of us."

"Okay. To business," Yva agreed, though her face still pulsed with nervous energy. "So he didn't just fall by chance. That's obvious, right? It happened right in front of us, but we know from Bianca he'd been hanging there for ages. What we saw was meant to be seen."

That made sense – it certainly wasn't a coincidence – but Alex felt there was something missing. It had been quite difficult to see Dry Diver hanging there, and the only reason any of them had known about it was because Bianca just happened to look through the right window at the right time. Alex didn't see how the sighting could have been planned. But if it hadn't been, then what *was* the plan?

And that wasn't the only problem. "Everyone was there with us," she said. "Nobody could have let him down."

"Wrong. There's one person," Yva corrected her. "George Sanderling."

George... The previously unknown tenth person, who'd been hiding in the building for a good forty minutes before showing himself. It was definitely a tempting theory – and he really did seem like the only person who could have caused the body to fall.

But Alex was suspicious of only choices. Besides, there were major problems with George as the culprit.

"George is an old man, though," she pointed out. "He may look tough for his age, but could he really have hauled Leo's body four floors up? With or without a head injury? I don't think I believe it. Also," she gathered pace, "Bianca saw George injured on the stairs *after* seeing the Dry Diver costume outside the window, with Leo in it! George couldn't have been holding the costume up the whole time!"

Yva fidgeted on the spot. "I knew that," she said at last. "I was just testing you."

The thing about Yva was that that could, absolutely, be true. But Alex had thought of something else. "Also, George is almost certainly telling the truth about when he arrived in the building – like he said, it's verifiable," she explained, "but that would have been only minutes before we found Matt's body at the end of the tunnel. He couldn't have had anything to do with it."

"It's easy to criticise," Yva said. "People criticise my stories all the time, but I'm not obliged to respect anyone who can't come up with a better story themselves. So," she jabbed Alex square in the chest, "what's your theory? How was Leo let down in front of everyone?"

It was a very Yva response; but, Alex had to admit, a fair one. It wasn't as if they could just pin the blame on Dry Diver. "What about a mechanical device?" she asked. "Some sort of arts-and-crafts, remote action, physics gimmick thing? Isn't that your speciality?" She kicked at the wire. "We have the fishing-wire right here, after all."

"Hm. Tempting," Yva admitted. "The problem is the cleanup. If Leo was hoisted up on a long length of wire, that should've been left dangling down right next to him when we found the body, and we'd have found the whole apparatus still set up in here. Neither was true." She turned and gazed down the length of the room, slowly sweeping her torch from wall to wall. "I could *probably* think of something, if it's possible, if I had long enough..." She ran a hand down her face. "Bleh. I'm getting tired, but I can't afford to let my brain slow down now. Give me a minute, I need to splash water on my face."

Their two pools of torchlight met again in the adjacent corridor, where Alex was gazing out of the window along the rain-wet, weed-ridden concrete roof of the north wing. "Anything in there?" Yva asked, gesturing to the remaining door nearby.

Alex shook her head. "Just another empty dusty room."

"Perfect," Yva grinned, and seized her arm. "Get in here."

"What are you…" Alex was practically pulled off her feet and into the unlit room. Bewildered, she let herself be pushed into a chair before Yva slammed the door behind them and sat opposite, putting down her torch with an eruption of dust.

"Time to get down to business," Yva said, her expression as serious as if this were a job interview. "The fact is, we're now at the end. Once we get back to those idiots in the foyer, there can't be any more developments or any more clues. We need to have some kind of a theory to bring back to them if we want to look good."

So, they were solving the case, here and now… or trying to, at least. A dark and dingy and dusty room as far as anywhere from their friends wasn't an encouraging place to work; but at least it was space to think.

"Okay. Let's do this in order," Alex said, and tried to wrestle some semblance of sense and logic from the tangle of events taking place that night. "Leo… I've still got no idea how he got out of the typing room. We've talked about the video footage being faked, but it doesn't make a difference to the problem."

"Agreed," Yva nodded. "It's so frustrating! We both saw him walk in there. There must be something we've overlooked."

"What happened next is a bit clearer, though," Alex went on. "At some point he got into the Dry Diver costume. That implies that, whatever he did, he didn't go far. It might be…" The thought made her queasy to think about. "It might be that he'd been in the Dry Diver suit all along, any of those times afterwards when we looked into the storage room and saw the costume sitting there."

"He really *was* a creep," Yva agreed. "But that clears up one thing, and that's that it probably *was* him in the video with Matt. That means Matt must have been in on it – obviously Leo couldn't attack anyone in that costume, the arms don't really work! Matt deleted his own footage of himself and Bianca, and he and Leo must already have set up the fire exit to let Leo get in from outside. They faked the 'attack', and then left together."

"And if that's the case," Alex said excitedly, "it's starting to make sense that they were the victims! They had a secret plan, and either someone betrayed them, or fought back against what they were trying to do."

"Even the motive fits!" Yva marvelled. "Okay, what next. Leo goes back to the storage room and disguises himself as an empty suit. Just as a reminder, he was able to go walkabout in the first place because Viggo got Chase upstairs and out of the way – that was probably part of the plan, too, something Leo told him to do. As for Matt, he just hides himself wherever. Probably sneaking about behind our backs like a coward."

"But then we have a problem," Alex said. "When did they die? We had almost everyone under observation."

Yva leaned back in her chair, thinking. "Viggo and Chase split up again, when we told them to..."

"You're right," Alex realised. "In that window, one of them *had* to have killed Matt – no wait, there's also Leo! Forget *how* Matt was drowned – we're doing really badly on howdunnits – but Leo could have killed Matt and hidden him in the tunnel while everyone else was busy in the north wing or upstairs. Then, after everyone split up, Leo went around to the courtyard for some reason, attacking George on the way, and..." She stumbled. "Died... somehow? And was pulled up by someone else?"

"A chain murder – Matt was killed by Leo, who was then killed by someone else. Chase? And then a fourth person killed *him*," Yva summed up. "That would be really cool, but... even to me, that sounds unlikely. That's the sort of twist people flame my fanfics for. It's too elegant for reality."

"'Elegant' is not what I'd call it," Alex said, feeling herself growing obstinately attached to the idea. It simply *had* to be the case that there was some kind of conspiracy... "Either way, it seems like Leo had to die in the courtyard, right? He had to be there, dead, in the Dry Diver suit, to be hauled upwards. Someone could have put the suit on him after wearing it themselves, but *why* would anyone ever do that? Unless George was wrong about seeing somebody wearing the costume..."

"Ahhh!" Yva screamed and tipped forwards in her chair, the legs striking the floor with an echoing clap. "I've got it! I've got it! I've got whodunnit and it's really clever!"

"*What?*" Alex was almost as shocked by Yva's declaration as she was by her explosive scream. "Okay, um, if this was a book I'd ask for a hint, but it's not so just spoil it for me. Who is it?"

"George, of course!" Yva declared, with a grin. "Stop! I know what you're about to say, but I have addressed the Matt murder criticism! In fact, Matt's death is the crux of my theory!"

Alex felt as if her brain was curling up in frustration. She was about to complain anyway that Matt's murder was the hardest part… when the image of Great-Aunt Cornelia suddenly came to mind. It was as if the world's greatest armchair detective was in the room with them, grinning knowingly at what Alex had been about to say. "Anything which appears to make things harder for the murderer," the old lady's image said, "is secretly making things easier…"

Matt, at the end of a dead-end tunnel to the outside world. A tunnel which was a dead end because somebody had padlocked it from the outside. And a suspect who had been outside the Pitchwater Building when the disappearances had taken place.

"I think I just got it," Alex whispered. "You're right. Matt's death would have been easy for him…"

Yva looked momentarily disappointed, before her smugness reasserted itself. "Congratulations, you got there almost as fast as I did," she said. "I knew I was right to choose you as my Watson. Yes, it's really quite simple: We've been assuming that the woods hatch was padlocked *before* Matt's death – but there's no reason it couldn't have been *after*."

"Matt's body was never moved. He went down the tunnel himself," Alex began, spelling it out. "When he reached the far end, he climbed up and met George in the shack in the woods; by George's own timing, if he came from town the shack would've been only a few minutes out of his way. There, George drowned Matt somehow –"

"If George is the culprit, he can freely enter and leave the building," Yva added. "He could have used some obscure piece of equipment still hidden in the woods."

"Right," Alex nodded. "George drowned him outside the shack, then dropped the body down the hatch and padlocked it behind him. That's where the other injuries came from. Then he walked back through the woods to the front gate, let himself in at who-knows-what time, and met Leo, who was dressed as Dry Diver, in the courtyard – and killed him, too. Anything he used to do that, he then left and hid in the woods, before locking us all in and throwing his own keys and phone through a gap in the fence. Then he must have set up a harness around Leo for an accomplice to pull up..." She paused. "What about his head injury, though?"

"Self-inflicted, obviously," said Yva. "Anyone with the steel to commit a murder has the steel to give themselves a serious injury as a cover story. I should have known – anyone who survives a murder attempt is secretly the culprit."

"Only if it was *actually* a murder attempt," Alex corrected her, thinking back to some cases she had encountered. "But okay – regardless, George was probably telling the truth about crawling injured around the building, because maybe he was more hurt than he expected. Certainly Bianca and Tara saw him – unless one of them was his accomplice, and the other is just covering for them? Well, whoever his accomplice was, the point is he ended up taking over for them to drop Leo down once he heard everyone in position; he could have stayed as close to the fourth floor as he dared, ready to run back to the bathroom at any time..."

"And then all he had to do was follow us downstairs before putting on a performance as an impartial figure of authority," Yva concluded. "It all works – and it's really clever, too! Worthy of me! Wow." Her face went slack, and she suddenly looked very awkward, as if she didn't know what to do with herself. "I... I don't know what feeling I'm meant to show. This has actually never happened to me before."

"Solving a mystery?" Alex asked, tilting her head. "Isn't that normal? Most people never get involved in a real murder mystery." Slowly there came to mind, though, an instance in their first meeting when Cornelia had levelled a particularly biting criticism at Yva. "Wait, you mean in books too?"

Yva gritted her teeth. "On my own, I can come up with amazing ideas. But when it's someone else's idea, I just can't ever see it. The only ideas that come to mind are... uncreative." She abruptly tipped her head up with a look of haughty disdain. "Look, I'm an *author*. I create problems, I don't solve them."

"Well, now you can say you do both!" Alex said, touching Yva on the arm. It was strange, feeling genuinely happy for her. Yva's mind had once seemed genuinely alien. But once you saw through her bluster and difficulties with empathy, then underneath there was a vulnerable person who desperately wanted to prove herself.

Indeed, having arguably proven herself, Yva now looked uncertain that it was all for real. "Obviously, there are still a few outstanding holes –"

"The accomplice," Alex began counting them out, because their feelings wouldn't change the facts. "What happened to Chase. How Leo escaped from the typing room – and, of course, the motive."

"– But no mystery novelist seriously expects you to get *everything*, even if it's technically doable," Yva continued. "You only have to figure out enough to be proud of yourself, and the confession will do the rest. So, what are we waiting for?"

It was true that there was more left to solve – more even than Alex realised – but she thought it could wait. "We've got enough to go back with," she said. "This is important." Especially important to one person, she thought, as a dark idea crossed her mind. "…What should we do about George after this? He might get violent."

"He's just one old man, he won't do anything stupid. We'll shut him in a cubbyhole or something and dare him to vanish like Chase did," Yva declared. "And if he objects, we'll tie him up! We can use the wire. I'll get it."

Yva came out of the bathroom winding the wire around her waist, zipping her coat up over it. Alex was bouncing on her the balls of her feet, ready to be gone. They'd exceeded their stated half an hour by a good ten minutes or so discussing theories, but would easily make it back within their final deadline and any worry on the part of the others would be worth it. The deep stairwell of the Pitchwater tower rattled with their footsteps, twisting down and down in a spiral and leaving them almost dizzy. Alex regained her balance and increased the pace yet again, as much from eagerness to solve the case as to be past these places which were familiar to her; the break room where the empty Dry Diver suit had so mysteriously appeared, the tunnel hatch beyond which Matt's body waited, the east wing corridor with its boarded-up windows hiding Leo's body, the typing room where he had seemed to vanish into thin air and the neighbouring storage room with its stacks of chairs and dripping sink… A few last turns, and they were bursting into the foyer where four people waited in agony.

"The detectives make a glorious return!" Yva cried, her face shining with triumph. "We've solved the case!"

Alex was just about to add her typical clarification to Yva's boast when something made her pause, and sweep her torch across the room.

Four people waited in agony.

They had left five.

CHAPTER TWENTY-FIVE
THE MOST LIKELY SUSPECT

3:24am

Four people in the room, where there should have been five.

George, arms crossed and face grave, watching shadows –

Bianca, huddled quietly on a chair in a corner –

Tara, standing anxiously above her with a protective air –

Viggo, his gaze flitting from one door to another –

Yva noticed it, too, if only from the general lack of excitement; and her face gradually fell into darkness. "Where's Reef," she said, without even the inflection of a question.

The four people left in the room looked uneasily from one to another, until at last George slowly cleared his throat. "Said he wanted some fresh air," he muttered. "Went out on his own. A little while ago now."

Alex could have screamed. Yva really did. "You *people!*" she gasped, pronouncing the word like an insult, torn between fury and astonishment. "I give you *one job* –"

"It's you we were worried about!" Viggo interrupted. "It's not like we lost him, he's just in the courtyard. And besides –"

This time he interrupted himself; and stayed quiet, looking around as if somebody else had spoken. As if he wanted somebody else to speak.

"And besides what," Alex said, giving him his interruption. "And besides *what*, anyone?" She looked around at the four of them, their faces closed like doors; like the doors of the courtyard standing a way off, shut to all but the pattern of rain. "Look, I know we've kept things from you sometimes –"

Tara spoke up, her voice strangely cryptic. "And there was something we wanted to keep from Reef."

Alex and Yva looked at each other. "You wanted to keep something secret from *Reef*?" Alex asked.

"After a fashion," George rumbled.

Tara explained. "There was something we could only discuss without him being here to hear it."

"Stop being so cagey already and spit it out," Yva scowled. "Being cryptic is for detectives. I couldn't wait to start dropping hints about my brilliant theory that George is the culprit."

George looked up. "Hey, I resent that."

"I'm sure it was a clever theory," Viggo said. "You two *are* clever. But you're also wrong."

"Oh?" Yva's temper flared. "Wrong how, exactly? We haven't even started our explanation!"

Her anger flared and flickered like a candle's flame as the room went silent. Slowly Bianca lifted her head, and from across the room she met Alex's eyes; and then her shaking voice quietly spoke.

"Because Reef's the killer, isn't he?" Bianca said.

And Alex's thoughts began to race.

"*Excuse me?*" Yva exclaimed. She'd gone right through anger and come out jeering, mocking to hide her incredulity. "That's your dumb amateur know-nothing cryptid-credulous *theory*? That it's your *ex-boyfriend*?"

"Reef's always just out of sight when someone disappears," Bianca said. Now she'd started it was as if she couldn't stop, and the words just tumbled out of her. "He chased me and Tara up the stairs and then he just vanished. He insisted on going out even though you'd told everyone to stay together –"

"Reef has perfect witnesses for the entire period people went missing in," Yva declared. "Including me. Including you!"

But Bianca, for all that she was shaken and terrified, held absolutely firm. "Reef was up to something tonight," she said, her voice growing gradually more confident. "I've been pretending this whole time, hoping he'd slip up, because I *knew*. I knew, I've always known, because of what Chase told me –"

"Chase never had time to tell you *anything*," goaded Yva –

"Hold on," Alex interrupted. "I don't think she means *here*, in the Pitchwater Building." She met Bianca's eyes again. "She means in the car park where we first met the two of them, right? When we were with Matt."

Yva froze as the memory came back to her. "That's right. She'd gone there by mistake..."

"Not by mistake," Alex said, "was it, Bianca? You acted confused, but when we met Viggo he said that you'd texted him to explain where you were. But I didn't see you do that *after* we met you. So it had to be before – before you were told you were supposed to be somewhere else."

Viggo nodded slowly. "She texted long before you showed up," he said. "It came in while we were still driving to our rendezvous point – and we were meant to be there early."

"You and Chase planned to meet up ahead of the rest of us," Alex concluded.

Bianca gave a faint, humourless smile. "Got it in one, detective," she said.

Yva had listened to this in silence, simmering. "This I hate," she said. "You had clues before we even knew there was a mystery. Fine – make up for lost time. What did Chase tell you?"

Bianca couldn't help whirling a quick glance over to the courtyard doors, where no one stood. Tara squeezed her shoulder, and she drew a fluttering breath. "Chase had been acting weird for days," she began. "The two of us... still talk, regularly, even after what happened with the vlog and the breakup. But he started missing our video calls and wouldn't explain why. At last he asked to meet ahead of the official rendezvous – something too important to say over text or anything. I didn't get it, but I thought he seemed... afraid, somehow."

Chase had known, Alex realised. Somehow he had already known, or guessed, or some mixture of both, what terror would strike in the Pitchwater Building that night...

"I knew I was right when the two of us met in person," Bianca went on. "He was worried, it would've been obvious to anyone who knew him. Anyway, what he told me was that something was going to happen during the crossover filming. Some kind of prank."

"The disappearances," Alex filled in.

But Bianca shook her head. "I don't know. Probably. He wouldn't say. But the point was, the whole thing was being set up by Reef... and by someone from Team Silver. He didn't know who, he got all his instructions from Reef. Because Chase was being blackmailed into going along with it."

"What *blackmail*?" burst out Yva. "And why would Chase tell all this to you?"

At least some mysteries were easily solved, Alex thought. "Because you were in love, right?"

Yva and Viggo looked surprised, but Bianca seemed to have been expecting it. "I guess we weren't careful enough," she said. "It was only really meant to be a secret from Reef, but that meant not making it obvious to anyone else."

"If you knew what to look for," muttered Tara, "it wasn't subtle."

Yva's smile was back. She must have had the obvious idea. "And how long had this state of affairs been going on?" she asked, and for once her cynical mind had seen through to the human answer.

Bianca hesitated, and looked away. "Since before I split up with Reef," she admitted.

Yva's grin widened like a torn seam. "How very interesting!" she crowed. "So it's *Reef* who was the injured party, after all."

"Hold on, Yva," Alex interrupted. "Let's hear her out. The whole story." She turned back towards Bianca. "I'm kinda guessing Reef is maybe not a great guy to be with."

Bianca shook her head emphatically. "He frightened me – still does, even tonight. He's *so* jealous... If I so much as talked to another guy, he'd just go wild. He never hurt me, to be clear," she said suddenly; "I'll give him that. But I'd believe he'd hurt anyone else. Sometimes he did..."

"And being around Chase was the only time you could relax?" Alex asked.

Bianca nodded. "Reef trusted Chase," she said. "I think he thought Chase was gay, but whatever it was, he didn't get mad at Chase being around me – though it still felt like we were on thin ice when the three of us were together... But then one day me and Chase were alone at his place, waiting for Reef to show up, and... well." She shot a conciliatory glance at Tara, and skipped the details. "It was so crazy and stupid, we were both *so* afraid of what Reef would do if he ever found out, but we couldn't stop seeing each other. It was exhausting – acting all the time... In the end Chase gave me the courage me to break off with Reef and put some distance between us."

"But you and Chase were still together afterwards, right?" Alex said. "And *that* was the blackmail."

"Yeah," Bianca sighed. "It was when we first started to talk about a crossover. Obviously I thought it was a terrible idea – if I never saw Reef again it'd be too soon – but neither me nor Chase could risk saying anything, and Matt Silver was all for it. Anyway, around that time Chase started getting a bit paranoid; said he thought he was being followed. I..." Her voice trembled. "I teased him about it. Said he'd been watching too many spy movies. I thought at worst it was probably a Dry Diver fan who recognised him."

"This is insane," Viggo murmured. "What is all this? Stalkers now?"

"More like a private eye," Yva said. "So I imagine this alleged blackmail involved telling Reef about you two."

"That's what Chase said me when we met up," Bianca explained. "Somebody had e-mailed him from an anonymous account. They had pictures of us... Whoever it was, they were going to send them to Reef unless Chase agreed to go along with the prank. And we were terrified of what Reef would do if that happened."

"And the blackmailer was Reef's partner on Team Silver?" asked Alex. Who could it have been – Viggo, Tara? Or one of the two members who were dead?

"Dunno, but the upshot was that Chase had to help when Reef let him in on the prank – *had* to, and act like it was his own opinion," said Bianca. "And obviously, that rattled Chase no end. It made him suspicious that there was going to be more to it than just a prank after all, that it was going to involve something criminal. That's what he wanted to warn me about in person – that I should be really careful what I did and who I trusted tonight, especially around Reef."

"Did Chase tell you anything about what this prank involved?" pressed Yva.

Bianca shook her head. "He didn't have time to tell me. Matt noticed us in the car park, remember? He was just about to tell me everything, but there wasn't time, and then – and then we were never alone again." Her voice trembled as she spoke, and Alex realised that tears were glistening in her eyes. "And Reef killed him for it," she wept. "I really think Reef must have killed him, like he killed the others! I don't know how he did it, but it's the only thing that makes any *sense* –"

"Let's get a little perspective here," Yva spoke up.

She spoke with an authoritative tone, or at least a loud one, and the room fell silent around her. Alex had forewarning of what she was going to say, because it was her founding philosophy:

Doubt everything. Trust no-one.

"The only evidence we have as to the existence of this prank is the statement of Bianca Marsh," Yva began, "who in testifying admitted to hiding information from everyone involved since before we even got here."

"That's true," interrupted Alex, "but she really did meet Chase early, and it was meant to be a secret. We saw them, remember?"

"And even if Bianca reported everything truthfully," Yva continued, managing to combine a direct rebuke to Alex with an air of having ignored the interruption altogether, "*her* only evidence as to the existence of this prank is the statement of Chase Ferrier, who in testifying admitted to hiding information before and afterwards."

"What's your point?" cut in Tara.

Alex looked from one of them to the other. "Her point is she wants to throw out the prank idea. Treat Bianca and Chase as unreliable and ignore them."

Instant uproar, and everyone spoke at once.

"You can't just ignore her –"

"Call yourself a detective?"

"That doesn't make any sense –"

"I'm telling the truth!"

"But Yva, shouldn't we at least *consider* the idea?" Alex demanded, staring into Yva's face of stone. "It might explain everything!"

"And it might be a cunning red herring," Yva retorted. "Consider the following scenario: Bianca is the culprit and is trying to throw suspicion onto the person she hates the most. Ditto Chase. The whole thing could be a frame-up by either of these two, even both!"

Yva had grown more heated than Alex had seen in a while, the sort of heat she had only expressed before when clashing with her detective idol, Cornelia Crow. Why was she so mad? Alex struggled to think. Did she care about Reef after all, even a little bit? No, that really was impossible –

"Why does this matter so much to you, Yva?" Alex asked bluntly. "Is there a problem if Reef is complicit? If he murdered someone?"

Yva bit her lip, as if she at once wanted to answer and hated to do so. "It matters because –" she began, and hesitated. "Because…"

Alex was amazed. Yva was actually so upset she was struggling to speak. "You can tell me, Yva," she said, lowering her voice. "We're friends, right?"

And for all that *that* had seemed impossible, in speaking the words Alex felt for a moment that it might be true despite everything.

Yva met Alex's eye, and her resolve slackened. Disgusted, she looked down at her feet. "It matters," she muttered, "because the murderer is… because the murderer is *cleverer* than me." She looked up sharply. "And Reef Evans isn't that!"

"That's it?" Alex was momentarily underwhelmed; but Yva lashed her with a look, and Alex realised that of course that was it. Yva was the proudest person she'd ever met. Her whole identity was bound up with the idea that she was the cleverest, and any blow to that idea shook her to her core. "I get it now," Alex said, and touched Yva's arm. "I'm sorry, Yva. I see why it upset you."

"She has a point," Bianca admitted, her voice still shaking. "Reef was *never* this clever; that's partly why I didn't say anything, because it seemed so unlikely that he could have come up with all this…"

"So what's the problem?" George interrupted, sounding baffled. "Kid's dumb, so his accomplice came up with the plan and fed it to him. Big deal."

Alex's gaze was locked with Yva, and they both saw each other's eyes widen in the same instant. If somebody else came up with the plan – meticulous Tara Gill, for instance, or the enterprising Matt Silver –

"Let's think this through," Yva said abruptly. "Let's take it seriously for a second. If Reef was an accomplice, what would that explain?"

Alex was ready. From the moment Reef had been seriously mooted as a suspect, her brain had been bubbling with ideas. "How Leo got out of the typing room."

Yva actually gasped, and the others cried out –

"No, listen, I think this really works," Alex said excitedly. "When the door of the room was open, we couldn't see anything down the corridor, right? Because me and you and Chase were bunched up on the outside of it. So if Reef was in cahoots with *Leo*, Leo could have walked right out and tip-toed down the corridor without any of us seeing him!"

Yva was thunderstruck. "Right in front of us? I would hate it so much if that worked! But it's possible, I admit. Then there's Matt – if we just vary my George theory a bit, Matt goes to the end of the tunnel on his own, Reef breaks off from chasing Bianca to sneak down there and kill him at the end, then leaves through the hatch and padlocks it – and then goes back around to the front of the building and gets in after it's unlocked by George!"

"Hey, that pretty much requires me to be part of the plot, right?" interrupted George. "That's starting to add up to a lot of accomplices. Even if only one or two were set on murder, there's no way too many others would keep their traps shut. I'd say you're allowed one unwitting accomplice, tops."

"We can work out the kinks later," Yva said dismissively, although as it happens George was quite right. "But the point is it could have been something along those lines. Reef might have prepared a ladder outside the fence, or climbed a tree – the details will come later."

"But it's the same with Chase, right?" Alex spoke up excitedly. "The two of us had our backs turned while we were interviewing George. Chase could have left the room then, or even been dragged out by Reef!"

"Again, that puts me in on the conspiracy!" George roared. "I'd have seen if anything was happening behind you! You had the place lit up like a Christmas tree!"

"Valid objections," Yva admitted, "but we're not obliged to answer them until we're sure we have all the necessary evidence. Just having a compelling theory is good enough for now – and even I'll admit..." She paused, and took a deep breath, as if even she needed to compose herself. "That it's enough to confront Reef."

"Really?" Alex was taken aback. "You're okay with that?"

"Of course I am," she said, as if she hadn't been arguing just a minute ago to do no such thing. "It's one person's word against another's, so it's fifty-fifty as to who's telling me the truth. If Reef is lying, confronting him with this might be enough to get him to confess. We can even lie ourselves and say Bianca recorded the whole conversation with Chase, just so he can't pin it on her. At the very least it will provoke a reaction."

Being a detective sometimes involved a certain degree of trolling their suspects.

"So we're all agreed?" Alex asked, looking around at the others.

Viggo nodded. "Let's do this," he said. "If Reef had anything to do with killing my brother, I want to know about it."

"The rain slackened a while back," George said, and indeed the raindrops on the windows were pattering only quietly. "If you need any help dragging him back in, I'm willing to join you."

"If he's still out there, that is."

It was Tara who had spoken, and the whole room turned to look at her. She didn't seem in a hurry to clarify her remarks, but perhaps that's because everyone knew in an instant just what she meant.

Once again, somebody had been alone in a room.

"Tara," Bianca whispered, "there's only one way out of there, you know…"

"Yeah, like that's ever mattered this whole night," Tara said; and her sarcasm had an undercurrent of something dark. "The guy went out nearly an hour ago. That's a long time to be standing alone in the rain."

Slowly, silently, six pairs of eyes turned towards the double-doors to the courtyard; two tarnished metallic faces with windows of wired glass which might as well have been a cloud of dense fog for all you could see through them. Anything might have happened on the other side. Anything might be happening at that moment.

Perhaps it was hysteria, but they made for the doors in a rush, six bright torches at the ready.

George was right; the rain *had* slackened. It was still drizzling, that kind of fine drizzle which is little more than a mist and which leaves a damp film on the skin without the feeling of having been rained on. The place was more or less as Alex had left it, the concrete ground turned to one big puddle, the statue smashed and shapeless, the walls so high they seemed to lean in ready to fall and crush them. As torchlight danced in all directions, these features leapt out like an attack.

At first glance, there was no sign of Reef. But then Yva let out a small noise, and marched towards the trashed filing cabinet.

That old thing was still there, a metal cuboid spilling water; and Leo's body beside it, ghastly and wet in the Dry Diver costume. A little way away was the broken torch Alex had kicked on her first arrival in the courtyard, the one she had surmised belonged to Matt; but rolling nearby and pointing brightly at the wall was a working torch, obliquely angled to illuminate a small metal object lying discarded in the rain, and a rather larger object slumped alongside Leo's body.

Alex's pace quickened even as her heart plummeted. Behind her she heard gasps as the others saw it; they hung back at first, but then tentatively began to follow, as if they wouldn't believe it if they didn't see it with their own eyes...

Once again, a semicircle of six stood in the corner of that stone well staring down at a body. But this time it wasn't Leo's, and it wasn't in a costume.

Whatever Reef had come out into the rain and the courtyard for, he hadn't found it. Instead he had found only his death, and now lay with half his face in the water and his eyes bulging at nothing.

Chapter Twenty-Six
The Fourth to Dive

3:37am

"Well, so much for *that* theory," Yva said. For all that Reef's death put him among the victims of the case, trashing the theories they had just been working on – and for all that he was supposed to be her boyfriend – then her face was alive with ideas.

Alex didn't even try to comfort her. Yva neither needed it nor wanted it. But it was saddening to see just how badly damaged her sense of empathy was.

The others weren't taking it nearly so well. Alex looked back at them, and saw that each of them looked absolutely terrified – and it wasn't hard to guess why. Disappearances aside, and appearing bodies aside, this was the first time outright murder had been committed practically under their noses.

"There are two ways in here."

Alex looked up in surprise. Yva had begun to speak, her voice calm and measured.

"There's the foyer door, of course, through which Reef came," she said, still facing the body and with her back to the others. "But there's also the fire exit. Alex?"

Alex knew an instruction when she heard one, and hurried over to the fire door in the wall of the north wing. It came into view through the darkness as she approached, flush with the wall and firmly closed, without even so much as a handle. It did have that small hook on the back, which could once have been used to pull or hold it open; and Alex pulled on that hook now, and heard the bolt of the fire door clank in the lock. "Still closed, still normal," she called back.

"The fire door requires two people to open, and the number of unaccounted people is one. The fire door can't be opened from the courtyard, and Reef would have been suspicious if he had seen someone setting up an escape trick. So in the end, there is only one way in and one way out – the one you four were guarding," Yva said, and now she faced them.

"We know," Viggo answered. Not bothering to wipe the rain from his face, he looked almost truculent in the face of a nonsensical reality. "We know that none of it makes any sense. We know it's impossible. You don't need to stand there and *explain* to us when we can see that what's happening can't have happened!"

"Indeed. Your story *is* impossible," Yva said – and pointed. "And that's why I'm giving you all one chance to confess."

"To what?" Tara retorted.

Alex felt queasy. At some point, it was going to come to this – to the point where it was easier to say that *everybody* lied. "To the four of you killing Reef together," she said.

Tara and George only flinched; they, at least, were clever enough to have seen that this was a real possibility. Viggo and Bianca, on the other hand, recoiled as if Yva had thrown a snake at them.

"Of course not!" Viggo cried. "Why would we..."

His voice trailed off, and the alarm on his face grew sharper. Motives weren't hard to find.

Yva had the look of a shark smelling blood in the water. "You suspected Reef – you've admitted that much to us. Taking him to trial is a different matter. So why wouldn't the four of you just kill him right here, while the detectives were away?"

"Even I can see the sense in that," Alex admitted. "You'd be protecting yourselves, avenging the people you loved..."

"That didn't happen!" Viggo yelled urgently. "None of us left the foyer! None of us killed Reef!"

"Then where's the killer?" Yva swept her hand around the entire courtyard. "Even if the killer was already waiting here, there's nowhere for them to hide now."

"Maybe they waited for us to come out," Tara said, "and snuck behind us while we were distracted by Reef's body."

Her flat tone suggested that she didn't really believe this.

"Here's another idea, then," Yva said. "Even if it's true that none of you left the foyer, even if it's true that none of you killed Reef – you wouldn't have objected if someone else did it for you, right?" She gave a grin that was frightening in its ghoulishness. "If Chase reappeared, and spun you a tale that confirmed all your prejudices, wouldn't you have let him walk right through the foyer, kill Reef out here, and then leave as he came? Can you guarantee we won't find him alive and well elsewhere in the building, feigning innocence, perhaps sporting a nice ugly wound to 'prove' it?"

"No! No, I won't have it!" roared George, the rainwater flying off him. "Nobody came in or went out the whole time you were off gallivanting except the dead boy! I'm not lying for any kids, I'm the one with all the authority here!"

Yva's only answer was a sneering shrug. "Then tell me this: Whodunnit?"

They had no answer. It was the same whether or not they were telling the truth, Alex realised. If they were guilty – and she didn't buy, quite correctly, the idea that all four of them were in on it – then they could admit nothing; but if they were innocent, they could admit nothing either. After all, hadn't they all had that experience tonight? Of standing outside a room where something inexplicable had happened, and somebody had lost their life as a result?

When miracles happen often enough, people stop looking to humans for an explanation. And more than once, Alex saw each of their eyes flash to the corpse of Leo lying nearby – or rather to the costume of the phantom, Dry Diver, that he wore.

The fact was, they were ready to believe in fantasies.

"Go back inside," Alex told them. She wasn't used to giving commands, and didn't like the almost curt way her voice came out, but nothing good could come of having the others stand here with two bodies and an accusation they couldn't disprove. "Go back inside, and hole up somewhere safe – preferably with just one exit and no wriggle room. Actually, go to the break room near the tunnel; that doesn't even have windows. You'll be as safe there as it's possible to be, and we'll join you when we're done."

As it turned out, they didn't need telling twice; they didn't even argue back. It was the command they'd been waiting for without even knowing it. Bianca went first, barely holding herself back from running, then Tara at her shoulder, their teammate Viggo following them, and George stiffly turning away without a word.

But as they left, Tara took one look back – but it wasn't at Alex or Yva, or even at either of the corpses. It was too low to the ground for that.

Her last look back was at the small metal object lying in the edge of torchlight, and Alex realised, with a start, that it was a camera.

Well, it fitted the pattern. But it stretched credulity to think that all of these unnatural videos were natural. Could there really be a fourth recording of a fourth attack by Dry Diver? And could they really believe it if there was?

Yva had seen the camera too. But Alex got there first. She picked it up gingerly, shaking water off as though it were acid. "It's still working," she said, switching it on; letting the bright glow of the digital screen wash over her. "And the playback has..." She looked up at Yva in disbelief. "*Three* videos?"

"Don't get excited," Yva said. "Remember that Reef's one of the few who did any legitimate filming tonight."

Alex sighed in relief, and flipped through the three thumbnails. "You're right. The first clip is the typing room where he was meant to film with Leo."

With one hand shielding the screen from the rain, she set it playing. A chest-high perspective showed a familiar door opening, and the camera advancing one step into it, a beam of torchlight playing around the empty room. Alex jumped as a faint voice whispered off-screen, "*Are you real, or just another hallucination?*"; and after a few moments more the camera receded a step again and turned to look behind the door, torchlight shining full in the faces of Yva Dysart, Chase Ferrier, and, looking small and uncomfortable with the light in her eyes, Alex herself.

"I'd forgotten," Alex, in the present, murmured. "But that's exactly how it happened, isn't it? This video, at least, is the real thing."

"No doubt about that," Yva nodded, "but it does tell us one thing that's important: Leo didn't tip-toe out and down the corridor while only Reef was watching."

"Oh! ...Oh," Alex said. "Darn. And I thought my idea was really clever, too."

"Welcome to my world," Yva said. "Play the next one."

The thumbnail showed another dark and unrevealing room, but things became clear almost immediately, as the camera turned in the wake of a torchbeam and fell upon a human shape – Bianca, spinning around and standing like a mirror image with her own torch and camera pointing forwards. It was the argument scene, and Alex let it play out for half a minute before fastforwarding to the end – to Reef's final, furious cry of "Admit it, *you cheated on me!*", and

Bianca with her face screwed up from crying turning on her heel and belting it for the door as Reef's hand came up to turn the camera off.

"At least we have one copy of that scene, for what it's worth," Alex said.

"What it's worth is nothing," Yva replied.

Alex sighed, and advanced through the menu. "And the final clip is –"

The thumbnail showed a dark figure outlined in torchlight, without a head. Alex's heart tightened – but it wasn't Dry Diver. It was the statue, and that meant that this video had been filmed in the courtyard...

Alex switched the camera off. "Let's watch that with the others," she said, and thrust it into her coat pocket. "We all need to see it."

Yva scowled at the pocket, as if she wanted to wrench the camera right back out of it; but she conceded with a nod, and Alex was relieved. Perhaps Yva actually felt just how she did, Alex thought. It wasn't just that they all needed to see it at once, not really. It was that, right now, she just couldn't face it. She dreaded to think what the final video showed.

"Still, there's an upside to the impossible," Yva murmured, as if there was someone to overhear. "It might be just what we need."

"As the last piece of evidence?" Alex asked.

But Yva shook her head. "As proof against the only theory that explains his death," she said darkly: "*Wedunnit.*"

Alex's heart thumped like a punch to the chest. Two people whose actions were entirely unaccountable – a fire door which took two people to open – two people who could have propped that door open with a chair, and with their combined strength overwhelmed Reef –

"Oh," she said, in a tight, quiet voice.

"Just this once, Corby, I know that feel," Yva nodded. "Still, there's always the forensics," and she pulled her gloves a little tighter as she turned back to the body. "You can leave that to me."

"Wait."

Yva paused as Alex spoke, and looked at her curiously.

"Just so we can verify things with the police later, I should stay and..." She cringed. "Watch."

Yva cocked her head. It was a very Cornelia-ish mannerism, bird-like. "I thought you were one of those normal people who were squeamish about such things."

"I *am* normal," Alex said. But she couldn't help noticing that she felt curiously insistent about it, as if it wasn't Yva she was trying to convince.

Yva sighed dramatically. "You keep telling yourself that. It makes no difference to me." She strode over to Leo's body, and knelt down in the rain and the grime.

Alex reluctantly scooted to her side, a place which had the unfortunate advantage of being also to the side of not one but two corpses. Reef's body lay practically alongside Leo's, which still stared horribly from the ruined diving suit, and his damaged face was a nightmare to behold. But while Alex was trying not to look at one body, she found herself noticing something odd about the other.

One of Reef's coat pockets was bulging.

Although it was one of those things they always did in mystery novels, it hadn't occurred to Alex to go through the pockets of any of the victims. It was partly that she was trying not to disturb the crime scenes, of course, but it was also that she didn't see what there was to learn. She already knew who all the victims were, she didn't need to look at their wallets, and she doubted very much that any of them would have a packet of incriminating letters sewn into the lining of their jackets. Incriminating texts on their phone, maybe; but even if their phones hadn't been destroyed, guessing a passcode wasn't likely to happen.

Still, she was curious. And the investigation was in serious need of more clues.

"I'm going through his pockets," Alex announced. "Do you have a problem with that?"

Yva, who had been probing around Reef's throat, looked back at her. "None whatsoever," she said. "In fact, if we're interfering with the corpse, it's as well to be hanged for a sheep as a lamb!"

She got her hands under the body, and heaved it over onto its back. Reef's head lolled to the side, and Alex glimpsed a raw and ugly line cut into the flesh around his throat. "That's not a drowning mark," she said, grimacing. "Was his throat cut...?"

"Don't be stupid. Where's the blood?" Yva said, scowling at her. "That's strangulation; or garotting, if you prefer."

"That's awful." Alex half-glanced at Leo's body, lying just next to her. "Matt and Leo didn't have marks like that…"

"Yes, and that's how we know they were drowned, not strangled. Nothing blocking their airways, either. Process of elimination," Yva continued. "Bloodless crimes – this killer's smart. They know better than to risk bloodstains. Honestly, I don't know how the Carver's Rest killer managed to avoid being covered in the stuff."

Indeed, Alex reflected, this was a very different criminal to the murderer at Carver's Rest. That person had acted recklessly, insanely, deliberately leaving clues. With a creeping dread, Alex realised that she was on far more dangerous ground with her enemy in the Pitchwater Building; with Dry Diver, who was coming into view as a person both careful and ruthless…

But she was getting away from herself. She'd been meaning to go through Reef's pockets, and go through them she would, starting with the bulging pocket at his side; and deciding, at last, that not disturbing the crime scene was a luxury of those not trapped in a lonely building with a serial killer, she bent down and reached inside.

The thing in the pocket was a torch. Alex took a swift glance back across the courtyard, to where another of the generic torches, still bright, had rolled to a stop sending its searchlight beam in her direction; and beyond that was the torch with the smashed bulb they had found when Matt had gone missing. That sent her mind back to earlier in the night, and she remembered where the torch in her hands now must have come from: Leo had also left a broken torch behind after his disappearance, and Alex had concluded at the time that Reef must have pocketed it to avoid giving anything away to Viggo. She remembered seeing Reef staring at it, looking into the bulb and flicking the switch uselessly.

She flicked the switch, and stumbled as light blazed straight into her eyes.

"What are you doing?" she heard Yva ask, as she steadied herself and pointed the torch away.

It took Alex a few moments, blinking the dazzle from her eyes, both to locate Yva and to put her thoughts together. "I was expecting this torch to be broken," she said. "No – it *was* broken, before. Reef tried it right in front of us."

She caught Yva's outline tensing. "What's your point?"

"My point is –" Alex stopped, not actually sure what her point was. She didn't see any reason for the torch to have magically fixed itself. But the only other torch Reef could have introduced to the courtyard was working perfectly, too; she and Yva were standing in its beam right now.

There was still the other broken torch, with the shattered glass, that Matt had left behind. Alex pointed her own torch over to where she remembered it being, and indeed there it was, just as she remembered kicking it. Setting the extra torch down, she approached the broken one and picked it up, finding it quite empty of glass; and this time, flicking the switch did nothing.

Discounting George's heavy-duty lamp, there had been nine torches of this make in the building, right? They'd each started off with one. Some of them had changed hands or been discarded now and again, Yva had broken one herself, but last she'd looked she could still match each torch to a person.

There should have been six of these working torches in the building, and three broken ones. So why had the numbers changed?

Alex had a feeling she was on the brink of something really important. So – she shelved the thought. If it was really that important, she wanted to think about it when she was back inside and had time to think, not while she was in the middle of an investigation. She wasn't done. After all, if Reef had one important clue in his pockets, why not another?

Yva seemed to have got bored of Alex's silence and had turned back to the body. Alex did the same, avoiding looking at the swollen face and putting her hands in first one pocket and then another. There was no sign of any other obvious large object in any of his pockets, but –

But probing into another of the coat's outside pockets, tucked away beneath a camera strap, Alex felt her fingers close upon a small, flat object. It was smooth to the touch but had a faintly irregular shape, with rounded sides but sharp corners. Alex quickly pulled it out, but it took several moments of examination in torchlight for her to understand exactly what it was.

It was a large coin wrapped in a short strip of tape.

"What the heck is this?" she asked out loud. It looked as if somebody had torn off a strip of tape, put a fifty pence piece slap in the middle of it, and then folded the ends over. She couldn't see the use of it – and that alarmed her. No way was some random bit of arts-and-crafts anything other than a vital piece of evidence.

"What's that you've got now?" asked Yva, without obvious interest. She appeared to have finished her examination of Reef, and now had her eyes tracked on Alex's hand. Alex showed her the coin.

"Odd," Yva said, taking it and turning it over in her hands. "Just about the shoddiest piece of evidence I've ever seen. More interesting than a cigarette butt, but that's not saying much." After a few moments of further contemplation, she shrugged and pocketed it. "But I don't want to risk getting paranoid about tape just because of what happened at Carver's Rest. It's probably junk Reef's had in his pocket for months."

Alex was incredulous. "Do you really believe that?"

Yva sighed. "I'm a mystery writer. I can turn *anything* into a murder weapon, even the most ordinary household object. Doesn't mean somebody else had the same idea, though."

A murder weapon wasn't quite what Alex had in mind, but then again she didn't know *what* she had in mind. Unlike the torch, she had a feeling this required not a feat of logical deduction but something more creative. What could you do with a coin and tape?

The remainder of Reef's pockets produced nothing of interest, and Alex was glad to be done with it. If Yva's clinical attitude had one thing to recommend it, it was that it prevented her fear and horror from being wound up any further than necessary; but there was a limit to how long she could bear to spend in a stone tomb with two corpses.

They stepped into the foyer. It seemed like a very long time ago that they and the others had gathered here for safety – first six others, then five, then four… Now the room was quite empty, dark and deep and echoing as a cave. "What did you get out of your examination?" Alex asked, as they stood there shaking drizzle from their coats.

Yva pursed her lips. "Exactly what I anticipated," she said. "He was garrotted, probably not long after we left him here. No stunning blow to the head this time, unlike Matt and Leo." She paused, and seemed to be weighing her next words carefully. "And the killer was probably taller than him," she said.

"Taller?" Alex repeated. Reef's wounded neck flashed through her imagination, and it seemed to her that the markings did angle sharply upwards towards the back. "How many people here are taller than him?" She'd seen everyone standing together on multiple occasions, of course, but didn't exactly have a photographic memory. The only person who obviously came to mind was George. Then again, face value wasn't everything. "How tall is Chase?" she asked. "You spent time with both him and Reef. All I could really tell was that he always seemed to be slouching."

"Permanently bent over from too much time in the Dry Diver suit – and the boot of the car," Yva said, with a smirk. "Good question, Corby. Unfortunately, all I ever thought was important was that they were both taller than me, so I'm not sure about the specifics. But," and she held up a cautionary finger, "I did just say *probably* taller. I can't rule out a short person who just tricked Reef into kneeling down..."

If it wasn't nobody, it was anybody. In this scattershot case Alex felt like her suspicions were everywhere and nowhere, like a net she had cast at too many targets and was now reeling in empty for her pains. "Let's get back to the break room," she sighed. "We have a video to watch."

How many times had she passed up and down this one corridor that night? How many times had she shone her torch into the black depths of the east wing, a corridor of cold and featureless stone with barricaded windows on one side and yawning doorways on the other? Even as the night advanced towards dawn, she felt the darkness grow deeper with each time she retraced her steps. It was closing in on her like a pair of invisible jaws in a missing head; and her eyes flashed this way and that as she advanced deeper into the mouth, first to the storage room full of discarded chairs and the leaky tap, then to the windows where bars held back sheets of plyboard that might easily be torn away to show two corpses, and then to the typing room which had swallowed up Leo and spat him out dead...

And then they were into the winding corridor that turned away from the tunnel's mouth and finally around towards the break room, where torchlight from within the empty doorframe was casting a bright rectangle on the opposite wall. Having a door to shut might have been more secure, but Alex supposed that nobody's nerves would stretch to hearing somebody outside knock. Indeed, she and Yva arrived to find four pairs of eyes staring at them; mercifully, all were present and correct, no more disappearances, though they all looked worse the wear for the wait.

She couldn't help noticing that Bianca was at least a head taller than Tara. Taller than Viggo, too…

"You're back," George said. "Any news?" His voice became a sneer. "Know whodunnit yet?"

Alex and Yva exchanged a dejected look. "No," Alex admitted.

"Not *yet*," Yva corrected. "We're still reviewing the last pieces of evidence. We'll sit and think for a while, and then put our heads together, and I'm sure we'll come up with something."

The other four didn't seem to have much confidence in their heads, alone or together, to judge from the silent reception this received.

"I think it was Dry Diver," Viggo said at last. His voice was very quiet. "It had to be. A human couldn't have done all this."

Bianca was sitting with her back against a blank wall; and involuntarily looked over her shoulder.

"No way am I accepting a second-rate Slenderman rip-off as the culprit," Yva snarled. "I'd never hear the end of it from my mentor. Roll the film, Alex."

Tara looked at her. "So there *is* another video."

Alex nodded. "Reef filmed something in the courtyard, after his footage for the crossover. The earlier videos are legit, but we haven't seen the new one yet."

"Well, what are we waiting for?" broke in George. "Maybe someone actually caught the killer on camera for a change."

The room was still all set up for an event, chairs circling the rickety table in the centre of the room where Yva had cut the birthday cake, so many hours ago. She must have been dying to solve the case, Alex thought. There was nothing she wouldn't do to show off. Alex set the camera in the centre of the table, and by unspoken agreement the six of them each took a seat around it, Tara moving chairs for herself and Bianca so they could get a better view. Alex and Yva took what passed for the best seats, and Alex became conscious of her heart jumping wildly in her chest.

This was it. The final piece of evidence, the last link in the chain. The tension was almost overwhelming; what this video showed could either make or break the case against Dry Diver…

At last, they were all seated. There could be no more stalling. Yva had already turned the camera on and flipped to the right video; and even her finger shook as she pressed the button to set it going.

Within half a minute, Alex knew everything.

The murderer had made a mistake. They should never have permitted this video to be recorded, much less played in front of anyone who might understand what it meant. Because once you understood what you were really seeing, the whole façade fell apart – Dry Diver and every other illusion Alex had fallen for that night.

The deductions wouldn't stop coming. All their theories had been wrong, although some had come dangerously close. Alex knew now the breathtakingly audacious manner in which Leo had been made to vanish, and that Matt had never touched that fire door. She knew how the killings had been committed, as well as what Matt had meant when he spoke of drowning on dry land. She knew why the door to the tower bathroom had seemed to be stuck, and which room had a second exit she'd looked at over and over again without really seeing. She even had a shrewd idea of where to find Chase, though the prospect filled her with dread.

And she knew about the culprit.

It was one of the people in the room with her. It was completely unbelievable, but there was no possible doubt. This person was the mastermind behind every death in the Pitchwater Building that night, and the motive for their crimes was even more horrible than Dry Diver. And Alex knew who it was.

Alex could already see just what their next move would be. She also knew that she was the only person who could counter it.

THE DRY DIVER DROWNINGS
"ENTRY 10"

A dark figure is outlined in torchlight, without a head. But it's just a statue, the camera level with the head it doesn't have, and the camera view slowly turns with the torch left and right to show an otherwise empty courtyard, nobody visible, certainly not the person who must be holding the camera. They're tucked into a corner, and though the camera shows a whole row of boarded-up windows one way and another beside a fire door the other way, it doesn't dip to show the corpse beneath its feet – save for the merest glimpse of a trailing hand in a clawed glove.

Then the camera tips back, a single drop of rain having time to hit the lens as it arcs upwards to where the rooftops vanish into the night –

And suddenly it jerks level, but twisting wildly from side to side like a fish on a hook; and muffled choking sounds gasp from above.

It's obvious within moments that something is wrong. The torchbeam jumps and dances wildly with a splash from below; hands flash up and scrabble futilely out of sight, forearms filling the viewpoint. The digital readout counts painfully drawn-out seconds of struggle when there's suddenly a scratching of fabric and metal around the camera itself. It comes loose and trembles in mid-air, making to turn towards the person holding it; but their nerve or their grip fails, and the viewpoint goes plummeting and spinning down into the water.

But somehow, on its last journey, the madcap spin of camera and torch synchronise to show something astonishing.

At an inch from the ground the camera slows in its turn; and the torch rolls to a stop. For just a second, they are pointing in exactly the same direction. They show the corner of the courtyard – a body in a diving suit lying still in the water – a fallen filing cabinet with its side sheared off – and just behind them, full in the centre of the spotlight –

Reef Evans lifted off his feet, legs thrashing, hands at his throat.

And behind him, nothing but empty air and a blank wall.

There is the tiniest splash as the camera hits the water, and then the impact with the concrete beneath jars and shuts it off.

CHAPTER TWENTY-SEVEN
IN PURSUIT OF TRUTH

3:50am

"Well, damn," Tara said at last, breaking the stunned silence. "I guess I believe in monsters now."

"There was nothing holding him up," Bianca whispered. "It must have been Dry Diver – putting its arms through the wall –"

"It'd be one thing if there was a window there," George said, his eyes wide. "But I know this place. Ain't nothing behind him except the tower wall."

Alex let this chatter wash over her. Her brain was still busily firing off ideas, linking up pieces of evidence, reeling from the enormity of the deception. She knew Yva must be thinking hard, too.

"So, ah, there any ways you can defend against this Dry Diver thing?" George was asking. "Just to be sure, mind."

"The only people who could tell you are all dead," muttered Viggo. "Matt, Reef, even Leo – they're the ones who cooked up the lore."

"What are we going to *tell* people?" Tara broke in. "We can't just say they were all vanished or killed by a monster from the internet! Nobody's going to believe us."

"There's the video –" Viggo began.

"The police will say we faked it somehow."

It was Yva who had spoken. Of course, her cynical ideas would give her the clearest view of the way in which they had all been trapped.

"The police will say," she went on, her face as calm as deep, dark water, "that we killed them all. That we got into a fight or an argument and people ended up dead. And that we then faked the videos after all, or lied about the circumstances in which they were filmed."

Bianca looked terrified. "She's right. You thought it yourself, Tara, that the videos were faked in advance. If *we* thought it, even though we saw it all happen, what will the police think?"

"We're going to go to prison," said Viggo, numbly.

"No, only those of us who are tried as adults," corrected Yva. "Most of us would be put in young offenders' institutions."

George looked shellshocked. "If I go to prison, I'm not ever getting out. Not at my age. I'll be leaving in a wooden overcoat."

"You will if anyone sees those videos," Tara said. "We'll never see each other again. Our careers will be over before they've even started!"

Bianca grabbed Tara's arm. "We can't let those videos get out. We can't, Ta!"

"What, are you suggesting we destroy the evidence?" Yva asked sarcastically. Then she paused, and seemed to consider the idea. "Normally I wouldn't approve," she mused, "but if the truth can't be proven…"

Viggo started, the light of hope flaring in his eyes. "If we can get rid of the videos," he said, "we can tell the police anything we want! We can come up with a story that gets us off the hook!"

George angled an eye at Yva. "What d''you think of that, detective?"

"I think you need to be realistic," she replied. "You can't just delete the videos, the police will pull the data off the cards. The cameras are too big to just flush down the toilet or drop down a drain, and we'd still have a bunch of empty camera harnesses – and if we got rid of those too, we'd have to explain what we were all doing here."

"What about just the memory cards?" Bianca interrupted. "Those would flush!"

"I brought spares!" declared Tara excitedly. "In case of emergency! Right here in my pocket! We'll just swap blank memory cards into the cameras and drown the suspicious ones!"

"Now *this* is starting to sound like a plan," George said, looking for all the world like a man in a shipwreck with floating driftwood in reach. "Send someone out to flush the cards, and we'll hammer out a new story which the police will swallow."

"So, um…" Viggo trailed off as he looked around the room. "Who's volunteering to go out there?"

"I'll go."

Alex had finished drawing her conclusions some time ago, and had since been letting things play out. Seeing if the discussion went the way she suspected it would – with a little push from the culprit. It had; but she couldn't let them have their way.

It had been so long since she had spoken that the others had almost forgotten she was there, and her voice made them jump. Yva looked the most surprised of all. "You sure, Corby?" she asked. "I wouldn't have thought a goody two-shoes like you would care for this lying-to-the-police plan. I know for sure that Cornelia won't."

"I've been telling lies all night. Why stop now?" Alex asked her right back. "I'm sure we'll solve the mystery one day. But right now, we have to think of ourselves."

Yva grinned. "I knew you'd see things my way eventually." She began to climb to her feet. "I'll come with you –"

"No. You stay here," Alex interrupted, and Yva looked more astonished than ever. "Like I said, I still think the mystery can be solved – which means one of us needs to stay and watch our suspects. If the culprit's among us, they might still have some trick up their sleeve."

The culprit *was* among them, as Alex knew full well; but she didn't dare accuse them openly. It was too risky, right now; it could easily backfire on her. In any case, she'd calculated that she didn't need to. Once they were all securely in police custody – more to the point, once she could check her solutions with Great-Aunt Cornelia – then it would be the time to talk.

"That's settled, then," George spoke up. "Better give her the memory cards."

Tara reached out and picked up Reef's camera from the table, her hand hesitating only a moment before she grasped it. "Here," she said, sliding the memory card out in a dextrous movement and handing it to Alex. "And the others are…" Her expression became troubled.

"You've got them, right, Yva?" Alex asked.

Yva gave a startled nod. "You're on form tonight, Corby," she said quietly; and reaching into her coat pockets, produced first one camera, then a second, then a third… "Given the circumstances, I thought I had better make a point of collecting the evidence before it disappeared," she explained. "Ironic, given that we're now the ones making it disappear."

Within moments, Alex had four tiny memory cards in her palm. Clutching them tight, she carefully transferred them to an inside pocket of her coat and zipped them in.

"Well, that's me," she said, trying not to betray her nerves. "Help the others come up with a story for the police, Yva. If I know you, you've already got something in mind."

A delighted grin flashed onto Yva's face. "Fictional murder plots *are* my forte," she purred, and turned immediately to the four others in the room. "The safest story is one that keeps we six survivors together as much as possible, whilst providing an outside murderer who conforms to the police's prejudices. An eleventh person, a petty criminal who followed us down the tunnel and later escaped the same way…"

Unobtrusively, Alex slipped out.

The nearest place to flush the memory cards away was the bathroom at the top of the tower, which the stairs on her right would take her directly to. Alex turned and immediately began to hurry in the opposite direction.

Destroy the evidence? As if. The contents of those memory cards clearly indicated who was responsible for the murders in the Pitchwater Building. Rather than destroying them, it was imperative to get them outside the bounds of the Pitchwater Building as quickly as possible – and along the way, she could confirm a last couple of deductions in her chain of evidence…

Her first stop was the prep room in the north wing, the one where she and the other girls, Yva and Bianca and Tara, had killed time whilst Matt was supposed to be filming in the conference room next door. There was something she would have liked to examine there, too, for completeness's sake, but without a second person at her side then opening the fire door was out of the question – out of the question now that Matt had been murdered, that is. Instead she cast her torch over the prep room windows, a long row across the back of the room with bars and broken glass that couldn't shut out the pooling rain. The building's mysterious repairman had only got around to boarding up one of them.

And with very good reason, Alex thought. The east wing had had its windows smashed and boarded up, too, the plywood board fitted on the outside in broad sheets, so that from inside you saw it behind the bars. But she'd never seen bars in this particular window, either from the inside or the outside; and she'd looked on numerous occasions. She'd always just assumed they were on the other side of the boarding, but actually, how did she know they were there at all? She'd always just assumed that the plywood board was firmly attached, too.

Alex walked up to the boarded window. The board was made of a single piece of ply, carefully cut to fit roughly into the deep window frame, but it leaned at a slight angle and had a noticeable gap at one side. Alex reached in and wrenched –

And the whole thing came down with a clatter, the giant wooden square dancing at her feet. Behind it was another piece of boarding, identical in size and shape but leaning slightly inwards. And what both sets of boarding had been leaning against was a row of solid iron bars –

Of which the middle three had been roughly cut out, leaving a gap a person could comfortably climb through.

It was foolish of her. They'd investigated so carefully the rooms which people had vanished from, but given no consideration to the rooms the suspects had been in. Even after she had understood that the whole building was a stage carefully adapted to murder, she hadn't thought to ask why this room in particular was important.

Purely for the sake of argument, Alex lifted up the dislodged sheet of plywood – large, for sure, but the light and flimsy material had been selected for just this purpose – and attempted to fit it back into the window frame. It wasn't difficult to restore it to exactly how it was. Suddenly angry at herself, at her short-sightedness and gullibility, Alex ripped it out and let it fall, thrust an arm through and shoved out the other bit of boarding too. Then she climbed up and jumped between the bars.

The rain outside was worse than ever. It had given them the briefest of reprieves for which to investigate Reef's murder but now had redoubled its efforts, torrenting down like an avalanche of hammers. Uselessly pulling up her hood and soaked in seconds, Alex hurried across the courtyard as fast as she could, every footstep splashing an inch of water up her legs. They needn't have worried about disturbing the crime scene, really; the rain was doing its level best to interfere with the place of two murders. This was part of why it was so important to preserve the memory cards. The crime scene was being washed away, and the stain of guilt upon the culprit with it…

Alex hauled open the courtyard doors and stumbled into the foyer, dripping like a fish or a rising diver. The foyer was pitch-black before her; she couldn't even make out the frosted security glass in the pair of doors opposite, the ones which led to the true outside world and the woods and the fence and the chained and padlocked gate. That was Alex's ultimate destination, where she intended to take her coat and throw it, with the memory cards inside, all the way over the fence. Just hooking it on top of the fence would do, so long as it was out of reach of anyone inside the Pitchwater Building. Even if worst came to worst, the police would notice. Someone would notice, and figure out what had happened.

But first, she had one other task in hand – one final investigation. It was a task which filled her with horror. Perhaps because she was so reluctant she steeled herself to doing it first, to not putting it off just because it was so scary. But she should have put it off. She really should have tossed the coat first…

Alex entered the cubbyhole; the one Chase had vanished from, though the door had been under constant watch. The one Chase had *supposedly* vanished from. Because really, of course, it was impossible for him to have left the room; they had proved that quite effectively. And since he had definitely entered the room, he was therefore still inside. And there was only one cavity big enough to hide him.

Alex turned to the filing cabinet. Yva had checked each drawer for any trace of the missing boy; but there was never any way he was going to fit in those. But there was more to a filing cabinet than the drawers, of course; and when they had entered the room, the drawers had already been halfway out. They still were.

Grimacing, Alex put the toe of her foot to one of the open drawers, and slowly pushed it in as far as it would go. It was perhaps three-quarters of the way back when it hit a soft resistance, and stopped.

Sometimes, Alex hated being right; in this case most of all. But she hated even more what she had to do next. She grasped the handle of the second drawer from the top, and gently pulled it all the way out, jiggling it free from the cabinet and lowering it two-handed to the floor. And then there was no avoiding putting her hand on her torch and pointing it into the hole in the filing cabinet, knowing that what she was about to see would give her nightmares for weeks.

There was a face in the hole.

It was Chase, his eyes confused and bulging and still. It was like seeing a decapitated head left to stare. But his whole body was there, too, shoved behind the drawers as deep as it would go, and then the drawers replaced to conceal it – though of course they couldn't be pushed all the way in. The gamble had been that nobody would think to fully close the drawers again; too tidy an instinct in an abandoned building in the middle of a mystery. Possibly there'd been some plan to move his body later, most likely to the courtyard, since its location pointed squarely to his killer and was unlikely to have gone undiscovered forever. There was certainly no mystery about the manner of his death – like Reef, he had been garrotted, a thick wire mark sunk deep into his neck. It wasn't hard to guess what had been used. Alex had noticed before how the telephone's spiral cable had been pulled slack.

Alex found herself breathing as hard as if she'd run a marathon. That was all. It was time to go. Nothing mattered now except smuggling the crucial evidence out of the Pitchwater Building and to safety. She hurried out of the cubbyhole as fast as her legs would carry her, closing the door as she left as if Chase could follow – and froze in her tracks.

The front doors of the Pitchwater Building were lit up, but not by her torch. A glow was approaching the building from the outside.

This was coming far too late in the day for Alex to have a hope of taking it well. An eleventh person was arriving at the Pitchwater Building? It was a coincidence too far. George turning up seemingly out of the blue had been bad enough, but who could this new person be? One of his associates, or a police officer? Yva's mysterious petty criminal? A hitherto unknown ally of the murderer?

There were too many possibilities, and Alex's nerves were too tightly-wound to know on the spot what to expect. She had only two options: Stay and meet them head-on, or hide and watch from afar.

She chose the second option. Flicking off her torch, she ran full-pelt to the corner and the door to the south tower, and hid behind it.

Whereupon she became aware of a second problem: Footfalls echoing somewhere in the corridors to the north, and getting louder with each step.

Alex could have screamed.

One job! They had one job, up there, the five of them packed into the break room. Forget all that rubbish about coming up with a story to fob off the police, their *real* job was to stick together like glue so the murderer couldn't come after her. Of course, there was no guarantee that it *was* the murderer coming down the east wing and entering the tower now; but realistically, who else could it be? Alex was fairly sure that the person she was thinking of had seen through her ploy of destroying the evidence – if not immediately, then before long. She couldn't afford to be cornered by them, not before she'd got the memory cards out of the building.

The eleventh person on one side, and the murderer on the other. They were like Scylla and Charybdis; but Alex had a third way out. Still without risking turning her torch on, she crept away down the branching corridor and raced for the stairs.

How far up to go? That was the question, as Alex breathlessly pounded up the stairs, feeling her way up the banister and trying and failing to make as little noise as possible. She didn't want to risk getting trapped at the top of the tower – but with two people after her she could be trapped almost anywhere. Returning to the break room was out of the question while she still had the memory cards; and besides, the murderer had already predicted once just where she would be. There was only one thing to do, Alex decided: Stick to the plan. Get the memory cards away from the building. And on the fourth floor, she'd be above the line of the fence.

She reached the fourth floor and veered away from the stairs. A risky blink of torchlight revealed the open door of the south wing ahead of her. If she could smash a reasonably central window, she could hurl her coat right out and over the fence and into the middle of the overgrown drive leading to the building. The police, or anyone else for that matter, couldn't miss it. Just so long as she could pull that off, there was the faintest hope that the murderer might give up. She had to cling to that hope as tightly as she clung to her torch, unconsciously holding it like a weapon.

A few steps took her into the south wing, closing the door behind her and switching on her torch. Like its counterparts on the floors below, this wing took the form of a single wide-open room, lined with row after row of desks and chairs. Perhaps it had once been occupied by more typists, typing up endless letters and reports for filing elsewhere; but all Alex cared about was that it had windows. The north windows looked out onto the courtyard and were, like the others on this floor, all unbarred; but the south, outside windows retained their bars, and moreover were annoyingly narrow. Even on the brightest summer days, very little light would penetrate this place. Alex's own hopes were just as narrow, just as dim… She sprinted to the middle of the room and picked the most central window she could find, and, aiming directly between the bars, struck the glass as hard as she could with the handle of her torch.

Her arm rebounded with a jolt, and the glass held firm.

Alex stared in disbelief. All that hard work, and this was what stumped her? A window? She tensed her arm and struck again, to no effect except to make her wrist hurt. But the place was full of broken windows! How did Yva make it look so easy?

She gave it one last blow, and the glass again wouldn't shift but her torch flickered alarmingly. Reflecting that she couldn't afford to lose her only light source at this stage, Alex instead followed up with an awkward and unpractised kick. If her leg could flicker alarmingly, it would have. Was she that weak – or had they doubled down on security with tougher glass for the external windows? Desperate now, Alex was on the verge of grabbing a chair –

When off in the dark, untouched by any torchlight, there came a low, grating noise. It was the sound of the room's metal door slowly grinding open.

In the moment of crisis, Alex felt strangely calm. Deep down, she had suspected it would come to this. When everything she had tried to do on that night had failed, it was only natural that her plan to deliver the evidence to the outside would fail, too. That wasn't fatalism. It was simply recognising the calibre of her opponent.

This was only ever going to end with herself and the murderer facing each other alone.

Alex shone her torch across the room. The beam cut through the shadows like a knife through cobwebs, and settled on a person waiting patiently in the doorway. It was exactly who she'd thought.

"Don't worry, it's me," the culprit said. "I was worried about you alone out here, so I convinced the others to let me go. Here, give me the memory cards; I'll take care of them."

The enemy stretched out a hand. It might as well have been daubed with blood.

"You know I can't do that," Alex replied. There was the faintest tremor in her voice.

Her opponent raised an eyebrow. "Why ever not? You trust me, don't you?"

Alex shuddered.

"I did trust you," she said. "That's the worst part of it. I trusted you all along, but you're the one behind all this! You're a murderer!"

Silence fell between them. The pair watched each other, waiting to see who would move first, and what their next move would be. Then the hand drew back, and slowly closed the door. And the murderer smiled.

"Lucky guess," said Yva Dysart.

CHAPTER TWENTY-EIGHT
THE WRECKERS

4:01am

"Lucky guess," Yva repeated, "because it *is* just a guess, isn't it?" She spread her hands and grinned mockingly. "How could I be the murderer, who was never out of your sight or your guard?"

"Not *never*, not out of my sight," Alex said. "And while you planned the murders, you only committed one of them yourself. Reef's two working torches told me that much."

"The torches?" Yva asked. "Is that all?" It seemed even she hadn't worked it out that far yet.

"Here's how I figure it," Alex explained. It was strange, spelling out her deductions to the person who should have known it all. "There were nine of those basic torches in the building, all identical, and we each started with one; George's is unique and we can ignore it. But then you broke one, and Leo's was also broken – and Reef took it with him. Now, when we gathered for the questioning, everyone except you had a working torch. And after Chase's disappearance, everyone *still* had a working torch, with Chase's going to you." Alex rested for a moment, to let those details sink in. "Which means that there's only one person Reef could've got a second working torch from: Matt."

"No, you're forgetting," Yva interrupted. "Matt's torch was broken during his disappearance. We found it in the courtyard, you even stepped in the glass."

Alex shook her head. "We were wrong. The number of torches only adds up if that was *a previous broken torch* – that Reef had swapped Leo's broken torch for Matt's working one." She glanced towards the courtyard. "But the only time Reef could have swapped torches between taking away the broken torch and us finding it again in the courtyard is while you were alone in the prep room with him. And if Reef secretly left the prep room during that time, met Matt, and ended up swapping torches with him – then the only way I see that working is if he's Matt's murderer. The broken torch in the courtyard had a shattered lens, which didn't match the one we'd seen before – but that's exactly why Reef had to swap it. Matt had been struck on the head; Reef used Leo's broken torch and the glass smashed in the attack, and if later we asked to see that torch, we'd have noticed the damage and put two and two together – so Reef had to take Matt's working torch to pass off as Leo's broken one." Alex fixed Yva with a glare. "But he could only do any of that with you covering for him, then and afterwards. And I don't think you would *ever* cover for someone in a murder plot unless you came up with it in the first place."

"*That*, at least, is true," Yva said, with a nod. "I certainly wouldn't trust anyone else to come up with a murder plot for me." Her face went blank, a sure sign that she was really thinking. "As for your deduction... I admit that it's interesting. I could probably come up with another explanation if I had time to think. But it's you who's been doing the thinking, isn't it?"

She took a step closer and Alex's heart caught in her throat; but Yva was only pulling out a chair. She sat down facing Alex, between her and the door.

"So," Yva said, making herself quite comfortable, "you finally have a complete theory. Now we really are playing detectives!" She leaned towards Alex, grinning. "And when you have a theory that good, you can't help but share, can you? So go on – share. Four murders in a haunted house – whodunnit?"

"You and Reef," Alex answered without hesitation. "Almost all of it was about him – even the others could tell that much. The torches mean he probably killed Matt; their use as a weapon suggests he also killed Leo. And he's the only one who could have killed Chase... just like you're the only one who could have killed *him*."

"Whilst he was outside and I was inside," Yva replied, "and four floors apart, and with you, and a recording showing nobody near him."

"Of course," Alex agreed. "This is what you do, you invent problems and try to make them unsolvable. You'd never have compromised yourself unless you were certain there was no risk."

"And that's true, too! Anyone would think you understood me," Yva said pleasantly. "But what about the other spooky shenanigans, then? Invisible men running down corridors, Dry Diver hovering out of a window and dropping like a stone right in front of us. Reef can't have done those."

"No, but he helped – or really, those were someone else helping him," Alex replied. "It was Chase, of course. We practically knew this already – it's exactly as he told Bianca. He'd been blackmailed into helping Reef play a prank on everyone. He didn't like it, and he suspected there was more to it, but he had no idea murder was involved until he set eyes on Leo's body – and he pretty much shut down after that."

"What about the Team Silver co-conspirator?" Yva asked. "Remember, Reef and Chase were meant to be working with someone from the other team."

"Someone Chase didn't know, who he never set eyes on, who contacted him anonymously," Alex played back. "Because the Team Silver co-conspirator was just a lie he was told – one more step you took to cover up your own involvement, and so Chase didn't get suspicious when Team Silver members started disappearing."

"In other words, Team Dry are the culprits, and Team Silver the targets – that's your answer," Yva jeered. "Even though there are just as many dead on both sides!"

"But only you ever knew that that was how it would end up," Alex answered. "Of course Team Silver were the targets – that was Reef's motive. Like Bianca told us, he was dangerously, violently jealous; it's been obvious all night. But this wasn't just about Bianca; he was also jealous of *Silverfish*. Reef and Chase and Bianca were just amateurs, but they had actually been successful with *The Dry Diver Drownings* and had got a lot of attention… and then Matt came along with *Silverfish* and swept it all away, even getting Bianca onto his team. Reef must have hated that; and by killing Matt and Leo, the creator and lead actor, he took revenge on those he felt had taken his role and crippled *Silverfish* as a production… and punished Bianca, too. That's why Chase also had to die." Alex shook her head in despair. "The irony of blackmailing Chase with photos of him and Bianca together was that Reef must already have known."

Yva's eyes narrowed at her. "This is the whydunnit, now," she said. "Motives…" Her lip curled into a sneer. "Reef was jealous. Chase was blackmailed. So, what about me, Corby? Why did I do all this?"

Why, why, why… Alex had an idea, but it was so horrible that it made her ill. "Well, the reason you came up with this exact plan was to eliminate anyone who could incriminate you. First Chase, then Reef," she began uneasily. "But as to how it all started – I'll come back to it. Later." She couldn't think about it. Not yet. "After all, there are some things even you don't know the whole truth about, aren't there?"

"As a perfect innocent, I can freely admit to not understanding *everything*," Yva shrugged; but Alex had plainly caught her interest. "But I suppose we have plenty of time. Nobody is going to find us here. So go on – tell me everything, right from the beginning, and…" Her eyes sparkled. "I'll help you out if you get stuck."

So that was how it was going to be, was it. Alex had thought it might. Yva was too risk-averse to openly admit to what she had done, but she would tacitly confess quite cheerfully if she could do it under the guise of a theory. At the end of the day, she couldn't resist a chance to show off how clever she was.

"Let's start at the absolute beginning, then," Alex said; she wouldn't risk sitting down herself, much less taking her torchlight off Yva, but she leaned against a table as she spoke. She was so tired. "*The Dry Diver Drownings* had been going on for a while and was quietly successful. Then Dry Diver's creator, Matt Silver, came along with *Silverfish* and stole their thunder – and their lead actress. Reef and Chase had to continue on their own, trying to compete with a far more professional effort. And that's where you came in – spotting an opportunity to get in on a creative project that might help your writing career."

"They were desperate," Yva filled in. "Not that I couldn't have forced my way in if they *weren't*; they both acknowledged that I was the real deal as a writer."

"But you weren't just a writer. Reef was still smarting from Bianca leaving him, and he turned to the first girl who came along to soothe his feelings." Alex was being brutally blunt, but on this subject, she knew Yva wouldn't care. In fact, she would probably entirely agree. "I doubt it was ever your plan to date him – I'm sure it never occurred to you – but you went along with it, even though neither of you were really serious, because it helped cement your position."

"What would 'serious' really look like, anyway?" Yva asked. "I've only ever seen it in books. So melodramatic! Real people couldn't have feelings so intense."

"That might sometimes be true," Alex confessed. "I wouldn't know either, if I'm honest. But you wanted a bigger advantage, so you did something else to cement your position. You had Reef on your side; and you immediately set to digging up dirt on Chase, so you could hold it over him if ever you needed to. And you hit the jackpot with Bianca."

"It was elementary," Yva shrugged, so modest that Alex knew it was true. "Reef was completely blind to what they were up to, but a little social media stalking and slightly more actual stalking soon got me to the truth. I didn't tell him right away, though; I held it in reserve." She hesitated for a moment. "That doesn't incriminate me. It's fine if you know."

Yva would be admitting a lot more than that before they were done, Alex thought. "What happened next is that *Silverfish* made waves with Bianca, and her role in both big series inspired a crossover – and with that opportunity in hand, you and Reef agreed to go through with a murder plan targeting Team Silver. That's when you told Reef about Bianca and Chase, and began your blackmail plan. It meant you could use Chase as a tool and then get rid of him afterwards. You went with Leo and Tara to do some location scouting in the Pitchwater Building, and that gave you enough material to start planning in earnest."

"You can't deny that the place has potential," Yva said. "I was thinking of setting a book here."

Alex ignored this and continued. "Between the location scouting and the filming, you finished your planning and sent Reef and Chase in here to prepare the ground. We know from George that lights had been seen here more than once before – the extra time was when they came to modify the building... and pre-film the disappearance videos. It would've been quite a bit of work, and at least some of it will be traceable. All the wood, the tools, anything you needed to buy I can only assume came from Chase and the workshop he mentioned; he didn't know that it implicated him in a crime, but in any case he couldn't refuse. The large sheets of plywood could be slipped between the gaps in the fence; for everything else, Reef had one of the keys to the tunnel. They put up the graffiti to put us on edge; smashed and boarded up the windows on the east wing, so nobody there could see what was happening in the courtyard; smashed the windows and cut a few bars in the north wing prep room, and used a couple of boards to hide the escape route; smashed the glass in the cubbyholes and boarded those up too; and recorded, with their digital cameras set to the wrong date and time, the disappearance videos."

"I take it you've gone with the fakery explanation," Yva remarked. "But Leo spoke in his video, the fire door needed two off-screen people to operate it in Matt's video, Chase knew too much in his – and Reef wouldn't have collaborated in *his* if it showed his death."

"Reef's was real," Alex said. "I'll explain why later. But of course the others were fake – an idea you stole, I'm guessing, from your own hidden mystery explanation for the Dry Diver storyline? But I took too long figuring out what bothered me about them. We couldn't hear the sound of rain on the windows in the background. It must have been a dry night when the fakes were recorded."

"Tonight's weather is the worst in a few days," Yva admitted. "But there wasn't much they could do about *that*, was there?"

"As for Leo's voice in his video, I'm sure it was just a clip from a *Silverfish* episode," Alex continued. "I'll talk about the fire door in a minute, but the glitches in Matt's video were an editing trick disguised as file corruption, so you didn't have to worry about excluding Bianca. As for Chase knowing too much in his, of course he did – because the whole thing was planned by you! You always intended to act as the detective once the murders were discovered, and stage interviews in the foyer with the team members in the cubbyholes. I remember particularly that that was *your* idea."

"Ah, but there's an alternative theory!" Yva broke in excitedly. "The conspirators might have recorded multiple variations of Chase's disappearance, and just selected on the night the one which fitted the situation."

Alex glared at her. It was very likely that this was what had actually happened, and Yva was making sure she didn't miss it. "They did that as well, then," she said drily. "But the fact is, the only way Dry Diver could attack Chase through the boarded-up screen was if it *wasn't boarded up yet*. And that proves Chase was in on this part of the plan. And as for Matt, there was a simple way you could make the fire door easier to open – with just one slight alteration to the shaft in the doorframe."

Alex pointed to Yva's pocket. Yva took her cue, and pulled out the coin with the tape across it. "The part with the shaft is called a 'strike plate', and the bolt is a 'latch', by the way," she elaborated.

"Thanks," Alex sighed. "But you know that this alone was enough – a large coin taped over the strike plate so that the latch couldn't enter it. The fire door was never really locked in the video – and it was never really locked tonight, either, or not until after Matt's disappearance. All anyone had to do was to pull the hook on the outside."

"Ingenious," Yva beamed. "And presumably you have an explanation for how these video files made their way onto other people's cameras?

"Simple," Alex said. "The cameras may be unique, but they all use the same type of memory card. The killer, Reef, would have had all the right memory cards on his person – maybe a different pocket for each so they wouldn't get mixed up – and whenever he attacked, he simply took the victim's camera and swapped out the memory card for one with a pre-made video."

Yva clapped. "Brilliant! And so simple," she enthused. "But a perfect device for making it appear that either the videos were authentic no matter what they showed, or the victim had to be in on it. That's why Chase's had to be done so carefully, of course."

She was on the brink of admitting it, Alex noticed. Pretty soon she'd give up the pretence. Not that it mattered at all. This was just stalling on Alex's part; and she'd play it out for as long as she could. "You carefully kept yourself out of the preparations," she said, drawing out her words. "But there was one thing you personally needed, to be sure of your own safety: Someone to vouch for you… as a detective, and as a human being. Somebody outside of Team Dry, a complete outsider to Dry Diver, and a stranger to everyone – and who therefore had no reason whatsoever to lie for the benefit of people like Reef and Chase or to help anyone with a murder plot. Somebody like Great-Aunt Cornelia – or like me. That's the real reason you invited us…. Your ulterior motive itself had an ulterior motive."

It was awful to think about. That all along, her own presence in the Pitchwater Building had been purely as a fig leaf for Yva, a giant red herring draped in front of Yva's guilt…

And behind even that, there was an even worse possibility. One she wanted to put off thinking about for as long as she possibly could.

"I'll come back to that, too," Alex said quietly. "That brings us to tonight – crunch time. And for everything that went right, there was quite a bit that went wrong, wasn't there?"

"You tell me," Yva said, giving nothing away.

"Well, right from the start there was Chase confessing his role to Bianca," Alex pointed out. "He didn't have time to give her the details – and you'd spiked his information just in case, so he dobbed in a Team Silver member rather than you; but even so, it was a huge slip. And it's clear that Matt's murder went completely off the rails – but that's later." It was a complicated story, but telling it in order helped to keep things straight. "Where Matt met his end was where the tricks began tonight: Right at the hatch, the one we can't escape from. Earlier we were theorising – or at least, *I* was – that the forest hatch was only padlocked after Matt's murder, right? But once you know that Reef and Chase are involved, it's obvious that it was done long before. They were the last people to come through the hatch, shutting it behind them; and it was while the rest of us were talking at the bottom that one of them got out that chain with the padlock. With these heavy coats, one padlock and a bit of chain could easily be hidden in a pocket. Whichever of them was last down just had to let the hatch lid rest on their arm while it was nearly closed, and reach through the gap to feed the chain through the clasps and snap the second padlock on. I wouldn't be surprised if the key was somewhere just within reach of the hatch, but where you wouldn't find it just scrabbling around at random."

"A basic precaution in case anything went *really* wrong," Yva yawned. "Complete plausible deniability for anyone who found it, too."

"The next weird event happened while the two of us were collecting up people's phones," Alex continued. "This was when you started being careful never to get separated from me, so that you would always have an alibi – but because you were pretending to be the detective, you could frame it as giving an alibi to *me*."

"Of course, it's another of Knox's mystery rules that the detective can't be the culprit," Yva said. "But I'd never violate those. Good thing I made a point of you being the co-detective, don't you think?"

Alex stared at her. "Are those old rules that important to you?" she asked. "Isn't one of them that mysteries can't have Chinese people? Even that?"

"*Actually*, that rule is against racial stereotypes," Yva retorted, not entirely convincingly. "But on that note, did you see how I weaved in the fact that Leo and Viggo were twins?" She brightened perceptibly. "They were such a good red herring! Of course, that they were twins was really totally irrelevant – they weren't part of the plot, they couldn't be *forced* to act suspicious – but it was useful to spread a little suspicion around in case it sparked any theories."

Was Yva even able to distinguish fiction from reality? Alex shook the thought from her head, and got back to her point. "We're not talking about this, we're talking about when we got back to the break room – and found Dry Diver there. Nobody would admit to moving him there; but of course it was probably Chase, the moment we left for the north wing. And the footsteps we heard in the corridor, that ran away towards the east wing but where Reef said he'd seen nobody? He just lied; that was Chase, too. He hid in the typing room for a few seconds, then came out not saying anything in case we noticed he was out of breath, and carrying things to excuse it if we did. I think he wanted to see where we put the box of phones; destroying those was probably another of his duties."

"That's just basic division of labour," Yva replied. "If Chase couldn't be let in on the murders, he had to take charge of muddying the waters. He couldn't object, just so long as the idea was that he wouldn't get caught."

"I see…" Alex nodded. In her own bizarre way, Yva really was trying to help. "And so that brings us to Leo's disappearance – or rather, his murder."

"Ah, now *this* I am looking forward to," Yva said. She leaned forwards in her chair, an especially attentive look in her eyes. "The really impossible part. Go on, then, Corby; impress me." Her smile took on a distinctly hungry cast. "How did Leo escape from a room with us guarding the only exit?"

Alex had been very close with her original theory. She just hadn't taken it to its furthest extent. "He didn't," she said. "Because he was never in that room at all."

Yva's eyes narrowed, like a hunter's. She looked like she didn't know whether to be pleased or annoyed. "But we saw him enter the typing room," she said. "We saw him jog up the corridor and go right in –"

"No, we didn't," Alex corrected. "You kept on saying that we did. You emphasised it at every opportunity. But do you remember my theory that Reef let him out of the room? That, while Reef held the door across the corridor and we couldn't see past it, Leo just tip-toed out? It's just as true whilst Leo was meant to be going *in*. Chase called for Leo, and he turned off his torch and held the typing door wide open. We couldn't see down the corridor while he was doing that. We *heard* someone jogging up; but it wasn't Leo, it was *Reef* – with Leo's camera and the broken torch. He rolled the torch in, set the camera down just inside the doorway, and then crept back the way he'd come, while Chase bought him time by closing the door as slowly as he could."

It was that easy. A trivial illusion that would have worked even if Yva wasn't in on the secret; but which relied absolutely on complicity and simple lies.

"Bravo," Yva murmured. "But you have to take it all the way, Corby. Where was Leo during all this? Why didn't he answer his cue? Why did he play along, if he wasn't part of the plot?"

A trivial illusion, but one that masked a deeply unpleasant truth.

"Because he was still in the other room," Alex said, "being murdered by Reef."

And Yva's eyes went narrower still.

"I remember now. Leo wanted to talk about his performance, and you instructed Reef to help him while Chase got the Dry Diver costume," Alex recounted. "Reef could've talked Leo through his lines anywhere, but instead he took him to the storage room. I think probably the first thing Reef did in there was to get behind Leo and club him with his torch as hard as he could. That knocked Leo right out – and broke the torch by accident. So he took Leo's torch – the broken torch was Reef's all along, for all we later thought it was Leo's and then Matt's – and also his camera, swapping in the memory card with the disappearance video. Around that time, Chase came back with the costume – and you very loudly announced their return. That was Reef's prompt to come out and take it off him; you couldn't let him see Leo knocked out on the floor, of course."

"I suppose you've guessed where Leo's body was all along, then," Yva scowled. "But that was so obvious I'm amazed nobody thought of it."

"He was just where we found him," Alex agreed: "In the Dry Diver costume. The moment he was out of sight again, Reef put the costume on Leo; it wouldn't have been easy, but he had five minutes, and if Leo started coming around Reef could have hit him again for good measure. The only time he had to break off was when Chase gave Leo's cue, and he had to act as Leo, running up the corridor. I'm sure Chase wondered why Leo was going along with this, but he probably figured Leo was the non-existent Team Silver prankster."

"None of this drowns Leo, I notice," Yva remarked.

"It does... once he was fastened into the suit," Alex said. "Because I remember something Chase told me – that the costume has a breathing tube because it's fully airtight. And when we next saw the costume, Reef had set it up in front of a sink."

Yva sat back and folded her arms. She'd conceded the point.

"The Dry Diver costume itself was the murder weapon," Alex continued. "With the mouthpiece fitted to Leo, and the end of the breathing tube attached to a tap, an endless stream of water was piped straight into his throat. Even if the mouthpiece came detached, there was no other source of air in the suit. You told me yourself that drowning is hard to diagnose, but it's basically just lack of oxygen. The amount of water in the suit and in Leo's system would make drowning the obvious conclusion, even if he actually just suffocated. And that would ensure he stayed unconscious, wouldn't it, even if he was coming around from the blow to the head?"

"That's entirely accurate," Yva answered. "Very clever work, Corby. You're a better detective than I gave you credit for."

Which was something else that had gone wrong.

"But what about Chase?" Yva continued. "I stuck him in that room to mind the costume. What if he noticed something?"

"Of course you thought of that," Alex said. "I'm guessing you had the perfect excuse for him: That the costume was meant to be filled with water. It was going to be further involved in the prank later, when Dry Diver dropped down into the courtyard. Chase wouldn't have been happy about that, either – it would have destroyed the costume, which he was proud of – but like you said, he literally couldn't object. I expect you even had him turn the tap off after a while and detach the breathing tube."

"It's not as if he didn't have his petty rebellions," Yva said, with a frown. "Spilling the beans to Bianca – and then going off with Viggo for a little walk! At least he did *something* useful there."

"He pretended that the bathroom door was stuck, right?" Alex said. "In the north tower. That room was deeply involved in the plan, so it was best to pretend it was shut up tight."

"Makes sense, doesn't it?" Yva replied. "But in the meantime, we were downstairs getting mixed up in Matt's disappearance. Tell me about that, Corby."

It wasn't surprising that Yva was keener to talk about Matt's murder, even if it was one of the points which most clearly implicated her. About this murder in particular, even she didn't know everything.

"So we left Chase and Viggo in the east wing, where Chase was meant to stay and where you hoped Viggo would too," Alex resumed. "Actually, they both got bored and went for a walk – but the point was that they were somewhere where they couldn't interfere with what was about to happen in the courtyard."

Yva nodded slowly, and gestured for her to continue.

"The two of us, plus Reef, ended up in the north wing just in time for Bianca to be done filming with Matt, leaving him alone in the conference room," Alex remembered. "What happened next relied on the precise timing of the filming schedule. Reef was supposed to be alone in the corridor five minutes from that moment; in the meantime, he insisted on talking with you alone – supposedly about his Viggo-Leo swap theory. The two of you shut yourself in the prep room, but you instantly reopened the door to grab my arm, supposedly so you knew where I was – but actually it was the reverse, wasn't it? I was giving *you* an alibi, while you were giving Reef an alibi – which made it seem like I was also alibiing Reef. But

I wasn't, really. From the moment he stepped into that room, I never saw Reef – or even heard him. All I could hear were whispers… which could easily have been you playing two roles. So until I saw Reef leave that room again five minutes later, he had no alibi."

"The fact that he was in a room with no exit except the one you were standing outside should have been good enough," Yva replied. "But you've already discovered that room's secret."

Alex nodded. "As I said earlier, the bars on one of the windows have been sawn through, and disguised with boarding. What actually happened was that Reef crossed the room, took down both bits of boarding, and climbed out into the courtyard. It was raining out there, but if he left his coat inside until he got back, then in the darkness and torchlight we wouldn't have noticed how wet he was."

"There's a reason I never proposed how wet people's clothes were as a potential clue," Yva agreed. "Let's face it, we couldn't really tell. Even footprints were meaningless, the place was full of wet footprints the whole time."

Alex pointed at the window she'd been attempting to smash through. "It's raining hard tonight, and that helped to create the ominous atmosphere you wanted – but it's not like you could have predicted that reliably; not with this country's weather, anyway. We might just as easily have had clear skies and moonlight – which made it all the more imperative to board up the east wing windows, to eliminate any chance of Chase and Viggo witnessing something."

"Sets up the more purposeful use of boarded-up windows elsewhere, too!" Yva insisted.

Alex drove ahead. "At this point it's easy to see that Reef is the culprit. He had around five minutes out of sight, he had a way from the prep room into the courtyard – and he had a way from the courtyard into the conference room. The hook on the fire door, and the coin you'd taped in the doorframe, made it the work of seconds to burst in on Matt while he was filming." She paused, playing out the scene in her mind. "I don't think Reef attacked Matt immediately… Matt's bigger than him and if he put up even a tiny bit of resistance the game would be up. Besides, we found shattered glass from the torch in the courtyard, not in the conference room. I think Reef probably used the element of surprise to spin a story that would get Matt outside. He'd be so startled that just about anything would do – and it didn't need to work for long."

"Think how you'd react in that situation," Yva supplied. "A friend or an acquaintance pops up somewhere he shouldn't be, acting panicked and urging you to follow. If you had no reason to be suspicious already, you'd want to know what it was all about." She shrugged. "That's what Reef said, anyway."

It would have been a surprisingly subtle psychological touch to come from Yva; Alex wasn't surprised that it was someone else's idea. It was yet another telling point that this was a criminal conspiracy and not a solo crime. "Well, however it was done," Alex resumed, "Matt took a few steps into the courtyard and Reef brained him with the same torch he'd used on Leo. That shattered its glass, so he swapped it for Matt's torch so there would be no visible difference. He got Matt's camera out of its harness and swapped in the memory card with the faked video, and chucked it back into the conference room before ripping the taped coin out of the doorframe. He wasn't worried about fingerprints; he was the one who pointed out that everyone here is wearing gloves. Then it only left dragging Matt the few short metres to the murder weapon."

"The murder weapon, huh," Yva mused. "Another one we never found." She flashed a wolfish grin. "Because people let their preconceptions run away with them."

Alex grimaced; she'd been one of those fools not seeing what was right in front of her. "I was imagining something like a deep sink or a hole in the ground; if the courtyard had a fountain instead of a statue, that would've done it. I never gave that overturned filing cabinet a second thought... even if it was full of rainwater." She shook her head ruefully. "I thought it was a coffin when I first saw it. But that wasn't such a crazy idea. I'm sure you'll tell me that the five-minute window for the crime isn't nearly enough time to be sure of drowning someone to death, even if you ignore the time spent messing with windows and cameras – but if Matt could be forced face-down into what was effectively a tight bathtub, the idea was that he could just be left there and he'd never regain consciousness."

"That would be the idea, yes," Yva agreed. "But I'm sure you see the problem, right?" Her voice grew high and mocking, as if their showdown was an enormous joke to which only she knew the punchline. "Let's say all that was true, that Matt was left in the courtyard to die while Reef showed his face inside. It's a good plan! But..." She suppressed a giggle. "But we were out there in the courtyard not ten minutes later! You looked right inside that cabinet-bath and saw nothing but rainwater!" Now she did laugh, high and wild and unrestrained. "Where did Matt's body go?" she cackled. "Where did the corpse go, when nobody was there to move it? Leo was dead! Chase and Viggo were romping about upstairs! And you, me, Bianca, Tara – we were all in a room together! Reef was in the corridor while Tara watched him every second! And George wasn't even *here* yet! Everyone has an alibi!"

"There is one person who could have moved Matt's body," Alex said.

Yva stopped dead, mid-cackle – but her eyes lost none of their ghoulish interest.

"There are a few interesting things about the courtyard, actually," Alex went on. She wasn't quite changing the subject, for all that Yva looked faintly impatient. "One is that you didn't want us to go out there – you tried to convince us not to bother. The second is that you didn't want me to look at the filing cabinet. You stood blocking my sight, and given how dark it was, if I hadn't pointed my torch that way then I wouldn't have noticed it at all. And the third is that, when you saw the cabinet was empty, you were scared stiff."

That took the wind out of Yva's sails. She glared at Alex, plainly resentful for her having pointed this out. "And your deduction from this is?" she prompted.

"That you fully expected Matt's body to be in there, didn't you?" Alex asked. "*That's* what the falling Dry Diver stunt was really about – to draw our attention to the courtyard, whilst also destroying the murder weapon. Moving Matt's body was never the plan. And frankly, I think you would have taken a lot of pleasure in having us find both Matt and Leo's bodies there at the same time – and later, Reef's as well. I'll bet you'd even hoped for an opportunity to get Chase's body to appear there."

"It would have been extremely elegant," Yva confessed. "So what, then? Who moved Matt's body?"

Alex met Yva's eyes. "Matt did."

CHAPTER TWENTY-NINE
COMPLICITY OF CORPSES

4:17am

"A dead man walking…" Yva mused, her tone sarcastic but her eyes never leaving Alex's. "How convenient that would be for a murder mystery author! I'll have to remember that one."

"Come off it, Yva!" Alex snapped. "The fact is, you don't know exactly what happened to Matt either – but you've already figured out it had to be this, haven't you? The truth is that we were slower getting to the north wing than you'd have liked, and it cut into the time Reef had to set up Matt's murder. He botched it – and while there was nobody in the courtyard to see, Matt came around and managed to get out of the filing cabinet."

Yva sat back in her chair, looking sulky. "It's the only way out of the problem you've set up, that's for sure," she admitted. "And as for Reef botching things, that's annoyingly plausible, too." She recovered her poise, and cocked her head. "So, what then? Play it out for me."

"What then is that Matt was still badly injured," Alex said. "I can imagine it: He'd been cracked on the head, he'd almost died of drowning – he was groggy, in pain, not getting enough air… and he was scared." She could almost *feel* it, how terrifying it must have been – to be in pain, to not understand what was happening, but to know that someone had tried to kill you… "What he did next was obvious," Alex said. "He legged it."

"He legged it?" repeated Yva, with obvious disdain. "He turned tail and ran? Without even an attempt to get help?"

"If it had just been an accident, he'd have tried to go for help," agreed Alex. "But he must have remembered enough to know that he'd been tricked and attacked. He didn't know who he could trust or where the next attack might come from. The safest way forward was to run – to get out of the Pitchwater Building." A thought occurred to her. "Of course, as a diver, he probably also knew exactly what kind of medical help he needed – and knew he couldn't get it where he was."

"So he ran," Yva fenced, "and didn't meet a single person?"

"Of course not. Where would he?" Alex asked. "Matt would have taken the shortest route back to the tunnel, and there was nobody on the way to run into! The only way out of the courtyard was into the south wing, which was empty, and then up through the east wing – which, despite your plans for Chase and Viggo, was also empty. Leo was dead, and hidden in the Dry Diver suit for good measure. The rest of us were all in the north wing, where there was no reason to return. So nobody could have seen Matt on his way to the tunnel."

"Fine, point conceded," Yva agreed. "Matt made it to the tunnel – to the end of the tunnel, even, where we found him. But what then?" Her eyes began to gleam. "Are we back on George, or Reef, or our mysterious petty criminal killing him there somehow, and then leaving the tunnel and locking up behind himself?"

This was the critical point, Alex realised; the most impossible part of the whole mystery. So long as she could resolve this problem, the rest of the case was straightforward – almost obvious, even. But she had no idea if what she was thinking of was actually possible at all.

Yva would know, though. This kind of medical research was her forte.

"Yes, Reef killed Matt," Alex murmured. "But he didn't follow him down the tunnel; he didn't have to. He'd already killed him… it just took until the end of the tunnel to work."

Yva stared at Alex as if she was mad. "…Do you mean poison? Reef put poison in the water? Because I'll be very annoyed if he could get his hands on poison while I've never been able to. Tell me, Alex!" she cried. "What are you talking about?"

"Dry drowning," Alex answered.

Yva stared at her, eyes round, blinking in confusion. And then the light began to dawn.

"It's something Matt mentioned when we first met him," Alex explained; "that you don't have to be in the water to drown. I remember hearing about that now, in swimming lessons years ago. Once you begin to drown, it damages your lungs and airways. Even once you're out of the water you might still have difficulty breathing; and without immediate medical attention you would still be in danger – and I can only imagine how much worse that would get if you were panicked and tried to run." And Matt would have known that, too – but panic is panic, and danger is danger. "He got as far as the ladder… and that's where his body gave out on him. It's like you said, Yva – he was a dead man walking."

Yva let out a long, gushing breath. "Dry drowning," she repeated. "That's an outdated term, by the way; your knowledge really is behind the times. Medically, drowning is a *process*, one that might kill you or might not, immediately or… later. But you're right that this *can happen* – rarely – though it would be obvious to any witness that something was wrong." She shrugged. "Not that there were any witnesses, as you've pointed out!"

"It was an absolute fluke," Alex concluded, "one that could have ruined everything… but instead it almost sealed your innocence."

Now that Yva had had it explained to her, her mood took another swing upwards. "Honestly, Matt's disappearance from the courtyard gave me real grief," she confessed. "It's not often I feel scared! I had no idea what could have happened – but like you said, it was a fluke, not part of the plan. I certainly couldn't have predicted it, let alone relied on it! But I'm sure you're right. Well, it's that or Dry Diver." Her eyes glimmered. "And on that note, shall we continue? What happened next, my dear detective?"

Alex sighed. So many hours still to cover, of crime committed under her nose. "What happened next was that Tara decided the show must go on," she said. "That suited you down to the ground; as you told us at the time, it was just what you'd been about to say! And you'd also anticipated that the Reef-Bianca argument scene was the obvious thing to move onto." Yva had practically announced her intentions at the time, now that Alex thought back on it. "You boasted that you'd scripted the scene to play on Reef and Bianca's real-life breakup. That was deliberate; and while you complained about Reef ad-libbing and the scene breaking up, what you *wanted* was an upset that would scatter people through the building and give your accomplices time to get on with the next stage of the plan. The idea was for Reef to torment Bianca into running off – and if that failed, I'm sure he would have stormed off himself."

"It wouldn't have taken much," Yva admitted. "The guy had *very* poor control of his emotions." She rolled her eyes. "I notice boys can get away with that, but when it's me I'm being 'irrational' and 'acting like a little girl'!"

Any other time, Alex would have sympathised. Now was not the time. "The point was that the first floor was cleared," she continued. "Bianca fled, Tara went after her, and Reef went after them – or put up a show of doing so, anyway. Viggo was already hanging around upstairs. Then there was Chase, who we'd met a couple of minutes earlier; I was surprised not to find him guarding the costume, right after you'd told him to do just that – but that wasn't his real task, was it? You'd emphasised that he had a job to do… and though he wasn't clear on whether or not you were in on the prank, that was his signal. The moment our backs were turned, he went and damaged our phones by pouring bottled water over them. That's the only real window of time when that could have happened, as everyone else was in check until the filming broke up – Reef might have had time once the filming broke up, but it wasn't reliable. Afterwards Chase hared up to the top floor of the north tower, still while filming was ongoing, and locked himself into the bathroom. He had a job to do in there, and couldn't risk anyone realising the room was available – which was why he'd pretended to find the door stuck when he visited with Viggo, and why Viggo subsequently tried the door and found it locked."

Yva nodded impatiently. "There was never any denying that that bathroom was where the rise and fall of the Dry Diver costume – and Leo's corpse in it – was managed. The fishing-line used in that bit of engineering was left there when Pitchwater got its makeover."

"The two ends of the wire were knotted into small loops," Alex reminded herself. "Chase hung both on the coathooks – I think the missing one hadn't been ripped out yet – and threw the slack out of the opposite window. Then he had to wait for somebody on the ground floor below: Reef. Instead of chasing Bianca and Tara, as he claimed, he'd actually hung around near the ground floor waiting for us to get out of the way. Then he had to lift and carry Leo's body, in the costume, way around to the courtyard; it wouldn't have been easy, but both he and Chase were better-built than the Karswells. Chase couldn't be trusted with the carrying part, though; he'd have realised he was dealing with a body, not a costume filled with water. But on the way, something totally unexpected happened."

Yva smiled bitterly, reflecting on an unforeseen event that nonetheless hadn't hurt. "The night watchman showed up to make life interesting."

"Right. George Sanderling, who we'd also encountered at the bookshop," Alex recalled. "He arrived through the front door – and immediately saw what he described as a person in a diving suit exiting into the courtyard. Of course, what he actually saw…"

"…Was Reef, carrying the costumed corpse on his back," Yva grinned.

"But given the power of George's torch, Reef would've seen himself outlined in the glare and realised he'd been spotted," Alex said. "That wasn't part of the plan at all – but it was easy to improvise. He got into the courtyard and out of sight, and dropped Leo immediately. Then he just hid behind the doors and waited for George – and gave him a violent shove that threw him to the floor and knocked him out."

"George isn't exactly in the first flush of youth. I wonder if Reef thought he'd killed him?" Yva pondered. "Of course, if George had shown any signs of recovering, Reef really *would* have had to kill him. George got off easy, all things considered."

"Regardless, that's about as far as George's role in the story goes," Alex said. "Reef went right back to what he was doing – dragging Leo over to the corner of the tower beside the filing cabinet, where the fishing-wire was hanging down from the bathroom up above. With both ends hooked up there, the slack simply formed the long end of a loop. Reef hooked that under the costume's arms and wrapped it around a few times, enough to secure it without tying an actual knot – and that was him done. Of course, for good measure he took the chance to go through George's pockets for his phone and his keys and hurl them over the fence where we couldn't get our hands on them. Then he probably did exactly what he claimed he did later – went and hung around in the break room until he got wind of us."

"Having our little argument with Viggo about Matt's death," Yva said. "Calling him 'Leo' there was a nice touch, by the way – for you and for Reef."

"Meanwhile, Chase was stuck with the real hard work – hauling Leo's body up as high as it would go," Alex resumed. "It was a lot heavier than an empty costume, but like I said, he'd probably been told it was full of water. The idea was that he would keep it suspended like that until he got some prearranged signal; maybe someone calling in the courtyard, which he'd have heard with the window broken. And he thought he did hear it, once, I think."

Yva frowned at her. "What do you mean? Do you mean when Bianca saw it?"

Alex nodded. "I think he probably kept the bathroom door wide open half the time, so he could listen out for any signals in the corridors; he only needed to close up and lock it if he heard anyone's footsteps nearby. Now, what Bianca said was that she saw Dry Diver, and it lunged for her and she cried out – almost at the same time. I actually think she got it confused in her mind... She cried out, just from having seen the costume rising up – and that made Chase's hand slip, jerking the costume suddenly. Bianca put it together the scariest way possible, but really, it was nothing important."

"Makes sense," Yva admitted. "But aren't you brushing over the strain of holding this thing hauled halfway up a building? And when it fell, Chase was right alongside us, remember? We sure didn't find any fishing-line hanging down to the courtyard, either. How do you explain that?"

Alex sighed. "I was hoping you would," she said, grudgingly. "Moving parts with string and things like that aren't what I'm good at. But I'm guessing it's important that one of the coathooks had been ripped out of the wall, and the taps had gone wonky. I figure they were all used as tethers to take some of the strain off Chase while he was just waiting for his signal... and were also used as a kind of timing mechanism, too, so he could show his face in front of us at the same time as the body fell."

Yva let out an exaggerated sigh. "Leaving me to do the hard work? What kind of a detective are you, anyway?" she complained. "But... as it happens, you've got it already. It's not easy for everyone to visualise this sort of thing without trying it out for themselves, but basically: The two coathooks were next to the sink, with the two ends of the wire attached to them. As Chase pulled, he looped one side of the slack around each tap, helping to anchor it and bearing some of the weight. That meant he could let go for a moment if ever he needed to shut the door, for instance." Yva's face was quite serious, but calm, in a way. She seemed at ease with the technical parts of a mystery. "The timer mechanism was a bit more improvised. One of the coathooks had been ripped off the wall by the time we got there, remember? It had a screw loose. That was deliberate; one of the screws had been removed beforehand to weaken it. If the coathooks were left to bear the weight of the body for any length of time, that weakened one would eventually pull from the wall – loosing that one end of wire and sending Dry Diver tumbling down to ground level." She sat back in her chair, deliberating. "The thing to remember is that, as you rightly said, the wire wasn't actually knotted around the body – just looped. So when one end of the wire came free, Dry Diver unspooled himself in his fall." She flashed a grin, suddenly proud of her cleverness.

It all fitted in with Alex's rough imaginings. She could take the rest from there. "You actually had to change plans a little here, if I'm right," she interrupted. "The only reason we ended up witnessing the fall from the fourth floor was because Bianca had seen the costume there – but you couldn't have predicted that and it really just made things more obvious. You relocated that part of the plan after learning what she'd seen, maybe even from the courtyard itself."

"Why settle for anything but a front-row seat?" asked Yva innocently. "I could have lured you out there somehow, and you'd have seen no more nor less than I wanted you to."

Alex nodded to herself. "With the bathroom window broken to allow the wire to pass through, Chase could have heard any shouting in the courtyard, even above the rain. Something like that was probably the signal; I remember that he showed up right after Reef had yelled his name – something he'd avoided doing until then – and if Reef didn't think to give the signal himself then you probably elbowed him in the ribs to make it happen."

"Guilty as charged," Yva said, with an irreverent air.

Alex glared at her, and continued. "You smashed the window, just to make sure that we saw – and the timer came off just as planned, dropping Dry Diver right in front of us. In fact, it probably worked better this way; if we *had* been in the courtyard, I don't think

Chase would have quite had time enough to leg it down to us and we might even have noticed the fishing-wire."

"A fair point, but it's not like it was the sort of thing we could practise," Yva conceded. "So, do you have any idea how it is that the two of us found the fishing-line neatly off the hooks and pushed into a corner by the time we got there?"

"Simple," Alex shrugged. "Chase only needed an alibi for when the body dropped; afterwards we weren't paying the same attention. We all just raced downstairs in a muddle – but the thing is, I don't remember noticing Chase in the courtyard until the last second before George caught us. I think he deliberately detoured upstairs at the first opportunity – back to the bathroom to haul the wire in through the window, unfurling and unhooking it and dropping it in the corner. Then he raced down to join us." She thought for a second. "Chase couldn't have got out through the fire exit alone – but Reef knew what was going on too. He probably waited by the fire door until the rest of us were out and then propped it open with a chair for Chase. It's not like any of us were looking in that direction."

"Indeed you weren't," said Yva.

"But when Chase did arrive, he finally realised that he'd been an unknowing accessory to murder," Alex said. It was really no wonder to her that Chase had gone very, very quiet after that; she couldn't imagine how horrifying a revelation it had been for him. "Keeping Chase out of the way also had the advantage that he had no idea what was going on – but once the situation changed, you and Reef had to silence him permanently. You could bank on him keeping quiet for a while, as he tried to figure out what had really happened and whether he could safely confess his role in events; but he'd always be a threat to you. And besides… you'd already given away Chase's secret to Reef. To him, what Chase and Bianca were doing was the ultimate betrayal; and if he wouldn't lay a finger on Bianca, he'd take it all out on Chase."

"What happened to Chase is really straightforward," Yva confirmed. "The only mysterious part was what happened to his body."

"But before that happened, George finally showed up," Alex said. "That threw us all into a muddle – probably you especially…

You and Reef had had no opportunity to confer, so your only previous hint that George was even a factor was Bianca and Tara's ghost story. Reef had managed to deal with George without giving anything away; but in retrospect, the fact that the attack he'd suffered had no trace of impossibility or even ingenuity about it was always a clue that he was genuinely uninvolved – and that whoever attacked him wasn't the same person as masterminded the murders."

"But in the end, George was actually quite useful!" Yva pointed out. "He went along with our detecting and added an air of legitimacy to the proceedings. Without him, people might have been suspicious of the fact that I'd put Reef and Chase alone together in an unobservable spot."

Alex sighed, disgusted with herself. "You really had me hook, line, and sinker," she said. "The whole idea of detecting and interviewing witnesses and seeing them alone – it all looked so reasonable… but really, it was set up purely to kill Chase. Even the order you interviewed people in was important – you were out to buy time for Reef to commit the murder, to strangle Chase with the telephone cord and set up his camera and hide his body in the filing cabinet. You even went and brought Reef out from the cubbyhole yourself, because me or George might have noticed that Chase was already missing."

"The filing cabinet thing was a gamble," Yva said, with a thoughtful air. "Because it was such a simple problem – Chase couldn't have left, and the filing cabinet was the only place he could have been hidden. Pretending to check the drawers even drew attention to it! If I hadn't been playing along, I'd never have fallen for it. But because of all that work establishing an atmosphere of the supernatural and the impossible, people lost their wits. They stopped thinking." She gave Alex a half-apologetic, half-mocking smile. "Including you."

"Including me," Alex groaned. "But the biggest deception – the biggest trick you played on me this whole night – came a little after, when we left to investigate the towers."

Yva frowned at Alex, and got serious. This was the point at which her culpability crossed the line between conspiracy to murder… and actual murder. "Our investigation of the towers was just the epilogue," she said shortly. "They're as far removed from the scene of Reef's death as possible. Not that I'm not interested in your theory – but I'm warning you now, if you're anything less than completely sure…"

"I'm sure," Alex broke in. "You killed Reef. The way it happened tallies with everything else that's been happening tonight. And the towers certainly aren't as far removed from the scene of the crime as possible – because the place where Reef was killed was the same place the Dry Diver suit was lifted from! And the fact is," she went on, with the sense that she was striding into the lion's jaws, "you used exactly the same method to murder Reef."

"We were never apart," Yva said quickly. "I couldn't have done anything without you seeing –"

"That's not true, and you know it," Alex interrupted. "We were apart twice, and if it wasn't for long, it was still as long as you needed."

"It takes ten, twenty minutes to be sure of a strangulation –"

"Here's how it happened," Alex said firmly. "The way Chase's death was arranged showed that you'd planned out our detective activities, so it follows that going to the towers was the same. And Reef finding some excuse to go outside was transparently part of some plan."

"It could have been just to dispose of the memory cards he'd taken," Yva protested. "He'd have dropped them down the drains – after stamping on them, of course. Data security is important!"

"Again, he did that too," Alex said shortly. "But it wasn't enough. See, despite all the alibis you arranged for Reef, the fact was that he *was* the most obvious suspect, and you would have known that well in advance, and so would he. So long as the murders were impossible, alibis counted for nothing, really. So the idea was that there'd be one last trick to draw suspicion off him: An attempt on his life."

Yva tutted. "So stupid. Everyone knows that anyone who survives a murder attempt is secretly the culprit."

Alex had already rebuffed this principle once, and didn't trouble to do so again. "Even so, Reef might not have known – and anyway, who's going to put any stock in a murder mystery cliché in real life?" she countered. "The point is, the idea of a faked murder attempt was just a lie you fed to Reef; your plan was always that he would die."

"Now, why would I do that?" asked Yva. "He was such a useful accomplice! I do the planning, he does the execution, we both come out smelling of roses, it's win-win. Also, he was my boyfriend, which probably counts for something."

Alex shook her head. "You killed him *because* he was your accomplice. It was just like Chase. You couldn't risk having someone around who knew your secrets – and certainly not someone as volatile as Reef. You could only trust him while he had a motive to kill, but who knew what he'd have done after that? Or if he'd still have protected you if the police managed to pin something on him?" She remembered the words of someone who knew Yva a lot better than she did. "It's just like Great-Aunt Cornelia said: Your friendships are transactional. Reef was just a murder weapon to you; and once the murders were over, you disposed of him."

Yva rolled her eyes. "Fine. So I had a motive, in your theory. Well, motives don't count for anything. Howdunnit is all that matters."

"Fine. Then this is how you dunnit," Alex retorted. *"Hanging."*

Yva flinched, and bared her teeth.

"You gave me all the clues. You were scrupulously fair, even if it was just because it was a risk to lie," Alex went on. "And what you told me was that Reef had been garrotted by someone taller than him; in other words, the wire mark on his neck cut upwards at the back, right? And the final video showed him suspended in the air. A noose attached in the tower bathroom would have done it, exactly the same way as lifting Leo's corpse."

Yva's eyes went dead as she scrambled for a response. "I had no opportunity –"

"After we'd searched the north tower bathroom, you let me go on ahead while you supposedly splashed water on your face," Alex answered, quick as a whipcrack. "Actually, the moment I left you hooked both ends of the fishing-wire onto the remaining coathook and threw all the slack out of the window. It wouldn't have taken half a minute. By looping some of the slack around the tap again, the whole thing could be made to hang down just a little higher than it did when it was used on Leo."

Yva's face was rigid. "Go on," she said.

"Down in the courtyard, Reef noticed the cable – or rather, he'd been expecting it," Alex said, "and, as he did with Leo, he coiled it – around his neck. The idea, as he understood it, was that he'd let himself be strangled, long enough to leave a mark, and then you'd let him go. This explains why he filmed that last video at all – he was setting the scene, establishing that nobody else was in the courtyard who could have helped him. The camera perspective was higher than usual, so he must have been standing on the edge of the filing cabinet with the noose already around his neck. All he had to do was tip back. It would hurt, but it was a small price to pay for freedom from suspicion."

"But Reef died," Yva pointed out. "So something went wrong."

"No, everything went according to plan," Alex pointed out right back: "*Your* plan. Reef's survival depended on you loosing one end of the wire after a very short time, dropping him like Dry Diver. His life was literally in your hands. But you had already gone." Alex found herself blinking back tears of anger, of humiliation. "Because you'd run off after me to lounge in an office and theorycraft about the murders!" Yva was silent. Alex couldn't see her at all, because she was blind with sobbing. "That's it, isn't it? You used theories as a murder weapon! You used *me* as a murder weapon! Just to buy time for Reef to choke to death!"

Yva shifted in her seat. Alex could hear her, even if she couldn't see. When her voice came at last, it was a simple, plain statement: "They were good theories."

"Good theories?!" Alex wiped her sleeve across her eyes. It barely helped. "Here's a theory: Reef realised something was wrong! That's why he used the last of his strength to pull the camera out of his harness! He was trying to show the noose – to show that you'd betrayed him too!"

Again, Yva was silent. She was just a blurred shadow in the dim torchlight.

"You ducked into the bathroom again as we were returning," Alex finished. "You even said it was to get the wire! Like with Leo, if one end was unhooked then the whole thing would unravel and could be pulled up. That's another half a minute. From my point of view, you were only away for so little time that I barely noticed…

but so long as Reef's death looked like it needed minutes, you only ever needed seconds."

Alex wiped her eyes again, and saw clearly. Saw Yva, hunched in her chair, no longer lounging impassively, no longer boasting; no longer even meeting her eyes.

"It's the only possible explanation. The *only* one," Alex said. If she could have pleaded with reality for another, she would have. "Are you… going to say something?"

A pause, and Yva lifted her head. She looked more dejected than Alex could have predicted. "Damn. When did you get so good at detecting?"

"I learned from the best," Alex replied. "But – be honest with me, Yva. You were helping, weren't you? You were dropping clues and hints *this whole time.*"

CHAPTER THIRTY
WHYDUNNIT

4:32am

"Helping?" repeated Yva. Her voice was scornful, but only half-heartedly so. "Why would I do that?" she asked, with something desperate in her eyes; as if she truly yearned for an answer. "Why did I do any of it?"

"Why…" Alex echoed, and looked into the shadows. "It wasn't for love or money. You couldn't care less about Reef, and Dry Diver is finished once all this comes out. Your real motive was something I had a hard time understanding. I knew immediately, but I struggled to believe it. It was just so strange. Like a cryptid's motive."

A low, bitter noise came from Yva's mouth, stifled behind her hands.

"Listen, Yva," Alex said. She almost wanted to cross over and put a hand on her shoulder. "I don't know why, but other people aren't real to you. You're the genius, and everyone else is just the audience; and what you've decided you're best at…"

"…are murder mysteries," Yva answered.

"Right," Alex nodded. "Writing murder mysteries… and solving them, too. You have to know a bit about solving mysteries to write a detective character, after all. The only people you've ever shown any respect for are the people better at detecting than you – and one person especially: Great-Aunt Cornelia. She's not just better than you, she helps *you* to get better, and that's the most important thing, right? Because you're constantly having to prove yourself, *to* yourself."

Yva could only nod. She had a look of faint comprehension on her face, as if Alex was putting into words something she had never realised about herself.

"But then," Alex went on, "Carver's Rest happened."

The immediate downturn of Yva's whole expression was almost palpable.

"Carver's Rest happened, and there was a *real* murder mystery," Alex said, thinking back to the dark hours in that death-touched castle. "But… you weren't the detective. You weren't even the murderer. You were a red herring. It must have been humiliating."

"I was fine," growled Yva, through gritted teeth.

"And that's as strong an undercurrent to the Pitchwater murders as anything else," Alex continued, ignoring yet another obvious lie. "Losing at Carver's Rest – insisting on having a detective with you here – squandering all the progress you'd made with Team Dry... there's only one thing that makes sense."

And, Alex reflected as she faced her, it was awful. It was a motive a normal person couldn't ever have; but Yva had never been normal.

"You did it because you could."

An expression of astonishment so pointed it was like panic flashed up on Yva's face; and she half-leapt to her feet, but her legs went from under her and she fell back hard in her chair. Somehow, despite everything, it seemed as if she hadn't seriously expected Alex to understand.

"You did it," Alex followed, "because you saw *how* you could do it, because you had people who could be *made* to do it, and most of all, because if you pulled it off, you would feel well and truly *validated*. You just couldn't help yourself; you had to prove that you were the cleverest. And that's why you needed a detective alongside you, so you could beat them fair and square – which is why you came to *the* armchair detective."

"Cornelia Crow..." Yva muttered softly, with some of the old spiteful energy. "The best detective I know – well, the only one, but she'd *still* be the best. What a risk!"

"But nothing could match the reward," Alex replied. "Nobody would believe she was an accomplice of yours; even as your friend, she's brutally honest and would have given you no advantages. The fact that she's a bit slow on her feet might have helped, too. You only needed to pull the wool over her eyes once or twice, and so long as you kept your hands clean otherwise, you'd be untouchable. Your endgame was to tell a completely fake story to the police so there'd be no chance of *anyone* working out the truth – but with Great-Aunt Cornelia, even if she solved the mystery..." Alex took a deep breath. What she was about to say didn't sit easy with her. "...*She might have kept your secret.*"

A silence, in which Yva Dysart nodded slowly.

"Cornelia Crow never lies," the murderer said quietly. "Prides herself on it, even. But she's got no scruples at all when it comes to being *clever* with the truth. Anyone who can't logic out what she's really saying isn't worthy of her time. And by the same token…" A rueful smile twitched at her lips. "Just knowing the truth doesn't mean she'll share it. She doesn't care about justice or sentiment. She just wants to *know*. Yeah, one way or another, I thought I'd be safe with her."

"But instead," Alex said, with a weary shrug – "you got me."

"Yep… you," Yva sighed. "At Carver's Rest, you didn't have a clue when it came to locked rooms and howdunnits. You were the whydunnit girl – but I never thought *anyone* would understand me. I figured you'd be just adequate enough a detective to look convincing without catching on – and depending on how things shook out, maybe I could even gull you into a false solution." She uncurled in her seat, looking thoughtful. "Underestimating you is one of two real mistakes I made."

"What was the second?" Alex was genuinely curious. Matt's temporary survival, George putting in an appearance – these weren't things Yva would blame on herself.

Yva remained silent for a while, her expression blank as it always was when she was really thinking. When she did continue, it wasn't at all what Alex expected.

"Reef was a psychopath," she said bluntly. "I may not be very good with people, but I got that pretty quickly; there aren't many romantic subplots in books that are just one party venting constantly about everyone who's wronged him. Bianca this, Matt Silver that; how he'd like to kill anyone who laid a finger on her. And there I was, getting ideas for how to make it happen." Her lip curled, ever so slightly, into the familiar grin. "You know, it took us a while to figure out that we were both *serious*…"

Alex couldn't help but be saddened by how toxic a relationship it had been – two people matched in bringing out the worst in each other.

"Chase disliked me from the start," Yva went on. "Maybe he saw through me, or maybe he preferred it when it was just him and Reef, but either way he made clear I wasn't welcome. Leo was a slimeball; the location scouting experience made that very clear.

And Matt Silver – you know, you talk about *empathy*, but I could actually see where Reef was coming from! Matt had one good idea, Reef actually made something worthwhile out of it, and Matt came muscling in to try and own it." Her expression was almost righteous. "They were a write-off, all four of them. Trash humans who weren't worth my time. So long as I was safe, I didn't see a single reason not to go through with the plan." She made a scything gesture, like someone sweeping chess pieces from a board. "But tonight, I made my second real mistake."

Alex was starting to uneasily get it; and it was all the more disturbing for the fact that it involved her. "You saw something more worthwhile."

Yva seemed to struggle with herself for a moment; but then she gave a helpless gesture, and spoke.

"I had fun."

Her voice was so quiet that Alex almost missed it.

"I had fun. Detecting with you," Yva admitted. "Running around, interviewing people, coming up with theories – I thought I would just be acting the whole time, but I've never felt more like myself. It actually made me… happy. Happy enough to wish that it was real, and that I wasn't the culprit."

For the first time in a while, Yva stood up. Her expression had shifted instantly from one almost nostalgic to one of frustration.

"In retrospect, I don't know what I was thinking," she muttered. "Why was I so careless as to compromise myself for those idiots? I should've just given Reef some general pointers, warned him that he couldn't expect any help on the night, and then you and me could've detected our way to catching him and nobody would believe anything he said about me afterwards. It wouldn't have been as interesting a mystery, but it would have been real, and it would have been safe." She looked up at Alex. "And… we could've both walked out of here, on the same side."

In a way, Alex could see the awful logic in Yva's actions. Whatever the cause, all the people she rubbed up against had filed the soft parts off her and left the hard edges; from her parents, to her boyfriend, to her teammates… and even, though Alex didn't like to admit it, to the one person in her life who had been anything like a positive influence and a friend: Cornelia Crow, old and remote and filed to the sharpest of points. Even Alex had written Yva off as too strange, too spiky, to really make the effort – before the mystery of the Pitchwater Building had forced her hand. She couldn't possibly have known it was a mistake, but it was a mistake, all the same. "I'm sorry," Alex said mournfully, "that we didn't have a chance to become friends any sooner."

"Never thought I'd say this, but… I'd have liked that, too," Yva confessed. "You're a goody-two-shoes, but you accepted me as I am when nobody else would. The murdering should have stayed on paper."

And that was all. The air was clear. Whodunnit, howdunnit, whydunnit. The only three questions that mattered had been answered.

Which brought Alex to the moment she'd been afraid of all along.

Facing Yva across the room, she cleared her throat. They could still get a happy ending out of this. "Does this mean… you're willing to turn yourself in?"

Yva blinked. Then a bitter, ironic smile began to cross her face. "Let me answer your question with another question, Alex. Are you willing to lie for me?"

Lie for Yva? Lie that she killed someone? Lie that she plotted the deaths of three more, and saw them through? Join the great lie that would destroy all the evidence and fob the police off with a fake story and leave the truth unprovable forever, and them all walking away scot-free? It was tempting, Alex admitted. She was surprised, now, at how tempted she was; now that Yva had bared her soul.

But it wasn't right. She wasn't like Cornelia Crow. Just knowing the truth wasn't enough; there had to be some justice in the world.

Slowly, she shook her head.

Facing her, Yva gave an equally slow nod in acknowledgement. "That's what I thought," she said. "Just like you've already thought that my answer is the same."

Alex gave a deep sigh. "Yeah," she admitted. "I didn't really think you were going to go quietly. But we had to ask, didn't we both? Even if we knew the answer."

Yva gave a shrug, with an expression of faintly amused resignation. "If we could choose differently, we wouldn't be who we are, right?" she said. "But, you being you, and me being me – there's no way forward."

She unzipped her coat. Beneath it, still wrapped around her waist where she had tied it up earlier – was the fishing-wire. Yva found the end and began slowly unspooling it in her hands, never taking her eyes off Alex.

Now Alex was terrified.

This had never just been a friendly chat. This had never just been theorycrafting. This was being cornered alone in an abandoned building by a murderer and explaining that you had them lock, stock, and barrel. Alex felt her breathing grow faster and faster, felt the hammer of her heart, her fingers tight around her torch as she backed clumsily away down the room, and Yva gracefully, casually followed her, winding the wire around her two fists until she had a length of it bared tight between them.

"I really am sorry about this, Alex," she said, and she sounded almost surprised by how much she meant it. "I'd have loved to go on Holmesing and Watsoning with you through an unending number of inexplicable bloodbaths. Guess I'll have to settle for putting you in a book someday."

The room was a long one, but Alex was all too aware of the concrete wall getting gradually closing on her back. She wasn't a fighter. She'd never been physical with anyone in her life. She would try to run if she could and struggle like a wildcat once caught, but there was absolutely no doubt in her mind which of the two of them would come out on top. "Y-you don't have to do this –"

"But we both know I do, don't we," Yva answered, her expression quite cool and composed. She'd killed once without giving the slightest hint, after all. Once she was committed, nothing could stop her. "It's Reichenbach Falls time, Alex," Yva said, drawing the wire taut as she drew closer step by step. "It's either you or me."

Alex let out a gasp as the wall hit her back. Death was only a metre away –

"Having fun, are we?"

For a split second, Alex sincerely believed she had hallucinated it. Yva's expression was what told her she hadn't. It was rigid with horror; and for a second the two of them locked eyes not as predator and prey but as two people united in common disbelief. Then Alex stepped to the side and Yva turned on the spot so they could both look back down the long room whose far end was sunk in shadow.

And striding out of that shadow, impossibly, inexplicably, like a dream or a nightmare or a monster, was the eleventh person in the Pitchwater Building: Great-Aunt Cornelia.

"Pardon the intrusion," she said sardonically, her cane casually resting on the floor as she put away a narrow torch of her own, "but I'm afraid I cannot approve of this activity. Alex, I presume you are quite alright?"

"…Yes?" replied Alex, too stunned to ask anything remotely meaningful. Part of her still thought it was a hallucination.

"Good, good," Cornelia nodded, as if they were still chatting away over a cup of tea. "Now, Yva dear, would you care to explain what you are playing at?"

Alex heard a thump beside her, and saw that Yva herself had backed into the wall. Her features had started working again, after a fashion, and she was mouthing in slack-jawed disbelief; she looked *caught*, red-handed, and Alex had a momentary image of her as a child found with her fingers in the biscuit tin. "H, ha, how – how are you here –"

"Oh? Haven't worked it out yet?" the old lady sneered. "So slow. Why don't we see which of you is the detective, then, and which is the murderer. Alex, if you'd care to explain…?"

How *could* it be explained? How had the old lady appeared out of nowhere? But suddenly, Alex was firing on all cylinders. What sort of motive and what sort of method might propel Great-Aunt Cornelia from the bookshop to the abandoned building – if you could just trace a path…

"It's been hours. Hours and hours without contact from us," Alex realised. They had spent so long isolated in this netherworld that it had been easy to forget that time still passed outside. "If you tried to ring us, you wouldn't have got an answer – no, with our phones damaged, you'd have gone straight to voicemail. You were…" It was almost a shock, after she and Yva had been discussing Cornelia Crow, the cold and calculating woman who might just overlook murder. "You were worried about me?" Alex whispered.

Cornelia's eyebrows rose. "But of course, Alex. Surely that goes without saying? Do go on, now."

Her great-aunt cared. She actually cared! It gave Alex the energy to keep going, to rush through the last deductions. "So then – you knew we were still local, somewhere lonely and creepy, you could have asked the bookshop staff if there was anywhere that fitted the bill," she ran on, "and someone would have told you about the Pitchwater Building, and then you just needed to look at a map – and the route George took, that takes about half an hour… And once you got here," Alex cried, with an air of triumph, "the gates may have been locked, but George's keys were lying in the middle of the drive!"

"Very good!" Cornelia said, tapping her cane on the ground in the manner of light applause. "An unpleasant walk, but it was really very straightforward, you know. Even convenient."

Yva's staring eyes lashed back and forth from one to the other of them, her mouth wide and frightened…

"So – you were the eleventh person, at the front door when I passed," breathed Alex, throwing her mind back to that moment of blind panic in the foyer. "If I'd just stayed – but from there, there's only one way to go; you found the south-east door unlocked, you'd have heard mine and Yva's footsteps ahead of you, if you followed you'd have arrived just in time –"

"To stop the door with my cane when Yva thought she was closing it – and hear everything," finished Cornelia, with an agreeable air. "So straightforward. So convenient. Don't you agree, Yva?"

The pair of them turned to Yva, who was twisting the garotte reflexively in her hands while her eyes sought doors and windows. "I, er, yes, um – oh look, forget all that!" she roared, at last finding her voice. "CC. This is important. Literally a matter of life and death," she went on seriously. "I need you to convince Alex not to turn me in."

Cornelia's eyebrows rose in surprise again. "Whyever would I do that?" she asked. "I'm going to turn you in myself, you understand."

It must have been a strange picture for the old lady, to have one girl gazing at her in ineffable relief whilst the other stared in naked despair. "But – but why?" stammered Yva.

The old lady sighed rather grandly, and gave a slow and regal shake of her head. "Oh *dear*, Yva, you really are a sad case, aren't you?" she said. "We'll never know, will we, whether I'd have sussed you out, or agreed to keep your secret. A little vexing, if I'm quite honest. But attempting to murder Alex – not just threatening, mind you, actually *attempting* – is really beyond the pale!" She shook her head again, more forcefully this time. "You *have* become a little unhinged if you thought I could overlook that."

Unostentatiously, Alex stepped away from the wall and moved to stand at her great-aunt's side. She could have slapped her past self for ever worrying about Great-Aunt Cornelia's integrity, or her love. The old lady looked down her hooked nose at Alex, and nodded in acknowledgement. The two of them were a strange team, but they were, undeniably, a team.

And Yva had become an outcast.

"Please, CC, understand my position here," she said, a picture of desperation, looking ready to get down on her knees and beg. "You're basically asking me to kill *both of you*. One was bad enough!"

"You don't have to kill either of us, Yva!" retorted Alex. "You can turn *yourself* in. It's the only thing you can do now that will help you – and you *need* help." Somehow she was no longer afraid of Yva's threats. Rationally, it was certainly the case that Yva could kill both of them; in physical terms Great-Aunt Cornelia was an even bigger pushover than George, and that left her and Yva back where they were. But with Cornelia Crow on her side Alex suddenly felt invincible.

"But I'd go to prison," Yva said. "I'd have no life. No future. I can't do it!" She was shaking now, and Alex could not tell whether it was with misery or rage. She suspected that even Yva did not know.

"That, Yva, is a little something called the consequences of your actions," Cornelia replied. "But whether you would kill us or who would turn you in is a moot point. The horse has bolted, Yva; no use closing the barn doors now. *I've already turned you in.*"

Already – !   Alex and Yva both whipped her a look of astonishment.

"W-wait, CC," sputtered Yva, recovering a little, "I know you never lie, but – *that's a lie*. I know your phone isn't a smartphone, not because you can't afford it, like me, but because you think they're beneath you.   And there's no reason you'd have had any special equipment with you.   So you couldn't have been recording our conversation from outside the room, and you couldn't have made a phone call without us hearing it.   So it's a lie, isn't it?"   Her expression was electric, devilishly gloating at Cornelia for having unbent.   "You've broken your unbreakable principle.   You're bluffing!"

"Once I make a resolution, I keep it," Cornelia snapped at her, like a dragon's bite.   "I turned you in before I even entered the building."

Yva's took it like a boxer's blow, and stood dazed.   This time it was Alex who asked.   "But… how?   You didn't know anything until you got here."   How had the old lady's deductions leapt so far ahead?

"Oh, it was trivial," Cornelia said dismissively.   "The instant I realised, back in that noisy little bookshop, that the two of you had gone off-grid was the instant I knew Yva was responsible.   The moment a single suspicious thing happened, her entire role became suspicious.   Inviting me out of the blue to watch her film a horror series in some lonely and treacherous place?   It really made no sense… unless I was being lined up as a witness to some devilry of her devising.   So, yes – even if I didn't know the details, I was quite sure.   And just so," she gestured with her free hand, "I was right, as I always am."

"So, what did you actually do?" asked Alex.   It wasn't as if she'd come flanked with constables.

"You remember all those police officers who came to Carver's Rest after the end?" the old lady enquired.   "I had prevailed upon one of the more important of them to give me her contact details.   It seemed like it might be useful one day.   Well, before I set out, I left a message on her telephone: *I believe Yva Dysart has committed a serious crime in the Pitchwater Building.*   She'll remember you, of course," Cornelia finished, addressing Yva with pleasant understatement.

Yva looked aghast. She stood like a bombed-out shell of a person; nothing but a husk without hope.

"I… I don't see a way out of it," she whispered. "If it was just one of you I could get away with it. Even both of you, I could come up with a story. But if I'm already a suspect before the police even get here, I'm done for. There's no story I could tell or that I could get the others to tell that would save me."

Her arms fell to her sides; and momentarily the wire linked her wrists like handcuffs before that, too, slackened and fell away. And in the same moment, Alex felt the weight of the world lift at last from her shoulders; felt that she was free.

"So, you're giving up?" she asked. It seemed as well to be sure. "You're really surrendering? You're not going to try to kill us?"

"I don't want to kill you if I'm not going to get away with it," Yva said dully. Something of her old bile rose as she muttered bitterly, "I didn't want to do *any of it* if I wasn't going to get away with it!"

"*That,*" said Cornelia Crow acidly, "is the sort of thing you should have considered before you took action; recalling that in theory, you may fail as many times as you like, but in practise, you have only the one chance." Some of her crusading force left her, and she let out a sigh. "I *am* sorry, Yva."

The electric tension had fled the room; and in the darkened space lit only by dying torchlight on the one hand and the faintest glimmer of dawn on the other, they were only three exhausted people who had fought their last battle to a checkmate.

A faint sound plucked at Yva's throat, and she straightened up; and forced her eyes wide open and to an illusion of their former unflagging energy, though pinprick tears glistened at the corners. "I-I," she stammered, looking from Alex to Cornelia and back again, "I guess there's no shame in losing to the best."

Alex felt the tears touch her own eyes again, too. It seemed unjust somehow, as if she, too, had lost; had in one breath gained a friend and lost them again. Yva had given in to her own darkness and now would never be free…

"Was it at least –" Yva croaked, and stopped to draw herself stiffly together. "Was it a good plan?" she said, in a pleading voice. "Was it *clever*?"

"One of your best," Cornelia said, and her voice, at last, was full of regrets. "You really should have written it down."

Yva turned to Alex for affirmation; and in Yva's disturbed world, there was only one compliment Alex could give that she could live with herself for. "If it had been a book," she agreed at last, "there wouldn't have been a problem."

With those words, Yva's expression grew calm. Her expression was the same as when she had given up on solving the Carver's Rest murder; one oddly at peace. "I can live with that," she said quietly.

And she spun abruptly on her heel and charged for the unbarred windows.

"No!" Alex screamed, but Yva had moved quicker than thought and before Alex could take even a single step she had cannonballed out through the glass and vanished into the night. "It's the *fourth floor –*"

A bony hand shot out and seized her hard around the arm: Great-Aunt Cornelia, her eyes urgent, delivering a stiff shake of the head. "Too clever for her own good again," the old lady said, and sagged over her cane. "She always was a natural at finding another way out."

Beyond the shattered window, a rising peal of sirens drew steadily closer…

CHAPTER THIRTY-ONE
DECOMPRESSION SICKNESS

A few days after

"Alex?" The knock on the bedroom door was repeated, slightly louder this time. "Alex, dear, may I come in? I've brought tea."

Alex was lying on her back on the narrow bed in her cramped bedroom, staring at the ceiling and trying, for once, to think of nothing. The day before the Pitchwater Building, she'd been halfway through a book, but now it sat on her bedside table untouched. She didn't feel like reading right now. Actually, she didn't feel like anything right now.

The knocking was repeated yet more firmly. Great-Aunt Cornelia had used her cane this time. "Alex?" A pause, and then, "An old lady might begin to worry, you know…"

It was a hypothetical, which meant that even a person who only told the truth might be playing a trick. Alex could tell that she meant it, though. "Okay," she said, just loud enough to be heard, and turned over.

Behind her back, the door squeaked open, and her great-aunt tapped her way in. Alex didn't feel like meeting her eyes right now. "I'll leave your tea here on your bedside table, Alex, so be sure not to knock it all over your book," the old lady's croaking voice echoed around the bookshelf-walled room. "I, ah, I added all those things you like in your tea when you're in a low mood…"

It was a nice gesture which it was hard to appreciate. Alex twitched her hand in acknowledgement. There was silence in the room for a few moments; and then, with a rasping sigh, the end of Alex's bed sank down a little as the old lady took a seat.

"I say, Alex," she said tentatively, "you're not still blaming yourself about Yva, are you?"

Alex stared into her pillow. "I don't want to talk about it."

"Well, yes, it's not my favourite subject either, but nevertheless…" Cornelia went silent for a few moments; and Alex could picture her staring at the wall and twiddling her thumbs in thought. "But you know, Alex, it's really not your fault that those people died!" she resumed. "Yva was her own person who made her own decisions and kept them secret from everyone! You didn't control her!"

"But I did make it easier." The accusation that had been rattling around in her head for days now spilled out easily. "I was trying to be a friend to her, but she was just shuffling me around the board like everyone else. Like just another pawn."

"A pawn who crossed to the other side and became a queen at the end," Cornelia corrected. "You're the one who caught her, don't forget."

"Yeah, and look what happened!" Alex wanted to punch her pillow, but it was too much effort, and she let her clenched fist slump. "And anyway, I couldn't stop her," she muttered into the duvet. "I didn't make any difference."

"You stopped her from doing it again."

"Letting her do it once was enough," Alex sighed. "I should have suspected. I should have seen something sooner."

"Now Alex, you know full well that there was precious little to see until very near the end…"

"Then I should have seen into her soul!" Alex cried, and the words reverberated in the room like a tolling bell. "Even you saw that!"

There was silence in the room for a long minute after that, but for Alex's breathing gradually returning to normal. The sudden rush of blood in her ears took that long to die down, so she almost missed the old lady saying, in little more than an undertone, "If anyone is to blame, I believe that I, actually, am the one."

Alex was so surprised that she actually turned over. She needed to see for herself that the old lady was serious; and there she was, not staring dead at the opposite wall as Alex had imagined, but looking down upon her great-niece with an expression Alex didn't recognise. It took a few moments to see it as a mirror of her own guilt.

"But you weren't there," Alex said. "You didn't do anything."

"I did everything short of pointing at the murder weapon and saying, 'Go,'" Great-Aunt Cornelia said. "Who knew her first, Alex? Befriended her on a website for mystery fanatics and gave her pointers in her writing? Recommended one whodunnit after another for inspiration? Pointed her to the kinds of grisly resources she would need to get a basic grounding in forensic science? Noticed her glaring deficiencies as a human being and, if anything, encouraged them?"

Alex hadn't thought about it that way. "But you thought you were being a positive influence."

"Not especially," Cornelia confessed. "You did, though."

"Great-Aunt —" It was the strangest thing. As hard as it was, struggling against the currents of the sea of guilt, it seemed almost as hard to make Great-Aunt Cornelia see how lost she was. "She used me as a human shield for her murder plan," Alex whispered.

Her great-aunt sighed, and looked down at her with a softer expression than Alex had yet seen. "You were Yva's pawn," she said gently, "but I taught her to play chess."

Maybe they were both adrift in that black sea, then. But it didn't mean they had to drown. They were there together, after all.

"You're wrong," Alex said. "Whatever you taught her, it wasn't to be a killer. She chose that on her own. But..." But it was all part of the picture. The things they knew they were doing; the things they couldn't have known. "Maybe there are things we could both have done differently," she conceded.

"Yes..." mused Cornelia, looking adrift in her own thoughts. "Take it from an old, old lady, Alex. Hindsight is a wonderful thing. But it only comes after, Alex!" She tapped Alex sternly. "It only comes after."

It only comes after. No matter how good a detective you are, you can't deduce the future. You can't see everything. Maybe, Alex thought, it was enough to reconstruct the past, if you could stop it from being repeated.

"Feeling better?" the old lady asked, after a minute or two in their own thoughts.

"No," Alex said. "But... less worse." She pulled herself up. "I think I'd like that tea now. Thanks, Great-Aunt."

Cornelia Crow made an impressive gesture, as if it was nothing, nothing at all... Alex knew better. The house creaked. She knew how long her great-aunt had taken on those stairs.

"By the way," Cornelia said, as Alex was drinking the oversugared, overhoneyed, overeverythinged tea with gratitude, "you had a telephone call earlier."

"From my parents?" They had responded to the tragedy of the Pitchwater Building in much the same way as to the disaster at Carver's Rest: By trying to pretend it was nothing to do with them. "Or – not from the newspapers?" Having her life dissected for the prurient scrutiny of tabloid readers was one of Alex's worst fears.

"Of course not. You're a minor, remember?" Great-Aunt Cornelia replied. "No, it was from one of the other young folk who went along with you that day. Tara, her name was, though she said she spoke for the others there as well."

"Team Silver?" Alex asked. She wondered how Tara had got her address and phone number; but then again, she seemed pretty savvy. There probably wasn't much she couldn't find out. "What did they want?"

Alex hadn't seen any of the others from the case – Tara, Bianca, Viggo or George – since leaving them in the break room that night. She and Cornelia had met the police at the doors of the Pitchwater Building, and after that everyone had been taken to the police station in separate cars for interview in separate rooms. Alex didn't know how much they knew, and even the media had thus far only got a vague and highly inaccurate version of events.

"They want to talk about what happened," Cornelia explained. "Young Tara said they got the gist of the truth from the questions the police asked, but they really need a fuller account in order to understand."

That made sense. The four of them must have got the general idea once the police started focussing on Yva's involvement and her movements; but they had the right to know it all. Alex wasn't looking forward to what they would make of her role, though.

But Cornelia was still talking. "And the girl also said..." The old lady smiled, as if she had anticipated Alex's fear. "That none of them blame you."

Alex blinked. "They don't?" Didn't anyone?

Alex's great-aunt shrugged her bony shoulders. "Tara expressed the view that you must have been the most deceived out of any of them."

Alex leaned back on her pillows, and looked up at the ceiling. She wasn't ready to let go of her guilt, not yet. That would take a long time; it might take her whole life. But perhaps she needed to remember not to victim-blame, either. If it had been anyone else but her, she wouldn't have blamed them; so why make an exception for herself?

Being wilfully deceived, wilfully ignorant, is one thing. But to be lied to is not a sin.

"Maybe I will talk to them," she decided. "But… not just now. I'm not ready yet."

Cornelia Crow nodded in understanding. "When, do you think?"

Alex looked towards the window. Rain was falling steadily. "When the sun shines," she said.